THE FRENCHWOMAN

THE FRENCHWOMAN

Jeanne Mackin

ST. MARTIN'S PRESS, NEW YORK

For Helen and Richard Mackin

THE FRENCHWOMAN. Copyright © 1989 by Jeanne Mackin. All rights reserved. Printed in the United States of America. No part of this book may be used or reproduced in any manner whatsoever without written permission except in the case of brief quotations embodied in critical articles or reviews. For information, address St. Martin's Press, 175 Fifth Avenue, New York, N.Y. 10010.

Design by Glen M. Edelstein

Library of Congress Cataloging-in-Publication Data

Mackin, Jeanne.
    The Frenchwoman / Jeanne Mackin.
    ISBN 0-312-03346-X
    1. French—Pennsylvania—Asylum—History—18th century—Fiction.
2. France—History—Revolution, 1789–1799—Fiction. 3. Asylum
(Pa.)—History—Fiction. I. Title.
PS3563.A3169F74 1989
813'.54—dc20   89-32756

$\mathscr{P}$ROLOGUE

Pennsylvania 1836

$\mathscr{I}$ dreamed of the fall of the guillotine last night. Its cold metallic breath whispered against my neck. My heart pounded out a drummer's tattoo that changed into the heavy marching rhythm of the "Marseillaise." When I opened my mouth to scream a sigh came out instead.

It is a familiar dream, one that has visited me every autumn since that blood-filled year of 1793. It was autumn when Marie-Antoinette lost her throne, autumn when she lost her life. And between those falls, it was again a season of downward-spiraling red leaves when her son was stolen from her, never to be returned or found.

The slow-motion fall of Samson's blade awakens me, as it always does. But not before the other parts of the dream have gathered in my consciousness like dew gathering in the flower, sweet and fragrant. Charles awaits, a misty phantom grown more dear with the years, not less. I am young again, not grandmama or even mama, but only Julienne, molding herself into the curve of her beloved's embrace. The death tattoo becomes the sound of his heart beating against my ear. I awake to the feel of Charles's arms around me, but the sensation disappears with the chill reality of the Pennsylvania night. I shiver and pull the quilt to my chin. The Susquehanna rushes beneath my window; I pretend it is the same music the Seine composed when I was young, a child of Paris.

Three hours to dawn. This is my time, when the rest of the sleepers are tangled in the fine webs of their dreams, and I can remember, can inventory moments and years like a mother calling her children to her knee, fearful that one will be lost. Memories are easily lost and they are all precious, even those that carry fear on their shoulders like pallbearers.

I remember, and then I know why the dream has come, although it is spring and not autumn, the season of dreaming. Today, the Queen's House will be razed.

The refuge we built for the Queen of France will be taken apart log by log, stone by stone, until only a raw foundation is left to jut out of the fertile ground like an unrealized hope. Who will be left to remember that those rosewood staircases, those carved doors large enough to admit a goddess, were designed to please Marie-Antoinette?

v

Only the meadow will remain, a silent observer of the foibles of history, the ancient meadow where we built French Azilum. We dreamed we could build a rustic Versailles in the wilds of Pennsylvania. We were foolish; we were desperate. We had lost too much to imagine we could lose yet more—our Queen, our history.

The clock chimes. Its ticking is an announcement of time passing that I would rather not hear. But it brings me back to one of the earliest memories, back to when I was a child, dirty and hungry as my American grandchildren could never comprehend. Clocks were the rage then. Paris was entranced with time, as if immortality itself could be locked inside cunning metal cases and tamed.

The universe was a giant mechanical clockwork ticking away in an orderly fashion. Or so Paris believed in 1774, the year one King Louis died and another took his place; the year Marie-Antoinette wound the clockwork that would be her destiny and mine.

PART

The Old World

Paris 1774–1793

"Although God decreed that I should be born in the rank I now occupy, I cannot but marvel at the dispensation of Providence thanks to which I, the youngest of your children, have been chosen to be Queen over the finest realm of Europe."

—Marie-Antoinette

"So the sweet voice of Nature is no longer an infallible guide for us . . . peace and innocence escaped us forever, even before we tasted their delights."

—Jean-Jacques Rousseau

1

. . . a king is buried, a pauper is born . . .

"Where there is no mother, there is no child."
—Jean-Jacques Rousseau

In the Cité we measured time by degrees of darkness. So crowded were our narrow streets, our poor dwellings, that daylight could not penetrate. In the wealthy faubourg St. Honoré, the roofs of the hotels were gilded with gold trim and sunlight; we in the Cité lived in constant twilight.

I pressed my damp, hot forehead against the rough lattices of the attic window. Sticky tears dried on my cheeks as I watched the scurry of activity below in the rue des Anges. Monsieur Pirent, a gardener at the Tuileries, shuffled home trailing his cart of hoes and spades. His brother, Petit Pirent, a wine-cask cleaner at the quai de Bercy, sang jovially enough that the entire neighborhood guessed he had been sampling the cognacs again.

Others I didn't know by name made their tired way down the congested alley dangling baskets of vegetables from Les Halles for the evening soup. Children scurried in the black mud of the gutter, trying to stay out of the way of sedan chairs and donkey carts. In the distance, the towers of Notre Dame hovered over us like a benediction, but at the base of the great cathedral mean hovels leaned against its buttresses like mastiffs begging their master for table scraps.

My Paris was a city of people, rich and poor . . . mostly poor; happy and wretched . . . mostly wretched. It was a city of noises, of clomping horses and iron wheels ringing over cobblestones, of merchants yelling their wares in the street, everything from oysters to chamber pots with Ben Franklin's face painted at the bottom, of children laughing in games or crying in hunger, of men and women quarreling, whispering, cuffing each other, kissing.

Paris, in 1774, was a city where women wept if a pet dog was crushed in the turmoil of commerce, but turned their backs if a beggar were struck down by a hurrying "whiskey," those fast and sleek carriages of the young noblemen. It was a city where thousands of stomachs rattled with hunger, while the noblesse feasted at tables groaning under the weight of peacock pies and creamed potatoes, that dish of the exotic new world vegetable that only the rich and daring could eat. We dressed in limp cast-offs, while they wore suits encrusted with pearls and diamonds and embroidery that took years for half-blinded seamstresses to complete.

I did not question such discrepancies when I was but six. It was not injustice on a grand scale that brought my tears, but the more immediate injustice of the stinging slap that my grandmama Mathilde had given me. I, accused of crime, knelt on scabby knees in the garret alcove that gentle Louise called my asylum. It was there I went when in trouble, which was often.

Paris, that day, was preparing to bury a king. I was plotting the revenge I would take on my grandmother.

"I'll starve up here. I'll die. She'll be sorry," I told the mouse who crept in the overhead rafters.

What would it be like to be dead, like King Louis XV, who had left his earthly turmoil behind the day before and set all the church bells in Paris clamoring in frenzy? Would Mathilde smear ashes on her forehead and pay the curé to ring bells for me? Probably not. She, mean and frugal as a Friday in Lent, would waste no money on masses for the dead. My tears dried faster as I realized that death would bring me no comfort but only more problems. Didn't Saint Peter beat with a broomstick little girls who stole?

Below, in the street, I watched careless Madame Mouret drop a bright apple from her shopping basket. A group of ragged boys pounced on it, claiming the prize that should have been mine, for it had been dropped in front of my doorway. Would that I had been there, rather than self-exiled in the attic.

My belly grumbled with hunger. I stuck my dirty thumb in my mouth and sucked hard, trying to ignore the yeasty smell of fresh-baked bread wafting up to me from Monsieur Mouret's bakery.

4

It grew darker. The fluttering shadows reminded me that I was afraid of the dark, and the more I thought about death, the more upset I became, and eager for companionship.

Mixed with the sweet smell of bread was the acrid fragrance of Yvette's cologne, powerful enough and worn in such quantities that it could weave its way up three floors to where I crouched with my thumb in my mouth, my begrimed cheek against the wood-lattice window.

Smells of hair pomade, sweat, manure, and beribboned bouquets of spring violets crowded into my hiding place, the familiar everyday odors of the world around me. Odors from the evening before—brandy, wine, male musk and the sharp smell of unwashed women—hovered in the air like spirits, waiting for the new evening to come and make them strong again. After supper, Louise and Yvette would open the doors to the boudoirs, there would be footsteps up and down the stairs, the slamming of doors, giggles. . . .

I thought the whole world smelled and sounded like that. Only later did I learn that a *maison de joie* has its own distinctive realities.

Yvette was already beginning her evening toilette. I heard her arguing with the water carrier, who was trying to cheat her of a full measure. Jacques, the cobbler, passed by and his son, Mathieu, tripped and dropped a full sack of tacks. Jacques roared his anger, drowning out Yvette's high-pitched protests. The caged songbirds on Louise's windowsill tittered nervously.

I waited, straining to hear one more sound, the most important one.

"Julie! Come down!" My grandmama's voice was weary and authoritative at the same time. Finally, she had missed me.

Turning my back to the window, I pressed one red eye over a knothole in the ancient wood floor. She stood underneath in the room below, her hands on her big cushiony hips, her face upturned to the small hole in the ceiling.

"No," I said.

She frowned and uttered an obscenity that I was not allowed to use. In the same breath she reached for her workbasket and sat down to sew. Mathilde was not one to waste time in cajoling or apologizing, especially not to a worthless chit of a girl who couldn't even sew straight seams yet.

Seated, she had moved out of my line of vision. All I could see was the tip of one worn and muddy sabot. Her faded, ragged skirt was an unhappy contrast to the wealth of sumptuous blue satin that billowed across her lap like a miniature ocean.

Mathilde's leg did not swing back and forth as she worked, as Louise's did, nor did the toe of a slippered foot glide suggestively up and down the other calf, as did Yvette's. Mathilde, old and grey and solemn, sat as still as a granite statue. Only her hands moved quickly, as quickly as Louise's caged songbirds, skimming over and under the blue satin gown she was working.

The small room she worked in was also the room where my grandmama and I slept. It was lined with baskets filled with cloth and ribbons of every color and texture. Empty gowns in varying stages of completion hung against the wall like shy girls at a dancing class. A huge embroidery hoop draped with cheap muslin stood at attention in one corner. I hated that hoop. It was my worst enemy, next to the devil and Monsieur Mouret. I hated the needlework my grandmama was teaching me, and the hatred showed in the blood-splotched, crooked ABCD that sprawled against the white cloth like drunks on the Pont Neuf.

Mathilde, concentrating on her work, forgot me again. I was amazed at how long Grandmama could sit in silence like that. I wondered what she thought about. Louise had told me once Grandmama had been very pretty, and before she took up sewing she had been a popular public girl, with many wealthy clients. But wealthy clients, like fresh skin and thick hair, tend to disappear as a public girl ages. Never in my lifetime had Mathilde opened her door to a chevalier or even a broom seller.

My hiding place grew darker and I knew evening was coming. The street outside quieted again as our neighbors sat down to their watery bowls of soup. Just when I thought I could stand it no longer, that perhaps I did not want to die after all, Louise entered the room below. My heart leapt with joy and relief.

As young and pretty as Grandmama was old and grey, Louise was my favorite, my first love. She would plead with soft words for me to come down, making it possible to surrender with some pride left. She would be sorry that Mathilde had hit me.

I knew, though, that I had deserved the cursory blow. That morning I had broken the strictest rule of our household, that I never touch the garments my grandmama stitched and repaired. But Yvette's shawl had been so lovely, so tempting. I grabbed it from its hook over our straw mattress, draped it over my shoulders, and ran to show Jeannette, my best friend, the baker's daughter.

Its silken fringes trailed through the mud of the gutter as I twirled and danced, oblivious to the damage I wrought on the delicate garment. Jeannette, crouched on the stoop to await the charcoal seller, jumped up in alarm when she saw me pirouetting in Yvette's best shawl.

"Oh, la! You'll get a beating for this," she pronounced gravely, pointing to the big splotches of black Paris mud now hiding the shawl's embroidered roses. Paris mud would not wash out, we knew. It clung stubbornly as mortal sin on the unshriven soul.

Jeannette's own pale face was still discolored from her father's latest beating and her alarm for me was well warranted. Grandmama may have lacked the enthusiasm to give me the routine cuffs and slaps that were the daily fare of the other street children, but Yvette did not.

I stopped, disheartened, in the middle of a swoop and the shawl flopped over my bare feet. Just then I heard shutters fly open across the street and the dreaded owner of the now torn and muddied thing looked out of her window. Yvette crashed down the stairs and into the street as if the devil himself were riding her. Loosened orangish hair and slack ribbons flew fearsomely in the wake of her anger.

She was on me before I could make good my escape. She wrenched me by my hair and dragged me after her back up the stairs. I kicked and screamed uselessly, like a witch splashed with holy water. Injured vanity can give even the smallest of women incredible strength, and my foe was not of delicate size. Yvette, not even panting from her exertions, dumped me at Mathilde's feet.

"Look at what the brat's done! Ruined my shawl, the one you promised to mend today!" Her voice was shrill with wrath.

"Apologize to Yvette," Grandmama said quietly. Her eyes were stony.

"No. She has many shawls. I have none," I whined from behind the safety of Mathilde's skirts. "Yvette owes me for sweeping out her room."

"Ah! We have an insurgent who would redistribute the shawls of the world!" Yvette shrieked. "You'll have a job keeping this one out of the cells of the Salpêtrière, Mathilde. She'll end up wearing the fleur-de-lis on both her shoulders."

The fleur-de-lis was the brand the King's police used on thieves. An insurgent, according to my meagre store of knowledge, was an American who dumped tea into harbors. The connection between the two I could not grasp. Mathilde could. She, without hesitation, boxed my ears.

Dizzied from the blows and humiliated, I ran to my attic asylum to soothe my burning cheek and heart with spittle and self-pity.

Soft-hearted Louise, as I had anticipated, pleaded with me to come down.

"I'll give you a new ribbon," she promised, her voice threading up to me through the cracks in the floorboards. "Besides, it is time to go, Julie. Do you want to miss the parade?"

Parade. I had forgotten we were to go see King Louis be buried.

7

Curiosity won over pride and I scurried back down the wooden ladder to where Louise and Mathilde waited.

Even the Dauphine, Marie-Antoinette, who would soon be Queen, was not as pretty as Louise, I thought. My friend's flaxen curls were piled on her head in a two-foot tall cascade, and enough feathers to awe a peacock bobbed over her ears. Four gilt timepieces, only two of which actually worked, criss-crossed her bosom with golden chains and dangled from gilt chatelaines. No woman of fashion wore fewer than three timepieces in those days. Some sported half a dozen or more, and you could hear their merry, ticking approach long before you could see them.

Even more alluring, though, was the way Louise's pink satin skirt ballooned in front. She was going to have a baby soon.

"Voilà!" she exclaimed, tying the promised ribbon around my head so that it pulled back dirty black curls. Satisfied, I gave a hand each to her and Mathilde and we made our way down the dark stairs into the street.

We turned our backs to Notre Dame and headed in the direction of the rue St. Denis, where the King's funeral procession would pass, cutting through narrow alleys and unnamed backways. It was fully dark then, and Louise carried a torch to light our way.

In the dim light I saw bed linens and petticoats hung overhead to dry, flapping in the sooty night air like ghosts. Feathery bouquets of bound chickens—tomorrow's dinner for the well-to-do merchants of the Cité—clucked sadly overhead. I crept closer to Louise and Mathilde. The Cité was dangerous after nightfall. Beggars and orphans were sometimes rounded up and sent to work on farms in Canada, never to be heard from again. Children could be stolen and sold to jaded, rich men who had no taste for mature flesh. There were rumors that some children were killed, their blood used to nourish fading countesses and princesses.

Even the old King Louis had been said to develop a bedroom taste for child-flesh, a taste his mistress, Madame du Barry, helped to satisfy by bringing pretty street children to his private retreat, the infamous Deer Park.

But now he was dead. And Paris, who had grown to hate the King it had once called the "Well-Beloved" was burying him at night, in disgrace.

All the taverns on the rue St. Denis were filled to overflowing. Vendors sold hot cups of sweet coffee, cold sugared water and sweet rolls. The smell of chickens spitted over hot coals made my mouth water. It was like a holy day feast, not a day of mourning.

A girl smaller than myself, her eyes wide and black with hunger, approached us. Louise purchased three rolls from her basket. Mathilde put hers in a pocket for the morrow, but I swallowed mine in four bites.

At the corner, a late-working barber was pulling a tooth from a portly man who squirmed and yelled in unabashed pain while a small crowd cheered him on. Next to him, a young woman, oblivious to his agony, stood tiptoe on a crate, trying to be heard above the uproar.

"Your fate awaits you!" she screamed. "God has sent a sign, he has struck down the King! Will we bow to yet another who will rob us of life and freedom?"

Mathilde put her hand firmly on the back of my neck and I saw her exchange glances with Louise. She nodded towards a group of uniformed men who stood in deep shadow, out of the torch lights.

"The King's men," she said. "I wager that fool won't be here tomorrow with her silly ravings, or ever again, for that matter." The group of men moved toward the young woman. She stopped in mid-sentence, skipped off her crate and into the crowd, disappearing into the darkness. The King's men scattered in five directions, angry and confused.

At the next corner we had to stop and lean against the damp stone wall of the Conciergerie, for Louise was panting with fatigue.

"Does it hurt?" I asked, putting my hand over her round belly. The thing inside kicked under my palm, and I jumped back in alarm.

"Only in the purse," she laughed. But her face was pale and strained in the dim, flickering light.

"Do you think it will be a boy? I would like it to be a boy."

"Doesn't matter if it's a boy, or girl, or donkey," Mathilde said. "It won't be staying." I watched Louise panting, and the night felt newly sad. A dank breeze carried the scent of the Seine up to us, a smell of refuse and decay and hopelessness.

While we waited for Louise to catch her breath, we saw Monsieur Mouret, followed by Yvette and Jeannette, advance towards us. The street was busy with torchlit figures, all eager to see the old King buried. Louise sighed, her eyes watching the bulky, drunken figure of the baker as he approached. She loathed Mouret as much as I did.

"Come to say *au revoir* to Louis the Well-Beloved, hey?" Mouret sputtered his words. He smelled of cheap wine, yeast and sweat, and his clothes were flecked with greyish flour. With bulging eyes, swollen red nose and thick, slobbering lips he looked like one of the Notre Dame gargoyles come to life.

"Well-Beloved, my ass." Yvette giggled. "I hope the filthy bastard rots in hell." Yvette was offended by the fact that she had never been invited or abducted to participate in one of the Deer Park orgies. She took her calling quite seriously.

9

"Careful," Mathilde hissed, nodding at the sentry who stood at attention at the gate of the Conciergerie. He ignored us.

"At least this new Louis won't be leaving a trail of bastards behind him like his father," Yvette continued. "He's impotent. Spends his nights making locks. Poor Marie-Antoinette! Poor little Dauphine! No bread in the oven!" She and Mouret burst into loud guffaws. At a time when even serious philosophers spent considerable energy achieving and then boasting about sexual exploits, France had a dauphin, now a king, who could produce no child, legitimate or otherwise. Louis and Marie-Antoinette of Austria had been wed for four years and her flat belly was the talk of Paris.

Jeannette crept close to me between Mathilde's and Louise's skirts. "Impotent," she repeated, and we puzzled over this new word. It must have something to do with locksmithing, we concluded.

"What happened to the shawl?" Jeannette whispered.

"I gave it back," I lied, watching as Mouret put his huge hand over Louise's breast. She slapped it away.

"Nothing like a whore for putting on airs," Mouret yelled.

"I am not a whore," she often told me, "I am a courtesan. There is a difference. A big difference. It is a matter of fine and important distinction. No one calls me a whore."

But Mouret did. I blushed for Louise and edged further away from him.

Above Mouret's laughter we could hear the sound of carriages approaching, the quick pace of horses' hooves clopping down the street, the iron rims of the wheels ringing louder than church bells. Revelers poured out of the taverns and cafés and Mathilde, showing enthusiasm for a change, yelled "Look! The procession! It comes!"

Jeannette and I clambered onto a stone wall, eager to see the parade as it passed by on its way to the Church of St. Denis, a church I had never seen.

St. Denis was the patron saint of Paris, the first one we learned about in our catechism. He had been beheaded by the heathens for his faith. After the executioner's stroke he had picked up his head, tucked it under his arm, and walked to where he wanted his church built. In later years I often wondered at the irony of this. The king whose reign would be followed by years of mass beheadings was laid to rest by the holy, beheaded St. Denis of Paris.

The boisterous crowd in the street forced the procession to slow down and we were able to get a look at the trappings of royalty. It was not often that banners with the golden lilies of France floated our way. It was disappointing. I had expected the whole court to turn out, to see the nobility dripping with ermine and lace and diamonds. Instead, three plain hunting coaches trundled down the congested street. Even the horses seemed embarrassed. There were few royal mourners, no show of exquisitely liveried guards, no blaring of fanfares. King Louis, his body already so decayed and foul he was put inside three coffins, one inside the other like a Chinese box to contain the smell, moved quickly down the street in ugly disgrace.

"Rest in peace, filth of the ages," Mouret yelled as the coaches forced their way through the slow-to-part crowd. As quickly as one cloud slips over the moon to be replaced by another, the mood of the crowd changed from rowdy excitement to angry resentment.

Hoarse shouts rose up like pigeons taking to wing. Louise pulled me from the wall to stand closer to her. I couldn't see the first handful, but suddenly the air was thick with smelly lumps of Paris mud. They landed on the sides of the coaches with thick, splattering noises. The horses snorted in surprise and reared.

"Time to go home," Mathilde said wearily. Louise took me and Jeannette by the hand and we squirmed and pushed our way through the crowd, laboriously at first and then faster where the mob thinned at the edges. When we broke free we ran, with Mathilde and Louise each holding up their skirts with one hand and pulling a frightened little girl behind them with the other.

Behind us, in a rising crescendo of hatred, we heard the yells of the Parisians who had turned out to curse their dead king, not mourn him.

Louise's labor began that night and lasted till early morning. Mathilde sent me to stay with Jeannette, not to protect my childish sensibilities but simply to keep me out of the way. Not wanting to find myself in Monsieur Mouret's way, I instead hid again in my attic asylum.

I listened to Louise scream for several hours before I finally fell into a troubled sleep filled with bad dreams. At dawn I dreamed that Mouret, atop a black, fire-breathing horse, was galloping towards me, trying to crush me. I leaped over the side of the Pont Neuf and landed not in the cold, refuse-laden waters of the Seine, but on a barge. The boat was loaded with coffins, all open and filled with skeletons wearing crowns. From deep inside one of the coffins I heard a high-pitched wailing.

Awake, I sat up quickly, wide-eyed and covered with cold sweat. I still heard the wailing sound, but it had a sweeter quality to it. Louise's baby cried in the room below.

"It's a boy," Mathilde said, pointing to a tiny bundle that rested at Louise's side in bed.

11

I walked to where she lay. She pulled aside the wrappings so I could see the newborn's red, contorted face. Delighted, I touched the tiny nose, the cheeks smooth as fine silk.

For two days Louise huddled in bed, her meowing, red-faced bundle at her breast. I poked at him often because he would stretch and quiver like a kitten when I placed one of my grimy fingers under his chin.

Mathilde ignored the baby, only handling him as much as was necessary to change his swaddling, and then tossing him about so gingerly that Louise and I watched, breathless, fearing she would drop him.

The room filled with the smell of blood and illness. The birth had torn something inside her, Mathilde said. There would be no more children, and for that she should thank the Virgin. But Louise did not look thankful. Buckets of water turned pink with blood stood waiting to be thrown into the gutter. Strips of torn rags hung from the bed posts, waiting to be thrust under the sheet between Louise's thin, white legs.

"You look awful," I told her on the third morning. "Are you going to die?" The thought of Louise dying brought quick tears to my eyes. I'd had enough of funerals.

"Hush!" Mathilde snapped. "There's no need to talk of dying. Not if you get off your lazy backside and go get bread, as I told you to do hours ago."

"I went for bread. Mouret wouldn't give me any. He said to come back with money."

"A pox on Mouret," Mathilde grumbled. She went to the bag where she stored her coins, knowing already that it was empty. She turned it inside out and then flung it to the bare wood floor.

"Go back to Mouret. We must have bread. Beg if you must. But don't come back empty-handed."

I pretended not to hear her. Beg from Mouret? The thought made me fidget with fear.

"Do all babies cry this much, Louise?" I slid my bare feet in the direction of the bed, hoping to start a lengthy conversation that would take their minds off food.

"Henri is hungry because I don't have enough milk for him," she said.

Mathilde, pulling out her sewing basket, grunted. "All the more reason for him to go, and quickly."

"Ah, Mathilde! I know you are right. But pity me, please. He is so little, so helpless. Let him stay a week, then he will go. You remember how hard it is to let go, you had a baby . . ." Louise's voice trailed off weakly and then stilled as Grandmama rose again to her feet. Her face was dark, her eyes glittered menacingly. I held my breath. It was forbidden to mention my

12

mama. I did not even know her name, so rarely had she been mentioned in our household.

"Shut up, Louise. And you, with the big ears . . ." she turned and pointed at me. "Go get bread before I lose my patience and sell you to the gypsies."

I fled the room, but paused at the top of the stairs, hoping to hear more.

"You think he'll send money for the babe?" Grandmama was yelling. "Show me an aristo who claims his bastard son by a whore! No, let me show you a whore who's out of her mind."

"I'm not a whore. I'm a courtesan," she weakly protested.

"Think, Louise! You know you must send the baby away, or you'll be just a beggar. God forgive you."

Later, when I knew more of the world, I realized that God had to forgive Louise not for having a bastard—that was common enough—but for wanting to keep him. That went against all the rules of our society, for even whores must follow rules.

"Just a little longer, Mathilde, let him stay with me a little longer."

My mama wasn't mentioned again, so I crept outside and down the corner to Mouret's bakery. The morning air, heavy with the threat of rain, felt dismal on my face.

Jeannette was huddled within the bakery doorway, her back curved like that of an oft-beaten dog, but she smiled when she saw me.

"Julie! Guess!" she called, brightening.

"Your mother gave you some bonbons?" I asked, jumping into our game with enthusiasm, to put off the encounter with Mouret.

"No," she giggled. "Guess again."

"You have learned to write out the Ave Maria and now Père Roget owes you an apple." Père Roget was the round, stuttering priest who attempted to teach the neighborhood children their catechism and alphabet. We met on the steps of Notre Dame in good weather, and in one of the side chapels if it was bad, and listened to him stutter his way through the Credo and Pater Noster until we could repeat them. We stuttered and coughed in the same places he did to make fun, but he only eyed us sadly and gave us fruit when we were good. He spent little money on fruit.

"No," she said. "Only one more guess."

"Your father is at death's door and won't last the morning," I asked hopefully.

"No. You lose."

I held out my hand for Jeannette to give it the customary loser's thwack. It stung, but not much.

"I'm going to Versailles. With Papa," she announced, twisting jubilantly from side to side.

My mouth dropped in jealousy.

"You can't," I hissed. "Only ladies and gentlemen go there, not bakers and bakers' daughters."

"I can," she insisted, turning red. We're going to the Salon de . . . Salon d'Hercules. Anyone can go there. Papa said so. He has to rent a sword at the door, and then we can go in."

"If anyone can go, then what makes it so wonderful?"

"You're mean, Julienne. You're . . . you're covetous. Old Mathilde won't ever take you to Versailles. I'll get to see the orange trees in the silver tubs, and the gold mirrors big as walls, and the white dogs with the diamond collars. I'll see them, and you won't." Jeannette finished her unusually lengthy speech by sticking out her tongue at me.

"That's a lie, Jeannette. Even if Mathilde won't take me, my mama will come back, and then we'll live at Versailles. I'll give the Dauphine her morning chocolate and she'll give me one of her puppies. The best one."

"Your mama has run off and will never come back. All you have is old Mathilde!"

"No, no, no! Now I have a brother, too. I have Henri." I stamped my feet and pulled Jeannette's lank brown braid.

"He's not your brother! He's not even your cousin!" Fighting back tears, she turned on her heel and fled. I wanted to run after her and knock her down, but I still had my errand with the baker. It was that that had made me so mean to the baker's daughter, my best friend.

I opened the door to the bakery and crept in, hoping Mouret wouldn't be there. He was. The counter was level with the top of my head, and I stood with my hands behind my back to make it less obvious I had no money with me.

He was piling loaves of just-baked bread onto his shelves. He turned when he heard the door swing behind me, and laughed in a way I imagined the devil laughed.

"You again," he sneered. "Have you brought the money Mathilde owes me?"

"No." I couldn't look at his face. I studied the floor. "Grandmama says we must have bread, though. Louise is sickly."

He came out from behind the counter and sat on a stool. He was so fat his buttocks hung over the seat like sacks of flour resting on a too-narrow shelf.

"Come here," he said.

I stood by his knees and tried not to smell the stench of his breath as he lifted me from the floor. His lap beneath me felt hard and soft at the same time, like a pear that has started to rot even while it is still green. I tried to curl up within myself.

"You want bread? Give me a kiss." He pressed his face close to mine. His hand was already moving under my skirt.

I was saved by Madame Mouret. She came through the heavy curtain that separated the shop from her own kitchen, and the baker jumped up. I slid off his lap to freedom.

"How is Louise?" she asked, ignoring her husband. "She has had a son, yes? How nice."

Everything about Madame Mouret was grey. Her hair, her eyes, her clothes, even her skin. But she was the kindest grown-up I knew. Louise said that Madame Mouret was a saint and that Monsieur Mouret was her martyrdom. Truly, she had a wispy, unreal quality that I associated with the saints in heaven. Grandmama said she was simpleminded.

"A son," she repeated, smiling and humming a little to herself. "You must take some bread to her. As a birth gift. And some for yourself, and Mathilde." Oblivious to the look her gargoyle husband gave her, she heaped four fresh loaves into the waiting basket of my arms. Then, she gave me an unnecessary push in the direction of the door.

Outside, safe again in the cool and sooty air, I heard the baker curse and storm. "Bitch!" he screamed. "You gave that beggar the best loaves. White bread you gave her, and from today's baking! You couldn't give her last week's loaves?" There was the sound of flesh hitting flesh, and I knew that tomorrow Madame Mouret would wear the same black and blue eyes that often adorned her daughter's face.

I ran back to the safety of Grandmama's room, enjoying the warmth of the bread pressed against my chest, and the smell of the yeast rising through the hungry, morning air.

But outside our crumbling wood and plaster dwelling I saw a carriage just beginning to pull away. The driver, in a great hurry, raised the whip and brought it down heavily on the horses' backs, so that they jolted into a harried trot. Laborers and housewives jumped out of their way. But old Lily, the rag collector, got her skirt caught under a wheel and it ripped away, leaving one ulcerated leg exposed to the knee.

"Out of the way, old hag!" the coachman yelled to Lily. "I've a long ways to go today."

An ugly sensation circled my heart, driving away the pleasure of my armful of bread. I climbed the stairs slowly, already knowing what I would find.

Henri was gone. The room, freed of his tiny wails, seemed quieter than it had ever been before, and forlorn.

"Sit," Mathilde told me. "I'll get you some broth."

I huddled next to Louise in her bed, and swallowed the thin soup in gulps. Louise shed silent tears that dripped into her bowl. Underneath me, in the depression of the mattress, I felt the remnant heat of Henri's small body grow gradually cold.

Even now, I remember the taste of that bowl of soup—a taste of betrayal and loss.

2

... traversing a shadowed bridge ...

*"The sense of our weakness stems less from our nature than from
our cupidity. Our needs bring us together at the same time as
our passions divide us, and the more we become enemies of our
fellowmen, the less we can do without them."*

—Jean-Jacques Rousseau

he Cité, in the early autumn morning, was filled with a grey, somber
light that presaged rain. It was past dawn, but the "white hour" had
not yet arrived—that busy time when all the barbers and hairdressers of
Paris hastened to their first appointments, trailing powder on the cobblestones like spills of gauzy lace over dirty cloth.

Mathilde stood at the basin splashing water on her face while I leaned
restlessly on the windowsill, waiting for her to finish her scanty morning
ablution. She no longer seemed gigantic to me, my grandmama. I had grown,
and when we talked we met eye to eye.

"Grandmama, quickly," I pleaded, eager to be out. It was Monday and
the Fair of the Holy Ghost, which was held every week at the Place de
Grève, would start any minute. The square was the same one where criminals
were hung, but on Monday there were no executions. Instead, the ragpickers, seamstresses, and other low-born women of Paris collected there to
haggle over carts mounded with used clothing.

17

Early arrival could mean acquiring for a few sous a lace petticoat discarded by a duchess, or a pair of satin dancing shoes once worn by one of the Queen's ladies-in-waiting. Thanks to the Fair of the Holy Ghost, even a poor servingwoman could dress in satin and lace finery if she were willing to risk the fury of the mobs that gathered there. To arrive late, however, meant consoling yourself with items that even a slop carrier would disdain.

"I'm hurrying," Mathilde answered, moving slower than ever.

Outside, beneath the window, a liveried man on horseback stopped at the door. I watched a now familiar routine as Louise stepped outside to greet him and hand up a package to his huge satchel.

"The post is here," I called out, although Mathilde and I had never received nor sent anything by post. "He's taking Louise's gift to Henri."

Her son was ten years of age then, and for ten years Louise had sent him monthly packages filled first with good linen swaddling, then long dresses and tiny jackets, and now real shirts with lace cuffs and breeches that tied at the knees. I tried to imagine what he looked like, but could not. Louise had never received a letter nor any kind of likeness of him from his foster family. They did not even acknowledge the packages. But Louise still thought of him as her son, and I still thought of him as my brother. Somewhere beyond the tax collector's barriers of Paris I had a mother and a brother, and the thought cheered me on days when nothing else would.

Those ten years had conveyed me from childhood to adulthood, not easily or quickly, for time is long to a child, but as surely as a leaf rides the current of the Seine.

The winters had been calamitous times for us, drawn out by months of cold and hunger. The summers had been better, filled with days of filtered sunlight and hot, humid evenings when the women of the Cité would sit on their stoops, fanning themselves with their skirts and gossiping amiably.

My hated muslin sampler had been long finished and replaced by a better one done on real silk. Then the samplers had been put away and Grandmama gave me a petticoat to quilt, and then a bodice to embroider, and a long series of dancing dresses to sew and trim, and when the dresses were done I looked out my window and noticed Jeannette passing below. She was grown and so was I.

Time did not pass that quickly, of course, but memory tends to condense our private histories. I remember being nine years old and thinking the short space of time between the feast of the Sacred Innocents and the Epiphany an eternity I could not survive, for Monsieur de Bracy had promised me a New Year's gift.

Would that time passed as slowly, now that there is much behind me but little awaiting me ahead.

That morning, as I waited for Mathilde and listened to the post carrier trot off towards the Pont Neuf, I saw Jeannette come out to wait for the charcoal seller. She waved up at me, a smile on her pale face. In the dim light her new gilt necklace glittered around her neck, her first gift from an admirer.

Jeannette was in love. I would have been grievously jealous—she had a tender mother and a handsome beau, and I had neither—except that she still had her father, Mouret, to torment her. That misfortune outweighed any other blessing life might give her. And while her Jacques was dashing in his uniform, his army livery also meant he could not marry her for four more very long years. To be ruled by Mouret and pine for someone she could not marry . . . no, I preferred Mathilde and my embroidery hoop. I had long since outgrown my childish hatred of needlework. Indeed, I even enjoyed it when days were damp and evenings long and lonely.

My impatience grew as Mathilde slowly dried and dressed in her grey work gown. Her fingers were nimble over the fastenings; age had not swollen her joints and for that we were both thankful, for it kept us from begging. Her needlework was as fine as ever, although mine promised to surpass it. She had grown increasingly silent and entire days would pass wherein she said only, "Pass me the needlecase," or "'Sweep the floor, good-for-nothing." My mother had not been mentioned since the day Henri was taken away.

"Ready?" I asked.

She nodded without smiling. I picked up the heavy basket of cloth remnants we had to sell, and followed her down the stairs. I had earned ten sous sewing for Madame Mouret the week before, and the coins clinked happily in my pocket. With them, I could buy an old gown, some discarded ribbons and feathers. Then, I would go to the Garde-Meuble where the Queen's gowns were displayed and make sketches of the latest fashionable trimmings. I would attempt to duplicate that style, and then sell the gown next week for fifteen sous.

The challenge was to duplicate a style and sell the gown before the next style arrived, for fashion changed as quickly as the weather. Marie-Antoinette was the deity who decreed whether skirts should sweep the ground or expose the foot, whether bosoms would be shown or covered, and how deeply the lace at the elbow should hang. Paris was not enamored of Marie-Antoinette who was, after all, a foreigner, worse an Austrian, but Paris was enamored of her style.

I had never seen the Queen, only her publicly displayed dresses. By the time I was grown enough to brave the streets alone and attend the holy day processionals that paraded the haughty court of France down our streets, the Queen had ceased most of her appearances in Paris.

She spent most of her time in the Petit Trianon, her private château at Versailles, where even the King, her husband, needed permission to visit.

The French court had never warmed to Marie-Antoinette. They disliked her Austrian accent, her informal manners, her love for the golden youths with whom she surrounded herself, for it was said she hated all old things. And the court was filled with old courtiers. They resented her; she mocked and ignored them.

She had triumphed in one thing, however, The beautiful, gay, Marie-Antoinette had lured her laggard husband away from his locksmithing long enough to produce two children, one of whom was a son, destined to be our next king.

Gossips said otherwise, of course. Was ever a royal son born when his parentage was not aspersed? "Can he, or can't he?" asked one tavern song about the King's bedroom prowess. The last line of the song, after naming the King a cuckold and his children bastards, advised Marie-Antoinette to go back to Austria. Would that she had been able to, even then.

Even before the troubles really began, Marie-Antoinette was in trouble. She was accused of everything from squandering the national budget to having sapphic love affairs. I paid little attention to the gossip. I knew how the fishwives of Les Halles and the prostitutes of St. Denis slandered each other. No wonder they elaborated when discussing the Queen. Gossip is most titillating when it involves the highest of the land and gossip was one of the pleasures of Paris, just as the Queen's pleasure was to keep to her private palace and play cards with her small and racy circle of friends, rather than feigning politeness to a court she disdained. It seemed harmless. It was not, we realized later.

The Place de Grève was already a seething mass of squabbling women when Mathilde and I finally arrived. Even so, Yvette found us instantly in the crowd.

"Ah! My good friends!" she shrilled, throwing her arms around me and leaning so close I could smell the turmeric she used to color her scanty yellow hair. The powder bled down onto her face, giving her skin a jaundiced tint. "I forgot my purse," she sighed. "You can lend me some money. I'll pay you back tomorrow."

Four years ago that terror of my childhood had been arrested for prostitution. She had been too bold, had tried to procure right at the gate of Versailles itself. Instead of a wealthy, titled protector, she earned a term in the harlot's block of the Salpêtrière and a disease from the prison warden that destroyed her health and looks.

I squirmed out of her embrace. "No," I said. "Lending money to you is as profitable as throwing it in the fire."

Yvette stared evilly at me before turning away, her head high and wobbly and garish as a giant marigold. The hatred in her eyes made them glitter.

"Take care not to end up like that one," Mathilde muttered, watching her go.

"I'd volunteer for forced labor in the colonies, first," I agreed. It was not the immorality of Yvette's life that turned me against her and it, but the ugliness and discomfort of it. I had no wish to have my complexion and health ruined, nor my youth spent following a career that would leave me miserable and wasted even before that youth was over. I had higher hopes. I would be loved. And cherished. I would wed, and have many children, all of whom would stay with me. I would work hard with my needle and my faceless but oft-dreamed-about spouse with his hammer, and we would have a house with a garden and apple tree. Such was my ambition. It seemed not much to ask. It's just as well I could not see the future, nor know how far I would have to travel to find that garden, that apple tree, those children.

"There's Madame Dupré," I said, pushing Mathilde ahead of me through the thick and jostling crowd. "Last week she sold a gown cast off by the Princess Lamballe. Let's see what she has this week."

I plunged into her stall, swimming through layer after layer of cheaper goods to find the gems she buried at the bottom of her baskets. A half-hour search produced an arm's length of wondrously fine lace decorated with seed pearls.

"I've seen better lace wrapped around a donkey's tail," I said to Madame Dupré, holding the lace gingerly, as if it stank. It would take much skill to obtain it for the five sous in my pocket.

"A donkey!" she shrieked. "That lace was worn by the King's own aunt!"

"In the privy she wore it!" I yelled back, and on we went for the better part of an hour, exchanging insults and gossip, till finally she sold me the lace for my sous and a promise to mend four shawls for her next week.

The seed pearls were only painted glass and the lace was badly torn, but with a little work it would be perfect for Louise's new brown gown, which we were trimming à la Suzanne, after a popular stage heroine.

Fashion, that season, made obeisance in all things to Pierre-Augustin de Beaumarchais, whose play, The Marriage of Figaro, was the new rage. It had taken the King's former watchmaker over six years to move his play past the long noses of the royal censors and to a public stage. Finally, the Queen herself interceded on his behalf, for she found the play highly amusing.

The fact that the play poked fun at nobility—a daring and dangerous concept—did not daunt Marie-Antoinette, although now we can look back and say, "It should have." Thanks to the Queen, the people of Paris were given royal permission to scorn and laugh at the court and its nobles for the first time.

I have since heard rumors that Beaumarchais was a spy who helped filter French gold to the American insurgents—by then they were doing much more than dumping tea. They had warred against King George III of England and beat the mighty Cornwallis. Just the year before, the Treaty of Paris had been signed, giving America freedom from England. France hated England, our most ancient of enemies, and we had danced in the streets for weeks to see Fat George so bested by the upstarts.

But that day we were thinking of fashion, not politics, as I trimmed Louise's new gown à la Suzanne, and dressed her hair à la liberté. She was thirty then, close to old from my vantage of sixteen, but still beautiful. Time had been kinder to her than it had been to Yvette—time and Monsieur le Comte, her protector, whom we simply called Monsieur de Bracy. Monsieur, I had guessed, was also the father of Henri, but that subject, like that of my mother, was locked in darkness, like the secrets in Pandora's box.

Monsieur de Bracy visited every week and always brought gifts. Louise's room was filled with gilt mirrors, brocade hangings, and a score of gay songbirds in cunningly wrought cages. An artist had been brought in to paint her walls with flowering vines and murals of Diane, the huntress. Floor-length mirrors had been centered in each wall, so that when I walked into her room I saw myself endlessly reflected.

"Ah, the seamstress arrives," she exclaimed, rising gaily from her marble dressing table. "Hurry, Julienne, monsieur will be here any moment." She danced in excitement when she saw the new lace.

"Then hold still," I said, trying to arrange and pin the lace in folds that would conceal the rents I hadn't had time to repair.

As I worked, she sang in her high fluting voice and set all her birds to chirping. I loved her voice; it had provided the only bedtime songs of my childhood.

> "As I rode with a loose-hanging rein,
> Alas, but my heart is in pain,
> The Queen passing by said, "Pray tell me why,
> You ride with a tear in your eye . . ."

"I shall ne'er see my true love again," I sang in response. "I shall ne'er see my true love again. Voilà!" Finished, I dropped to my knee and played her swain.

"Bravo," Monsieur de Bracy exclaimed from the doorway. Our boisterous song had concealed the sound of his footsteps. "Louise, you sing sweetly enough for the stage. But our little Julienne had better discover other talents."

He strode proprietarily to Louise and planted a smacking kiss on her mouth. She swayed in his arms like a seedling caught in a breeze. It was required, then, for ladies to swoon, given any reasonable opportunity to do so. Louise had practiced that graceful half-faint for many an hour in front of her looking glasses.

As curious as any other sixteen-year-old virgin, for such I was, thanks to Mathilde's fierce vigilance, I watched them out of the corner of my eye as I packed my sewing case. Neither of them minded my presence. I was a servant, one of those people who are invisible until needed for some errand or other.

I must have watched them too intently, however, because monsieur broke the embrace and sent Louise off to finish dressing for the opera.

"Sit down, Julie," he said, taking one chair at Louise's little ivory game table and offering me the other. "Oh, come now! Why hesitate? You used to dangle on my knee and eat jam off my fingers. Now you're grown and you won't sit with an old friend?"

His heavy jowls shook as he spoke. Because he was quite bald (Louise had confessed it to me) his curled and powdered wig was often askew on his slippery pate. But there was humor and sympathy in his watery blue eyes.

I liked Monsieur le Comte, although he was the reason Henri had to be sent away. He was often fatherly with me, and would tell me about his six children, of whom he was fond, who were at home with the countess, of whom he was not fond. The fact that he had a son he had never seen bothered him not at all. At sixteen I thought I would never map the twisted labyrinths of the human heart. At sixty-six, I know for certain I never shall. The depths of that most mysterious of organs shall always be terra incognita.

I sat, and de Bracy pulled a small box out of his coat pocket. "Does it please you?" he asked, opening it to reveal a set of tortoise shell combs and hairpins. "Now you can put your hair up as befits your advanced age. Although I must say, I prefer it like this, loose and without artifice. You look like Diane herself."

"Mathilde says I look like a harpy," I said complacently, twisting my hair into a coil and trying to pin it up. I had not yet loved; I had not yet a purpose for vanity.

"Mathilde doesn't have eyes in her head, then. What will you do with your life, now that you are grown? Do you think about the future?" His voice had lowered to a conspiratorial whisper so that Louise wouldn't hear us from her dressing room.

"Sometimes," I whispered back. "I think I would like a husband." As if acquiring a husband were as easy as knitting new stockings. I knew the facts of my life. I had neither family nor position nor dowry. Facts matter little when you are sixteen.

De Bracy laughed loudly enough that I took his laughter for insult rather than merriment.

"Don't blush so, Julienne, or we'll have to fetch the surgeon to let blood," he reprimanded, when his great belly had ceased heaving. "And be realistic. A husband is not in your cards, my dear girl. Consider the other options."

"But what of love?" I thought of Jeannette and the way her pale face shone when she spoke of Jacques.

"Love if you must, although it is not an emotion that comes highly recommended." He took out his gold and enamel snuff box and inserted a large pinch into each nostril. Had Monsieur de Bracy been disappointed in love? I tried to imagine him young and slender and despairing, filled with a great and impossible desire. Then he sneezed with relish, and the illusion was gone.

"Never confuse love with reality," he said in his fatherly tone of voice. "Duty and pleasure are separate realms. Fulfill your duties, and then you will have the time and means to take your pleasure. I married, to secure my estates with progeny and a wealthy wife . . ." (his wife, I knew, was fifteen years older than he and ugly as sin), ". . . then I found pleasure." Henri. He was talking of Henri and Louise in this businesslike way. They were pleasure. The son he had never held, the mistress who lived for the four hours a week spent in his company. That was the reality he wished for me.

"I have no estate, no name. According to your scheme, then, I have no duty."

"Don't twist my words. Your duty is to yourself. You're pretty, Julienne. Not in a fashionable way, but the right man could do well by you."

I looked up into Louise's mirrors and saw scores of dark, young women in shabby but well-fitted garments sitting across from the expansive girth of scores of Monsieur le Comte. The diamond on his finger glittered and made constellations in the looking glasses. The look in my own eyes was a familiar one, I had seen it in the eyes of scores of other women, strangers, who sat in public taverns trying to look at ease and happy while their escorts made crude jokes and exchanged news of the families waiting for them in front of the home hearth.

"I know such a man. I will introduce you. You are of age," he said.

"Mathilde would beat me to within an inch of my life."

"You mean that for a suite of your own rooms, a splendid wardrobe filled with new gowns, your own opera box, you would not be willing to risk your old grandmother's wrath?"

It did sound tempting. Maybe there would even be a small garden with an apple tree. I saw myself, dressed in fine printed lawn, a stylish and new straw hat on my head, sitting under that tree enjoying long afternoons freed from the drudgery of the needle. I saw myself alone under that tree.

"I couldn't keep my children with me, could I?" I said. It was not a question, but a reprimand. Monsieur le Comte's eyes grew stormy. He dropped my hand as if it were hot to the touch. Louise returned in time to see his ominous frown.

"Oh, la! Have we quarreled?" She gave me a quick glance of warning.

"No. Monsieur is too kind . . . too generous . . ." I stuttered, wanting only to flee the room. Help arrived in the garish, overdressed form of Monsieur Barbeau, the hairdresser, who arrived in the doorway in a burst of song and powder. He waved at us, and his hands, with their polished, long nails, flapped delicately.

"Tenderly each day I sing. From love for you I hope nothing . . ." he crooned to Louise, going on bended knee, putting hand to heart. But it was Monsieur de Bracy he ogled from the corner of his eye. Louise tittered from behind a large fan, but Monsieur de Bracy was not amused.

"Get up, you fool. We will hear better voices at the opera. If you will do us the great honor of attending to madame's hair. That, I assume, is what your outrageous fees are for, not your theatricals."

"Bien," Barbeau sniffed in a high and sulky voice. He snapped open his voluminous leather case and quickly enveloped Louise in a white sheet to protect her dress. Then, producing two huge swansdown puffs and a box of talc, he quickly reduced Louise's head, indeed the whole chamber, to a whirling storm of powder.

"Tonight," he promised, speaking from the heart of the storm, "Madame Louise will wear a coiffure à la jalousie! It will have no less than sixteen rolls of curls and in the center of all, three grey doves . . . three, do you see? The eternal triangle. Three doves with outspread wings, sitting on a branch of roses. Even Leonard, the Queen's dresser, will die of envy when he hears of it."

25

I heard de Bracy sneeze several times as I found the door and exited, unobserved.

Sixteen is an age when women step out of that linear doom that is called time, and waver between childhood and womanhood like hummingbirds deciding at which lily to enjoy the nectar. One moment I was considering my future with the cold-bloodedness of a banker; the next I was sitting on Jeannette's pantry floor cramming a sweet roll down my mouth.

"You mean, he actually suggested . . .?" Her eyes were large in her thin face as she licked the confectioner's sugar from her fingers. We whispered, hoping to remain unnoticed and hidden in Jeannette's busy household, protected by the closed pantry door. It was cool there, and the room smelled of jam and smoked hams.

"Exactly. He was going to make an arrangement for me. An introduction, and then . . ."

"How exciting. Perhaps he would be titled, young and handsome."

I doubted it. De Bracy himself had said I was not pretty in the fashionable way. More likely he would be old and fat, like Monsieur le Comte. And in that case, what would a title matter? Besides . . .

"Mathilde would kill me, Jeannette." My grandmama shared my ambition for marriage. We hadn't talked of it, but I knew she had so fiercely watched over my virginity for a purpose.

"Ah, well, that's true." Jeannette grew silent and thoughtful. I, still hungry, waited to see if she would reach up for another roll. She did not. "Papa has been making arrangements for me, too. Monsieur Dalmas has asked for my hand for his son. They are coming tonight to discuss the nuptial agreement."

"Dalmas? The baker on rue Dauphin? The one with the son whose face is covered with boils, who stumbles and stutters?"

"That Dalmas," she sighed. I understood why she had lost her appetite for sweet rolls. "Papa wants us to marry immediately after Easter. Just six months away."

"What about Jacques?"

"Papa won't even consider it. He won't let me live in his house for five more years, he says. He won't provide for a woman who is old enough to have her own household." She was close to tears.

"I won't marry Dalmas fils," she said. "I won't."

I could see fresh bruises on her face and arms. They had already quarreled about it. She would resist for a while. But in the long run, Mouret would win. I, too, was no longer hungry for another sweet roll.

The rain clouds that had scurried across the sky all day dispersed in the evening, leaving the little patch of sky visible between the bakery and the cobbler's shop a clear, inviting blue. We did not sew after twilight, as we were not able to afford candles, so I went outside to sit on the stoop and think.

At the age of six I had not questioned injustice. At sixteen, I was beginning to. And it seemed to me that the world was unfairly hard on women. Jeannette was to marry against her will; I, who wished to marry, was denied the possibility. Given those contradictions, how could men then turn about and decry the scarcity of virtuous women? If you force a girl to tolerate the embrace of a man she cannot love, do not be surprised if the woman looks for consolation elsewhere. I, of course, have never forced my daughters to marry, or marry where their hearts could not abide. I did try to guide their choices, of course, as is a mother's duty . . . but I get ahead of myself.

"You look deep in thought," a shy voice said from the gloom that evening. I looked up and saw Mathieu, the cobbler's son, peering down at me. He was eighteen then, tall and gangly with his bony wrists hanging several inches below his jacket sleeves. But his eyes were nice and his deferential manner pleased me. There were those who called me the "whore's daugther." Mathieu called me mademoiselle.

I made room for him next to me on the stoop. We often shared such evenings, sitting in companionable silence and speaking only when the impulse came. Lately, he had begun to court me, in his shy, frightened way. I neither encouraged nor discouraged him. That evening I tried to imagine him sitting beneath my apple tree.

He put his thin arm about my shoulders.

"If Grandmama saw you do that she'd throw the bedpan over your head," I warned.

"I'm not afraid of the old witch. Besides, I saw her leave on an errand several minutes ago." He pursed his mouth for a kiss.

"We were children, before, Mathieu," I said, pulling away. "It's different now."

"All the more reason," he said, nibbling at my ear when I turned my face away. It tickled. It was pleasant. His arms tightened around me.

"Stop, Mathieu, or we won't be able to receive the Eucharist on Sunday." The threat of sin, like my grandmama, however, carried little weight with the cobbler's son. No longer shy, he whispered a quick "I love you" and pressed forward the attack. His mouth closed over mine, his hands clutched at my waist. Safe from the prying eyes of the neighborhood gossips because of the darkness of the evening, I relaxed and thought that perhaps I should let Mathieu begin my instruction.

But my first lesson in love was not to be so pleasant. He was not the only one who had been watching and waiting for Mathilde to leave.

I smelled Mouret before I could see him. His sour odor of yeast and wine engulfed us. Mouth still flattened against Mathieu's, I saw Mouret's huge arm reach down to the cobbler's son. He grabbed him by the back of his neck the way one handles an alleycat, and pulled him to his feet. Mathieu winced in pain; Mouret slammed him into the wall. Mathieu slumped unconscious to the ground.

I had never seen Mouret so drunk. Saliva foamed at the corners of his mouth, his eyes were wild. He stepped over Mathieu and came toward me.

"Slut," he said, smiling. "Whore."

He stood between me and the door that led to Mathilde's room; there was no escape that way. I turned and ran into the dark street towards the Pont Neuf. I had no doubt of his intent.

"Don't go out alone during the dangerous hour," Louise had always warned me. That was the witching time between day and night when all Parisians, rich and poor, have finished the day's events but the night's have not yet begun. The streets are deserted then, the night watch not yet out. It is time for pickpockets and drunks and child stealers. It is the time for rape.

I ran towards the Pont Neuf. There, perhaps, there would still be some crowds; there, perhaps, I could lose him, or find protection behind a merchant's solid door.

I ran, and Mouret pursued with dogged purpose. My heavy, ragged skirts weighted me and I knew I could not outrun him, but there was nothing to do but run and try to reach safety.

Mouret guessed my intent and ran faster. He was two steps behind. His pace was surprisingly agile and sure-footed for a man so drunk. My heart pounded against my rib cage, my ankles felt limp. Now he was one step behind.

At the foot of the Pont Neuf, where the traitor Molay had been burned at the stake and where his restless ghost still frightened lonely Parisians who dared cross the Pont Neuf on the nights of full moon, Mouret caught me.

His hands twisted in my loosened hair, he pulled me backwards, away from the safety of the bridge lanterns, back into the darkness of the night. He picked me up and slung me over his shoulder like a sack of flour. Even Molay's apparition would have been welcome at that moment, but we were alone in the darkness. I struck at him, but he only smiled. He was enjoying himself. I kicked, and when I tried to scream he put one large hand over my mouth and pressed so hard I couldn't breathe.

Behind a decaying wall used by the beggars as a pissing spot, he threw me to the ground and wrested my skirts up to my waist. He fell on top, his arms thrashing, but still he smiled. I felt the dirt and grit of the street, the stench-filled dampness, scrape against my bare skin and then another pain, sharp and ugly, as he thrust between my legs.

I kicked and struggled and tried to scream; in short, I unwittingly did all those things which bring further pleasure to a man who enjoys violent sport. This was my instruction from Mouret.

When he finished—a moment he announced with a yell of delight—he rolled off me. I leaned over and retched as the repulsive feel of blood and semen trickled down my legs.

"Bastard!" I said, and my hatred of him made me retch again. Mouret rose to his knees and held my head for me. I slapped his hand away.

"Touch me again and I'll kill you. Bastard."

"You're the bastard," he pointed out, lacing his pants. "Or have you forgotten, whore's daughter?" His face was red and swollen with exertion. I struck out at that hideous, bulbous nose. Blood flowed, and I was pleased.

He looked at me in sincere surprise, and then anger. He grabbed my wrist so tightly my hand went numb.

"Let me go," I said, trying to rise to my feet. "If you don't I'll . . . I'll go to De Crosne. You'll rot in prison."

De Crosne, head of the King's secret agents, had offered a reward for information about certain thefts occurring in Paris at that time.

"What would a whore have to say to De Crosne?" Mouret asked, wiping at his bloodied nose with his sleeve.

"I'm no whore, and you know it." I spat at him. "What I would say to De Crosne is this. I know who is stealing flour from the Corbeil warehouse. I know who comes back late at night, his cart loaded with sacks of stolen flour. Yes, I've seen you. And how many years do you think you'll rot in the Bastille, if I tell?"

His expression changed and I wished then I hadn't said so much. I had only guessed at the truth, and Mouret was looking at me as if he would kill. It was true. He would rot in the Bastille.

He raised his arm and landed a blow on my face that made blood spew from my lower lip.

Blinded by the pain, I stumbled towards the bridge and, too weak to go further, missed my footing and fell into the quickening traffic. Paris was coming alive again, the bridge was filled with carriages and people afoot, all in a hurry to be other than where they were.

Horses' hooves crashed down within an inch of my head and I knew I must get up, but I couldn't do so.

"What's going on here?" The carriage driver's voice was peevish.

Mouret stepped from the shadows and pointed to where I was struggling to my knees.

"My daughter, sir," he said, his voice indulgent with false good humor. "Caught her with the 'prentice boy and was teaching her better." He bowed obsequiously to the driver, who was dressed in the rich livery of a servant to nobility. The carriage was profusely adorned with plumes and gilt scrolls and crystal vases filled with hothouse roses. It was a closed carriage; I could not see who was inside.

"He lies," I said, getting to my feet, but the driver gave me a look that silenced me. I was aware, then, of the blood from my lip that had stained the front of my dress . . . and blood that trickled down my legs to the cobblestones.

"You are being a bit rough on the girl," the driver said to Mouret. "You canaille should keep your quarrels at home." He flicked his whip and tried to maneuver the horses around me.

"No!" I yelled. "Don't leave me!" I jumped up on the filigree footstep of the carriage and clung to the door with my returning strength. The catch released and the door opened. A tide of perfume washed over me.

Inside sat three shocked ladies and their escort. They peered at me through black, concealing masks, their startled eyes moving inside those masks like caged animals, busy and frantic. One woman raised two dainty, lace-mittened hands, squealed, and slumped back against the rose satin cushions.

The escort, heavily painted with powder and rouge and wearing more lace than I had ever before seen on one person, fluttered his handkerchief at me as if I were a fly at an afternoon picnic.

"I say, begone," he said in a voice surprisingly deep and at odds with his foppish appearance.

"You must help me," I said, clinging to the swinging door. I addressed myself to the woman who sat in the midst of the others, calm and serene. Her coiffed curls shone auburn in the lamplight. They towered so high that the ceiling of the carriage had been cut open to accommodate them. The skin of her exposed shoulders and bosom was as white as Louise's alabaster statue of Cupid.

"What is it, child?" she asked in a voice not unkind.

"He will kill me," I said. Indeed, my bruised and bloodied face might have made that already apparent. Her eyes, flashes of blue which shone through the slits of the mask, assessed me cooly.

Then, "Monsieur, be so kind as to help this child into the carriage. She is in distress. You . . ." she pointed at Mouret. "Go away. Be off."

With a great show of distaste, the fop assisted me into the carriage. The door closed safely behind me. Mouret, shoulders slumped, headed off to the nearest tavern.

"Now, wipe your face here, and tell me what happened." My lady rescuer handed me a lace handkerchief to clean off the blood. I hesitated, not wanting to soil such fine lace, and she wiped my face for me. I kept that handkerchief for years. Somewhere in my travels it was lost, and I mourned it the way others will mourn a friend.

"She's probably just a whore who was quibbling over a price," the escort with the outrageous lace cuffs and collar said, yawning with boredom. The medals and crosses laced over his green silk jacket said he was very highly placed, perhaps even a prince. I was awed. But still angry.

"I am not."

The lady in the middle watched with calm, knowing eyes. "She's a child, monsieur. And it appears she has been ravished. You will refrain from further coarse comments, or you will displease me."

"Oh, la! Ravished! Do tell!" the other ladies exclaimed. "This is more exciting than the opera!"

Ravished? Is that what they called it? I huddled into the satin cushions, angry and intimidated at the same time. The auburn-haired woman leaned towards me.

"It's true, then?"

I nodded.

"This is a problem. Are you married?"

I shook my head.

"Do you have a family? Can your father press the scoundrel to marry you?" I shook my head again.

"No. I will not marry him. I hate him, and he already has a wife. I would kill him before I would marry him."

"It seems," the painted escort drawled, "that the scoundrel feels the same about you, mademoiselle. This would not be a marriage made in heaven." His voice was thick with sarcasm.

"Is there a midwife you can go to?" my auburn-haired rescuer asked. "Yes? then you must go immediately. Tonight. Ask her for the *poudre jaune*, the

31

yellow powder, and do just as she says. You may prevent the greater dishonor that could follow some months hence. You understand?"

The other passengers opened their mouths in shock, but she tapped her fan impatiently at them. "Do you think I know nothing of these matters?" she asked, her voice imperious. They snapped their mouths shut so that the disapproving Oh's of their rouged lips became straight red lines.

She took a small cloth purse from her larger reticule and gave it to me. The coins inside made it lay heavily in my hand.

"That will pay for the powder and the midwife. And for a new gown. That one is quite ruined. And now, if you feel safe, go, and we will proceed on our way. The evening grows late, and I am expected elsewhere."

"I will pray for you. Every night and a Mass on holy days," I promised.

There was sadness in her laugh. "Your prayers may do me more good than you imagine. Remember me to the saints. Tell them Marie asks their help. And occasionally, their forgiveness." She laughed more brightly.

Life is paved with broken vows, but that one I kept. Marie still gets her Mass on holy days, all these years later. I descended the carriage with no assistance from their disapproving escort or driver and waved thoughtfully as they pulled away. No one waved back. The men in the tavern made catcalls at me and hooted, but I ignored them.

The flickering, alive shadows of the night no longer frightened me as I walked back to the rue des Anges. Childhood and innocence were behind me, thanks to Mouret, the thief who had ended one, and my lady rescuer, whose sad smile at hinted at the futility of the other.

3

. . . the cold winter of departure . . .

"Be fair if you can, wise if you will, but be circumspect you must."

—Pierre-Augustin de Beaumarchais

The grim, rainy autumn of Mouret's rape gave way to a winter that the French of my generation still refer to as the year of the great cold. A colder year would follow, but it would be made memorable by other events.

The autumn rains did not cease but were merely transmuted by the dark magic of nature's force from wet droplets to huge, silent snowflakes that fell for days at a time. The whole world turned white and frozen.

Refuse-laden alleys of the Cité were buried under drifts that reached my hips, and cold winds tore down the streets, sweeping up skirts and cloaks in their icy grasp. Well before Christmas the Seine froze over and all river commerce ceased. There were was plenty of ice, but little water; clothes and linen could no longer be washed, and all things that came by barge, especially food, became scarce.

In Mathilde's room, lacy patterns of ice formed inside the windows, making miniature white landscapes that invited contemplation of what it might be like to freeze to death, out there in the bitter street.

We stuffed the numerous chinks in our walls with wind-torn pages from

33

old journals, and lined the walls and windows with all the clothing and fabric in our boxes and baskets. The room looked like a gypsy camp, yet our breath frosted as we spoke and it was hard, sometimes impossible, to ply the needle with our blue, stinging hands.

The cold was as absolute as God's justice, and there were those who did consider the great cold a punishment on France for her evil ways. Of course, why God would punish homeless beggars who froze in our doorways, rather than the sinful rich who toasted in front of the fires, was not explained. I wonder what Doctor Guillotine was doing, in that winter of 1784? Was he playing with the toy death machine he had found described in an ancient and dusty history of the Egyptians? Would that he had frozen to death, along with the thousands who did.

There was little to do that winter but wait. For spring. For firewood. For food. To be relieved of the burden of Mouret's bastard.

I hadn't gone to the midwife, as my auburn-haired rescuer had instructed. As terrified as I was at the thought of having Mouret's bastard, I was more frightened by the thought of dying.

"I've heard of the yellow powder," Louise admitted when I questioned her about it. "The Duc de Montpensier's mistress used it last year to rid herself of the consequences of an affair she didn't wish the duke to know about. It worked for her. But sometimes it kills the woman. Remember Anna-Marie, the housegirl from Arles that Madame Mouret had a few years ago? That's how she died. From the yellow powder. It was a terrible death."

The white plume of Louise's breath ceased for a moment and then continued. "Why do you ask?" She eyed me speculatively.

"No reason," I said, putting my face close to my sewing. So. A woman before me took the yellow powder to be rid of Mouret's bastard, I thought. Well, I would not be the next to die for him. But neither did I want his child. And I had not had my courses since the night of the rape.

I had told no one about the rape, and no one had questioned me about my torn and swollen lip, which took weeks to heal. People had more pressing issues on their minds—where to find wood to burn in the hearth, and which baker had not yet tripled the cost of bread, as Mouret had.

The hardness of life and the shame of what had happened kept me silent. The guilt was Mouret's, but the shame was mine, and it was cold and harsh as the winter winds that made the curtains dance in a macabre, chilling frenzy. Nor did I go to De Crosne as I had threatened. Who would he believe—a respectable baker, ah well, at least a baker, a man of commerce, or a whore's daughter?

So I kept that secret, as well. I realized that the knowledge of Mouret's warehouse thefts was more useful as a threat against him than as a tool for revenge. He was keeping his distance.

I avoided his daughter that winter. To Jeannette, my closest of friends, I could not lie or even hold my tongue, and I did not want to shame her with what her father had done.

Mathilde, who had complained often and bitterly of my laziness, had no complaints of me during the cold year. I was content to sit indoors and sew for many hours a day, from the first to the last dim light. At my sewing I thought only of the arabesques and furbelows of the opera gowns and dancing dresses I worked, not of other matters, which would have made my hands slow and my heart heavy. I wove elaborate romances about the women who wore those gowns. They were, in truth, only public girls with short and sad careers ahead of them, but I turned them into young princesses who would twirl in the arms of a handsome and loving prince. They returned home from the ball, and were greeted by sweet, tender mothers and protective fathers. I made stories about all I had never had.

And at night I dreamed of a faceless mother who had no words for me, only a haunting smile, and of another woman with red hair who rode in a carriage pulled by winged horses.

I realized, that winter, I must leave the Cité. My childhood was over, and to become an adult there would mean to be like Mathilde, prematurely old and bitter. Nor would I be like Yvette, who had taken to leaning against damp walls until early morning, taking any customer who would look her way. Or like Louise, who lived her life in a constant state of waiting, and worrying that her waiting would be in vain.

Monsieur de Bracy did not come often to Louise in the frozen winter. His wife, the countess, had rented a hôtel near the Palais Bourbon, and she required his constant attendance, now that she was in the city. When he was able to steal away for an hour or two, he was distracted and short-tempered. Louise was often in tears and the cold, even in her more luxurious rooms, made the tears freeze on her eyelashes. She only lighted the hearth when he was there, to save her wood. She was too proud to ask him for more money, to point out that firewood was now as dear as the King's private stock of smoked venison.

It was Monsieur de Bracy who guessed my secret. Once when he came, he invited me to share a meal with them. I accepted thankfully, for hunger crept close on the heels of the great cold, and I had eaten nothing since the day before.

"You have changed," he said, peering closely at me while Louise ladled a thick bean soup into my bowl. Normally I would have served, but it was his whim that I be treated as a guest that day.

"It is the cold," I said, avoiding his eyes. I had grown thinner, not fatter, yet my monthly courses were still as frozen inside me as the waters of the unmoving Seine. Could he tell?

"No," he insisted, "there is something more." He took my chin in his chapped, fleshy hand and tilted my face to his so that our eyes met. I lowered mine.

"As I thought," he said, releasing my chin so quickly I tilted backward in my chair. Often he was gentle, but when angry de Bracy used the same brisk mannerisms he probably showed his hunting dogs and horses.

He slurped at his soup. "When did it happen?" he asked between gulps.

"I'm certain I don't know what you are talking about," I protested.

"That false innocence—it is false, now—convinces me even more, Julie. I had such hopes for you. And you have thrown them away!"

"What has been thrown away! I assure you, my treasure, we waste nothing here," Louise said, coming in with a small loaf of bread. She had grown thinner, too, and wore a cape garnished with shimmering peacock feathers to hide the bones that stuck out in her shoulders.

"Her maidenhead," he said angrily. "She has become coy, she does not meet my gaze openly. In a word, she is no longer a virgin." He poured himself a glass of port and slammed the glass onto the tabletop. The wine spilled, and a red stain spread over Louise's expensive brocade cloth. She was too frightened of his anger to move, but only stared at it.

His anger woke mine. I jumped up and quickly poured salt over the stain. No need to spoil the expensive and pristine cloth, just because monsieur now considered me spoiled.

"I had no say in the matter," I muttered. "I was forced. It was no doing of mine."

"Forced? Truly? Then I am sorry, Julie. But you should have heeded what I tried to tell you some weeks ago. You were no longer a child, even then, but ripe for the taking. By not making a choice for yourself, you left the choice to someone else. I won't ask who your lover is. I'm certain he is no one I would know . . . or approve."

"That is unjust. He is not my lover. He raped me." Louise dropped the serving ladle into the soup and a thick green stain met the red one. I left it. Damn the cloth.

We sat in silence for some moments. I waited, but de Bracy made no more offers to introduce me to the right gentlemen. I knew why not. To begin a good career, a girl must go into it a virgin. To begin that most deceitful and hopeless of relationships, an illusion of innocence is required.

A new thought occurred to me. Was that why Mathilde had made such a show of guarding my virginity? I felt very alone.

"What will you do now?" he asked.

"I don't know," I said.

"Excellent soup, my dear," he said to Louise.

Later, after I had finished clearing the table—I was servant again, no longer guest—and Louise was changing for the opera, de Bracy took me aside. His bad humor had passed. The meal had concluded with a very pleasing apple tart, and he was in a mind to be kind.

"Take this, and say nothing of it to Louise or your grandmother." He handed me a folded and sealed piece of paper.

"What is it?"

"A letter of introduction. Should you need to, show this letter to a certain Dr. Albert. You will find his rooms near the Hôtel des Invalides. He will shelter you, and then make arrangements for the child. The letter is not addressed to him—he requires a certain amount of discretion in his business. It says only that I will speak for your honesty and good nature."

Dr. Albert would get rid of Mouret's bastard.

"For your own sake, wait till the child is born. Do nothing before. Childbirth is nothing compared to one of Dr. Albert's abortions," de Bracy said.

I put the letter in my pocket and then, back in Mathilde's room, hid it at the bottom of my sewing basket.

In December, Mathilde and I ran out of wood and the money with which to buy more. Our teeth chattering, our hands blue, we sat in despair for two days, wondering what to do. Finally, I traded my tortoiseshell combs and pins for an armful of twigs, and when that was gone Mathilde and I roused ourselves from the lethargy caused by cold and hunger, and trudged to the Palais Royal, with the other beggars. Food and wood had become so expensive none of our clients had money for new gowns. We were out of work.

Many were trudging in the same direction; paths had been worn through the deep, sullied drifts leading across the Pont Neuf and down the rue St. Honoré to the charity bonfires of the Duc d'Orléans. It was there that those who could no longer heat their rooms gathered. The duke was a prince of France, almost as highly placed as the King himself . . . and much more popular.

Marie-Antoinette and Louis also lit bonfires in the gardens of Versailles, but those bonfires were not as well-attended as the ones in the Palais Royal. Parisians made political decisions even when it was a mere matter of keeping warm.

The convents and monasteries of the city handed out bread to ever increasing lines of supplicants. Supply carts no longer made their daily arrival at Les Halles because the farmers could not force their donkey-pulled carts through the ice and snow. The bread shortages that would plague Paris for the next decade began.

I continued to go to Les Halles for a long while, just in case some wrinkled apples, an egg or two, or a scrawny chicken might be found and traded for some piece of embroidery I had slaved over for days. I believed that as long as we were not reduced to begging, we could yet be all right. Increasingly, I went home empty-handed and each day when I returned the lines in front of Mouret's bakery would have grown longer. Our credit with the baker had expired long ago.

The day came when Mathilde and I, silent and morose, took our place in the begging lines in front of the convent of the Sisters of Charity. After hours of waiting we were given a roll each. We ate them then and there, tearing into them and swallowing as quickly as the other beggars, and we almost choked on them, that first time.

The dyings started early and finished late, that winter. The youngest, children so small that the drifts towered over them, were the first to die. Then the beggars who slept in the frozen doorways and bridge buttresses died, their bodies littering the snow like fallen, grey tree branches, so thin were they. The old died, and those already weak with illness and poverty before the cold and hunger came. Winter was like a ragpicker, picking up and putting into her basket those remnants of humanity who had not the strength to fight through another day.

But that winter the dyings did not stop with the very young and very old. Middle-aged and even young people began to cough one week, spit up blood the next, and take to their beds the week after, usually not to rise from them again, nor leave their shelters except on a mortician's plank.

So it was with Madame Mouret.

Jeannette came to me one day in December, after Mathilde and I had begged for our bread and come back to sleep under the bed linens that hadn't been washed for two months. It was the middle of the day, but there was nothing to do but sleep. It was too cold to sew, or even to sit and think.

Jeannette was hurt that I had avoided her, but as old friends do she overlooked the slight when a more important matter came up.

"Mama's dying. Please come," she said.

Huddled under one of our blankets, Jeannette and I dragged ourselves through great piles of snow to her house and the death room. Her brothers and sisters sat in a long row of chairs, red-eyed and sniffling; the youngest still crawled on the floor and played with a rattle.

Mouret was there, slumped in a chair and looking as if he hadn't slept in some time. He was thinner. The hunger had reached even the baker. But he was drunk as ever, and great tears of self-pity rolled down his face. He was losing his most hard-working servant, his wife. He looked at me once and then looked away. I gave him no greeting. The hunger had consumed my rage and fear; all that was left was an anger that was even colder than the winter.

Madame Mouret was already unconscious. She roused only once to cough so hard I thought it must cast up her heart and lungs, and then she lay back down, a grimace of pain and distaste pulling at the corners of her mouth. After an hour, the grimace left her face and her gentle smile returned. Jeannette arranged her arms over her chest in an attitude of prayer and closed the eyes.

The children old enough to know what was going on set up a great wailing. Jeannette went into the pantry to begin dinner preparations. I followed and watched as she diced turnips and withered carrots and threw them into the stew pot. She was older. Her hands moved in the same quick, sure gestures her mother had used.

"Have you heard from Jacques?" I asked.

"I see him tomorrow. We meet under the belltower of St. Roche. He has rooms near there." She smiled. "They are nice rooms. I have already seen them many times."

"What of Monsieur Dalmas and his son?"

"Papa is still busy with the contract. They haven't agreed on some of the terms. My papa's greed is giving me more time, and for that I am thankful. But the marriage will not take place. I belong to Jacques now. Stay and have some soup, Julie. And some bread. If you eat in the pantry, Papa won't bother you. I think for today, at least, you are safe enough."

She knew.

We embraced, and then she set about feeding the children.

I learned the next day that Madame Mouret had been with child when she died.

"Just as well," was Mathilde's comment on her death. "This is no winter to be birthing. It was an easier death she had now, than she would have had later."

I put my hand over my stomach, trying to feel if it was yet different. All I felt was the hunger ache.

That night Mathieu came and threw a stone against my window. I had not seen him since the night of the rape. I joined him in the street; his face and hands were covered in chilblains and he was so thin his shoulder bones showed through his heavy coat. A row of snowflakes rested on the sharp ridges.

"I've come to say good-bye," he said with a voice much older than it had been just months before. "I'm off to the quai de Ferrailles to join whatever merchant ship will have me."

There was a moon that night and it reflected brightly off the snow and ice. I could see his face clearly in that cold, shimmering light, the puckered spot on the forehead where Mouret had struck and left a scar.

"I don't blame you," he said. "Not for anything that happened. But I've had enough. There has to be better than this." He kissed me, a man's kiss, not a boy's, and turned and left. The little that remained of my childhood went with him.

Mathilde and I did not celebrate Christmas that winter. At least, not together. We stood in the begging line for our extra Christmas ration, and then Mathilde trudged back to the room while I attended a Mass at Notre Dame. I had need of solace, and knew not where else to turn.

It was warm in the cathedral, even cozy, thanks to the great press of worshippers. Incense and music filled the air, and there were huge white mums on the altar. I, no great believer in a God who would so botch things that he would take the gentle Madame Mourets from the world and leave to us the Monsieur Mourets, prayed anyway. Even if I survived the winter, what of the spring? And the summer? And all the seasons to come? I needed answers to many questions.

A more religious person might consider the next event a miracle. I think it had more to do with the extra food, the warmth, the sense of well-being that the familiar words of the Mass gave. But during the kyrie I felt a strong cramping in my stomach. And by the time the sacrament was being blessed, my monthly course was trickling down my legs, leaving red drops on the stone floor.

Those near me smirked and giggled at what they thought was my discomfort. But I had never felt such joy. Each cramp was a hosanna of thankfulness. I did not carry Mouret's bastard. I was free, the future was still mine to choose.

Many years later Delilah, my Indian friend, told me of such things

40

happening . . . a hard winter, not enough cornmeal, the squaws who would not have a monthly flow or conceive a child until times were better. "The Great Spirit looks over women," she told me. "He knows it's not good if she carries a child when there is too much hunger."

After the New Year, Mathilde started going out in the afternoon and coming back a few minutes later with fresh bread from Mouret's bakery, although we had neither money nor credit. I, as close to carefree as I had been for many months, assumed that one of her customers had paid an overdue bill or opened an advance account. I did not question our fortune.

I should have. After the Feast of the Epiphany she came home with her basket laden not just with bread, but also with sweet rolls and a meat pastry. My mouth watered at the sight of it. We hadn't tasted meat in weeks.

"I've been to see Mouret," she wheezed through blue, thin lips.

"So I see. How have you been able to purchase all this?" I couldn't wait for her to get her coat off, to sit at our little table, so we could begin eating.

"I didn't purchase it. It's a gift." She was slow as ever, and playfully held the basket under my nose to taunt me. She was in an uncommonly good humor.

"Jeannette is betrothed. To Monsieur Dalmas's son. The contract is signed, they will be married the first Sunday after Easter. Don't you think Jeannette is lucky, to be marrying a baker?" she said.

"No. She doesn't love him. Mouret is forcing her into it. Considering his meanness, I am surprised he sends us gifts to announce the engagement of his daughter." As good as the meat pastry smelled, I was quickly losing my appetite.

"It is time for you to think of marriage, too," my grandmama said.

"Gladly. But I have been so busy dressing for the opera I haven't had time to consider my many suitors," I said.

"Don't be glib, Julienne. You have a suitor. I have accepted in your name."

"Who?" I no longer smelled the meat pastry; I smelled a rat.

"Mouret will marry you."

"Mouret?" I would have laughed, but I was cold and hungry. And now, frightened. What had Grandmama done?

"Yes. Mouret. You are a lucky girl."

"No. I will not. He's old. He's a drunk. He's cruel." I thought of how the bristles grew out of his cheeks, his red nose and bloated face, his thin hair flecked with flour. I thought of the rape, and his beating afterward, how he had delighted in them. "I will not," I repeated.

"She will not! She will not!" Mathilde screeched. "I say you will. What else would you do? End up like Yvette? If you marry him you will be mistress of your own household, you will have a servant and eat fresh bread every day, as much as you want. And so will I."

"Grandmama. Mouret raped me. In the autumn. That is why I will not marry him."

"I know," she said, shrugging her shoulders. "All of the Cité knows. All the more reason to marry him." I should have known it was impossible to keep a secret in the Cité.

"I hate him."

"So hate him. But marry him. I command this, Julie. Tomorrow morning you yourself will go to the bakery and thank him for the great honor he is doing you."

She sat down and began to eat. I picked up my share of the food and threw it into the fire.

I went and sat by the window, and even the cold draft could not chill my anger. I sat and watched the falling snow and remembered when Mouret pursued me, when I knew I must run, and did not know where to go. Mathilde was making a sacrifice of my life. I sat and sat, and Grandmama finished eating and went to lie down.

I tried to work on a piece of embroidery, and the plan came as quickly as one of the winter storms. Run. I must run. My embroidery was good, even better than Mathilde's. I had worked for her all these years, why not seek employment as a seamstress elsewhere? And why not go to Mademoiselle Bertin herself, the Queen's seamstress?

It was a bold plan, one that a more experienced woman would never have considered, for to knock at Bertin's door was to knock at a door just slightly lower than the Queen's own. But my lack of sophistication—even my desperation—was an advantage. They made me bold, they nipped me forward.

I packed the piece of needlework and sat for another while, watching the flame of the hearth die. Mathilde was asleep, oblivious to my cares and fears. I covered her with the blanket we shared, trying to feel some tenderness for the woman who had loomed so large in those first sixteen years of my life. She was thin, her eyes were sunken into her face. Her eyelids flickered as she slept, and I wondered what she dreamed about. My mother? That one lover we all have whose memory won't fade away but stays to remind us all our days of what could have been?

She stirred and woke.

"Tell me about my mother," I said, kneeling by the bed and taking her hand. "I should know of her. It is my right."

"Your right. You will have a lifetime of misery if you must have your rights," she said with a snort. But she softened with the knowledge that we would soon be parted. Although it would be sooner than she thought, and for a different reason.

"She was like you, she thought there should be pots of gold at the end of the rainbow. I was at the end of the rainbow once. I found a pot of shit. You don't believe me. Well, someday you'll find out for youself. Your mother did. She was stupid. She wasn't raped. She went to it willingly. With a penniless aristo who couldn't give her name, protection, or even a roof over her head."

"She must have loved him very much," I said.

"Love." She sneered, sounding strangely like de Bracy.

"What was his name? What name did she go by?"

"De Marepois. She was called Angelina. Angelina from the rue des Anges." I smiled. At least once, for a short time, Mathilde had possessed some humor, some wit to help combat the hardness of life.

"What happened to her?"

"What do you think happened? She ran off with him. She got with child. You. She came back to her old mother for help with the birth. And when she wouldn't give him up, I told her to leave and never come back."

I jumped as if a spark from the hearth had burned me. She had thrown out her own daughter, my mother.

They say the truth can set you free. That truth freed me of any guilt I might have felt for abandoning Mathilde. She had disowned her daughter, and was sacrificing me.

I pulled the blanket back up to her chin.

"Go to sleep, Grandmama. And pleasant dreams," I said.

It seemed as good a way as any to say farewell.

4

. . . the sewing room . . .

"He who dares not speak well of himself is almost always a coward, who knows and dreads the ill that may be said of him; and he who hesitates to confess his faults, has neither spirit to vindicate, nor virtue to repair them. Thus frank with respect to myself, I shall not be scrupulous in regard to others . . . I shall paint them all in their proper colors."

—Madame Roland

There wasn't much to do. I threw the few things I owned into a basket, made myself as presentable as possible, and then, closing the door softly but firmly behind me, made my way down the dark stairs and into the street.

"Cold night to be out," called Pierre, the nightwatchman. His lantern lit his thin, lined face, casting all else into deeper darkness.

"It is," I agreed. "But I have an errand." I hesitated, and then stepped into the circle of his light so he would know me. "Please, when you see Louise next, tell her . . . tell her I said good-bye."

Pierre, kind and fatherly and witness to many a late night elopement, eyed me.

"Well, then. God go with you," he said.

There was a moon that night, just as there had been on the night that

44

Mathieu left. It was a good sign, it made it easy for me to pick my way through the alleys and paths that led to the rue St. Honoré. As I walked, trodding over snow that squeaked underfoot like new shoe leather, the streets became wider, the houses larger and in better repair. I walked from the architecture of poverty to the architecture of hopes and promise that night, and I vowed I would never retrace my steps.

Bertin's door, like the others in Paris at the time, had no number to identify it, but it was easily recognizable by the large sign hanging over the door. AU GRAND MOGOL. COURTURIER TO THE QUEEN. I stepped under that sign and prayed it would welcome me for many a day. Lights shone forth from the curtained windows. I had all but forgotten how festive candlelight could be, it was so long since Grandmama and I had been able to burn candles.

My first knock was timid and did not disturb the stillness of the silent winter night, for few people were in the street. The second knock was more forceful, and was answered by the sound of footsteps within.

A tall, fair young woman opened the door, so many pins poised precariously between her lips I was amazed she could speak through them.

"What is it?" she asked.

"I wish an interview with Mademoiselle Bertin. I come seeking work." I was beginning to shiver from my cold walk.

Another woman's voice, higher and impatient and not as friendly, echoed down the long hall to the door.

"What is it, Manon?"

"A woman. Come for work," Manon called back over shoulder, still not removing the pins. She looked me up and down, making a quick judgment that I hoped was in my favor. It was. She opened the door wider.

"Come in. But call her madame, not mademoiselle," she whispered to me.

My first impression of Bertin's establishment lingered long in my memory. Never before, or since, not even in the Queen's dressing room, have I seen such a profligate profusion of lace, fine as cobwebs, rainbow-colored taffetas and silks, baskets of feathers robbed from the most exotic birds of the world, and gilt and jewels piled high as my knees, waiting to find their way into embroidery rich as a queen's ransom. The room looked like a treasure trove which had been broached by pirates.

And the smells! The seamstresses at work in that shop numbered more than two dozen and they all wore their own favorite scent. Jasmine, rose, carnation, lily, hyacinth, all the flowers of last year's gardens wafted through the air, mingling with the smells of pomade and powder and the lingering, mouthwatering smell of the roast they had enjoyed for dinner.

As I stepped through the doorway I heard the sound of heavy footsteps, and then Bertin herself appeared, armed with her quill and ledger and a sample of yellow silk that trailed over her shoulder. She had once been a great beauty; the woman who stopped before me was of brief stature and thick build, and possessed of two chins more than are necessary for beauty's sake.

But she was quick-witted, Bertin. She was one of the most successful merchants in France, and a woman did not reach that position by being slow or soft. Her eyes ran the length of my figure, taking in the ragged hem on my dress, the weathered and wide cracks in my ancient shoes and, I hoped, the determination with which I returned her glance.

"Come in," she said finally. "Manon, put some paper under her or she'll drip all over the carpet." Manon placed a paper on the floor and I stepped obediently onto it.

"Now," Bertin said. "You say you've come for work? Even if I do need another seamstress—a point of which I am not convinced—why should I hire you?"

"I am one of the best seamstresses in Paris," I said.

"We expect nothing less of our girls." Bertin used the royal 'we,' to make it quite clear, as if all the world did not already know it, that her most highly placed customer was no less than the Queen of France. "What gives you the right to that claim?"

I took a bundle from my basket and gave it to her. "I cut this bodice from my own pattern. The embroidery is not my best . . ." It was, but I wanted to exaggerate my skill.

She examined it at great length, carrying it to the great chandelier to better see the oak trees and squirrels I had worked into the pattern. I had adapted the pattern from one on display in the Garde-Meuble. Of course it pleased her. She had designed the original herself.

"And where did you learn your craft?" she asked in a voice only slightly warmer.

"From my grandmother. She runs a small but popular shop. In the Auvergne." I must not admit to being from the Cité. I, and my low reputation as being the whore's daughter, could then be too easily traced. Bertin was a bourgeoise and known for her strict morality. The starving class could not afford fine morals and the rich did not need them. But the growing ranks of prim-mouthed bourgeoisie in Paris were a force to be reckoned with . . . as my Queen later discovered, when her own reputation was beyond repair.

"Do you have a letter of recommendation?"

I hid a sigh of relief. The work had pleased her. I handed her the letter from de Bracy, still sealed and unread by me. I hoped he had told me the truth about it, that it merely said I was honest and trustworthy, and nothing of the events that led him to write that letter. I held my breath as she ripped the seal and read it.

"It praises you," she announced. "But who is this de Bracy? He says he is a count, but we have never heard of him." Another bit of innocence was shattered. Louise's aristocratic protector, the only aristocrat I had known, whom I had feared and reverenced and considered to be a semi-deity in his own right, was unknown to a Parisian seamstress. To learn that there were as many classes of aristos as there were of commoners was a great revelation.

"Now tell me, mademoiselle, and be honest, for we can tell deceit, why have you left your grandmother to come here."

I took a deep breath and told my only truth of the night.

"My grandmother planned a marriage for me that was disagreeable."

She smiled benevolently. Bertin herself was unwed, and forced marriages were the one cause that could actually produce a feeling of sympathy in her tightly corseted bosom.

"We will give you a trial," she agreed, "if you are prepared to work with great diligence and perseverance. I am not a wealthy woman and the pay will be sufficient but not extravagant. You will have to live frugally, and within your income. I do not approve of credit for the lower class."

"Yes," I said demurely, stifling a smile and curtseying to my new mistress. And all the while I eyed the oil portraits on the walls, the floor expensively painted to look like yellow marble, the silver sconces that reached out from the walls. There were more candles burning in that one room than Mathilde and I had burned in our whole life together. And not one of them was cheap tallow with its odor of rancid fat; they were all of perfumed wax. Bertin, in her satin gown, with her rings on every finger, knotted rugs under foot, and vases of hothouse flowers, wanted me to sympathize with her hardships.

"I believe I can be suitably frugal," I said.

"It is only a trial." She wagged a finger in my face. The diamond on it was large as a pea. On the day I left, she again wagged that finger in my face and said, "It has been a trial, mademoiselle," thereby making the only witticism I heard from her lips.

"Just until the Queen's laying-in wardrobe is completed," she said. I had forgotten the news about the Queen's latest pregnancy. In the Cité we talked of food and little else that winter. I was thankful to Marie-Antoinette. She had chosen a good time to need a new laying-in wardrobe. As it happened, though, I was to stay with Bertin for years.

"But if you prove untrustworthy or lazy, out you will go. There is to be no scandal here, you must follow the highest principles at all times. Any gossip attached to my girls taints me, and the court through me. Understand?"

I nodded. I had no desire to return to the Cité. It was now imperative that I never do so. My life must begin anew, with no ties to the past. That was fine with me. What was there to go back to? Louise, with her endless waiting for de Bracy? Jeannette, who would be beaten till she married Dalmas fils, and then become feebleminded with regret, like her dead mother? Mathilde, who had banished her daughter and tried to sacrifice her granddaughter for a loaf of bread? The door was closed behind me.

Manon, the young woman who had opened this new door, agreed that I should share her room for the time being . . . another temporary agreement that lasted some years. I followed her on unsteady feet, for the heat from Bertin's many hearths was making me feel the fatigue of my long walk. We traversed a small courtyard in which many snow-encrusted statues of Cupid pointed their arrows at us, and then a narrow interior staircase, which led to the rooms in which many of Bertin's girls lived.

Manon's room was large, for she was the favorite. The walls were hung with green satin and the huge bed in the middle of the room was covered in the same rich cloth, and canopied with écru lace. It was much more splendid than Louise's room in the Cité. A new and very large tile stove sent out waves of heat, even though Manon had spent the evening in the workroom. I had never before seen a tile stove. It reached from floor to ceiling and the enameled tiles were painted with birds and flowers. A copper bed-warmer rested in a special alcove of the stove, ready for use. Manon followed my eyes.

"I can't stand the feel of cold sheets," she said. "Where are you from?" She handed me a soft, white towel to dry my sodden hair. My clothes, which had been stiff with frost and ice, had thawed and water ran in cold rivulets down to my ankles.

"The Auvergne," I said.

"You lie, Julienne. Your accent is Parisian." Manon twirled a golden curl around her forefinger and studied me. "But there are many reasons for concealing an identity. I will not press you for yours. What is your favorite color?"

"Red," I said.

"*Mon Dieu!*" she gasped, shocked by this choice in a way that my lie had not shocked her. "Do you know nothing? With a dark complexion like yours, you must never wear red. You would look like a gypsy. And the court favors pastels. So we wear pastels. Voilà. Try this."

She pulled from her opened clothes press a heavy winter brocade gown of palest yellow, the color of chamomile tea in a white cup, and measured it against me with her lively eyes.

"The color is good," she decided. "Try it on, and I will fit you. You are skin and bones."

Meekly, I permitted the authoritative Manon to push and pull me while she pinned the gown, although the need for sleep clamored in my body as persistently as children at a county fair.

"Bertin meant what she said, Julienne," she warned as she worked. "Cheat her of the time for which she pays, and you'll rue the day you stepped on her threshold. If you're late in the morning, she'll fine you. If your work is not good enough, she'll make you sweep floors and empty bedpans till you want to go back to . . . wherever it is you have come from. If you steal, God forbid, she'll have you imprisoned. I tell you this not to frighten you, but because I want to be your friend. Understand?"

I nodded. She finished with the gown and I lay down to rest in my still damp chemise. Morning, it seemed, came but a moment later. I woke to the sound of Manon singing as she splashed at the washbasin.

"Get up, lazy one!" she called cheerfully, "or the hot water will go cold again, and then you'll be sorry!" Hot water! I had felt nothing but ice water for months. The basin gave off spiraling whirls of perfumed steam, for Manon had put rose drops in it. Afterward, skin tingling, I dressed in the yellow gown. With it, Manon supplied stockings and leather slippers, and a thickly quilted petticoat. "It will help cushion your backside as you work," she said smiling. "The old slavedriver works us such long hours some of the girls wear two petticoats, one with a cushion sewn inside. Me, I only need one petticoat and no cushion. I am nicely built, don't you think?" She twirled in her chemise. Her vanity and pride was as open as a pretty child's.

"You're beautiful," I admitted. "But Manon, I cannot pay you for these. Not yet."

"You really think I'm beautiful? So does Raimond. But think nothing of payment. They are gifts. They don't suit me. And someday you will return the favor."

She pulled the cord and another miracle—breakfast on a tray, delivered by a silent, stealthy servant who knocked at the door before entering. Coffee pale and fragrant with cream, rolls still hot from the oven, a large wedge of cheese . . . I gulped mine down and most of Manon's too, for she drank vinegar for breakfast to keep her voluptuous figure from becoming overly so.

She watched me with open curiosity. She had never seen such hunger, her eyes told me. But she did not voice the questions she must have had.

Manon's watch, worn on a gold chain around her neck, indicated eight o'clock when we returned the way she had led me the evening before, back to the work room. I paused so often Manon grew impatient with me, but I wanted to admire the soft Persia carpets, the portraits and landscapes that hung over the many fireplaces and in stairwells, the spacious rooms hung with yellow satin festoons—I had since guessed that yellow was Bertin's favorite color, and Manon had done me a good turn by selecting that color for me.

Bertin had taste and the means to express it. Her shop was as luxurious and appealing as the court gowns she designed for the Queen. The rooms glowed with a soft richness and lightness, for that was the new style, a special airiness that conveyed the impression that the world, in general, was a very happy and carefree place, designed for dance parties and lunches in a rose garden. There were no dark corners, no heavy and bulky chests, but flowers, flowers everywhere and elegant, thin-legged furniture that did not look sturdy enough to support more than a vase or two. And everything was new, made in recent years by court-favored woodworkers and artisans. Marie-Antoinette, the taste arbiter for all of France, could not abide the old, the used, could not abide anything that was not to her own style of all lightness and pale pastel sweetness.

It occurred to me that the many old countesses, princesses and duchesses of France who clung to their ancient, dusty heirlooms either because of personal preference or poverty must be in despair over this new style. Queens are hated as much for their taste as for their politics. Perhaps more so.

One special portrait hung over the fireplace in the main reception room. It drew me as strongly as gravity. It was of a woman, dressed in a gold-and-blue court dress, with reddish-blonde curls piled extravagantly over a high and white brow. Her eyes were familiar, I felt I knew that sad smile that seemed to mock the beholder. Her regal posture, the auburn hair, the deep, forget-me-not blue of the eyes . . . they belonged to the woman in the carriage who had rescued me the night of Mouret's rape.

"Who is this?" I asked the impatient Manon.

"Silly. Don't you even recognize the Queen? Perhaps you are from the Auvergne."

"The Queen," I repeated. The revelation took my breath away.

"Have you truly never seen her before, nor even a portrait?" Manon was amazed.

"Never. At least, only once. She did me a favor."

"Lucky you. They say the Queen has a long memory, and looks to repeat favors. But hurry. We'll be late, and I've already been fined twice this month. And don't tell Madame Bertin the Queen once did you a favor. She, too, has a long memory and is prone to jealousy. Kindnesses from a Queen can be a double-edged sword." Manon, I believe, had a small but useful gift for prophecy.

When we arrived the workroom was already humming with activity and the noise of a goodly number of young women, all chattering at once with little regard to what others were saying. Each seamstress had her own worktable at which she sat behind great piles of cloth. Remnants of fabric littered the floor and younger girls, the ribbon pressers, swept the aisles regularly. If they didn't the room would soon have been awash with litter.

I sat at an empty table left for me opposite Manon. I hoped I would not be given anything complicated—I was stunned by the shock that I had been rescued by the Queen herself. I needn't have worried. Bertin, wary of my newness, gave me nothing but straight seams to do for many days. I was glad of it. I could concentrate on what was going on about me. I had much to learn in this new world. I wanted to belong, to know that I had been favored by Marie-Antoinette for a purpose.

I was quickly amazed by all that the seamstresses knew of Paris, the court and politics, as revealed by their chatter. Truly, if there were an inner sanctum of privileged information, it was that workroom. Later, when I was more experienced and allowed to fit customers, I learned that most people share confidences with their seamstresses as freely as if they were sharing them with their confessor. There is something about the intimacy, the serene and private atmosphere of a fitting room, that loosens tongues.

And Bertin's customers were far from being unremarkable. She received the cream of Paris society and most of the court in her shop; either an important title or great fortune was attached to a great many clients.

The chatter was often interspersed with the sound of the reception bell. We would hear the door open, the bell tinkle, and then one of the seamstresses would rise from her table and peer through the thick curtains that separated the sewing room from the public rooms. A good deal of curiosity went with the trade; gossip was the pleasure that made the long hours of work fly as quickly as our needles.

"It's the Duchesse de Chartres," a seamstress called Martine hissed early

51

my first morning, when I was still learning to concentrate on my stitches and listen attentively at the same time.

"Did you hear what her old goat, the Duke, did for her birthday celebration?" Martine continued with vicious glee.

"Old news, Martine, we all know," Manon sighed.

"I do not," I volunteered.

"He brought the governess in for the private family dinner!" Martine exclaimed with obvious satisfaction.

"Surely there is no fault in that?" I asked.

Manon smiled indulgently at my stupidity. "Madame Governess is also his mistress. His wife was most distressed," she informed me. "Martine, spy out again and tell us what she is looking at. Perhaps if her taste improved her old goat would spend a few evenings at home. Not that I would want him, if he were my husband. A more unappetizing man I've yet to meet."

The workroom filled with the giggles that quickly turned to solemn silence whenever Bertin came near.

The people we discussed in such a lighthearted manner (and who would have gladly put us in chains, had they overheard us) were among the most powerful in France. Hence, the most gossiped about. The Duc de Chartres, I quickly learned, was always a favorite topic of our insults. He, the rich and notorious son of the Duc d'Orléans (at whose charity bonfires I had warmed myself just weeks before), was a libertine with a reputation that addled the mind. It was whispered in matter-of-fact voices that he would willingly seduce anything—man, woman, child or animal—that still breathed. Manon said he once bedded thirty women in one night. But she believed that he hated women in the degree to which he professed to love them. She, sensible if vain daughter of a prosperous wine merchant, was not fooled by such demonstrations of virility.

"And he hates the Queen more than any other woman in the kingdom," she whispered to me.

This animosity between the Queen and her royal cousin were common knowledge, it seemed. She disliked his manners and pretensions, and had even publicly accused him of cowardice. He hated the fact that while he was from a family as old and important as the King's, it was Louis who sat on the throne, not himself. The Duc de Chartre's cause of discontent was an ancient and dangerous one.

He had also been Bertin's first sponsor, helping her years ago with the money and contacts she needed to establish herself. It was said she refused to be his mistress, saying instead she would sew his shirts, and her wit had pleased him. But the fact that Bertin's two best and most powerful customers, the Queen and the Duke, were mortal enemies, led to some tenuous and interesting situations in the workshop.

"Quick. The Queen's messenger is here," Bertin cried one morning after I had spent three weeks sewing straight seams and was getting bored with it. "Put the Queen's messenger in the pink room, the Duke's in the green, and don't let the two meet!" There was a scurry of activity; the two were successfully kept apart and peace was preserved.

But as hard as we tried to keep the two factions separate, it seemed they always came on the same days, and at the same hour.

The Princesse, Madame de Lamballe, was another favored client, and an excellent, inexhaustible topic of conversation. Once Marie-Antoinette's closest friend and companion, she had been usurped by the greedy Comtesse de Polignac. "As greedy as a Polignac," was a common insult those days, for the Comtesse was known to use the Queen's friendship in order to further her family's financial interest . . . at the expense of France. Paris disliked this, naturally, and looked with ill-favor upon Marie-Antoinette's involvement with this family of opportunists. We, loyal in our way to the Queen, would never have said this aloud, but it was rumored in the street that the Queen and her countess were lovers.

Paris did, however, approve of the Princesse de Lamballe. She was very beautiful, which always goes far when winning public favor, with pale blonde hair similar to Manon's, and a complexion that was a wonder of its time. A brief and mysterious dearth of pregnant bitches in that year of 1784 led to the conclusion that de Lamballe bathed her face with the blood of unborn puppies. I believed the missing dogs had more likely been stewed by starving citizens.

The rakish Duc de Chartres was said to be besotted by her. He had, according to workroom gossip, befriended de Lamballe's husband and led him so thoroughly down the primrose path that the youth had succumbed to various contagious diseases and died well before his time. Before the funeral was even over the Duke had set about seducing the chaste young widow. Whether he achieved his pleasure or not was a matter of speculation. Optimists tended to believe the Princess was firm in her virtue; cynics only shrugged and said, "Of course he's bedding her." No one knew for certain, especially not the Duke's neglected wife.

Such gossip made my head spin; those knowing *philosophes* of the sewing room, Martine and Manon, were capable of greater subtleties of thought and motive than the King's own ministers.

There was only one person immune to our chatter, and that was the

Queen herself. Even to mention her name without a proper tone of respect meant instant dismissal, should Bertin overhear.

It was not so much love that made Bertin protective of the Queen, I sensed, as the status of being the Queen's couturière and the need to preserve her position. As I more fully discovered later, those who seemed most loyal to Marie-Antoinette cared more for their own skins. When loyalty no longer suited them they abandoned the Queen as easily as last year's styles.

The remainder of that winter passed for me in a flurry of snow, gossip, hard work and instruction. There was much I had to learn to fit into my new circumstances. I memorized the difference between a fish fork and a fruit fork. I learned polite manners and the foundation of conversation, which must be witty at all times, although sincerity was not much called for. I learned to sit with a straight back and composed countenance for hours at a time, and to feign attention when the abbé came to read us his lengthy lectures on the virtues of chaste womanhood. I learned not to look at Manon on such occasions, for she would make faces that quickly and irrevocably banished solemnity. I learned to walk lightly as a dancer, and to flatter Bertin so outrageously that I blushed for it afterward. But Manon's instructions worked.

"You'll do," Bertin told me several weeks after my arrival. "Be circumspect in your behavior, keep a close tongue, and avoid slothfulness . . . and for God's sake do something with your hair. You look like a gypsy."

And so, under the mentorship of Manon, I learned to adopt those hairstyles that would distinguish me as a creature of fashion. It was one of my most difficult lessons. Coiffing hair à la liberté, or à la sphinx, required the patience of Job and the dexterity of Arachne; I had neither. Eventually even Manon gave up, and we elected a simpler style that required only four rolls of curls and a kind of curled horse's tail that hung over one shoulder.

The Queen's new son arrived in late winter, just as the snow-filled streets were showing the first muddy, brown patches of thaw. The Seine, held captive under a thick sheet of ice, broke free with a roar and flowed strongly under its thinning mantle. Promising green tips appeared on the winter-bare chestnut trees. In the Cité, it meant the dying time was over. In Bertin's workshops, we had our first taste of hothouse strawberries.

All of France had cause to celebrate, but none more so than I. Winter was passing, life was easier, even happy, and I was pleased with myself. The Cité seemed far away. But the past is never truly far from us; safety is an illusion.

The Queen's new son, her second, buoyed her popularity a bit, and I rejoiced in that, for I had come to regard her as my private saint. France celebrated the birth of the royal son with a wealth of activities, from special masses at Notre Dame to street dances. Bertin decided to open her rooms to the public and provided music and refreshments in honor of the Queen. We were to dress in new spring styles (she was, after all, a woman of business) in order to whet the public appetite. I was given a simple white muslin frock that had neither panniers nor train.

"I feel naked," I protested to Manon after slipping the thin thing over my head. "This is more like a nightdress than a gown."

"Don't be a goose. It's charming. You look like a shepherdess, all sweetness and light and innocence. Believe me, every woman who comes today will want one just like it. Which is, of course, Bertin's intent. Too bad your coloring is so unfashionable."

Manon had tried everything from lemon poultices to milk baths to lighten my complexion, but my skin stayed tawny as ever, and my already unmanageable hair grew even thicker with the hearty meals of Bertin's table. Decades later my looks would be known as the "creole style" and made all the rage by Josephine. But that was no consolation then, when I still had not known love but was learning vanity.

What Manon and I didn't know was that Marie-Antoinette had already ordered two dozen "shepherdess" dresses and, as revolutionary as the style seemed to me, its future was already assured.

The Queen's popularity was not. It lasted only as long as the first soft days of spring and then disappeared again as quickly as the thawing ice. As the streets became flooded with mud, the complaints about our Queen's extravagance and disdain for tradition filled the Paris air; one could keep neither one's foot nor one's loyalty free from corruption.

I tried. I was the strictest workroom enforcer of the rule that Marie-Antoinette remain unsullied by our busy tongues. Aside from that, there was little I could do. I enjoyed life, which was sweet and amusing, once hunger, poverty and disgrace were removed.

Since it was impossible to get about without the assistance of a carrier, a strong man was hired to carry one across the torrential streets, I gave in to that luxury. The first time I hired such a man and paid ten sous just to keep my feet dry I thought my life had indeed reached new heights. I was generally, however, considerably frugal, as I had promised Bertin I would be, and even acquired a nickname for my thrifty habits. I was the "Petite Franklin."

Goodman Benjamin Franklin, who had first arrived in Paris years before to enlist aid for the American insurgents, was still the most admired man in the city. He was quoted in churches, in taverns, by lackeys and princes. His portrait appeared on everything from fans to chamber pots and dining services.

Parisians, dressed in expensive laces and velvets, were enchanted with his plain brown homespun and stringy, uncurled hair. The Quaker look came in; velvets were out, just as Manon had predicted. Bertin's business throve, and her workroom was the eye around which the hurricane of fashion whirled. We produced work in huge quantities, and were paid well for it. By the time the spring waters receded I had a small purse of coins hidden in a flower pot in the room I shared with Manon.

And Manon continued her instructions. She came to regard me as her own private creation. She taught me to rub my hands with sheep's wool to keep them soft, to hold a fan to just below the eyes to indicate interest, and to snap it shut with a dramatic flourish to indicate rejection or warning. I learned to use many words to say little, for that is the essence of flirtation, and it was flirtation I was learning.

I was about to be elevated to the position of seamstress, one allowed to wait upon customers, instead of spending the long days over straight seams. For that higher position, I would have to mimic the manners of a lady, or be deemed a provincial, which was equal to ruination.

Flirtation was considered a skill of great importance. With it, one could awe female customers who might otherwise be troublesome. The advantage of being able to flirt with men successfully—and by success was meant receiving all you desired while giving nothing—need not be explained, except to say that many of Bertin's customers were men.

Princes, abbés, counts, dukes, gentlemen of the King's privy: they all ended up in Bertin's shop sooner or later, to purchase a tawdry fan to placate a complaining wife or an expensive gown to win a new mistress. Gifts from other establishments were considered inferior to ours. Hence, I must learn to coddle them, to please them, and encourage them to empty their wallets as completely as possible.

"It is expected," Manon insisted. "If some ancient fool with warts on his nose pinches you and rolls his eyes, are you going to scream 'Begone, ugly Methuselah?' Do so, and you'll soon find yourself transported to the street in no gentle manner. No, you'll say, 'La, Sir! How you tease! Don't you think madame would prefer this gown?' And then you show him the most expensive model we have. Understand?"

I learned to trust this sister-in-arms in all things, for she was worldly in ways I was not. And kind. When I finally pleaded with her to sew a cushion into the seat of my petticoat, she did so with good grace, never remarking that I ate like a horse and had little to show for it.

We worked hard, six days a week, twelve hours a day. But evenings and Sundays were our own. Manon spent many evenings at the ball. I spent the evenings alone, by my own choice usually, but not always. Life was becoming pleasant enough that I began to dream of lovers. But I remained distant from those few men who did approach me in that way, still afraid that I would do or say something that would give my past life away. And, I was afraid of something else: not that the reality of love would be similar to what Mouret had done, but that it would not be different enough.

On Sundays we attended chapel, and then we dressed in our best to promenade through the clipped green hedges and formal rose beds of the Tuileries. One was less liable to hear rude gossip about the Queen in that staid, traditional public garden.

Sometimes, for a change, we would promenade instead at the Palais Royal, the same place where less than a year, a lifetime ago, I had warmed my hands at the charity bonfires. This garden was not as lovely, for the Duc de Chartres had cut down all the ancient trees that had stood there, and clipped the hedges so severely that they looked mutilated. This penchant for destruction should have been a warning, but it was considered an aristocratic whim.

The Palais Royal gardens, despite their unattractiveness, were more popular than the Tuileries. Intellectuals gathered there to discuss Voltaire and Rousseau and the latest debate at Madame Roland's salon, so Manon and I went there to learn gossip of a slightly different nature . . . and to see, and be seen, of course. The Tuileries were lovely and traditional; the Palais Royal was lively and fashionable and for us fashion was more than clothing, it was a way of life.

In the Palais Royal, for instance, the women wore straw hats, not cloth or feather puffs. This signified their sympathy with the young Americans, and with republicanism. One would have thought that republican and democratic ideals expressed in a monarchy would have been prohibited or at least frowned upon, but our own Queen wore republican straw hats, along with her new shepherdess gowns. She had a talent, it seemed, for doing all she should not.

Aristocrats were fashionable, but only if they were both rich and witty; an impoverished or slow-witted aristo would be better off languishing in his country château than trying to woo Parisian society. Fidelity was as popular as a dull-witted, impoverished aristocrat. And much more difficult to find. It was expected that everyone be in love, but never with one's wedded spouse.

That was considered too dull for words, and wedded couples who showed mutual and public tenderness could say farewell to coveted social invitations.

Foreigners, unlike fidelity, were very much in demand, especially those from America. No house party or dinner was considered successful unless there was at least one American or Americanist (Frenchmen who had fought with the Americans) in attendance. Such men were able to go months without paying for their own dinner, and pretty girls trailed after them by the dozens. It was fashionable to have a lover, and if that lover were an Americanist, all the better.

Attendance at the opera, like an Americanist lover, elevated one's social position greatly—but only as long as you took your dogs, household servants, coffee service, and playing cards, and made a point of talking all the way through the performance. Attentiveness showed a dull mind.

Fashionable ladies suffered the vapors and refused to walk. When Madame Garais's carriage wheel broke, the story was circulated for days of how she hired another carriage to carry her back to her residence—which was just across the street from the disabled vehicle.

Gentlemen also refused to walk, except for the required promenades. Instead, they raced their small and swift whiskeys through the streets at breakneck speed, placing bets on the fastest carriage. What with the splashed mud and the constant threat of having toes or more run over, it was easily understandable why walking, except in gardens, was considered undesirable.

These same fashionable, adulterous and careless ladies and gentlemen often ended their hectic days by reading a chapter or two from Rousseau and shedding tears of delight over his maxims for a simple, unspoiled life in harmony with nature.

That was Paris before the revolution. The English author said it best: the world is truly a stage, crowded with play actors. And was Paris during and after the revolt any better? We are both angel and demon, all of us, and the worlds we create are both heaven and hell.

Even then, all was not the sweetness and light that fashion tried to create. Our Queen's preference for imported English muslin over French-made satins greatly damaged the southern textile towns and created massive unemployment. For a simple change of costume, weavers began to drink and children to starve. The textile guilds were among the first to rise in open defiance of the monarchy a few short years later.

But in that hot summer of 1785 I thought not of the weavers in the south, but of a single seamstress in the Cité. I, well-fed, well-dressed and already greeted by many of the famous names of Paris society thanks to my association with Bertin, was feeling a tinge of what others might call homesickness. Given different circumstances, I could have been one of those creatures who would have happily been born, wed, delivered of children, raised those children, and then died, all in the same city, same neighborhood, same house. As it was, I felt an urge to see Louise, my old friend, and my grandmama.

One hot morning I decided to risk a visit. If discovered, I decided, I would say I was delivering a charity basket—charity, too, was fashionable in a limited way.

Bertin's maître d'hôtel, an old man who was too deaf and nearsighted to be bothered with curiosity, packed a large basket of food at my request, and I covered the sausages and tarts with a new counterpane that would help keep Mathilde warm next winter. But as I was preparing to leave Bertin intercepted me in the hall.

"Mademoiselle, you have an air of stealth about you. What is this?" She poked inside the basket.

"I am visiting an ill friend," I replied too quickly.

"Kind of you," she said, but there was suspicion in her voice. "I will not pry," she decided. "But I have need of you this afternoon. When my errand is done, you may attend to yours." It was Sunday, my time off, but because I was the newest girl, the errand was mine. She put a bulky but light package on top of my basket. A gown to be delivered, probably.

"The Queen is waiting for this. She needs it immediately. Go there with good speed and then wait to be sure it is acceptable."

Bertin did not wait for an answer. The choice was not mine to make, nor was argument allowed.

I was to see the Queen. I was dizzy with delight and nervousness. Would she remember me? I feared that she wouldn't; I feared that she would. My heart thudded as heavily as the horse's hooves all the way to Versailles. My fellow passengers in the public coach watched me with concern, for I would alternately sigh and tremble, grow pale and then flushed. One young man went so far as to take the seat next to me and offer to hold my hand. "Is it family illness?" he asked with concern. He was unconscionably handsome and his eyes were kind, but my thoughts were of the quickly approaching audience. My fear, which he took for modesty, compelled him to hold my hand all the tighter, and for the first time in my life I felt that most reassuring of emotions. He was attempting to protect and comfort me.

We descended from the carriage together, but were soon swept apart by the currents of humanity that swirled through the courtyard of Versailles. Foreign ambassadors in exotic national costumes, black-robed magistrates, porters renting swords, flocks of gay sedan chairs, merchants and ministers bustled about behind the gilded gates. Versailles was, in truth, a city unto itself, with more than ten thousand people living within its confines.

Yet what most struck me was the palace itself. It was long and elegant and spacious—a rare commodity in crowded Paris—and contained so many long, sparklingly glazed windows it seemed that sheer will kept the seemingly fragile walls intact. Here was the epitome of sweetness and light.

I forced my way through the crowd to one of the Queen's guards, identified by his red-and-silver livery. He examined my letter of admittance and then led me over the smoothly paved courtyard and up a set of marble stairs. At the landing, he saluted smartly and left me in the custody of a new sentry.

Now I will see the Queen, I thought, trembling again. But no. This sentry led me through another courtyard, up a different flight of stairs. And then another sentry, and another and another. By the time I was conducted through the glittering Hall of Mirrors and into the less public rooms behind it, the Queen's rooms, my nervousness was almost drowned by fatigue and impatience.

I moved like one in a dream, admiring all I saw, from the intricate parquet floors to the abundant pink cupids painted on the vaulted ceilings, to the ladies of the court themselves, who stood in idle groups chattering much as seamstresses do. But these ladies were dressed in formal court dresses that were wider than even the wide doorways of Versailles, and they eyed me with haughty disdain. I had not thought to powder my hair and face; my darkness made me stand out among them like a weed among flowers.

Even after reaching the Queen's private rooms, it took another staff of sentries to lead me to the final door, behind which the Queen of France awaited her gown. I have heard it said that in the old days if Marie-Antoinette wished a glass of cool water it changed hands so many times; and followed such a rigorous protocol, that it was an hour before her thirst could be quenched, and the water arrived warm and flat. No wonder she was impatient with the formality of Versailles.

A femme de chambre led me to the last door. I raised my hand to knock.

"No, no!" she exclaimed, greatly disturbed. "One does not knock at Versailles. One scratches. It is much easier on the ears, more delicate than thumping."

Obediently, I opened my fist and scratched at the huge door.

It opened upon a scene I shall never forget, one I wished all Paris could have seen. Marie-Antoinette of Austria, Queen of France, sat childlike on the floor, her young son and daughter playing in her lap. Here was the "infamous woman," the destroyer of national budgets, the Austrian foreigner, on the floor playing at building blocks with her family. She was giggling and trying to position a too-large triangle over a round block. It fell, and she clapped her hands and laughed.

A lady-in-waiting gave me a push from behind and I was announced. Marie-Antoinette looked up and then, seeing an unfamiliar face, rose to her feet with a grace any opera dancer would have coveted. I curtseyed deeply three times as etiquette required, and kissed the small, white hand she offered. She handed her infant son to one of her women and reached eagerly for the package I carried. The basket of food had been left behind with a porter.

"Ah, just in time," she smiled. "I will wear it tonight." She reluctantly handed it to a femme de chambre who delicately undid the string; the Queen, despite her impatience, must not engage in labor even of that sort. The pink-and-silver gown was held up for her examination. It pleased her. She nodded, and the gown was taken to her dressing room to be freshly pressed.

That over, she turned back to me and gazed, first with indifferent eyes, then with growing recognition.

"It seems to me we have met before." Her eyes were unreadable. I waited. She held my future in her hands. Would she give me away?

"You are in better repair than when last we met," she said. "I am pleased."

The ladies-in-waiting stared. I heard a bored voice whisper, "Who is this grisette whom the Queen addresses in such a familiar manner?"

"Pay them no attention," said the Queen. "They will chatter about everything. It is the dreadful boredom of this place. So, relieve my boredom, petite, and tell me all that has happened since last winter." She sat on a blue satin couch, one foot tucked under. A little blackamoor, dressed all in white satin, stepped forward and proceeded to cool her with a huge fan made of ostrich feathers.

"I am employed by Madame Bertin," I said, conscious of the many heads now tilted in my direction. That much she had already guessed and my answer did not relieve her boredom.

"There is no husband?" Her question was direct.

"There was no need," I said blushing.

"A happy ending, then," she said with enjoyment. "But is Bertin kind? I hear she plays the tyrant. You are happy?"

"Yes, she treats us well." Does one tell a Queen how wonderful it is to eat twice a day, to have firewood even for the warm spring nights, to bathe in rosewater? No. "It gives me great pleasure to hope that my work will perhaps adorn the most beautiful woman of the realm," I said.

"You have learned flattery," she said, frowning.

"I am sincere," I said. The Queen's frown was a thing to avoid. And I was sincere, in this.

"You love me, then?" Her tone was like the one Manon had used when she asked, "Do you think me beautiful?" It was coy with vanity, but it came from the heart.

"I do, Madame. With all my heart. My joy would be to serve you."

"Well spoken. Perhaps someday I will remind you of that vow. Do you still pray for me?" But she turned away before I could answer. The interview was over.

I did not feel the ground beneath my feet, nor the jolt of the carriage and the hard bench under my backside, all the way back to Paris. The Queen had remembered me. I couldn't have been more impressed if the Virgin Mary herself had stepped from a cloud and given me her hand.

When the carriage made its stop at the Pont Neuf, however, I descended from the dream and back to mundane reality. I had another errand to complete.

A small, wondrously begrimed little boy stood by the towering grey statue of Henry IV, shuffling his bare feet through a pile of garbage. He stood just yards away from where Mouret had caught his hand in my hair and dragged me into the darkness.

"You!" I called to him. "Do you wish to earn a sou?" He ran to me with happy anticipation. "Take this basket to Mathilde, the seamstress on the rue des Anges. And bring back any message she gives you." The basket was as large as he was, but he ran toward the rue des Anges at good speed, eager for the sou he would get upon his return.

I waited, a lady on an errand of mercy, careful not to lean against the lamppost and sully my gown, holding my skirts out of the muck. Was it only six months ago that my ragged skirt had been even dirtier than the street itself? And now, I was just back from an errand at Versailles. The Queen had remembered me, and given me kind words. I was very pleased with myself.

The child came back quickly, looking worried. His errand had only been half-successful and he feared for his payment.

"No message," he said, hopefully holding out his hand. I gave him three sous instead of the promised one and pinched his cheek playfully in the way I had seen ladies do. I forced a half-smile that put a great distance between myself and the rue des Anges.

But my new pride was smarting. Grandmama had taken the basket. But she would not see me, for that had been my message, my intent. Like my mother before me, I had been cast out of her heart, out of her life.

Success is not as pleasant, when there is no one to rejoice with you. The Queen of France had kind words for me, but Mathilde did not.

5

. . . the affair of the diamond necklace . . .

"Yet for several months past flashes of lightning had been seen,
which were the precursors of the storm, but no one foresaw it. It
was thought that salutary reforms would put an end to the
temporary difficulties of our government. It was an epoch
of illusion."

—Comte Louis-Phillippe de Ségur

Though I soon learned my way around rose-lined paths and the marble staircases of Versailles, I never overcame the awe that the gilded palace inspired. My brief life had already been too filled with extremes, and it was difficult to reconcile the world that was Versailles with the world that was the Cité. I had ample opportunity to try, however, for the Queen availed herself frequently of my skills, much to my pride.

At least once a fortnight I ascended the public coach that bounced down the congested rue de Sèvres that ran between Paris and Versailles, carrying a package or sealed message from Bertin's. The Queen herself asked for me.

Madame Bertin began to look at me askance. "Her Majesty has requested that you trim this bodice for her," she would say, or perhaps it was a new straw hat to decorate, or a petticoat to be quilted with laurel wreaths. "She asked for you by name. Why?" Bertin grew perplexed and more than a little resentful. Manon had been right in two things. Bertin was jealous, and the Queen did like to repeat favors.

"Perhaps she likes my embroidery," I suggested demurely.

But the more the Queen praised my work, the less pleased Bertin was. Her original kindness to me, now made superfluous by the Queen's own favor, turned to dislike. I didn't care. The Queen knew me by name. I had no need of another patroness. But I grew wary, and stayed out of Bertin's way as much as possible.

I worked with great diligence and dedication, and it was many a dawn that found me already at my worktable, and even more sunsets that saw me still seated there, stitching and cutting and stretching my imagination to discover new ways of catching up flounces or arranging pleats.

It was hardly a life of all work, however. Because Bertin divided her days between her Paris shop and other workrooms in Versailles, we often made up excuses to leave our tables and run some errand or another. It was honor among seamstresses that these absences were never reported to our strict mistress.

One day Martine came in, pale and cold despite the heat, and vowing she was gravely ill and must see a physician.

I was tempted to remark that she had managed to come all the way across Paris in an open carriage without complaint, but kept my tongue. The carriage belonged to a young Americanist we were all wildly infatuated with, and my remark would have been construed as the result of jealousy—which it was.

Manon did comment that perhaps Martine could use a full night's sleep for a change, and a plate of red meat, for Martine, as round as a Rubens cherub and fearful of becoming rounder still, ate only infrequently. Meat was one of those uncouth substances that stylish ladies disdained. They swooned if anything as vulgar as a fillet of beef was set before them at table, and instead dined on "restoratives," soups of boiled down vegetables that looked like a nursery mess.

"Roast beef! Never!" Martine exclaimed with great drama. "How could you, Manon?"

No, she insisted, it was a doctor she needed, not a chop. And the doctor she wished to see was the great Mesmer himself.

"Ah! Mesmer!" Manon and I said simultaneously. That was a different story altogether. This was no ordinary bloodletter, but a physician so skilled even the court attended him in great numbers. The Austrian physician was said to use a powerful force called animal magnestism to heal the ills of body and mind.

"We will escort you, Martine. You look much too weak to travel alone," Manon declared.

Martine fluttered and fanned herself all the way to the clinic, trying to convince us she was truly ill. Manon and I cared not for the convincing; it was curiosity rather than worry that bestirred us on the adventure. Yet we hovered closely about her, solicitous, playing our roles. "Give her the salts," Manon ordered every few steps, and I would hold a vial under Martine's short pink nose as she sniffed delicately.

Despite the salts, we all three arrived faint with excitement. Manon the bold knocked for us. We waited, goose-fleshed under our summer gowns. A manservant opened the door to us and led us down a dark, long hall. He was tall and somber and dressed all in black for effect; when he gestured grandly at a curtain and said, "Through there, mesdames." I half expected the curtain to part by magic.

Manon hid her giggles behind a white lace fan. I bit my lip and wore the expression I had been accustomed to using with Mathilde to convey an attitude of gravity. We slid through the curtain one by one, into a room yet darker than the hall, so dark that even in midday it needed the assistance of many tall tapers to reveal its dimensions.

A full moon and constellations painted on the ceiling glowed eerily overhead. In the center of the room was a large copper tub of water, with many wires extending from it. Tethered to the end of the wires, neatly arranged in a circle around the tub, sat a handful of ladies in various stages of ecstasy, as Mesmer named the results of his bizarre treatment.

A man—Mesmer himself—dressed in a dramatic flowing black velvet cape approached on silent feet and led us to two empty chairs, the only ones left. I whispered that Martine and Manon should each take one, and I would watch. I had no need of treatment, but the session promised to be amusing. I took an armchair well outside of the circle. Martine and Manon sat tentatively, making much fuss with their skirts and arranging themselves comfortably before picking up the copper wires as Mesmer instructed. Once they were settled and solemnly, almost shyly, holding onto the wires, they looked as silly as the rest of Mesmer's clientele.

"Concentrate. Think only of the harmony of the universe. Concentrate deeply, ladies," Mesmer intoned. His voice was as deep and pleasant as notes struck on the great organ of Notre Dame. "Feel the magnetism as it flows from the copper vessel to your own fingertips. Feel it ascend your arms and reach the heart, giving you strength and good cheer."

I began to feel sleepy and quite strange. I had slept well the night before. Why, then, this sudden urge to rest my head on the cushioned chair, close my eyes, and sink into soft oblivion? His voice droned on, soft as a summer breeze, deep as blackest night, comforting. A tingle crept up my arm even though I didn't hold one of the wires; my head jerked back and my eyes began to close of themselves. I forced them open and stared straight ahead for focus. Straight into the close-eyed, dreamy face of the Queen.

Her head was tilted backward and she moaned softly, an expression of bliss playing across her fine features as she tenderly clutched the copper wire.

Now this will be terrible scandal, I thought, startled and worried. The Queen mixing in public with commoners, visiting a physician who, if wanted, should go to her, not she to him. And her expression. So exposed, so vulnerable, not demure and closed as a Queen's should be. My heart contracted with fear. I could do nothing but wait and hope she would leave before the others were aware of her presence. How could Mesmer allow such a thing?

When finally Mesmer announced the end of the session there was a general sigh of satisfaction, from all but me, who was barely breathing. A manservant came and lit the tapers.

And then I, too, felt relief. It was not Marie-Antoinette at all, but a woman of startling resemblance to the Queen. The same auburn hair, high pale forehead, graceful limbs, even the same tilt to her head.

"Who is she?" I asked Manon. Manon knew everything.

"I believe that must be Baronne d'Oliva," she whispered back. "She is an actress." Manon sniffed. She affected to dislike actresses but that was because her father had threatened to disown her if ever she approached the stage as anything more than a spectator. She had a gift for mimicry and a fine voice, but they could only find audience in the workroom.

Martine joined us, yawning and stretching with abandon. "I feel much better. Worlds better. I'll come again," she said. I decided I would not.

A fortnight later, in late August, I learned that Baronne d'Oliva had been arrested for impersonating the Queen, not at Mesmer's, or on the stage, but in a much more compromising situation.

It took weeks, months, even years to make sense of what had happened. In brief, it was this: a diamond necklace of tremendous value was missing, and the Queen, thanks to Baronne d'Oliva and other conspirators, was involved in the theft.

The events that became known as The Affair of the Diamond Necklace began earlier that summer. Monsieur Boehmer, the court jeweler, had offered a necklace of great value to the Queen. She refused it, saying it was too costly and she would not further strain the coffers of France for such an extravagant bauble. I think it would not hurt the Queen if I pointed out that the necklace had originally been designed for her father-in-law's mistress, the infamous Madame du Barry. Marie-Antoinette detested the woman, and would not condescend to buy her castoff jewels.

The first discussions about the necklace had taken place in the Queen's private château, the Petit Trianon. That little confection of a palace, Marie-Antoinette's own, was noted for its privacy and its lovely gardens. They, too, played a part in the conspiracy. She went there often to escape the boredom of court formalities, and had even built a Hameau, a little village with dairymaids and beribboned cows where she played at shepherdess. The grounds also contained several fountains, pavilions, a delicate white edifice known as The Temple of Love, and a private theater.

It was the Hameau I often thought of, later, when I first reached French Azilum, for our village was the harsher reality of the Queen's, which was but a stage set for a play.

When Boehmer went to the Petit Trianon and displayed the extravagant necklace to Marie-Antoinette, hoping to sell it and recover the fortune that had gone into it, the Comtesse de Lamotte-Valois was with the Queen. This woman was probably no more a countess than I was a princess. Indeed, when the scandal broke, we simply referred to her as "the Lamotte woman." She was a schemer of infamous talent. She had made herself known to the Queen to advance socially; that achieved, she decided to enrich herself at the expense of the Queen, by acquiring the necklace for herself. But first, she needed a fellow conspirator.

Enter the famous Prince of France, Cardinal de Rohan. A sillier man has yet to be born. The Queen hated him. He professed to adore her, and was stupid enough to think that he could, by cleverness, become her lover. Madame Lamotte went to this fool and told him that Marie-Antoinette coveted the necklace but her husband, the King, would not allow her to purchase it. Rohan was to purchase it himself, in the Queen's name. Madame Lamotte would deliver it to the Queen, and bring back to him her secret payment for it.

Cardinal de Rohan was a fool, but even a fool will occasionally ask for evidence. He asked Madame Lamotte to prove that the Queen was willing to become his friend, indeed, his lover, if he would do this favor. Money, after all, was at stake.

Madame Lamotte, not to be foiled by the Cardinal's new wariness, had already noticed the young actress, d'Oliva, and her incredible resemblance to the Queen. She hired d'Oliva to play her greatest role. She was to dress in a gown similar to the Queen's (did the gown come from Bertin's? Did I sew it?) and then merely stand in the Queen's rose garden in the moonlight.

When the Cardinal approached, she was to hand him a rose, say nothing, and quickly disappear.

It was a ridiculous scheme, but it worked. The Cardinal, seeing only Marie-Antoinette extending the rose of acceptance, was flabbergasted at his good fortune. The Queen would have him. The very next day he went to Boehmer and put a deposit on the necklace, purchasing it in the Queen's name. The great jackass then handed the necklace over to Madame Lamotte for delivery. It was never seen again. All this occurred without the Queen knowing anything of it, until the day Boehmer showed up at the Petit Trianon again, sheepishly asking for his money.

He arrived during a rehearsal for *The Barber of Seville*, which was to be acted in the Queen's private theater. I was there to fit her costume. She was playing the part of Rosine, the beautiful young mademoiselle pursued by the lecherous Count Almaviva, and was quite excited and merry about it. Her gown, I remember, was a simple, maidenly white one trimmed with silver-and-pink roses, and she was proud of the smallness of her waist.

"Childbirth has not ruined my figure," the Queen boasted. I quickly assented, having learned to speak through a mouthful of pins as well as Manon did. The fitting was interrupted by a trembling lady-in-waiting.

"It's that horrid jeweler again," she said, fearing, and rightly so, the Queen's wrath. I was quickly dismissed. Only later, back at Bertin's, for gossip traveled faster even than the public coaches, did I learn the rest of what had occurred that afternoon. Boehmer went so far as to accuse the Queen of taking the necklace without paying for it. He would be bankrupted, he said, if payment was not made. She accused him of being quite mad; she did not have the necklace, nor had she ordered it.

Boehmer, fearful for his business, reputation, and even life, revealed that he had given the necklace to the Cardinal de Rohan, who had claimed to purchase it in the Queen's name.

Heads were going to roll. Marie-Antoinette could be sweet and even patient, as she proved to me, but she had a temper that could shake mountains. And the mountain she would tumble was that fool, de Rohan. Louis was willing to pay for the necklace and forget the whole thing. The Queen was not. She bullied her husband and he gave in. The fiasco that followed was as much his fault as hers. Marie-Antoinette needed a strong husband who could give her guidance. Louis was not strong. He was weak, lazy and indecisive; he cared only for hunting and tinkering with his mechanical toys.

On August 15, after brazenly arriving at Versailles to celebrate a Mass for the Queen's name day, Cardinal de Rohan was arrested, at the insistence of the Queen.

It was a costly mistake for her. The Prince was short of sense, a libertine more prone to kneeling in ladies' boudoirs than in a chapel, a gambler and a rake, and quite handsome in a foolish way. In short, he was all that Parisians adored. Popular opinion quickly aligned itself with the Prince and against the Queen.

Women wailed in the streets and men muttered evil threats against the cruelty of the monarchy when de Rohan was charged with conspiracy and led away in chains.

The scandal of the necklace was all that was talked about for months; news of it was followed as closely as an important war. The affair dragged on and on, with no end in sight, but plenty of gossip, and all of it against the Queen.

"The jewelers in the Palais Royal are making glass copies of the Queen's necklace," Manon reported in October. Marie-Antoinette had never possessed the unlucky necklace, yet it was constantly referred to as the Queen's necklace.

"They say the necklace has been broken up and the diamonds are being sold in London, by agents of the Queen," Manon reported in December. By January it was rumored that the Queen had planned the scandal herself in order to shame Louis, who had not wanted her to buy more diamonds.

The Queen, who had made only infrequent public appearances in the past years, made even fewer that year. She had her little palace and the Hameau, her three children, her private card parties and theatricals. What did she need of Paris? was the attitude she conveyed. Ah, but she did need Paris. She realized it far too late.

Of course, she also had Count Axel Fersen, her Swedish lover. By then, after years of an unsatisfying marriage and after providing two royal sons, gossip was finally right about one thing. Marie-Antoinette had a lover to console her. A lover that the King not only raised no fuss about, but even seemed to approve. It was Count Fersen who attended, in the King's name, all the baptisms, weddings and dinners that the King himself did not wish to attend. Because Fersen was loyal, discreet, intelligent and of high birth, and a foreigner besides, the gossips found little of interest to report about this affair. It did not capture the public imagination as did the greater scandal of the necklace. It pleases me to know that my Queen and her handsome protector enjoyed some hours of peace and delight together.

I still visited Versailles, but not as frequently, and hid in my room for hours afterwards, else I would have been overwhelmed by the curious and sometimes cruel questions of the other seamstresses.

What would I have told them? She has lost weight from worry. She clings to her children for a second too long when she embraces them. There is fear in her eyes. Marie-Antoinette made many mistakes but she was neither witless nor insensitive. She was realizing, for the first time, the strength of the hatred that could be unleashed against her, and the force of it made her sway on her feet, as if a strong wind blew at her back.

But there was the man Fersen, who seemed always with her, who was protective as a lion, whose eyes rarely strayed from the face of the woman he could not claim except in the most private hours. I first learned of the possible tenderness there could be between man and woman when I, the seamstress still uninstructed in all but the crudest form of love, witnessed their great devotion for each other. It made me both thoughtful and restless with hungers I could not name.

In the spring, while the affair of the diamond necklace was still dragging on, Bertin finally allowed me to wait on customers in the public shop room. I enjoyed this change of duties, for the warm weather brought restlessness and a penchant for daydreaming which made the now-monotonous sewing room tedious. I could meet with customers and move about more freely.

The shop was busy, as usual. I waited on long lines of anxious mothers who needed lace fichus and feathered headpieces for marriageable daughters, and even longer lines of gentlemen who were eager to win back mistresses cast off during the gloomy winter months. Occasionally a gentleman would even buy something for his wife, but more often than not the wives—powerless in this matter of mistresses—simply selected what they wanted for themselves and had it billed to their errant husbands. It was amusing revenge, and it made for good business. Bertin often remarked that should fidelity become fashionable she would go bankrupt.

"No, no, nothing in grey. My daughter must wear pink," one particularly odious mother yelled at me towards the end of a long Saturday afternoon in May. "I heard that pink is the Cardinal de Rohan's favorite color," she announced to a hapless bystander who was considering the merits of a little chapeau strewn with silk daisies.

Too fatigued to argue, I spitefully fastened a deep pink velvet pouf on top of her daughter's boisterous red curls. The poor, pink-faced creature looked unhappily like a boiled lobster, as I had known she would. Her mother, finally having exhausted the topic of the Cardinal's favorite colors, as reported in the *Mercure*, turned back to her daughter and shrieked in alarm.

"You may try the dove-grey," she agreed, pointing at the hat I had first

71

suggested. The daughter and I sighed simultaneously. She was no more than fourteen, yet there she was, being outfitted for the marriage market. She made me very aware of my seventeen years and the long, warm summer nights ahead of me. And the many, many summers to come.

The afternoon dragged on and I found myself balancing first on one foot and then the other to help pass time and ease my aching feet, when the last customer of the day entered the shop.

Entered? No, he conquered. He was tall as the shop's highest shelf, and dressed in red satin coat and breeches bright as the Cardinal's cape. His waistcoat was so encrusted with jewels it was impossible to tell the color of the fabric supporting them.

He moved with slow determination, giving us ample time to appreciate his magnificence, this apparition, pausing often in mid-step as if expecting a court artist to appear and begin sketching him. It was immediately apparent that he was indeed a highly placed member of the court. The Duc d'Orléans, formerly the Duc de Chartres, was, however, the most dangerous enemy the court of France would face.

He would have been handsome, had someone had the courage to take a scrub brush to him. He was so coated with powder it had cracked like plaster around the lines of his mouth and eyes. His right cheek was adorned with numerous black patches in the shape of stars and moons; his lips were painted a bright, garish red. He was not yet forty, but looked much older, thanks to the princely paunch that made his coat slope forward from chin to hips in a decadent incline.

The three remaining ladies in the shop curtseyed and made eyes at him from behind their fans. As much as we wish our enemies to be ugly as Satan himself, I must admit that he did possess a small but certain charm, despite or even because of his foppish appearance, which was so at odds with his obvious masculinity. The Duc d'Orléans had the charisma that his cousin, Louis XVI, had never developed. And the cunning.

"Mademoiselle La Forge," he called to no one in particular. "Is she present?" He rested one hand on his sword hilt as the other carried a lace handkerchief to the painted mouth. "A warm day, ladies, *n'est-ce pas?*" he asked his small but attentive audience. They tittered.

The four men who followed in his wake began to amble aimlessly about the shop, picking over fans and poufs and ribbons. They were dressed in the Orléans livery and armed with swords and firearms. I began to fear for the safety of Bertin's goods.

"I am Mademoiselle La Forge," I said from behind the counter, admitting the name I had adopted. "And surely, you have no need of bodyguards in this humble and grateful establishment. We are your devoted servants. You might ask your men to wait outside." I had learned such subtlety from Manon. Left to my own devices, I would have yelled, "Get those royal pickpockets out of here before I call for the watch!" And I would have disgraced myself and Bertin forever.

The royal apparition smiled graciously and waved a hand at his retinue. They bowed with amazing insolence and shuffled out. A feather fan poked out of one's vest, but I counted that little loss to what could have been. Such retinues were worse scavengers than Paris's hordes of beggars. And who would dare press charges against them?

"How can I assist you, monsieur?" I made an effort not to stare, but it was difficult. I was seeing in person for the first time the infamous prince who had provided so many of the more scandalous stories of my childhood— tales of his black masses, orgies, and seductions had been among Yvette's favorite, well-discussed scandals. She even claimed to have attended a party in the Palais Royal, but no one believed her.

"I require a gift. For a lady," he said, stepping closer and peering at me down his very long nose. He smelled of expensive perfume used in great quantity. The three ladies, still wide-eyed and gap-mouthed, tittered.

"D'Orléans frowned. He unsheathed his sword and pointed it at the door, almost toppling one of Bertin's expensive vases with the grand gesture. "I believe I hear your husbands calling you, mesdames," he said. They filed out, one at a time and looking over their shoulders as long as they dared. He locked the door behind them.

"A gift," I repeated nervously.

"Something in forget-me-not blue," he specified, seating himself in a comfortable plush chair and putting his muddy shoes up on a small and fragile table. I rang a bell and a moment later a ribbon presser came in from the workroom.

"Tea," I said, relieved that the ringing of a bell would bring someone, even just a little girl, running, should I need assistance. The girl, not yet nine, rose on tiptoe to see him better. When she returned a moment later with the tea tray, he took her chin in his hand and pulled her face close to his.

"Promising," he said, flicking his tongue over his lips. The child fled.

"We have just received some new fans," I said, pouring tea into one of the two cups. "Perhaps your friend would enjoy a fan of blue feathers?" He, like many in France, was an Anglophile, delighting in all customs English. It was yet another way to show dislike of the French court . . . and the French Queen. Here, in person, was Bertin's first sponsor, and Marie-Antoinette's most vocal enemy. Her husband sat on the throne he thought should be his,

73

and she herself had declared him a coward. More to the heart of the matter, d'Orléans was possessed of great ambitions and little outlet for them. Such men are capable of anything; if not compelled to sainthood they become, instead, devils.

He lethargically examined the box of fans, pausing only to examine those that were richly encrusted with jewels.

"My cousin, Antoinette, has a great love for diamonds," he said in his deep but sulky voice. He held up a fan made of white ostrich feathers studded with large diamonds and pearls. "This would please her."

"The gift is for Her Majesty? Perhaps I could suggest something to complement a gown we are completing for her."

"I understand you do much sewing for the Queen. And visit her often," he said, not answering my question.

"I have that honor."

"You even visit the private rooms of the Petit Trianon." He held the fan under his eyes like a coquette, flirting. There was a hard glint in his eyes.

"That is so." I was growing very uneasy with this conversation. What was his point? And how had he acquired this information? Without difficulty, I realized. Paris was awash with spies. Why hadn't it occurred to me before that even a seamstress might be watched, should she be on speaking terms, no matter how slight, with the Queen? Favors from a queen can be a double-edged sword, Manon had warned. I had been naive enough to think she referred only to Bertin's jealousy. Already less naive, I knew what would be said next.

"I wish to hire you," he said in a tone of voice that indicated he was doing me great honor. "Pay close attention to all you see and hear at the Trianon. Who visits. What is said. And then simply repeat those things to me."

I poured him a second cup of tea.

"I must decline the offer," I said. "Alas, I have bad hearing and a worse memory."

"These small favors could result in much wealth for you," he said, ignoring my refusal. A smile, sly and hard, played on his face. The cracks in the face powder moved like eels writhing over white sand.

"Perhaps monsieur also has difficulty hearing. I refuse your request to spy on the Queen for you." I put the teapot on the table as gently as I could, still it spilled. My hands were trembling with anger and fear.

"Stupid slut!" He grabbed my wrist. "You refuse? You choose the royal whore over me? Over France?" It was the first time I had heard the Queen called a whore; the first time I heard it implied that loyalty to Marie-

Antoinette was disloyalty to France. I heard it often in the years that followed. He was hurting my wrist, twisting my arm so that I was forced to rise from my chair. Then he smiled again, and released me.

"I would suggest that it would be more profitable to ally with the house of Orléans. I can be a most unpleasant enemy." He sipped his tea. His moods changed with mercurial quickness; it is the sign of a spoiled and indulgent disposition.

"I have made my decision," I said. "I serve the Queen and no other. Do you wish the fan, or may I show you something else?"

He picked up the fan and tickled the end of my nose with it. "You are a problem. How I detest problems." He threw the fan on the floor and, standing, crushed it under his heel. Monsieur le Duc left that day without making a purchase.

The next morning Madame Bertin rushed into the workroom like her skirts were afire. Her cheeks were flushed with anger, her usually tidy hair sprang from her head in indignation.

"I will speak to you. In the hall," she said, stopping in front of my worktable.

"You have grievously offended the Duc d'Orléans," she accused, once the thick curtains were parted behind us. I knew Martine was already stationed behind them, listening.

"I ask your pardon. But how could I not offend him, considering what he asked of me?"

"Mademoiselle. We are not provincials here. We know how to comport ourselves. We are able to refuse a man without making ourselves, and our employers, look like jackasses!" Her voice ended on a high, angry note.

"Madame, I don't know what the duke told you, but it was no simple proposition he made. He wanted me to act as his spy at the Petit Trianon." I did not bother to keep my voice low. The workroom would soon know, if they didn't already.

"Oh, *mon Dieu! Mon Dieu!*" Bertin reached her arms to the ceiling and swooned so that I had to catch her in my arms and lean her against the wall while she dug into a petticoat for her salts. "Spy? Oh, you troublesome girl! Of course you mustn't spy! But the duke is so angry! Oh, *mon Dieu!*" She shook her head so vigorously her wig slipped loose and tilted over one small, watery eye.

"We are quite upset. Go back to your worktable. Stay there. Try to avoid further trouble." The black shadows at the end of the long hall swallowed

75

her retreating figure, and I returned to my worktable, thoughts of justice running riot in my head like a basket of tumbled ribbons.

The initial inquiry of the affair of the necklace closed and it was announced that Cardinal de Rohan would stand public trial, heard by the Parlement of Paris. And then the trial dragged on and on, much to the delight of Paris and frustration of the Queen. The city had ample time to enjoy each detail, to chew it over and then when its scandalous sweetness was exhausted spit it out as if the Queen's reputation were worth no more than Dominican sugar cane.

The enmity the Queen felt and displayed for the popular Cardinal de Rohan; the unrequited love he professed for her; the privacy of her gardens and their well-designed potential for assignations; her love for costly jewels— all these things were discussed openly in the Parlement, and in the journals and broadsheets available on every street corner.

Eventually, the Cardinal, still dressed in his handsome scarlet soutaine, was acquitted of any wrongdoing, without even receiving a reprimand. No one thought it notable that he had entered into a conspiracy against the Queen and sullied her reputation.

Baronne d'Oliva was also found innocent of wrongdoing, it having been decided that she had been an innocent dupe of Madame Lamotte, the orginator of the scheme. The fact that d'Oliva had given birth while locked in the Bastille, and appeared in court with her long auburn hair loose on her back and a pretty babe suckling her bare breasts did not harm her cause. The judges smiled upon her and placed bets as to who was the father of her child.

Madame Lamotte was found guilty, and sentenced to be branded and then imprisoned for life in the Salpêtrière, with sackcloth on her back and only prison bread on her dinner plate. She swooned when the sentence was read. She recovered and screamed, protesting her innocence and reviling the Queen.

The Queen was found innocent of any wrongdoing. That was the official verdict. But the city of Paris had its own opinion, and it was not in the Queen's favor. Ten thousand Parisians had cheered with delight when de Rohan left the courtroom. None cheered when Marie-Antoinette appeared, pale and trembling. She returned to Versailles in a closed carriage with the curtains tightly drawn.

Madame Lamotte, once imprisoned, never once dined on coarse prison bread. She became a cause célèbre, and many people visited her cell, bringing her gifts of food and clothing and condolences. Each visit, and they were countless, was a voice against Marie-Antoinette, a sign from those who favored a common criminal and imposter over their Queen.

The leaves on the chestnut tree outside our room were turning the same, soft yellow of the brocades in Bertin's reception room. It was Sunday, so Manon and I, resting sleepily in the large bed we shared, chatted of how we would spend the day. The early morning light still retained summer's golden intensity; it had a green cast to it and promised a clear, warm autumn day.

"We will promenade," Manon said, wriggling her toes under the counterpane. The orange kitten she had recently acquired jumped on her feet and batted them with silken white paws. I picked up the cat; we had named her Scylla, after the water nymph, for she enjoyed poking her paws in our water basins.

"And where will we walk?" I asked, petting Scylla. "Is there a place where, perchance, no one has heard of the diamond necklace, for I am wearied to death of the gossip around it."

"We would have to go to China," Manon agreed. "We must make do with the Palais Royal, I'm afraid, and take our chances. We will talk of the opera, and Madame Bertin's new carriage, and . . ."

"And Etienne," I finished.

Manon, then out of bed and standing behind the dressing screen, stuck her head over it and smiled. "Do I speak overly much of Etienne?" she asked. "If I talk of him at all, and I'm sure it's not often, it is only because he is so . . . easy to speak of. His virtues. His courtesy. His sparkling conversation . . ."

"His very pleasing looks. His great wealth," I added.

"You are jealous, Julienne." I heard the rustle of silk, dry and fragile as parchment leaves being turned in the wind, as Manon pulled a gown over her golden head.

"Yes, I am jealous." I could admit such things to Manon. We were as close as sisters. I had even considered telling her the true story of the first night when I had arrived at Bertin's, but had not. I picked up one of her pink dancing slippers and examined the sole. They were only a few weeks old, but they already had holes in them, so well-used were they. The room was littered with new fans, vases of flowers, baskets of fruit, and all were gifts of Etienne de Buzot, former protector of Mademoiselle Marianne of the opera, and now new suitor of Manon. She, newly arrived at her eighteenth year, had decided she did not want to spend the rest of her life in Bertin's sewing room. She would acquire a husband; a wealthy one, one her own father would approve of and from what I heard of that wine merchant, his tastes were as rigorous as St. Peter's on Judgment Day.

"Then you must do something about it," she called to me. "Give but one kind word to Abbé Lelache next time he comes to buy something for his mistress. Everyone knows he is wearied of her and eager to befriend you."

"The Abbé has warts on his nose and a disease or two we should not mention, should rumor be even half-reliable. I await a more promising offer." He was also fifty if he was a day, not at all the young and handsome lover I hoped for. I remembered the young man who had taken my hand during that first carriage trip to Versailles. He had had the look of a visitor; he had probably long since left Paris.

"If you wait too long you'll regret it later," Manon said. "The point is to let some escort take you to the right places. Then you'll meet others." She stepped from behind the screen, fully dressed and resplendent in blue silk trimmed with lilac, glowing with youth and beauty and hope. "Now, to chapel!" She pocketed a novel pasted inside a prayer book cover. Manon did not waste time on prayers and sermons; she had no need of them.

Later, we left Bertin's hôtel by the side door. We turned right, toward the Palais Royal, rather than continuing straight down the rue St. Honoré, to the gardens of the Tuileries. It was a quick decision, an easy choice, that I would long regret.

The Palais Royal, with its constantly growing crowds and expensive renovation in progress, was in a turmoil. The old palace had been rebuilt by the Duc d'Orléans, who wished to make his ancient home the social and political heart of Paris. The new structure was a three-sided, huge white façade, which accommodated shops, taverns, little theaters, game rooms and meeting halls. Between the tall Greek columns of the street level paused gaudy public women seeking clients, nosy journalists seeking gossip for their publications, and intellectuals who commented on the women and journalists and all else.

Promenading there meant smelling sawdust and wet paint and having to step around piles of lumber and other evidences of construction, in addition to the great crowds which always gathered there.

We made our way to the public gardens, although the lingering tree stumps of the felled oaks and stilted, overly clipped hedges were still more ominous to the eye than lovely, as a garden should be. After much searching we found a free bench along one of the gravel paths and sat contentedly, passing the time in idle talk and commenting on the people strolling by.

"Oh, la!" Manon giggled behind her fan. "Look at that creature." I turned my head in the direction indicated by Manon's eyes. The creature's dark scarlet dress—quite out of fashion—was cut in front to an impossible depth. A deep sigh or hint of laughter would loosen her charms for all to gape at.

Her hair was dressed so high we could see the tendons standing out on the neck that had to support the great weight of false curls and cotton rolls.

"The Comtesse de Feure," Manon whispered. "Hopeless, as usual. That gown, even if it had been made in a suitable color, was cut for a woman half her age."

The poor Comtesse, oblivious to the fact that a seamstress had found her badly wanting in taste, strutted past us on the arm of a young man whose eyes darted about him with the rapidity of a hungry squirrel, eyeing the many women who passed them.

"She should wrap a fichu high on her neck to hide all those chins," I whispered back to Manon.

And so the pleasant afternoon passed as we, lazy with the surprising autumn heat and content with ourselves, tore apart all that we beheld with the ease and callousness of youth.

The Palais was ablaze with sun, it almost blinded one, for d'Orléans had cut down any tree that might provide shade and protection. There was no gentle, dappled light filtered by overhead branches in those gardens. All was harsh revelation.

"Remember," Manon said, fanning herself. "When Etienne comes, we must seem surprised."

"Certainly. He will never know we spent the better part of the day waiting for him. I will make them put me to the test before I reveal you are wearing a new gown made in his favorite shade of blue. Shall I pretend to have forgotten his name so he won't know you mention it a hundred times a day?"

"Wonderful idea. I knew I could rely on you. Ah, marzipan, just what I was longing for!" She signaled to a sweets vendor who eagerly sold her a small quantity of the sticky sweet for a large amount of money. The candies were long pinkish lengths of marzipan filled with almond cream and called My Lady's Delight. The whores of the city knew them by another name.

"Don't look to your left, but your friend is approaching the bench behind us," she whispered a moment later.

"My friend?" I whispered back, puzzled. I dropped my fan near my left foot and, as I bent to retrieve it, took a quick glance over my shoulder. Through the black stems of the hedge I could see the Duc d'Orléans approaching. "This is no friend of mine," I whispered again. "Who is that with him?" He was two arm's lengths away, and separated from us only by a stunted hedge that barely reached the tops of our heads.

"The Princesse de Lamballe. Careful. They believe they are in privacy."

Why didn't we leave? Perhaps it was the sun, which had made us lethargic, or the mood of the day, which lent itself to whispered secrets. Perhaps it was simply because Etienne would look for us on that particular bench and we were loath to give up our place. We stayed, and because of that I made an enemy of a dangerous man who had before simply considered me a fool.

We sat still as statues, fearing discovery, already wondering what the princess, who was said to love the Queen, was doing with the duke, who was known to hate Marie-Antoinette. Was it true that Lamballe had been seduced by d'Orléans, that she was his secret mistress?

"Have you been to see our poor captive?" d'Orléans voice was deep and tainted with sarcasm.

"I have." Lamballe's voice was high and sweet. "And I had to wait in line to be received, so successful is your campaign."

"I will be more successful yet," he replied with assurance. "Once she has been freed, her talents and venom will destroy the little that is left of the Queen's reputation."

"Freed?" Lamballe's voice indicated shock and something else. Fear. "You never mentioned that. I was merely to visit, an act of charity. . . ."

Manon and I sat without moving. More words were exchanged, words whispered so lowly we couldn't be certain it wasn't just the rustling of leaves we heard. Then, the sound of a kiss, of a woman's skirts swirling into deeper folds as she stood to leave. Manon, more relaxed then, bit down on the lump of candy melting in her mouth.

She shrieked in pain, having just discovered a bad tooth. I closed my eyes in despair, heard the sound of Lamballe's delicate steps as she fled in surprise, the louder sounds of a man approaching our side of the path.

"Two grisettes from Bertin's," d'Orléans said, glaring at us. He feigned indifference, but his powdered curls shook with anger. "Your employer will be unhappy to hear you are eavesdroppers."

Manon, even in pain, thought quickly. "Eavesdroppers?" she asked with great innocence, pressing her fist into her throbbing jaw. "We have only just arrived, monsieur."

"I would have heard your arrival. No, you were here, listening." The glint in his eyes was even fiercer than the one the sun shot off the jeweled sheath of his sword.

Etienne appeared just at that moment, smiling and his arms filled with flowers. Manon, who had planned to ignore him for at least fifteen minutes after his arrival, fled to him, hoping the duke would not follow. He did not. But as I turned to leave, he caught me by my wrist.

"Beware, mademoiselle," he said. "You become ever more troublesome."

The next day the sewing room gossip was about de Lamballe. The Queen's oldest friend had herself gone to visit Lamotte in prison. It was construed as further evidence that the Queen was implicated in the scandal, else why would she send her friend to console the criminal?

"Perhaps someone else sent Lamballe. Lamballe could have made the visit out of simple charity, not meaning to harm the Queen. And the one who sent her used Lamballe's impulse for goodness," I suggested, keeping my head low over the sleeve I was embroidering.

Manon's eyes met mine.

"Perhaps d'Orléans," I said, but dared not say more.

A few days later we learned that Madame Lamotte had mysteriously escaped from her cell in the Salpêtrière. It was an impossible escape, one that would have had to be arranged for her. An unknown accomplice bribed her keepers and then assisted her onto a ship to England.

It was d'Orléans, of course. But many suspected the Queen herself.

6

. . . Venus arrives . . .

*"Either you have a rival or you don't. If you have one, you
must please in order to be preferred . . . and if you don't you
must still please—in order to avoid having one."*

—Pierre Choderlos de Laclos

*T*he shadows of night still flutter in the corners of my room. I can hear the strong sound
of the spring currents that quicken the Susquehanna as it flows beneath my window.
The river's sweet murmurs reassure.

All my life I have loved the sound of flowing water, the reminder that time, too, flows as
surely and will not strand us on one isle of existence, but will carry us along from where we
are to where we want to be. Sometimes, of course, the currents are stronger than we can control,
and we go where the river will take us.

Susquehanna. It was difficult at first to pronounce. Charles told me that the Gauls called
the Seine by another name, the Sequan. It is not so very different . . . Sequan, Susquehanna.
Charles gave me much information; he believed it was his duty to educate me. It was Charles
who insisted I keep a journal, to develop a sense of logic and philosophical aspiration, and
because it was fashionable to keep such a journal. How disappointed he was when I finally
allowed him to read a few pages. The lines slanted crookedly across the page like drunken ants
on a white cloth.

"It is all about me," he said, raising his eyebrows in disapproval.

"It is about love," I answered.

Finally, Manon is jealous of me, rather than I of her. "I have always wanted to became enamored in the spring," she said. "Oh, how lucky you are. And with an Americanist! What could be better!"

If he also loved me, it would be better. But as Manon points out, I have no reason to believe he doesn't love me. Nor do I have reason to believe he does. Shall I tear off the petals of a flower to determine my destiny? Or sleep with a piece of stolen wedding cake hidden under my pillow to see the face of my intended one? Time will tell, Manon says. How slowly time waits to reveal such things. How slowly the hands of the clock move, when meetings are anticipated!

The morning I met Charles, the mediocre dawn gave no warning that the day would be special. Such days do not forewarn. In fact, it started off badly, for I was accosted by Bertin in the hall. She had been cold, even rude, since the incident with the Duc d'Orléans.

"You are a fortnight late on the green satin gown and English riding jacket promised for the Marquise de Ste. Anne," she accused, searching hard in her memory for a thing with which to find fault.

"I am not," I protested, yawning. "She herself asked that I trim a new hat first, and then she would have a cape to match the hat. The gown is not needed until the new opera opens next week. She herself said."

"No excuses," Bertin insisted. Her brow creased like cheap muslin.

I watched her go, realizing that my time with her would have to come to an end, for it was becoming much too unpleasant. But where to go? Taking employment with any other seamstress in Paris would mean a retreat from ambition, not a step forward. I had vowed to take no backward steps.

In the workroom, my good humor did not return. Martine was reading the latest issue of *Mercure*, and the scandals they printed about the Queen were infuriating. On one page they accused her of eating strawberries in public, which was deemed a great sin on the Queen's part, while on the next page they accused her of secret orgies at the Trianon.

"The writer should make up his mind," Manon remarked. "Either she eats in public or feasts in secret. Which is it?"

"And see," Martine continued. "Several times they call her Madame Deficit." France was on the verge of bankruptcy because of the monstrous deficit under which the country was laboring—a deficit that had begun many decades earlier with the Seven Years War, and was made worse yearly by the financial privileges of the nobility and Church. Yet Marie-Antoinette was singly blamed for it.

"As if one woman could bankrupt a country. They blame her for they know not who else to blame," I said.

"They should look to the wealthy convents and the fat priests," Martine, daughter of an atheist, suggested.

"And to the farmer generals who pocket most of the taxes they collect," added Manon, daughter of a wine merchant. Even the workroom was becoming political. We who had discussed ribbons and what man was pursuing what woman, now discussed the tax structure of the country and Necker's "Account Rendered," the revealing report of the country's disastrous financial condition, which got him expelled from office in 1781 and then reappointed in 1788.

Marie-Antoinette's expenses had been laid bare in the "Account Rendered." She was extravagant. But what Queen has not been?

Marie-Antoinette forgave Necker that indiscretion. He claimed he could reduce the country's debt without raising taxes, and she was clever enough to realize that that miracle would help them all. The Queen had wept when Louis, at the advice of his jealous ministers, dismissed him. For once, Paris and its Queen agreed on one thing. "Necker will save the country," headlines in political journals claimed. It was the same Necker who later persuaded Louis to convene the Estates-General, so whether or not Necker saved the country is a question worthy of discussion even now.

"Guards have reported that a certain highly placed woman in the court—the highest—has lured several of their profession into a specially equipped private room. There, she drugged and abused them in ways that only the most debauched of females would have the cunning to display," Martine read.

"No," Manon said, throwing down her sewing. "That is too much. I will not listen to that infamous pack of lies. Everyone knows the Queen is faithful to Fersen."

Manon had become sensitive on issues of fidelity. Etienne had been forgotten and been replaced by a Jean-Pierre, who was then replaced by Antoine. She loved Antoine, she was faithful to him; she suffered for him. Antoine, a lowly printer's assistant, had been seen arm-in-arm with another woman in the Palais Royal gardens. Manon no longer needed to drink vinegar for breakfast, she had lost her appetite.

"Martine, you would better please us by reading a little from *Robinson Crusoe*," I suggested.

Martine put aside the paper and opened the popular novel that rested on her working table. She began reading where she had last left off.

" 'I caused Friday to gather all the skulls, bones, flesh and whatever remained, and place them together on a heap, and make a fire upon it, and burn them all to ashes. I found Friday had still a hankering stomach after some of the flesh, and was still a cannibal in nature . . .' "

We listened with relish, absorbed by the trials and travails of the shipwrecked Crusoe, just as women all over France were doing. People were not only becoming highly political, they were becoming restless and adventurous, and that is a most dangerous combination to established ways.

The morning hours thus passed in pleasant occupation, filled with the sound of rustling fabrics and Martine's sweet voice expounding on the evils of cannibalism. Just before the noon bells rang for the Angelus, Anne-Louise came in complaining of a stomach cramp.

"Julienne, it is your turn in the shop," she said. "I want only to sit today."

"You were at the opera until dawn. No wonder you are weak," Manon said in a dark voice.

"And you are just jealous because your sly printer won't take you there," Anne-Louise unwisely snapped back. I stepped between them before Manon, the larger of the two, could do damage to Anne-Louise's coiffure and gown. "I'll take your place in the shop," I agreed. "But watch your tongue or Manon may have it for lunch. We've been learning of cannibalism from Friday."

Anne-Louise laughed. Manon did not.

The shop was quiet at that hour. It was still too early for the nobility to be fully awake and about, but too late for the wealthy bourgeoises, who would be home supervising their servants over the midday meal. When the bell rang and a young man walked in I was caught by surprise, leaning on the counter and yawning.

It was the man who had held my hand during that first trip to Versailles. I had not paid him much attention at the time, my interview with the Queen being foremost in my mind. But since then, I had compared all other men I saw with this man.

He was about thirty years of age, but could have been younger or older by five years, depending on his mood and the set of his mouth. He was of medium height, well-formed, with green eyes and dark hair. His unpowdered hair was caught back simply at his neck with a somber black bow. His clothes were equally simple. In short, there was nothing remarkable about him, except that almost stern simplicity and his winning good looks. But the moment when he walked into the shop marks a boundary in my life as great as the one that marks birth and death.

"May I help you?" I stood as straight as possible, hoping to appear taller, hoping he would remember me.

"Ah! The public coach!" he said, remembering instantly, although much time had passed. He smiled, and his whole face, which had been a little sad and preoccupied, lit up. "Whatever caused you distress that day has been resolved?"

I nodded and smiled. I forgot all I had learned of flirtation. Such knowledge often flees when we most need it.

I grew shy; he grew serious once again.

"Well, then. I would like to purchase a gift for my mother." His accent was musical, including hints of the harsher American tongue and the lilting notes of the Auvergne, the place I had once claimed to have come from. I had long since given up that lie, finding that a secretive silence was more effective.

"Perhaps a red velvet pouf trimmed with fur?" he suggested, helpless in the way that men often are when faced with questions of fashion. His teeth were white and straight, his hands, which had gone to his head to indicate he wished to buy a hat, were sunburnt and looked capable of work. I rarely saw such honest hands in Bertin's shop.

"Alas, I must point out that poufs are quite out of style," I said shyly. "I would suggest instead a straw hat with a sash." I handed him the nearest one at hand. It was quite simple, trimmed only with a red ribbon upon which had been printed a repeated scene of American Indians gathered round a palm tree, with alligators curled at their feet. Such scenes of life in the New World were quite popular and much in demand. Women wore dresses printed with entire Indian villages and war parties at the hem and flounce.

He examined the chapeau with great interest. "Indians do not look at all like this," he pointed out. "It is greatly inaccurate."

"Indeed? What do Indians look like?" He was an Americanist! I felt faint with delight.

"Well, they are smaller, for one thing. About your size. And their hair is dark, like yours. But straight, not curly."

I did not know if such a comparison should be taken as flattery, but it pleased me that he had reached out and touched my hair. His fingers lingered near my cheek for a moment, and then hastily removed themselves.

"I do approve of the hat, however. It is the type of thing that the women of Philadelphia favor, simple and without pretension."

"Surely, it is the American style," I agreed.

"If you recommend it, I will take it," he agreed. "Inaccurate or not."

But when I told him the price he returned the hat to the counter and frowned.

"Perhaps you would like to open an account with us? We will send the bill later, and you may pay at your convenience." Bertin would rage for days, but let her. I will have his name, I thought.

"I generally don't approve of credit," he said. "But for this, I will make an exception. It is my sister's birthday." So. He had come in to buy a gift for his mother, and now it was his sister he sought to please? I was disheartened, until I realized that a man who denies having a mistress is already of a mind to obtain a different one.

"The name of the account?" I asked sweetly.

"Charles-Marie de Saint Remy." Charles. I have always liked that name, it is soft on the tongue, like something that must be whispered by moonlight.

"And now I am at a disadvantage, mademoiselle. You have my name, but I haven't yours."

"Julienne La Forge, at your service." A homeless gleam of April sunshine came in through a window and found refuge in his dark hair, giving it a fiery cast.

"Julienne," he repeated. The sunbeam danced over his face, lighting the depths of his eyes the way sunshine lights up a still pool. Those eyes had golden flecks as lovely as languorous goldfish swimming just beneath the water's surface.

"If I may, I will take the hat with me. Well, I am glad you are better than when we last met." He turned to leave, whistling a strange, foreign tune.

If he reaches the door and goes through it without another word I will run down the street after him, I decided.

He paused at a little table and fingered the snuff boxes on display. He turned back to me.

"Julienne, there are to be fireworks tonight at the Palais Royal, and a concert. Would you join me?"

In the four years that I had worked in Bertin's establishment, I had heard that question four score times and more, and always had said, 'no.' "What are you waiting for?" Manon scolded.

I was waiting for Charles.

"Yes," I said, "I will."

I donned cape and mask, for women who aspired to haughty reputations did not go out after dark without them. Swathed in deep folds of the popular new color of brown called "flea's belly," the top portion of my face covered by a heart-shaped mask trimmed with feathers, I slipped out of Bertin's side door to meet the future. At the corner, I hired a lantern-carrying linkman to light my way and escort me to the Palais Royal. I felt bold, daring, happy, and frightened.

Charles was waiting outside the Café Mécanique. He, too, was masked, but we recognized each other instantly.

He bowed, his swirling cape melting into the shadows around us, redefining the boundaries of the night and my life. When he stood straight before me and looked into my eyes, all was changed, would never again be the same. I was already forgetting what it had been like to live before Charles, before this aching, this glowing, that was love.

"Some refreshment before the music begins," he asked, giving me his arm and guiding me into the dark interior of the public café. I would have followed him into the inferno itself.

The café was a popular one for assignations, for there were no waiters to overhear private conversations or recognize unmasked faces. The tables had been cunningly built on springs and scaffolds. One wrote one's order on a slate, included the coins to cover the cost, and then pressed a lever. The table disappeared down a shaft, and then resurrected laden with food and drink.

I had never before been to the Café Mécanique and when the table disappeared, leaving a black hole between Charles and myself, I grew dizzy with the sensation of falling into that abyss. Charles, undaunted, smiled and drew his chair closer so that the rougher fabric of his breeches sang against the silk of my skirt.

"I have always been interested in mechanics," he said. "I have read all the papers of Franklin, Evans, and Jefferson. The Americans are much more advanced in this science. Although I would enjoy knowing how this device functions."

"I know nothing of mechanics," I said, greatly relieved when the table reappeared.

"It is the science of the future," he said. But his eyes carried other messages, unspoken words to which I clung with all my hope. He poured wine into two goblets and toasted to the evening.

We were both somewhat shy, and said little. There was more in the way his hand sought mine, later, when the musicians played for us under the stars. And even later, when he walked back with me to Bertin's hôtel and pressed his lips to mine for a brief, claiming kiss, and promised to seek me on the morrow. I sat up till dawn, remembering every gesture, every word, studying the landscape of this new country which is called love.

He is well-bred, gentle, educated and most attractive. He is of good family, his father being of the lesser nobility and possessing many châteaux and farms in the mountains of the Auvergne. How comes he to the age of thirty, and no wife to encumber him? Ah, thank God, there is no wife. This afternoon he came again to Bertin's. We sat in the parlor, a box of trinkets open before us in case madame should enter and suspect our true reasons for seeking the relative privacy of the sitting room.

"I have heard you are greatly skilled with your needle, and much sought after by many, including the Queen herself," he said. Ah, I thought. He has been making inquiries about me. That is a good sign.

"If I have won favor, it is only through her Majesty's kindness," I replied. His elegant, long-fingered hand sought mine amongst the brooches and necklaces with which we played.

"Tell me of yourself," he commanded, drawing my hand close to his mouth.

I took a deep breath and lowered my eyes.

"My family cast me out when I refused the marriage they had arranged for me," I said. "That is why I now employ myself as a seamstress, so that I will be independent." It wasn't a lie. It just overlooked some of the facts which I would rather he did not know.

"I admire you even more," he said, kissing my hand. "A woman of weaker spirit may have sought insincere refuge in a convent. I am fortunate you did not."

"And you? You have not married?"

"I was engaged once, many years ago, before I was yet sixteen. The girl died a week before our marriage was to take place." He spoke with little emotion, even coldly.

"I am so sorry," I lied.

"I was less than distraught. Our marriage, like yours, had been arranged by our families, and there was little love between us. I've wondered if perhaps she didn't willingly choose death over me. She was devout, and had hoped to remain within her convent, where she had been educated." Oh, foolish, foolish girl, I thought.

"It was difficult," he said. "I left before my family could arrange another such match. Since then, there has been little time or opportunity to pursue the softer companionship of women." He kissed my hand again. Like me, there was much he did not reveal. But I was content for the time.

"You look like a cat that has caught a canary," Manon told me this evening, when I repeated his words so that we could fathom all their nuances.

Manon's mother became ill, so she was called home to supervise her father's household. I missed her sorely in the weeks she was gone, for no one else had the patience or good grace to listen to my constant musings about Charles.

He gave me a gift, a leather-bound copy of Rousseau's *Emile*. I tried to read it quickly because Charles was eager to discuss it with me, but Père Roget's early tuition had provided me with only a halting grasp of such dense thought. I burned midnight oil and gave up sleep to blunder through the novel. Charles was, I could easily see, disconcerted by my lack of education. American women, he said, were educated as well as the men and were able to manage large farms and even political offices while their husbands had fought the British. It was the women, he informed me gravely, who had put the torch to New York when the British took the city. I failed to see how education had improved their ability to light a torch, but said nothing.

I quizzed him on how well American women cared for their appearance, and he admitted they were not as charming as the French women. "But they are strong and brave and educated," he said. "That is more important."

Was it? He seemed pleased with the new gown I made to wear to the opera. *Don Giovanni* bored him. It was too patrician, he said, but his eyes went often to the lace on my very low square neckline. He had spent many years campaigning in America with the Marquis de La Fayette, and had a soldier's love of pretty women dressed in fine lace.

On stage, the actor was busy seducing the maid and singing of the delights of love. In the balcony, Charles held my hand and discoursed on the evils of tyranny and the superiority of the American form of government, which included all men without regard to class or station.

I watched the light from the stage torches catch in his hair and heard his words, but did not comprehend. Speak to me of love, I asked with my eyes.

"I would give my life for freedom," he said solemnly and so loudly that the couple in the next balcony peered over the railing at us. I sighed and listened to the opera with one ear and to Charles with the other, and neither of them did I comprehend.

We spent many such evenings, they blur in my memory and out of the maze of reflections stands one image only: Charles, fine and straight as a tree, proud and fierce, looking beyond me to a new world.

He held my hand and and kissed my mouth, each kiss growing a little longer, a little warmer, but no other favors did he ask. My already feverish love fed on his hesitancy.

Manon returned to Paris in early summer, but she was greatly changed. Her mother had died and mortality, with its full, fearsome weight, had touched the gay Manon. I knew she had changed when she began to wear lavender mourning, a color that did not suit her pale beauty, and did not complain of it.

"Antoine likes lavender," she said. "He thinks it is a sensible color."

"Charles thinks mourning is hypocritical," I said. We looked at each other as through a windowpane, seeing but not touching. I had changed, too. I was no longer just Julienne, but Julienne who loved Charles and sought to please him in all things. His opinion mattered more than Manon's.

We could have parted then, but it was not yet time. Manon laughed and gave me a quick hug. "Indeed, I missed you," she said. "Now, tell me. How goes the battle? Has the castle been breached?" The castle, in the sisterly code we used, stood for the distance that still separates a man and a woman before they become lovers.

"No. Not yet." I helped her unpack her travel trunk and refill the clothespress, which had stood empty of her garments while she had been away. "And for every evening he spends with me, he spends four not with me, and I don't know where he goes. This is exquisite," I said, handing her a lace veil I had not seen before.

"It was my mother's. She married in it." Manon took it and lovingly folded it before putting it away. "But we must look into this matter and discover where Charles goes. First, though, I would much enjoy a walk through the Palais Royal, for I am weary of country lanes and sad thoughts. Maybe the Turkman who sells turbans will be there. I will buy one in a rose color, mourning or not."

"No one wears turbans," I said.

"They will. And I will be the first," Manon informed me.

Turbans were difficult to find that warm summer evening as we strolled in the Palais Royal and searched its many shops. But a certain book written by Madame Lamotte was available at every turn in the many paths. Once escaped to England, she had promptly written a volume of memoirs, as many ladies did in those days. But Madame Lamotte's memoirs were not filled with the usual tales of bedroom adventures and religious doubts.

She had written in great detail about the affair of the Queen's necklace and had taken great pains to implicate Marie-Antoinette. Implicate? No, she castigated, deprecated, accused, and faulted the Queen on every page.

"The Queen, realizing my blood line was of a line as noble as her own, took great care to appear to befriend me. Once I had sworn her my love and devotion, she used me in the devious plot to steal the fabulous necklace, which even now is hidden in the Petit Trianon," she wrote, ignoring the fact that many of the stones of the necklace, easily identified by jewelers who knew diamonds as well as seamstresses knew gowns, were being offered for sale in London . . . the same city to which she herself had fled.

The book was filled with lies, discrepancies, and inventions that even a child could discredit. But Paris read it; many chose to believe it.

Madame Bertin, who made frequent trips to England to purchase muslins and woolens, had herself been accused of smuggling some of the books into Paris, and that led to a definite chilling of her relationship with the Queen. I don't believe Bertin did any such thing. She was too practical to play those kinds of dangerous games. But for a while the Queen sent only for me, and would have no exchange with Bertin. That did not help my situation with my employer.

One day when the morning light was grey already with the promise of autumn and we had to light a fire in the tile stove of the workroom to warm our hands, Manon came in a few minutes late and took the table next to me.

There were blue shadows under her eyes. I guessed she had quarreled again with Antoine the night before; on such evenings she tossed and turned and woke looking more tired than when she went to bed.

"Charles did not lie when he said he was neither married nor engaged," she said in a low voice made private by the loud chatter of the other seamstresses.

"You are sure?" I asked, putting down a silk bodice I had been embellishing with silver embroidery.

"I am sure. I made inquiries through a friend. He is unattached. At least officially."

"And unofficially?"

"There is another woman. He visits her each Thursday."

The morning became even colder. "What will I do, Manon?"

"Whatever you do, do it quickly," she said. "But listen. There is more. He has joined a lodge. He is a Friend of the Constitution."

"A lodge? What do I care about clubs? It is this other woman that distresses me," I said jabbing at the bodice. The stitches were clumsy. I had to take them out and start over. Manon gave me a long, cool look.

"I tell you this, Julienne. In the long run, his activities with the lodge will be more threatening to you than any other woman could be. And you must never speak to me of this again. Antoine is also a member, and they are vowed to secrecy. They have pledged to work for a constitutional monarchy in France, as the English have."

That afternoon Charles came to the shop for the first time in many days. I almost stumbled in my haste to see him when Martine, who had answered the bell, whispered his name in my ear.

"Another chapeau," he said loudly enough for the others in the public room to hear; then he took my hand and pulled me to a more private corner where we were sheltered by a tapestry screen.

"For your mother?" I asked. He ignored the edge in my voice.

"Join me. This evening," he whispered, kissing my ear.

I pretended to hesitate a moment, then whispered yes. Whatever you do, do it quickly, Manon had said.

"But where have you been all these days? Why no message?" I asked.

"I was busy," was his uninformative answer.

Politeness and the rules of flirtation decreed I must drop the issue; love said I must press it. Fear, the image of another woman waiting for him, her arms open, made me incautious.

"Busy with what? You should have written," I insisted.

"Mademoiselle. You forget yourself. It is not your place to question me. Come tonight, but only if it pleases you." He drew himself up—angry men will always try to make women feel smaller—and left, with no further words.

I was devastated at my indiscretion, and his coldness. It was our first quarrel. If only it had been our last. When I returned to the sewing room I was unable to concentrate on the silver bodice no matter how often Bertin, glaring, paced in front of me to hurry my needle. He must come back, I told myself. He must come back.

Martine returned an hour later to call me again to the public room. My heart pounded with relief. He had come back! He would apologize!

But it was not Charles who had called for me, but the Duc d'Orléans. The pastel groupings of women had torn asunder once again to allow the duke the center of the floor, where he postured and bowed, preening like a cock of the walk.

He greeted me with great friendliness, which I found not at all reassuring, and asked to see a display of garters.

"You are expecting someone else?" he asked, as my eyes kept returning to the door behind him, looking for Charles.

"No. I expect no one," I sighed.

He only glanced at the tray of garters I had fetched from the large yellow cabinet; there was a restless air about him. I waited, knowing he would soon get to the real purpose of this visit.

"Tomorrow," he said. "You will be called to attend the Queen. No, do not look surprised. You will call attention to yourself. Show some sense for a change."

I stared at the buttons on his vest. They were of real gold, centered with a diamond in the elaborate Orléans crest.

"Don't ask how I know," he continued. "But believe me, my information is always accurate. You will go to Versailles tomorrow. I also know that you wish to leave Bertin's employ, that things are not well between you and her."

So. He had already found a workroom spy. "Thanks to you," I couldn't help but interject. He ignored me.

"I will give you another opportunity to be independent. You could be a wealthy woman."

"If I spy for you."

"Crudely put." His voice was sulky, still he smiled.

"I must refuse again, monsieur. Independence is not worth that cost."

"You grow more foolish, not less. I can ruin you." His eyes promised he would. When he left, Bertin watched with narrowed eyes.

Après moi, le déluge, I thought. Charles had been teaching me French history. It was still Charles I thought of, and in that d'Orléans was correct: I was growing foolish. I overlooked how easily, how disastrously those two men, one beloved, one hated, could be brought together, and there would be my real ruin.

That evening I slipped out the side door and found a linkman waiting for me. Charles had hired him to guide me; Charles wanted me to keep our assignation. I was faint with joy. The linkman, swaying his lamp, strode before me through the dark streets, pushing aside drunks and prostitutes so I could follow safely within the circle of his protecting light.

He led me to where Charles waited at the bookseller's stall. He, too, was dressed in cape and mask, but I knew him immediately, as I had on that first evening. He strode impatiently, back and forth, his cape swirling at his ankles like eddies of inked water. I mistook his impatience for continuing anger.

I ran to him without hesitation, and begged his forgiveness then and there for my bad temper. He begged my forgiveness for his rudeness. He held my hands between his and kissed them many times, vowing never again to be angry with me. Later, I would be better at anticipating the rapidity with which Charles changed moods; that night he caught me unaware, and I shed tears of relief.

We did not go to the Café Mécanique. Even the most private of public places would no longer suit our mutual mood. Instead, Charles hired a carriage and we drove through Paris to the faubourg St. Victor, to a small inn on the river. We ordered roast chicken and apple tart to be served in a private room, and neither of us could eat. When the untasted meal had been cleared away, I was the one who rose to lock the door and dim the lamp.

Our clothes whispered in the dark as we found each other and embraced.

"You would do this for me?" Charles asked. "Surrender this most precious of gifts?" He believed me a virgin. Manon had warned me, she had told me of the bladder filled with pig's blood I could buy from any barber, that would sustain the illusion of intact innocence. She, knowing woman that she was, had finally realized that my hesitancy in love was due to what she called a "previous experience that had not gone well." But I had decided against devious tactics. I hoped that passion would cover any fault Charles might find.

"For myself, too," I whispered.

His mouth was cool and soft, his silky black hair tumbled free across my arm as I unbound it. I heard his sword clatter as he began to undo his clothing, and then there were the softer rustlings of a woman's clothes dropping to the ground as he undid mine.

Moonlight bathed us on the couch, making our skin silver but providing no warmth. His green eyes darkened and then closed as I warmed him with the weight of my body, and soon neither of us minded the end-of-summer chill in the room, we were lost to all feeling except that which comes from within.

Manon had instructed me well in what I should do for delight, and what I should withhold, at least for a while, for modesty's sake. Charles, pleased, rewarded me with his own skills and pleasure. I vowed that night that he would never again wish to call on the other woman across town. Of the lodge, and the Friends of the Constitution, I did not think at all. But then it is always difficult to recognize the true enemy. Charles was my lover and my true innocence was this: I believed all battles between us to be over.

The next morning I had circles under my eyes deeper even than Manon's, but I sang as I washed and dressed.

Returning to the sewing room quickly fetched me from my cloud and back down to earth.

"You look ill," Bertin greeted me.

95

I laughed and said no, I was only a little fatigued. I gathered my skirts closer to me so she could pass, but she did not.

"You were not in your room last night," she accused.

"Madame. I understood our nights were our own."

"You displease me. Your work is not as ingenious as it once was, nor is your dedication to this establishment."

The only truth in her statement was the fact that I displeased her, and that through no fault of my own. Happiness made me bold and incautious.

"You are jealous that the Queen favors me."

Bertin's face grew white and then red with anger, her fat jowls quivered. "You are relieved of your duties here," she muttered through her teeth. "You will leave at the end of the week."

I watched, speechless, as she made her way down the hall to the door that led to her private rooms. She slammed that door so heavily the framed pictures on the wall shook with the force of her anger.

Too late, I realized that I had forgotten the most important condition of my employment with that difficult lady; due respect and appreciation of her tremendous pride. When I entered the workroom Martine did not even make the pretense of returning to her table from her eavesdropping position behind the curtains. All eyes turned to me, some with sympathy, others with glee and satisfaction, for Bertin was not the only person jealous of my frequent calls to Versailles. Manon's eyes were sad and worried.

At mid-morning the summons to the Queen came. That message both reassured and brought further worry. It meant that d'Orléans was privy to information that came from the Queen's own ladies-in-waiting. But it also meant that my dismissal had nought to do with my own foolishness. It had already been arranged by the angry d'Orléans. It was but a small satisfaction.

Knowing I would soon be unemployed and facing quick poverty—my sack of coins would last two weeks, I estimated—I hired a private cabriolet to take me to Versailles, instead of using the dirty and crowded public coach.

"I will taste a luxury or two before I am thrown into the street," I told Manon in decidedly un-Franklinish fashion. She shed the tears I would not cry, not while there was a chance that Bertin would discover my grief and revel in it. I was as proud as she.

The day was halted between summer and autumn, with fall's first red-and-gold leaves dancing down the streets of the city, and a taste to the air that promised colder days while yet reminding me of warmer ones.

When I thought of Charles and the previous evening, it seemed a beautiful day and even the beggar children seemed gay and pleasing. When I thought of the end of the week, and the poverty that would result, I noticed only the street gutters stuffed with ordure and rotting leaves, the misery and all-too-apparent hunger of the children playing in those gutters.

I would have to seek employment as a common servant, and even that would be difficult to find without the reference I knew Bertin would not provide. Charles, a noble, a soldier, a handsome Americanist . . . would he have anything to do with a servant? We were lovers, but had made no vows to each other and love, at least in the beginning, is as fragile as a cobweb.

By the time my cabriolet had passed the elegant hotels of the rue de Sèvres and the smaller houses on the outskirts of Versailles to pull up in front of the gilded palace gates, I was more than ready to weep.

"Hêlà! Julienne!" a gatekeeper called out. Jacques, who by then knew me by name, gave me the same warm greeting he gave to all women who were not so old and ugly they had to hide behind thick veils. He helped me out of the carriage.

"Let me guess," he said, pulling a long face. "You've lost an earring?"

"Nothing so small and easily replaced," I said, squinting up into his lined, ancient face. The heedless sun reflected off the gilded roofs and playing fountains of the palace so that the courtyard seemed afire with light. All that brilliance made me feel even darker within.

"Mademoiselle, you look unwell," the Queen said after I had finally been led down the long sequence of guards and ladies-in-waiting and curtseyed before her. She was enjoying the fine afternoon in a formal garden outside the Petit Trianon. Her friend and court artist, Madame Vigée-Lebrun, had asked her to sit for another portrait, and they had agreed to use the rose garden as the setting. She was seated in a graceful, relaxed posture, and the swirling lines of her gown, arranged by the artist, contrasted with the straight, classical lines of the Petit Trianon behind her. Her gown was the same color as the tranquil sky, her auburn hair had been left unpowdered and stood out against the white backdrop of the palace as brightly as a rose.

"Bring some water," the Queen commanded, and six different femmes de chambre fled to bring one glass. Marie-Antoinette was at the peak of her beauty in that respite of 1788. Disaster was but a year away, but aside from scandals and skirmishes it had not yet touched her beauty, her ability to spring back.

I was disheveled and perspiring from my long walk past the crowded Cour Royale, the splashing fountain of Neptune, down the side of the Grand Canal where members of the court and visitors leisured in long, abundantly pillowed boats, and through the many gardens and wooded paths that finally led to the Queen's secluded retreat. I wished to sit. But one did not sit in the presence of the Queen.

"Are you unwell?" she asked again, after I drank the water. It may have been cool at one time in the royal pantry, but by the time it reached me it had been passed from a score of hands and was tepid as bath water.

"No, Your Majesty," I lied.

She sighed with exasperation and turned to look full at me, so that the artist, who had carefully arranged the tilt to her head, clucked with impatience. "I command you to tell me what is bothering you," she said. "You are distraught. I have eyes in my head to see."

"I have been dismissed by Madame Bertin," I confessed, curtseying again for I knew not what else to do and was afraid of weeping before her.

Several ladies-in-waiting giggled and moved closer to hear in greater detail of my disgrace. I wondered which one of them would later repeat this scene to d'Orléans.

The Queen returned her exquisite head to the required tilt but made the artist yet more impatient by frowning. She was silent for several minutes as Madame Vigée-Lebrun tried to paint a smiling portrait despite that ominous frown.

"So," the Queen said, pursing her mouth. When she pursed her lips in that manner her Austrian accent became even more noticeable. It was, for a French queen, a disastrous mannerism. "So. Bertin knew this would displease me. I have taken you under my protection. Therefore, she has done this thing to displease me." She smiled. Women often smile when beginning a battle campaign.

"Oh, no! Your Majesty! It is I who have displeased Bertin!" I protested.

"Silence," the Queen ordered. All movement and sound in the garden, except for the singing of the birds which she could not command, ceased. "I tell you she has done this to displease me, just as last year she threatened to declare bankruptcy and disgrace me because of a few unpaid bills. So, the dressmaker is trying again to humiliate her queen. We shall see."

I knew the incident of which she spoke. It had puzzled us all, that sudden decision of Bertin's to state a bankruptcy which would embarrass the whole court. It had come during a time of frequent to-ings and fro-ings of d'Orléans's messengers. She, at the last minute, did not declare bankruptcy, but the harm had already been done. The Queen, Madame Deficit, was again accused of mishandling funds and of not even paying the bills for which she was accountable.

The Queen was silent for another long moment. Then, "Open the package you brought today," she ordered.

I carefully unfolded and held up a blue satin riding habit with golden lace ruffles and ruches. The hat was a flat pancake style, trimmed with a white

98

ostrich feather bent to echo the curve of the Queen's cheek. The underskirt was embroidered with purple and green peacocks, and seed pearls outlined the fan of their glorious tails. I had worked on the costume for many months, and was proud of it.

"You designed and created this yourself, did you not?" she asked. I nodded. "Then you are greatly skilled. And you shall open your own salon. This will show Bertin what I think of her tawdry tactics. But you must work hard, mademoiselle. You must be a great success, and not disappoint me."

Before I could reply, she had called for a secretary to bring her paper and pen, and had written a short note to her private accountant, authorizing him to bestow on me the incredible sum of four thousand livres. It was enough to pay a year's rent on a shop in an excellent location—even in the popular Palais Royal.

I fell to my knees. "You are my savior. Again," I said. "I will never forget this great kindness and generosity."

"See that you do not," she said. "And now, begone. Tell Bertin of this, quickly, I await with great pleasure news of her discomfort."

I left Versailles that day with my pockets heavy and clinking with the first installment of the Queen's gift. My heart was again light, my thoughts free to dwell on Charles and a delightful future.

I wondered what d'Orléans would think, now that his plan to ruin me had had just the opposite effect. The Queen had her small revenge on Bertin; I had mine on d'Orléans.

7

. . . new ventures and new hopes . . .

*"In private enterprise men may advance or recede, whereas they
who aim at empire have no alternative between the highest
success and utter downfall."*

—Tacitus

"Stop pulling at the covers, Julienne. I'm chilled," Manon protested.

"Then rise and warm yourself with activity. You promised you would help me today."

"When I made that pledge I did not know that I would spend the evening before with Antoine." She smiled, curling up to go back to sleep.

"If I waited for a morning that would not follow a night spent in delight with Antoine, I would wait in vain," I countered, pulling at her ankles. She slid over the sheets, dangerously close to the edge, when, kicking and laughing, she pleaded with me to release her.

"To be accurate, my hardworking petite Franklin, it was less than an evening of delight. I, too, my friend, have known hard work." She sat up and yawned. "We were printing, all last night." Then her face closed against me. She had said more than she should.

"Printing what?" I asked.

"Hurry with your packing. We should leave before the others are up and about, else Bertin will have sharp words for us both. She will not be pleased that I am helping you to remove to your new barracks."

100

"In a year I shall be rich, and you will come sew for me, so don't worry about the witch. You were printing more of the leaflets calling for a constitution. That's what you were printing. And if it's discovered who printed them, and who assisted, you will go to prison."

"We will not speak of it, Julienne." Manon stood straight and stern as an angry governess, no longer smiling. A cold barrier was between us, tearing asunder the friendship we had sworn would never be rent.

"Come," she said. "This is the day when your future begins. Why fret over small matters that have nought to do with you?" She laughed, and the moment passed.

We were—or at least I was—unaware that the many small revolutions already occurring—leaflets printed, tax barriers overturned and burned, convent walls smeared with red paint—would soon affect us all. Small trickles of dissatisfaction would soon become a raging river of revolt.

The quarrel had delayed us, so when we left Bertin was, as Manon had predicted, waiting in the hall. Her round, heavily powdered face was set in a grimace, her arms were crossed over the folds of expensive lace on her ample bosom.

"I hope you will remember all I have taught you," she sniffed. "And try to be more circumspect in your behavior."

"Yes, madame." I lowered my eyes and curtseyed. Bertin did not yet know I was retreating to no servant's position, but advancing to my own salon, one which I hoped would soon show hers some fierce competition. Manon looked away to prevent a smile.

For the last time I paused on Bertin's step and looked up to the overhead sign, Au Grand Mogol. Couturier to the Queen, remembering the winter night I had first stepped there. I had changed much since then. The beggar-girl from the Cité was wearing satin and about to become mistress of her own enterprise. And there was Charles, always Charles, waiting to thrill me, to distress me, for even when he wasn't with me, I thought of him constantly.

"I was the one who opened the door to you that night," said Manon with tenderness.

"Yes. And now we must open a new door, and quickly. I am eager to be off." For the second time in my life I hired a cabriolet rather than walking or taking the public coach. I'm glad I did. Otherwise I might have missed that particular pleasure altogether. Once the trouble began, private coaches became as scarce as loyal courtiers.

As much as I disliked and feared d'Orléans, I had rented a shop in the Palais Royal, his commercial property. More than anything, I wanted my salon to be a success. Not just for myself. Manon, through discreet questions to various people, had discovered that Charles was as poor as myself. Having been disowned by his father, he was dependent on the inadequate salary he earned as aide to La Fayette. I wanted success and wealth for Charles. And success, those days, was possible only in one area of Paris, the Palais Royal.

"All that you want to find in Paris, you will find in the Palais Royal," its enthusiasts claimed. "You can live your life here, a long life of perpetual enchantment, and say when you die, 'I've seen everything, known everything.'"

I thought those statements a bit exaggerated, even though the huge white quadrangle did house more than a hundred different shops, taverns, those new establishments called restaurants, gambling dens, and the new Théâtre Français. Everything new and fashionable could be found in the Palais Royal, including a new reckless and brazen atmosphere; inside those gates no King's guards were allowed. Here, at least, d'Orléans was the king, and the law.

Prostitutes, d'Orléans's favorite class of women, openly promenaded down the formal paths, displaying as much of themselves as they dared. Card games for ruinous stakes took place amongst the benches and fountains. Booksellers and pamphleteers who had circumvented the King's censors cried out forbidden titles. It was a pleasure palace for rich and poor alike.

My shop was No. 116. Its door faced the circus, an elongated oval building in the central gardens designed by d'Orléans as a theater for horse exercises. It would serve a more ominous purpose, later, as a rallying point for all the discontent in Paris. To the left of my entrance was a wine seller's shop; to the right was Madame Coulbert's marionette and peep-box theater. It was in Madame Coulbert's mirror-operated peep-box that I saw my first views of the American Falls of Niagara, and other new world scenes. They made exciting prints; never did I anticipate that one day I would see them firsthand.

The ground floor of my rented rooms consisted of a large reception area, already filled with display cabinets, tables, and a row of large fashion dolls dressed in costumes that could be ordered by the name of the doll: Céleste with her white shepherdess dress was always the favorite.

Behind that was a sewing room large enough for two: I planned to hire a second seamstress as soon as possible. A narrow staircase led to my private rooms—a sitting room, bedroom, and boudoir, all newly appointed with mahogany furnishings covered in good Utrecht velvet. My blood still sings sweeter in my veins when I remember the pride I felt in those rooms, those first possessions.

"Well?" I asked, turning to Manon. She was looking at her reflection in a large mirror installed in the bedroom. It was bordered with velvet streamers that matched the green bed hangings. Green gauze curtains hung at the window overlooking the gardens, filtering the strong sunlight into a shimmering, underwater quality.

"It is a mermaid's room," she pronounced, pleased. "It is charming."

"Charles says it is neoclassical," I said. "The simplicity of the ancients. It was his idea, to use low benches instead of sofas, and to swathe the walls with fabric rather than hang a picture gallery."

A woman reveals much when she reveals that the bed linens were selected to please a certain man. I had let Charles select the furnishings and colors of my room.

"And if you are to receive customers as soon as September, you will be stitching every minute, yes?" Manon asked, teasing. "No time for play?"

"I will take some time from my work for other activities." I smiled.

Charles arrived late that evening, after I had already given up waiting for him and gone to bed. I pretended to be angry.

"Julienne," he whispered, poking a bunch of wilted roses under my nose. The heat made their fragrance too fierce; I pushed them away. When his arm found its way around my shoulders and pressed me to him, I could not push him away, though, and did not even try. We loved, freely, extravagantly, until dawn lit the green curtains with a soft glow and the damp bed linens caught our legs in soft fetters.

In the misty light I rose on one elbow and traced with my finger the already familiar scar that marred his hard belly, running like a map's symbol for a river from his chest to below, where the hair grew black and curly.

He, supine with pleasure and fatigue, lay still beneath my hand. I already knew that the wound had been received in a place in Virginia called Yorktown, a place I knew nothing of except that my beloved had fought and been wounded there.

"My dearest," I whispered. "What kept you so long last night?"

"A riot. In the faubourg St. Antoine." His voice was sleepy, but ever alert. He disliked questions.

"What have you to do with riots?" I asked, rolling into his arms.

"I am not a man of leisure, though you would have me be one." He made to rise, but I would not let him. "La Fayette was concerned the unrest might spread, and what concerns La Fayette concerns me. Would you have me stay here and hold your yarn while you knit?" It was a reprimand.

"Hold me," I said.

He did, but only for a brief moment. Then taking up his shirt and getting to his feet, he was out of my arms, out of my reach.

A word portrait I painted of Charles . . .

"He is possessed of an appearance that turns all heads in his direction. Tall, well-formed, he walks with an air that says he knows at all times where he is going, and what his purpose is. But those who look deeply will see a hint of confusion in his eyes, a sense of misplacement, like a sleepwalker who is awakening in a strange room. He belongs to no one land, not the land of his birth, nor the land he claims as home across the ocean. And he belongs to no one person, not even the one he claims to love most devoutly. He is elusive and avoids capture, although he protests he is but too finally chained by his ambitions and his love. His heart and mind are ceaselessly restless. He welcomes all emotions, all ideals, but is content with none. He can shatter dreams as quickly as he invents them."

Such portraits were the fashion. I showed mine to Charles in a moment of anger, hoping to wound him.

"I approve the style," was his only comment.

"It will be bad weather today," he said, peering through the curtains.

I had learned not to discredit such announcements quickly. His travels in America had resulted in knowledge and lore that sometimes seemed prophetic to me. In actuality, he had been an avid student of the Delawares, and returned to France laden with Indian discernment, which allowed him to read skies and faces with equal ease.

I pulled on a wrapper and joined him at the window, where he was still squinting at the red dawn.

"Ah, Pierre is there." I opened the window and threw some coins down to the eight-year-old boy who leaned against the wall of my shop. "Pierre, fetch us some coffee and rolls from the café," I called to him. "And buy an extra roll for yourself. Two."

He grinned up at us and then trotted over to the Café de Joie, where Madame Moutier, yawning, was just rolling up her shutters. Slowly, the Palais Royal was coming to life and the silence of the night was broken by the sounds of gates creaking open, newspaper sellers calling the morning edition and a murmur of voices.

"I cannot stay," Charles said, pulling on his breeches. He hopped on one foot as he inserted one leg and then the other.

"Not even for coffee?"

"Not even for . . . that." He gave me a kiss that weakened my knees.

Pierre was quick, but even before he came with the breakfast Charles was retreating down the staircase. I was alone. I lowered a tray on a rope down to the ground, and Pierre put the steaming pot and basket of rolls on it. I ate slowly in the room that was still strange to me, comparing the high ceiling newly painted an ivory white with the low, smoke-darkened beam roofs of my childhood; comparing the woman in the mirror who ate expensive café rolls with the child who had scrounged for loose apples in the street.

The Cité was but a short walk away; it was a world away.

In the afternoon, as I was cutting the panels for a Céleste gown from a length of white silk, the workroom suddenly turned so dark I had to light candles. Rain came, heavy drops spaced closely that landed with the noise of pebbles against the summer-hard ground. The storm continued all afternoon.

I grieved for the tall marigolds, which had been broken under the weight of the storm, their golden yellow heads strewn against the green grass like miniature suns fallen from the sky.

Even as I grieved for something as slight as a bed of flowers, farmers outside of Paris stared at the sky and cursed the storm that had flooded the fields. They shook their heads and predicted food shortages. So did Charles.

My lover returned to me that night and most nights after, as I had hoped and planned. The small and large articles that surround men began appearing in my rooms—leather slippers by the bed, a razor leaning against the wash basin, boot polish in the chest of drawers. I came across them often during the day, indeed, sought them out, and smiled. They, at least, did not tend to disappear as did their owner.

There were days and some long nights, though, when he did not return, nor send any message. I tried to quiz him about those absences, but to little avail.

"I cannot spend all my time dallying here," he would say. "These are momentous times, there are many things to be done."

"What things?" I asked, not wanting to comprehend.

"La Fayette is a very great man. And great men need the assistance of smaller ones." More specific than that, my Charles would not be. He developed an interesting habit of evading my questions with caresses and kisses, and it was many weeks before my curiosity became stronger than my delight in those kisses. I learned little about his time away from me. Politics still seemed insignificant in my mind, compared to the image of the other woman.

My salon opened in September, at the beginning of the new season. The Queen did not come, of course, but sent a huge bowl of hothouse oranges and an order for three new gowns to buoy my courage. Bertin came, but did not enter the shop. I caught her peering through the large window and her expression gave me great satisfaction.

"Now you have an enemy," Manon said to me over her shoulder.

"I don't care, as long as I have enough custom to pay the bills," I said.

Moderate success followed my efforts and warmed me through the early autumn which turned quickly to cold. I found five seamstresses who would sew for me in their homes and hired chubby Lisette from Montmartre to help with the shop. This girl was a great trial to me; I constantly had to remind her to wash her hands or she would leave great greasy marks on the cloth, and she had a sullen disposition. But I could afford no better. Not yet. The mother of little Pierre, our errand boy, agreed to come in daily and sweep and dust, and fetch my midday meal.

Life was good, and sweet as the Queen's hothouse oranges. My days were filled with work, my nights with Charles. What cared I that the autumn disappeared too quickly, to be followed by a winter even crueler than the one we had known in 1784?

Snow fell in great, thick sheets, and the Seine froze again, this time even south of the city and as far north as Le Havre. River traffic ceased, and in France, the richest country of Europe, food became so expensive that even the aristocrats began to complain.

A roast chicken or dish of Pontoise veal cost as much as a length of the best velvet. I paid the price because Charles favored those dishes. Let others eat rotten turnips and rolls made with more sawdust than flour. Charles dined in comfort; his joy was my purpose.

In the poorer sections of Paris the dogs and cats disappeared from the streets to reappear in stew pots. And when they were gone and it was rare to hear dogs howl under the moon and cats make their boisterous courtships, the starving started again; not just in Paris, but all over France.

The hardship led to greater hardships; hundreds of thousands of people lost their work. Many, some days it seemed all, of them made their way to the streets of Paris. The streets had always been congested. Now they were almost impassable, so filled were they with beggars, entire families and even whole guilds, come to the heart of France only to discover things were as bad there as elsewhere. The curses and mutterings I heard in the streets bespoke of hot tempers and choler aimed at anyone still dressed in decent clothing and with abundant flesh on their bones.

The destitute ones were not going to go to a bridge archway and die without protest, as they had in 1784. They roamed the streets in dangerous bands, homeless and hungry and bitter. Many found their way to the Palais Royal, where long charity lines, paid for by d'Orléans, formed. With their free bread they got long lectures on the tyranny of the monarchy.

Grievances and complaints rose through the frigid air like blackbirds taking wing. The national deficit was the stone thrower that roused the birds of prey.

In the twelve years that Louis and Marie-Antoinette had ruled France, over twelve hundred and fifty million livres had been borrowed. I could not comprehend such a sum, nor could many others. But it rolled off the tongue with angry, warring sounds; it impressed. Where had it all gone? Not into wages. Not into public improvements. Not into hospitals or roads and not even to the fat army generals. The money went for new palaces and diamond necklaces, they said. And how would it be paid back? To that question, no one had an answer.

And because the King was interested only in watchmaking and hunting and he was a slow, heavy, and unsatisfactory scapegoat, the collective finger pointed at Marie-Antoinette, the Austrian woman, Madame Deficit.

The Assembly met to discuss the seemingly inevitable bankruptcy of France. But because the Assembly was made up of the king, the nobility and the clergy, and the only way to raise the necessary funds was to newly tax the nobility and priesthood, the Assembly proved futile. The nobility, claiming "ancient privilege, pointed a collective finger at the rich clergy, saying "Tax them!" And the cardinals and bishops put hand to heart and declared their importance as the salvation of mankind; surely that good and merciful work should not be taxed!

I smiled at many of the cartoons and satires published that winter; much of the posturing was comical. But while the priests and nobles and court quarreled, Paris starved. And waited for something to happen, as the winter dragged over the city like an old man too tired to lift his feet.

Manon no longer visited me two or three evenings a week, but came only on Sunday afternoons, for shorter visits. She ceased wearing silk and wore only simple cotton gowns. Antoine, a man of the people, preferred them.

"You'll freeze!" I protested. Manon, serious and gloomy, no longer the gay coquette, looked at me with steady blue eyes and lectured on the evils of luxury. I wished only to speak of love. I already knew firsthand the hardships she was then discovering. But of course, she did not know that.

One Sunday afternoon she arrived in a slightly gayer mood, with the announcement that she and Antoine were to be wed. I was to sew her wedding gown. It would be made of simple cotton, with no lace. Lace was a luxury.

"You cannot get married without lace," I protested. "I have a new pattern from the south called Constitution. Even Antoine couldn't object to that."

"Well, a little perhaps. At the throat," she agreed.

She was married in March, in a small ceremony that was attended only by her father and two younger sisters. There was no feast afterward. "How can we feast when so many are starving?" she told me. They were Antoine's words, not hers. I did not attend. As a loyal servant of Marie-Antoinette, I had not won Antoine's approval. Once wed, Manon left Bertin and took work with a milliner in the faubourg St. Martin, near the house she shared with Antoine's mother.

Gay Manon, the most popular beauty of Bertin's sewing room, the loveliest flower in that bright bouquet of womanhood, became a staid married woman, with boring work as a hat trimmer to lengthen the dull days, housekeeping chores to occupy her evenings—Antoine couldn't afford servants and therefore disapproved of them—a stern husband to please, and a complaining mother-in-law to placate.

Nevertheless, I envied her new title of Madame. Plots to win Charles over to the possibility of marriage filled my thoughts.

The object of my desire, however, had other plots on his mind. The King, realizing that he must give way on some point or another, announced that the Estates-General would convene in the spring.

Charles was ecstatic. It was, he informed me, the beginning of all that he and La Fayette had worked to achieve; a great new age of constitutional monarchy would be ushered into France. His step was light, his kisses quicker, his absences heartbreakingly more frequent. His work was just beginning. Politics consumed him, as love consumed me. Even so I, too, welcomed the coming great assembly.

I had my own reasons. It would bring hundreds of countryfolk into Paris, elected deputies from every city, town and village in France—all eager to send home Parisian gifts to their wives, daughters and sweethearts. It would be good for my business, which was laboring under heavy inflation and the ancient vexation of working for nobles who ordered much and spent large sums, but rarely paid their bills. Because of the beggars who bought nothing, and the nobles who disdained to pay for what they bought, my cash box grew lighter, not heavier.

I purchased a huge stock of cheap paper fans and hired an aged, perpetually drunk artist who camped in the slum courtyard of the Louvre, to paint them with likenesses of the King and La Fayette. The La Fayette fans sold well, but Madame Pugeau's fans painted with the leering visage of the Duc d'Orléans sold faster, and at a higher price.

The day of the great procession, Charles and I went to Versailles, as did all of Paris, it seemed. The rue de Sèvres was so jammed with carriages and sedan chairs that we finally abandoned ours and walked most of the way, making better time on foot.

Tense with excitement, we watched as the two thousand delegates to the assembly marched in crooked, jubilant file. They wore solemn faces that pulled into quick grins as children and spouses, watching from the side, called out names and messages.

At ten o'clock the King's chariot came into view, led by silver-robed pages and liveried riders who rode with straight, proud backs, carrying royal falcons on their sturdy wrists. The King himself sat smiling in the midst of his trappings, a fat, benign, middle-aged man who smiled sheepishly, regretting the spectacle which had called him away from his hunting dogs and mechanical toys. The crowd cried "Long live the King!" as he passed; he waved cheerfully.

Most people associate innocence with a young girl who has not yet tasted life. I think of King Louis, smiling and waving at the crowd that would soon have his crown and life.

All was silence as Marie-Antoinette passed by. She sat stiff and unsmiling, surrounded by her ladies-in-waiting who had dressed too richly, and who would not condescend to wave or smile. The crowd interpreted the Queen's narrowed eyes and griefstricken face as unfriendliness. In reality, her first son lay in his bed, dying from an illness that even a Queen's great wealth and power could not vanquish.

The Queen was capable of great vanity, and often of very poor judgment. Yet she was a truly devoted mother; how could she smile on a crowd which had called her from her dying son's bedside?

"The Austrian woman!" I heard a man yell. "Foreign whore!" yelled another voice. Marie-Antoinette shivered, despite the heat of the morning and the weight of her heavy court robes.

Charles half-rose from his chair, his hand went to sword hilt and then faltered. We were above the crowd, on a hired balcony. There was nothing he could do to avenge this slight to the Queen that would not make the matter worse. Friend of the Constitution though he was, he never wished harm to Marie-Antoinette. He sincerely believed that the reforms he and La Fayette campaigned for would aid the monarchy, not destroy it.

The nobility followed the Queen's carriage, rows and rows of aristocrats encrusted with jewels and ancient ribbons and medals of honor, their powdered wigs wilting in the heat and shedding clouds of white dust in their wake. They were followed, in turn, by the Second Estate, led by cardinals in brilliant red robes, whose huge crosses glittered in the sun like a warning of the fire to come. Worried by the talk of a tax to be levied on the Church and its rich holdings, they marched solemnly, at a pace usually reserved for funerals.

After the clergy marched the Third Estate, which was attending the Estates-General for the first time in over a hundred years. They, for the most part, looked self-conscious and clumsy, like vintners and farmers dressed in rented judge's robes, for such they were.

It was in this tawdry flock of crowlike merchants who wished to be legislators that I saw Mouret. He was fatter than before, and armed with a cheap sword that banged against his knee with each step.

I dropped my fan over the balcony, so surprised was I to see that my old enemy had been elected deputy. Bakers are often popular, though, in times of famine. Charles did not notice the tremble that went through me.

"That fan is lost," he said. "After this crowd has trampled on it, you won't want it back."

The Duc d'Orléans marched with the Third Estate, just four rows before the baker, Mouret. The crowd gasped with joy. With that very political and ingenious act of foregoing the pomp and glitter of the royal carriages to walk instead with the black-robed deputies, he had announced his loyalties for all to see. He had openly turned his back on the Queen and King; his beneficent smile was for the people. Triumphant shouts of "Vive le Duc d'Orléans!" greeted his every step.

The King, realizing that the Third Estate had already won the day, allowed its deputies to enter the Cathedral ahead of himself. The last shall be first. More cheers, more jubilation.

Charles approved the decision, but I had my doubts. Giving too much importance to people who are used to none can have unpredictable consequences.

And so, just days later, the King, harried and irritated by conflicting demands from the warring three estates, frowned, rose from his throne, and announced that the Third Estate, the last which had become first, was denied further admittance to the discussions of the Estates-General. His Most Benevolent Patience had already worn out. He, tired of all the conflicts, the words, words, words that buzzed around his uncomprehending head like hungry mosquitoes, could not kick out the aristocrats or clergy. Hence, the Third Estate must go.

But they would not. Refusing to be ignored or disbanded, they convened on the royal tennis courts and vowed to camp there until Louis welcomed them back to the negotiations.

The King gave in. Louis always gave in, whether it be on the matter of a new necklace for his queen, or a constitution for his country. The deputies returned and sat at his left side, across from the aristocrats, on his right. To be "of the left" became fashionable.

Warm spring became hot summer and my salon began to realize a profit. I sewed batches of gold and silver coins into hidden pockets of my petticoats and the weight of them reassured me with each movement I made.

Charles, too, was busy. La Fayette was sitting as a deputy from the Auvergne. Like d'Orléans, he wished to unite the nobles with the Third Estate. He put his plan to a vote, but it was voted against by the powerful clergy and those aristocrats who refused to see that they could best protect their interests by compromising on the wishes of others.

"They are fools," Charles muttered. "Great changes are in the making and they must go with the tide or be drowned in it." They chose to be drowned.

The city itself was awash with graffiti. "It is no longer a question of what has been, but will be," read one huge broadsheet hung in the gardens of the Palais Royal. "What is the Third Estate?" asked another. "The nation. What is it now? Nothing. What ought it to be? Everything."

Forbidden books that claimed to reveal in splendid detail the secret vices of the court proliferated like maggots on a garbage heap. Riots began to occur with surprising frequency, and the King's agents had more to do than monitor the reading habits of Parisians. Several factories were burned to the ground by irate workers.

I had thought that warm weather would finally lower food prices. It did not. Bread became so scarce that even the wealthy bewailed the lack of it. Rumors were spread that the king and his ministers were hoarding grain in order to drive prices up yet higher.

"Grain is being hoarded, but I think we should look closer than the warehouses of Versailles," Charles said one summer evening. He had just returned from another meeting at the Jacobin monastery, and was tired and worried. "I don't trust d'Orléans. He delights in trouble and I wouldn't be surprised if the shortages have much to do with him. He will stop at nothing to discredit the monarchy."

"Come to bed," I said. I paid scant attention to his talk, still preferring his caresses. Names—Robespierre, Desmoulins, Danton, Hébert—began to come into his conversation, but I waved them away as if they were no more than the black flies of summer.

On June 27 the noisy Third Estate was formally combined with the first and second; the people had won another victory. All of Paris celebrated and d'Orléans, the most jubilant of all, abandoned his titles and took the name Philippe Egalité. The glitter and glory of Versailles was fading like a lamp running out of oil.

"That's all very well," I said to Charles. "But I don't see him giving up the fortune that went with his titles."

"You won't. Half of Paris is in the employ of Monsieur Egalité. He needs every sou, for the loyalty he inspires does not come cheaply. He thinks to buy his way to the throne of France, once he has toppled Louis from it."

Marie-Antoinette and Louis were growing nervous. They surrounded the city with forty thousand Swiss and German troops. The monarchy was at war with its own people. Paris retaliated.

I was hemming a gown for a Madame Laquatra, wife of a deputy from Lyons, when I heard fierce shouting in the gardens of the Palais Royal on July 13.

A printer, Camille Desmoulins, was standing on one of the high tiers of the circus. A large, angry-looking crowd milled restlessly at his feet. I recognized Antoine, Manon's husband, among them.

"Enough talk!" Desmoulins yelled. "We have the greatest number on our side! We are the strongest! To arms!"

The shapeless crowd milled thicker and more determined and formed itself like a nightmare arising from the mist of sleep. Men and women, eager for arms, grabbed garden tools and then broke into shops to loot them for pistols and knives.

I closed my shutters and Madame Laquatra and I huddled behind a sofa until the afternoon grew quiet again. The mob had departed the Palais Royal, but had not disbanded.

Eager to find more arms with which to defend themselves from the King's army, they made their way down the rue St. Antoine. They stopped often to fortify their resolve with stolen food and drink. It was the next day, on July 14, that they reached their destination, the Bastille. Those fishwives, vintners, street sweepers and beggars took a royal prison. The Bastille fell, and with it the *ancien régime*.

"It is a revolt," the King said, when he was informed of the events of July 14.

"Nay, sir, it is a revolution," his minister informed him.

8

. . . a diamond reappears . . .

"I see that they are going headlong to destruction and would
fain stop them if I could."

—*Gouverneur Morris*

Paris grew becalmed under scorching summer heat which cast dust in our faces and filled both the poor hovels and the rich drawing rooms of the city with lassitude and choler.

I grew irritable and Charles became lethargic, overpowered by the sooty gusts that made everything hot to the touch. We slept on opposite sides of the bed, neither touching nor dreaming of each other in our separate, troubled sleep. The heat enervated us, and I grew absentminded with worry.

Fearful of losing Charles's already lagging interest altogether, I schemed of ways to hold him. I dressed only in those colors he preferred; I served meals planned to his tastes; I alternately smothered him with cheerful kisses and pouted, hoping to keep him off guard and more vulnerable. Marriage seemed to offer the strongest bonds, although it was a sacrament not much enjoyed by the women of my bloodlines. But I determined to bind Charles to me with vows made before God and man.

That same stifling season that Charles's lethargy filled my mornings with grey doubt was also when I first heard of an invention that a physician had perfected, the guillotine. It was said to dispatch criminals quickly and

113

mercifully. The progress of history can be told in the progress of our inventions of death. The "merciful" guillotine became the bloody toy of the revolution.

I had no such dreary thoughts then; I cared only about Charles, whose passion was melting like a wax candle left in the sun, despite my ploys, and about my salon, which was also not prospering as I had planned. Business slackened after the deputies bought up the cheap fans and hastily made gowns with which I had lured them into my otherwise expensive shop.

In truth, it wasn't just my business that was suffering. The fall of the Bastille had opened my previously insensible eyes; in the past year aristocrats had been fleeing France quickly, and in large numbers, taking as much of their wealth with them as they could. Merchants jested bitterly that the only items being purchased those days were travel cases and large trunks.

The possibility of bankruptcy added to my deeper fear of losing Charles. The fragility of my dreams was a new reality, and a harsh one.

"Ouch! Caution, mademoiselle!" a Madame Fauvrette complained one August afternoon when the sun outside my windows blazed as intensely as a thousand votive candles. "This is the third time you have pricked me today! If you aren't more careful I will take my custom to Madame Bertin's shop!" She was fat and her fleshy arms shone with greasy perspiration. I could smell the great quantities of garlic and onion she had consumed the evening before.

"Madame Bertin is in England," I replied, wiping a pin prick of blood from the fat arm. The Queen's seamstress, too, had taken a quickly planned and extended vacation to more peaceful England. And she wouldn't have refuse like you in her salon if she were here, I thought, but did not say.

Madame Fauvrette had come in to be measured for a carmagnole jacket, an odious red affair that women who supported the likes of Marat and Danton wore to show their allegiance. Her husband was a deputy from the Marais, and she carried on as though soon the Queen herself would be asking her opinion on matters of state. But she paid her bills promptly and ordered two new gowns a month.

"Forgive me," I said. "I will be more careful."

"It is so hot!" she complained, fanning herself with a blue silk fan painted with a likeness of George Washington on one side and La Fayette, hero of two worlds, on the other.

"Perhaps if you removed your jewelry?" I suggested, pausing to look up at the huge expanse of flushed bosom that confronted me. Madame, dressed only in her underclothes, was hardly a vision of matronly modesty, yet she had refused to remove the gaudy jewels her husband had recently purchased

114

for her. The large, greyish black stones, strung on cheap silver chains, fell into the cleft between her mottled breasts like souls being cast in the darkness of hell.

Madame, like other women from the faubourgs, had put her pearls in safekeeping and wore instead ugly strands of broken stone hammered from the walls of the Bastille. On her wrist dangled a relatively daintier string of sickly greenish beads called "prisoner's breath," calcified mold scraped from the walls of the ancient prison. Such ridiculous trinkets sold for a large sum and were already scarce, despite the abundance of stone recently available from the prison walls.

"I will keep my jewels on my person," she insisted. "Just hurry with the fitting. If only it would rain." She ended her high-pitched plea with a sigh. "It is so dusty in the Palais Royal, I think if any more dust settles in my throat I'll lose my voice."

Holy Virgin, you could do me that one kindness, I silently prayed, wearied of madame's long tirades on the perfection and political astuteness of Monsieur Fauvrette, who was bored with dealing in cowhides for cheap book bindings and would like to further his political ambition.

"He has joined the Jacobins," she announced proudly. "The club."

The meetings in the Jacobin monastery were no longer secret, and other political clubs, in addition to the Jacobin, had sprung up to further confuse Parisian politics. Every man, and many women, in Paris belonged to some club. It was fashionable. Charles was a Jacobin, as the Friends of the Constitution had renamed themselves, but was growing increasingly distressed by some of the speeches and goals of his associates.

"Danton is too extreme," he informed me one night when the sunset was orange with heat and dust and glowed eerily through the green curtains of our bedroom. "And that other, that lawyer from Arras. I don't like the look of his eyes, as though he were spying a rabbit through the sight of his rifle."

"He squints?" I asked. Charles pulled me to him. Our bare skins stuck together with the heat.

"No, unknowing one. The squint comes when the hunter is about to pull the trigger. Robespierre is not ready to pull the trigger. But I think he will be, soon." Rumors were already afoot that "Robespierre" was a form of "Robert-Pierre," the sons of Damians, the would-be assassin of King Louis XV. Damians had failed and died a long and extraordinarily gory death by torture, as prescribed by the reasonably offended King, who had not wanted to die. "Robert-Pierre has come to avenge his ancestor," the rumors whispered. "Robert-Pierre is here."

It was nonsense of course. All the more reason for people to believe it.

"And your husband enjoys his club meetings?" I asked Madame Fauvrette. With one last and desperate spurt of energy I jabbed the remainder of the pins into the neckline of her jacket and pulled it quickly over her head, not caring if she looked like St. Sebastian pierced by the hundred arrows afterward. I was weary of republicans and their frumpy wives, weary of the heat, weary of politics.

She screeched, but I smoothed the jacket and skirt with joyous exclamations that quickly convinced her that never before had a costume done so much for her beauty. She stopped squawking and instead clucked contentedly as she made her payment. The greasy paper money stuck to her palm. I plucked at it even as I herded her out the door.

"Go home Lisette," I told my shop girl.

"It's only three o'clock," she whined.

"I'll pay for the full day. But go home."

Paris

10 August, 1790

Charles returned yesterday covered with dust and sweat and that ominous silence that sometimes comes over him. He has been with La Fayette again, at Versailles, and the purport of that meeting is not good. The Assembly is considering removing the royal family from Versailles, which they feel is too isolated, too distant from Paris. As if the Queen and her children were no more than furniture to be moved from one warehouse to another. We quarreled over this, I protesting that it would unnecessarily distress the Queen, and he arguing for the move, saying the royal family would be safer in Paris. I, who had been learning something of French history to please him, pointed out that no king who had ruled from Paris had managed to keep his throne. Superstition, Charles said.

In the midst of that quarrel a messenger arrived with a note for me from the Queen. Charles took it from my hand. "You should not go to Versailles anymore," he said. "It is not safe."

I took the note back. "I owe the Queen more than a hasty abandonment in time of peril. You yourself have said that La Fayette is assuring the safety of the royal family. Surely there can be no threat, with the dauntless La Fayette in charge?"

He did not miss the sarcasm in my tone.

"Do as you will," he said.

He sat heavily in a chair and rubbed his eyes, which were red from the dust. I touched his forehead and it was too warm for my liking. A new fear: was Charles getting ill? All other matters shrank to the size of gnats as I fussed over him, but he laughed at my concern.

"It is nothing. I only wish it would rain," he said. "The city smells like a cesspool and tempers are short everywhere. It is cool in the mountains, in the Auvergne . . ."

He had a sickness I would learn much of later. He was homesick. I cradled him in my arms. He had no home left in the Auvergne, his family had dispossessed him, indeed, had even tried to imprison him with a *lettre de cachet* that night many years before when he had boarded ship with La Fayette for America. It is not just my old friend Jeannette, not just women, who can be bullied into undesirable marriages. But he had refused to be coerced into a marriage of convenience, he had waited, and now it was me he loved.

"It would be cool in the countryside. We could dine on stream trout and fresh peaches," I murmured.

"It is tempting." He closed his eyes.

"We could make it a wedding trip," I suggested.

"A wedding trip? That seems a long excuse for a short journey," he said, opening his eyes again.

The diligence to Versailles made good speed that afternoon, and successive trips became quicker yet. There were fewer carriages on the road, just as there were fewer customers in my shop. The people who owned the carriages, who could have made my shop prosper, were fleeing to the more favorable political climes of Poland, Austria and Belgium, where revolution was distant news, not a near threat.

The rue de Sèvres and wealthy neighborhoods of the faubourg St. Germain were marred with boarded-up hôtels. The once luxurious formal gardens were going wild. Lone, overbloomed roses swayed forlornly next to tall stems of invading weed, and grass grew high enough to conceal children at play. Statues of Diana and Neptune stood covered with pigeon dirt in the midst of fountains grown silent, their basins filled with garbage, their jets of water no longer playing their crystalline music.

The taverns of the city were overflowing with the gardeners, chefs, footmen and stablehands put out of work by the emigration of the aristocrats. Their discontent and poverty, bitter as fruit left to rot on the ground, added to the sultry, suffocating anger that rode the hot winds of summer.

Only the courtyard of Versailles retained its orderly appearance, the sun still blazed off the gilded roofs and trim. Guards in blue-and-silver livery stood at attention at every door and staircase. But next to them stood members of the new National Guard, recently formed by La Fayette. Most of these men were simple shoemakers or woodcutters, but they adopted postures and struts that made the normally pompous Swiss Guards seem modest.

The members of the new citizen militia, fearing that I had hidden an Austrian army or perhaps a cannon or two in my parcel, searched it thoroughly and then indicated they would search me, too.

"Touch me and I'll scratch out your eyes," I promised, grabbing for my parcel.

"Now, mam'selle," one of them complained. "Don't take on. We're just doing our job."

"And harassing women in the courtyards of Versailles is part of your glorious work? I'll speak with La Fayette about this." It was an empty promise, I had never met Charles's employer and idol, much less had conversation with him, but it worked. They released my arms and my parcel and parted ranks so that I could ascend the Queen's staircase without further interference.

"It would have been pleasant searching that one. Too bad," one of the men said behind me, loudly enough for me to hear. I made a rude gesture at him and went on my way.

Once safely inside that marble stairwell it required only a few minutes to be ushered into the Queen's presence, as there were fewer and fewer ladies-in-waiting content to wait out the revolution with Madame, Her Majesty.

"How fare you?" she asked from the rosy depths of a large loveseat. She wore a simple white gown; her face, despite the pleasant welcoming smile, was pale and strained, her Austrian accent more noticeable. The mirrors in the room were draped in black for her first son, who had died just weeks before.

"I am well," I said, making the three required curtseys before her. "And my business thrives." Why tell that grieving mother what she must already know, that the emigration of the aristocrats was emptying my shop as thoroughly as it was emptying her courtyards and reception rooms?

"We are pleased," she said. She glanced at a woman who approached us with graceful, gliding steps from across the vast expanse of parquet floor.

"Princess," the Queen called to her softly. "Pray join us. I would have your

118

advice on this matter." Princesse de Lamballe, the same woman I had espied in the private and ruinous conversation behind a hedge of the Palais Royal with the Duc d'Orléans, came to the Queen and kissed her hand gently. Let me state here and now: I believe the Princess was duped and used by d'Orléans, as was all of Paris, later. Marie-Antoinette and her friend clasped hands like sisters greeting each other after a long absence. I could not doubt the love in Lamballe's eyes.

"Arrange your lace samples," the Queen instructed me, pointing to a small table. "We must have private conversation, and mask it. Dearest Lamballe, can you think of some way to remove the other women?"

A half-dozen or so females of all ages peered sideways at us from behind their fans or from whence they sat at card tables, anxious to know why the Queen had stepped out of their genteel ranks to speak with a mere servant. In their own way, those remaining ladies-in-waiting were as formidable a guard as the loyal-to-the-death Swiss Guards of the King. Many already carried little daggers in their garters with which to defend themselves and the Queen. After the massacre of August 10, those dainty jeweled daggers became popular souvenir items. But I get ahead of myself. If memory is an exercise, it is one that must be performed diligently, with proper respect for chronology.

Their curiosity was based on loyalty and protection. All except for one, I knew, and the Queen must have known, too.

"It is warm, don't you agree?" the Princess asked loudly. "The ladies would be cooler and more comfortable, I think, if they were to sit closer to the windows." The rest was whispered, only for the benefit of the Queen and myself. "They would never leave the room altogether. But I will ask little Marie-Louise to play the pianoforte for us. She plays well . . . and quite loudly."

"You are right, as ever, my clever Lamballe," the Queen whispered back. "Do what you can, and give me a few moments of privacy."

I stood in uncomfortable silence as the Princess ushered the ladies into a group around Marie-Louise, who blushed with pleasure as she took her seat at the pianoforte. The Queen pretended to examine the lace. Marie-Louise opened the impromptu concert with an aria from Mozart's *Abduction from the Seraglio*. It was a noisy piece to begin with, but Lamballe insisted that all the ladies give full voice to the lyrics. The room filled with quavering song.

"Now, mademoiselle. Pay close attention," said the Queen. "I am about to ask a favor. No. Don't speak yet. The favor I ask will impose danger. Consider first." She continued her feigned examination of the lace, not meeting my eyes.

119

My heart went out to this woman. She, the most beautiful, at one time the most beloved woman, of Europe, must confide in a mere seamstress. What a strange world this is. But when I considered, it made sense. Who better to ask a favor of, than a simple woman who owed happiness, even life to her?

"There is nothing to consider," I whispered, keeping my fingers busy with the lace samples which frothed like cool snow over the rosewood table. "Even if I were not already in your debt, my heart and instincts would require that I serve you in any way you ask. I accept the task before you name it."

"I can trust you, then?" It was, I thought, already moments late to ask that question. She leaned closer to me and her rose and gardenia perfume filled the space between us, reminding me of the abandoned gardens of the rue de Sèvres. Had she seen them, those reminders of the troubles in her realm? I wished that Charles and I could be gone from Paris for a time.

"I pledge you my life and honor," I promised, sincerely hoping she would require neither.

The Queen caught the eye of a femme de chambre who stood waiting in a corner. She nodded and moments later the two remaining royal children were brought to us. Marie-Louise finished the aria and began another. The children giggled at the music.

Eleven-year-old Marie-Teresa Charlotte, known as Madame Royal, realizing she had displeased her Queen Mother, clapped her hand over her mouth and opened her eyes wide. She was a shy, timid child, even then, before her true troubles began. She showed no promise of beauty, possessing most of the characteristics that flowed to her from her father, not her mother.

Her brother, the Dauphin, was but half her age, yet he seemed the wiser of the two. Instead of rolling his eyes, he bowed to his mother and begged her pardon very prettily. She opened her arms to him and he went happily to that soft, maternal circle, no longer the prince, but only the child. He was dressed in a full suit adorned with ribbons and medals and a miniature sword, which seemed humorous at the time, but not in retrospect.

She, an arm about each, turned both children to face me. I curtseyed, and Madame Royal fled. Marie-Antoinette whispered something into her son's ear. At this cue, he produced from his pocket a box as large as his own hand. Stepping closer to me, he opened it. Within, on a soft bed of white satin, nested a yellow teardrop-shaped diamond as large as a quail's egg. I gasped. The Dauphin smiled mischievously as he took the diamond out of its box and handed it to me. My back was to the ladies at the pianoforte; they saw none of this strange transaction. Madame Royal was already playing with a basket of puppies in a different corner of the room.

"Darling son. Show mademoiselle the flaw." He, stepping closer yet, turned the diamond in my palm. He traced a line on the underside of the gem, a line thin as a knife's edge, where a facet had been cut. "It's crooked," he pronounced gravely, and his small finger rested alongside the flaw, a miniscule jag in the otherwise straight line of the facet. I could barely see it, would not have known of its existence, without his pointing it out to me.

He turned the stone back over and as he did so it caught a ray of light and returned it again as fiery beams dancing against the high ceiling. The Queen plucked the diamond quickly from my hand and doused its fire by returning it to the box.

That box she handed to me.

"Keep it. In trust, for me, and my son." She kissed the Dauphin and sent him to play with his governess. "Hide it away," she said, when he had left. "I hope never to set eyes on it again. And may the day never arrive when my son need see or remember it."

Not knowing what else to do, I pocketed the treasure as if it were nothing more than a box of pins. I hadn't come prepared to cart away a gem worth a king's ransom.

"That diamond is the central pendant of the necklace so foolishly purchased by the Cardinal de Rohan," Marie-Antoinette said, returning to her sofa with a soft whisper of silken skirts. "You remember that disastrous affair? Of course you do. Who will ever forget it?" Her hand went to her forehead, as if to rub away a headache. "I have always known the Cardinal to be of little wit. But I never realized how dangerously little until I heard he bought that cursed necklace, and in my name. As he claimed."

"Your Majesty was found innocent of intrigue," I said.

"I know the rumors," she said. "Many still say I have the necklace. I haven't. Only that one stone you now possess, and that I acquired in a most unusual manner. Soon after the Lamotte woman escaped from prison and fled to London, there was a small fire in my dressing room. I was at my escritoire, writing a letter, when a maid began to shriek that we were all to flee quickly.

"The letter I was writing was a very private one." She paused and smiled as she thought of that man the letter had undoubtedly been addressed to, her loyal Count Fersen. "Instead of leaving it behind, I took it and the writing box with me.

"I fled, but just outside the door something fell out of the writing box. It was the diamond."

She leaned forward and picked up a piece of lace to conceal the trembling in her hands.

"There was no fire that day. It was a ruse to get me out of my room. Once out, other people would enter. People who would know to go directly to my writing box and find the diamond. Because they had put it there. Imagine the scandal. 'Stolen diamond found in Queen's room.' " She held a piece of lace up to the light, pretending to admire its pattern.

Yes. I could well imagine the scandal.

"Now, mademoiselle. I am at your mercy." She eyed me through the lace.

"Others wished you to appear guilty. I believe more faithfully than before in your innocence."

"I fear a time to come, when I and my children will be separated. There are many who wish harm to my son, and many more will rise, not for any fault of his, but simply because he is my son, and the Dauphin. He may need to live quietly some day, out of the public eye, for his own safety. But once out of that eye, he may also be forgotten. With that diamond, you can help him claim his inheritance. By that diamond, you shall know my son, for only he will be able to point out that flaw, as a reminder of this day. He will have grown to a man older and sadder and if God wills, wiser than I have ever been.

"But no one else must know of this. Do you understand? Not even Charles-Marie de St. Remy."

She cast off her serious mood and smiled. "You are surprised? Remember this. D'Orléans is not the only person in Paris with an access to gossip! But I applaud your choice. He is handsome and well-bred. He could choose his companions more wisely, but then, who could not?"

She was referring to La Fayette. The Queen had never really cared for him, nor trusted him.

"I wish you luck," she said. And the interview was over. Did she refer to Charles, or the diamond? Probably both. For her, love and intrigue went hand in hand.

A full moon cast deep shadows when I returned home. I hired a private carriage rather than taking a public coach, aware of the weight of the diamond in my petticoat pocket. It was hidden under full skirts, yet I felt all must see it. Near the outskirts of Paris some of the shadows began to move; what would those beggars, who killed for a scrap of meat, do for a diamond as large as quail's egg? I urged the driver to reckless speed.

Charles was out. I spent a long and anxious hour trying to find the most secure hiding space in my rooms. Finally, I tore up a floorboard in my wardrobe, and placed the box in the recess between upstairs floor and downstairs ceiling. I replaced the floorboard and moved my clothespress over the spot, and still I felt, almost saw, the presence of that jewel. And so began a long and taxing relationship, not with a person, but with a stone, whose secret presence would never leave my thoughts for long in the years to come.

I was drifting in and out of sleep when my lover finally returned. Late night breezes still laden with heat ruffled the green curtains. Charles felt my torn fingernails, broken from my fight with the floorboard. "You have hands like a farmer's wife," he mumbled in the darkness. I hoped he meant it as a compliment, but wasn't certain it wasn't also an insult.

In August of that year, feudalism was abolished and the power of the great landlords of France was made into just so much dust under the bed. With one stroke of the pen, forced labor, slavery and the ancient inherited privileges of the aristocracy ceased to exist. With one stroke of King Louis's somewhat unwilling pen, Charles's family and thousands of others became virtually penniless. They owned their château and the land on which it was situated, but the surrounding farms and the income from them became the property of the peasants working the land.

In accord with the fickle chemistry of human nature, once the peasants acquired the land the first thing many of them did was stop working it. Free to do as they pleased, they did as they pleased.

"I don't have to worry about my lost inheritance, anymore," Charles jested. "The National Assembly has decided it for me." He was bitter, though. He, who had hoped to reconcile with his father, now saw little reason to affect that reconciliation. Or so he claimed. I used that bitterness for my own purposes, pointing out that titles and wealth no longer stood between us, we had been declared equal.

The tentative hand of the revolution touched our lives, sometimes in great ways, other times in little matters.

For instance, one day at market Melan fils suggested I could do something very indecent with the carrots he was selling, after I complained they were shriveled and limp.

"Watch your tongue, citizenness," the young man had growled. "We are all equal now, and the farmers don't have to put up with the crap you city rats gave us. If you don't like the vegetables, shop elsewhere."

Melan père emerged from the dusty, rickety tent arranged over the cart, his old bones creaking with age.

"Is that any way to talk to Mademoiselle La Forge, who gave you a bit of lace for your son's christening gown?" he protested through toothless gums. His son grimaced and turned his back to us. "What the world is coming to, I don't understand," the old man sighed. "You're right. The carrots aren't fit for pig fodder. But we had a dry spell and the marquis doesn't loan us his donkeys anymore for carrying water. He had to sell the poor beasts to raise his tax money when the Assembly said he weren't a marquis anymore, but only a citizen. Equality is good, I'm sure. But I'd rather have donkeys to carry water."

He leaned further out from the tent and hissed in my ear. "If you want better vegetables, come earlier. I can't put 'em aside for you anymore. And call my son 'citizen.' That will make him friendlier."

"Thank you, Père Melan. I'll do that." The old man, his face lined and leathery as a turtle's, retreated again into his tent out of the broiling sun.

I went home without carrots, thinking of lace for wedding gowns.

"Citizen, do you love me?" I asked Charles that evening.

"Yes, citizenness," he said, and his arms, more comforting than they had been for several days, went around me.

"Let's wed," I said. "I will give you the home you need. Marry me and you will prove the equality in which you claim to believe." I would use anything, even the revolution itself to gain my goal.

He hesitated.

"Do you love someone else?" I asked.

"No. But I had planned to return to America when this turmoil ends. That is my chosen home."

"Then take me with you," I said, although leaving Paris had never entered my thoughts.

Eventually he gave in, realizing he would get little peace until he did. He even offered to speak to my family, to formally ask for my hand.

"That would not be wise," I said, atremble at the thought of him meeting Mathilde, and what he would think of me then. A bourgeois shopowner is one thing; a whore's daughter another. "It would be most unwise. I have severed my ties with them."

I made the arrangements, as Charles was very busy. A certain enemy of the revolution had been captured and it was La Fayette's task, and therefore Charles's, to keep the man alive until his trial. Paris was eager to tear him limb from limb with no further ado.

Foulon was a sardonic antirevolutionary who had stupidly suggested quelling the riots in the city with mercenaries. That would have been as sensible as trying to put out a fire by piling more wood onto it. And when the citizenry complained they had nothing to eat, he had replied, "If you are hungry, browse grass. Eat hay, my horses eat it."

This answer so charmed the mob he was forced to flee rather hurriedly, hidden in a coffin. He was discovered, however, and returned to Paris with his hands and feet bound like a pig being led to the slaughter. They crammed into his forced-open mouth the straw he had suggested the citizens should eat.

La Fayette, pledged to keep peace, or the little that remained of it in the city, placed the man under lock and key, not to keep him in but to keep the hard-eyed mob out.

To no avail. The day before my wedding a crowd broke into the prison and hung Foulon from the nearest lantern. The rope kept breaking so stupid, terrified Foulon was hung not once, but thrice before he finally died.

I wished they had hung him sooner, before his witless, oft-repeated words were translated by the mob into "Let them eat cake," and attributed to Marie-Antoinette.

"Never has one woman been blamed for so many disasters," I protested to Manon, who had come to help dress me for my wedding. She flung a chemise over my head, but even through the many folds of cloth I could see the sun blazing hot and strong over the façade of the Palais Royal. There had been no rain for weeks, and Paris was a city of caked dust and fiery tempers.

"This is not the time to speak of disasters," she said, bending to smooth a stray furbelow of lace. "You should think only pleasant thoughts on your wedding day. Think of how beautiful this lace is. Where did you find it?"

"From a lacemaker in Marseilles. She calls it Love's Heart Pierced by Cupid's Arrow. She will give the pattern grid to no one else, but keeps it secret. Between you and me, she should charge more than she does."

The lacemaker was one of the first citizens of Marseilles to be beheaded in that city. Her crime was that of lacemaking. All that was in the future, I did not know her destiny on my wedding day, and for that I am grateful.

The complicated pattern died with her. I wish I could have saved a scrap of it to show my granddaughters, but they don't appreciate the difference between fine lace and the cheap netting that is worn now. Manon did. I remember the way she avidly studied the pattern and the way the lace hearts were strung together on a trellis of arrows, as though the key to her own heart was concealed in the pattern.

"If I had half your wits for trade, Julienne, I'd start my own shop instead of working for that slut, Madame Roulier. I vow on Genesis, half the men who come in are buying a tumble in the back room, and not a chapeau for their wives. The woman has no decency, or style."

"Is it terrible, Manon, to work there?" She looked pale and her eyes were no longer gentle but hard.

"Not terrible. But very different, you understand. Antoine . . ." her eyes

125

softened only when she said his name. Marriage had strengthened her passion, not diluted it. "Antoine says the revolution will solve the problems. He likes Madame Roulier. He says she has never bedded an aristocrat and she is a good citizenness."

"Is that what citizenry requires? I was unclear about that." But Manon did not laugh. There was a great distance between us, and I blamed Antoine for much of it. He didn't approve of me, or La Fayette, or Charles, for that matter, nor was Charles overly enthused about Antoine's extremism. Men come between women more after marriage than before.

Manon, unsmiling, dropped the wedding gown over my head. It was pale yellow.

"You have overcome your taste for scarlet," she said. "Just when it is coming back in style."

"Manon, I would never wear a carmagnole. Manon, what if Charles doesn't arrive on time . . . or come at all?" I stole a look in the mirror. That woman in the full, golden blossom of a dress could not be me. Where was Julie of the Cité? Gone, gone, I told myself.

"Your thoughts stray from one disaster to another. Control yourself, Julienne. Think of the pretty babies to come, a whole nursery filled with them."

The thought comforted me, but only momentarily. The nursery in Charles's home on the Auvergne would never welcome our babies. Charles's father, distressed by his son's marriage to a seamstress, had written to tell us so.

The letter, formal, cold, penned on thick vellum in writing fine and black as spider legs, was a simple one. "You continue to represent the most dismal disappointment to your family. Your disobedience when you voyaged to America against our wishes was one matter, although in that instance you incurred some military honors for yourself. But to wed a seamstress of unknown family, when you know how precarious is our own present status and fortune—your mother had almost convinced me of my duty to welcome you back to the paternal embrace. In light of these new circumstances I will not. You can never hope to reconcile with the family upon whom you have turned your back. Your sister has provided us with a grandson, who will be heir. I no longer have a son."

Did I care that Charles was marrying me as much to spite his father as to please me? Not at all. I loved him desperately.

"It is time to leave, Julienne." Manon's voice brought me back from that letter, the letter that had made Charles's face go ashen. After he read it, he refused to kiss me and then repenting of that hardness, had embraced me with such passion there were bruises on my arms after. Ours was a flawed union, but it was a passionate one. Now that all that is past, now that his Julienne is an aging woman who dreams of forbidden cups of coffee and new ways of tormenting her daughters-in-law to add spice to the day, she sits back in her bed and remembers the passion she inspired in one, tall man with hair black as a raven's wing, and she smiles.

We were wed in the new Church of St. Philippe-du-Roule, which was a monstrous masterpiece of neoclassical simplicity. I missed the familiar gargoyles and ornate decor of Notre Dame. The white expanse of the interior made me feel very small as I walked down the side aisle, past the Stations of the Cross, to where Charles waited with the priest. A marble tile had come loose in the central aisle and hence that portion was temporarily not accessible.

How strange, I thought, for a bride to follow the path of Christ's suffering and persecution to meet her groom. The gods will have their little jokes. When Marie-Antoinette first came to France to wed her sluggish Louis, the ministers had adorned her wedding pavilion with scenes from the tragedy of Medea. Imagine, a young girl of fourteen, away from home for the first time, about to wed a man she has never met, being required to study a tapestry of a woman who murdered her own children.

Our wedding party was small and more remarkable for who wasn't there than for who was. Charles's family was missing, as were Louise and Mathilde, whom I had not notified for fear they would come. Antoine, too, was missing, so a hired stranger stood next to Manon as our second witness. And while La Fayette had sent us a charming silver coffee service, he was, alas, overencumbered with duties. His regrets arrived, but he did not. Just as well. He was so popular then that had the "hero of two worlds" come, even that large, empty church wouldn't have been able to contain the crowd.

The Queen had sent a white satin coverlet heavily embroidered with gold thread. It was beautiful, but a strange gift to send in the midst of a heat wave. I could only imagine that she wished time to pass quickly, that winter could come and cool the tempers of her people.

Charles and I joined hands in front of the statue of Ste. Cecilia, the Roman virgin who had worn a hair shirt under her own wedding gown, and whose purity had made roses bloom in February. Her deep, obsidian gaze met mine over the shiny tonsure of the priest, and it seemed there was disapproval in her eyes.

The words we spoke that day escape me. I remember instead how Charles's hand trembled when he placed the ring on my finger, and how

Manon, overcome by the extravagant quantity of powder on her fellow witness's coif, had a sneezing fit just as I kissed my new husband.

Manon threw coins and ribbons as we left the church and climbed into the private coach that awaited us, courtesy of La Fayette. Standing there alone, ribbons tangled at her feet, she looked sad, like a stranger, when I turned to wave.

We journeyed to Montmorency to escape the stifling heat of Paris, to begin our wedded life in a pleasant inn surrounded by meadows and fresh breezes, where we could enjoy our promised trout stream and fresh peaches. The trip was a pleasant one, if overly quiet, for Charles was preoccupied and not given to conversation that day. I held his hand all the way and he would sometimes return my squeeze, sometimes not.

In our room, which was filled with flowers and bowls of fruit, I climbed out of my wedding gown and heavy, cumbersome panniers, anticipating the joy of the evening to come. I was eager, Charles was not. He, fully dressed in red silk breeches and waistcoat, looked away as my gown slid to the floor.

Perhaps he realized the weight of the vows we had just made and had the sense to be thoughtful, even if I was not. Or perhaps he thought of the wedding he should have had, surrounded by family and friends in the ancient chapel in the Auvergne. Perhaps he was fatigued by the heat and the journey. I determined to make light of his mood.

"Pour some wine," I asked, standing before him in my chemise.

It was golden in color and cool as water from a mountain stream. "To us," he said, touching his glass to mine, without a smile. He undressed with slow motions more revealing of distaste for the work ahead, than enthusiasm.

My groom's dark mood was making me wish Manon, or even Louise or Mathilde were in a nearby room to comfort and befriend me.

We embraced, hurriedly and without joy, barely mussing the white sheets or leaving our imprints on the feather mattress. There were no words of love.

After, when he was asleep and his back turned to me, with the moonlight gilding his legs, I slipped out of bed and walked out alone into the hot August night.

The sky was filled with stars, I had never seen so many before. Their brilliance made me feel as small and insignificant as a sparrow trying to wing across a vast ocean. A scent of flowers drifted on the night air, but I took no pleasure in the night. How could I when my beloved was estranged from me?

The air stirred heavily, shaking the leaves in the apple trees, and the first percussive notes of thunder sounded in the dark distance. The soil was spongy with moss underfoot. I knelt on it, but no comforting words of prayer came to me. I felt cold, despite the heat.

A twig snapped. Charles was behind me, dressed hurriedly in unlaced breeches, frowning.

"Julienne," he said. His voice trembled. "Forgive me. It's only . . ."

I should have let him finish. Now, decades later, I wonder what he was about to tell me. But I was young and eager and thought words were unnecessary for a love such as ours. I pulled him to me and closed his unfinished sentence with a kiss, glad only that he had missed me, he had sought me in the darkness.

I brushed back the long, black waves of hair that fell loose to his shoulders and smoothed the lines from his forehead. "I will make you happy," I promised. His arms went around me and we rolled together on the cushioning, warm earth, playful and passionate as our first wedded embrace should have been but hadn't been. He had come back from the distance that had separated us.

The stars winked overhead, flowers shed perfume and the earth itself slowed in its endless voyage as Charles and I loved. We melded together, I could not tell where his skin stopped and mine started.

"Now this would be a pretty scandal," I laughed, using my fingers to comb the moss and twigs from my hair. I tried to pull together enough of my ruined chemise to cover my nakedness. Charles smiled and tugged at the garment so that it, wearied of its unexpectedly difficult night, disintegrated and fell to my ankles in a wanton shower of rose-colored cloth.

"Never mind," he said. "I brought a cape. But not yet, hold still a while. There are little flowers tangled in your hair . . . you look like Hera herself, going to Zeus' bed. There." He plucked a daisy and twined it where flowers do not normally adorn women.

"Charles," I pleaded, aware now that the sun would soon rise and people would be stirring. "What if someone comes? Let's go in."

"Julienne, my Hera." His sweet face was alive with pleasure. "I will take you to a place where there would be no one to bother us from dawn to dawn."

"And where would that be?" I asked, struggling to my feet even as he tried to pull me into his arms again. "Surely not in any part of Paris I know." I wrapped his cape over my nakedness, and pulled Charles toward a side door so that we could enter the sleep-hushed inn without waking others.

"Not here," he agreed. "America. Pennsylvania . . ." and he continued to speak, but I paid scant attention, for the night porter and stable boy were gossiping in the shadows of the long hall. I was too aware of their curious, startled looks as we slipped by them, half-naked and still strewn with daisies.

The rain came that night sometime between our frolic and the dawn. We woke refreshed, and with the world made new around us.

9

. . . a parting forever . . .

*"Is an absolute prince, and the hereditary sovereign of the
ancient monarchy of France to become the tool of a plebian
faction who will, the point once gained, dethrone him for his
imbecile complaisance? Well, be it so! But before I advise the
King to such a step, or give my consent to it, they shall bury
me under the ruins of the monarchy."*

—Marie-Antoinette

I worked with great industriousness before my wedding; after it I
worked even harder. Not for me the long social afternoons spent
calling on friends, the late nights at the opera, the Sunday promenades. Even
during revolution people seek amusement, but my time was spent in work.
I had great hopes. Charles had great plans.

For the next two years, as I stitched or studied, my eye was caught by the
winking glitter of my wedding band. It kept me in mind of a quote from an
English novel. "Oh! How many torments lie in the small circle of a wedding
ring!" Torment. And joy. Charles provided an abundance of both and often
kept me guessing as to which I would receive.

They were busy years. Charles, as aide to La Fayette, was harried with the
need—and growing impossibility—of keeping order in the tumultuous, riot-
torn streets of Paris. It would have been as easy to stop a whirlwind in its
course or hold back the snows of winter.

I worked in the salon during all the daylight hours and some of the night, too, sewing the hateful carmagnoles and anticipating increasingly rare days when a customer would come, admire the fine silks and satins still stocked in the back room, and order a ball gown or dancing frock that would let my imagination and needles fly in beautiful fantasy once again. Most of the clothing being worn in Paris, like the carmagnole jacket, was so unlovely it made my heart sink. But what can one expect, when a farmer tries to dress like a duke, and a duke wishes to dress as a farmer?

If I had thought that my nights of wedded bliss would be filled with ease and pleasure, Charles soon laid to rest those lazy expectations. With the rigor of a country Latin tutor, he decided to overcome singlehandedly my educational weaknesses. He established a small but intimidating library where once my befrilled, friendly, sitting room had been. The smells of pomade and perfume were pushed out by the stronger smells of binding leathers and inks.

At dawn, before the salon opened and the day was more promise than reality, we rose and began our work with a study of geography. Still yawning, I would stand by the globe Charles had purchased, and trace the course of the Tiber as it flowed past Perugia to Rome, or sit in front of a yellowed map and examine the boundaries of Virginia. If Charles was already out and I rose alone, there would be a quiz later to be sure I had done the day's lesson.

The evenings were reserved for philosophy and that most fickle of tongues, English. If he were away in the evening, as he often was, I was allowed to amuse myself with a novel . . . selected for its worthiness by Charles.

I began to remember my days with Bertin with a certain nostalgia for those easier times. But when I would despair of ever learning the capitals of the colonies or the irregular past tenses of English, there Charles would be, smiling, prompting me with kisses. Charles, my reward. He was making me in the image of what he thought women should be, but I didn't care, I was as ready for his molding as the clay is for the artist's touch. I wanted him to be proud of me. I wanted to be able to enter the witty salons of Paris and make amusing conversation and perceptive, educated comments.

We did sometimes go to Madame de Staël's Friday nights, as she was a great admirer of La Fayette's and more than willing to receive his aide, Charles de Saint Remy. But that lady was so talkative no other other women in her sitting room need worry about making comments of any sort. I was a sort of oddity there, being of the working class and with no titled ancestors, no inherited silverplate nor fond memories of a court presentation. They tolerated me for the sake of Charles. And I tolerated them for the sake of

Charles. Although one night when the Queen's Count Fersen was present—imagine, her seamstress and lover in the same circle: republicanism had a startling effect on society—he paid me a nice compliment.

"Your serenity is most flattering," he whispered to me. "Indeed, you are better-mannered than our talkative hostess. And much lovelier, my dear."

"I am quiet because I am tongue-tied," I confessed. "I know nothing of the Illuminati and their prophecies about King Gustavus of Sweden." That had been the topic of conversation.

Fersen, taken slightly aback by my honesty, peered at me. "Indeed," he whispered. "But your candor is refreshing. Charles is fortunate to have such an open, veracious bride." He patted my hand. I smiled. Open. Honest. There was so much I hadn't told Charles. And what would this group think of me if all were known?

Whether or not I shined in the salon, Charles was relentless about my reading. My days were measured by those studies. It was the alarming history of Helen of Troy I was learning, and the wondrous disaster she and her lover, Paris, had wrought when I first heard the news of the "October Orgy." It was not really an orgy, but Parisians more than ever were prone to exaggeration, especially if the tip of calumny's arrow be aimed at the Queen.

Marie-Antoinette and her Louis had attended a feast held in their honor by loyal members of the Guard. Several tricolors fell to the floor and were stamped on, as the *Mercure* promptly reported the next day. As the tricolor had already been adopted as the symbol of the revolution, the Queen's well-publicized callous treatment of it was not well received by the masses.

The next evening a message arrived for Charles to proceed with all due haste to Versailles. The messenger, begrimed with soot and with bits of autumn leaves clinging to his boots and hair, peered at me quizzically as Charles read the short note from La Fayette. I had a veil draped over my head and bosom in the ancient Greek style; I cared not for historical accuracy but wished to distract Charles from the bookish fine print, which was wearying my eyes. There were, after all, other ways to spend an evening than in study.

But go to Versailles he must. I pretended to hand him a shield saying, "With it or on it," in the stoic fashion of a wife of antiquity. He accepted the grasp of air I gave him and bowed to me, hand on heart. The messenger, convinced he had entered a madhouse, flew back down the stairs three at a time.

I would not have been so carefree had I known that just a few hours later a crowd of enraged harpies—fishwives, whores and others convinced they should take destiny in their own hands—broke into the Queen's chamber, intending to murder her in her own bed. La Fayette's precautions for the safety of the royal family proved less than adequate on more than one occasion, as history proves. She had, however, made good an escape to the King, and avoided harm that night.

Lest the Queen's flight to the King's bedchamber be construed as cowardice rather than prudence, know this: later, when the mob gathered in the courtyard and yelled for the royal family to show itself, Marie-Antoinette, alone, went out on the balcony to greet the crowd that had just tried to murder her. Her courage shamed them.

Charles, too, reached safety, ducking through a double door and out into the night-dark orangerie, once he had seen the Queen shut safely behind the King's door. Several guards were murdered, and their heads paraded around the courtyard on a pike.

Louis, against the wishes of his wife, agreed that perhaps the royal family should remove itself to Paris.

I began to dream of red blood trailing down the King's marble staircase, like a streaming red ribbon on a harlot's negligé, vivid against pure whiteness.

The only happy outcome of the "October Days" was that the Assembly agreed to meet in future near the Tuilieries, where Marie-Antoinette and Louis took up residence. That meant Charles traveled much less often to Versailles; he had a few more minutes a day to tarry with me.

Louis managed to placate his people once again, and the rest of the autumn and winter passed in relative quiet, although the King proved slow and stubborn. The Assembly was pushing him to approve a constitution that would make France a constitutional monarchy; for a change Louis did not seem of a mind to give in.

This constitution was a momentous affair, requiring as it did the agreement of several hundred men. I did not envy Charles his interminable hours spent with the quarrelsome assembly, trying to reach a consensus on the fair value of an assignat, and whether or not God would be allowed to reside in the new France. God was eventually invited to apply for citizenship, but under a new title—the Divine Being.

Because the winter's revolutionary activity was limited to much talk interspersed with an occasional riot or hanging, Charles and I made some progress in my studies whether I willed it or not. We read through much of Voltaire and Rousseau, long sections of Diderot's *Encyclopedia*, and short sections of Paine's *Rights of Man*, for my English improved slowly and painfully.

"Fill my glass again, please," and "You are singing too loudly," were some of the first phrases Charles taught me, leading me to suspect he had learned his English in the taverns of America. He denied that accusation with righteous pride and made me conjugate ten verbs for voicing it. "He loves me. He loved me. He will love me," I began the exercise.

We were reading the story of Jason and Medea when it occurred to me that my monthly courses had not run for some time, and my breasts were fuller than usual and greatly sensitive. I closed the book and made him put it away, not letting him finish the story of that unnatural mother.

"It will mark my child," I said.

"Superstition," he said. And then, "Child?"

He danced me around the room, but then grew thoughtful and stayed thoughtful for many an hour after. I lost all interest in anything that happened outside of my own body, my own rooms. A new world, a new life was being created. How could a constitution compare to that?

By summer my belly had started to lose its flatness and swelled into more rounded contours. I admired it for hours, and when I dressed for the Feast of the Federation I wore a loose, slender white gown that exaggerated my new curves.

The feast was held in honor of the anniversary of Bastille Day, on the Champ de Mars, which had been newly graded for the occasion by ladies of the aristocracy and bourgeoisie who had wielded shovels and wheelbarrows all night. Hundreds of thousands gathered there to swear loyalty to the nation. I, dreamy and overheated, was more taken by the wild daisies that fringed the large field; they reminded me of my wedding night.

La Fayette, the hero of two worlds, rode up and down the aisles of booths draped with tricolors, his white horse prancing and jumping. The people gathered around him and, impressed as they were meant to be, yelled, "Vive La Fayette!" with gusto.

His followers, too, were in tremendous demand, and Charles was in constant conversation with men who sought his opinion on the nonjuring priests. Those clerics who refused to bow to the nation were deemed traitorous by France. But those who did take an oath to the nation were automatically excommunicated by Pope Pius. Nonjuring priests could celebrate Mass but had no church in which to do so; juring priests were given churches by the Assembly, but Pius would not let them celebrate the sacraments. It was a serious dilemma, and one that led to great religious strife in France for many years.

Horns, drums and fiddles provided a constant racket of music and the night was alive with gaity. It sounded festive. But added to the attending crowd of three hundred thousand people there was a fourteen-hour deluge that did not ease for a moment. I remember only being poked constantly by parasols and splashed with mud as great torrents of dirty water, rain and revolutionary talk poured over my hat.

The Divine Being, I believe, was not pleased with us that July and gave serious consideration to a new deluge, even though Talleyrand, Bishop of Autun, celebrated a Mass in His express favor. After the Mass, during which most of the three hundred thousand celebrants had continued to gossip and drink and pinch the nearest woman, La Fayette rose on the makeshift platform to address the crowd.

"We swear to be always faithful to the nation, the law and the King; to protect conformably with the laws the security of person and property . . ." La Fayette led the oath we had gathered to make. Charles would be pleased that I still remember so much of it. After the hero of two worlds finished his pretty speech the crowd yelled "I swear it!" It was deafening and meaningless.

Was Robespierre there, that evening? He would have melted into the crowd, might have been any one of thousands of fine-boned, pale men with powdered hair and silk stockings. In 1790 he had not yet begun to be identified by his sky-blue waistcoat with its brass buttons engraved with his own personal god, the guillotine.

Fireworks had been planned in honor of the American president, Washington, but were canceled because of the rain. Charles, reminded of his many Americans friends, grew sentimental. "If the child is a boy, name him George," he made me promise. I agreed, thankful that he hadn't considered the possibility of a girl and pledged me to the name of Georgina. We lingered in the rain and mud until midnight when I, pleading exhaustion, insisted we return home. As we left to go, a young man dressed in red, white, and blue, a human tricolor, pushed past me in pursuit of a pickpocket. I was knocked to the ground, winded, but not wounded, or so we thought.

Later, when we had climbed into our soft, dry bed, Charles was roused by a messenger. Sleepily, he pulled his damp breeches back on and went off to the faubourg du Temple, where a riot and factory fire had broken out.

I was alone when the pains began, and still alone several hours later when the bleeding began. Frightened, I sent a note to Manon but she did not come. I still think that Antoine kept my note from her. At dawn, still alone, I miscarried the child that Charles and I had conceived.

"There will be others," my husband promised. "Many young wives lose the first." He said it many times; each time I turned away from him to weep into the pillow. It was true, but it was not a consolation.

I gave myself up to grief, and time began to follow a different course. I went to bed on a summer's eve, and when I woke it was autumn. I swept leaves from the doorstep one day, and the next day the leaves were buried under winter's snow. I grieved, and the revolution increased its stranglehold.

The streets of Paris grew yet more congested with hungry discontents, while the avenues of the city grew less frequented by rich carriages and gay boulevardiers. They were replaced by donkey carts and dingy peasants released from the land to wander aimless and hungry in their freedom.

In the Palais Royal beggars and sansculottes roamed, harassing any person whose face or clothing displeased them. They were so aggressive I feared going out of my own door unless it be in full daylight, and even then only with a tricolor ribbon showing on my person.

In February, when I was reluctantly plodding through an eight-volume novel, *The History of Monsieur Cleveland*, Charles received a message from his sister saying the family had fled the château and gone into hiding. The Auvergne, like Paris, was in a state of chaos, and newly dangerous for those of aristocratic blood. Still hoping for a reconciliation between Charles and his family, I was pleased she had written. I did not intend that our children should grow up without the benefits of their natural grandparents—at least of Charles's family.

And, there were messages from the Queen. Not as frequently since she and her family had been moved to the Tuileries against her will, but Marie-Antoinette was a woman of great spirit and she would not change her habits or her style for the benefit of the sansculottes.

The first time I was called by her to the Tuileries it was a fine winter morning, quieted by a clean, thin blanket of snow not yet strewn with debris. The stillness of the Palais Royal subdued my increasing fear, for the Palais Royal was an indicator of the mood of the city, and the mood that day was calm. I did, however, walk rather than take a carriage, as pedestrians were less liable to be harassed than carriage passengers. It was dangerous to flaunt any comforts before those thousands who had none.

The Tuileries was situated off the rue St. Honoré across from the Place du Carrousel, one of the worst slums of the city. As I approached, the streets became narrower and littered with refuse and houses grew increasingly shabby. The square itself was scarred with ruins, and a garbage heap rose up from it in ugly, smelling profusion. Children in torn, filthy smocks played about the frozen corpse of a dog and beggars shuffled along in aimless, hopeless gait. One ancient man, his bowels loosened with disease, dropped his breeches and squatted over a pile of his own ordure, mindless of passersby.

I was thankful for the high walls of the Tuileries, which shut out these sights from the Queen and her children. The scene was not a pretty substitute for the luxurious gardens and playful fountains of Versailles.

Inside the Cour d'Honneur, under the shadows cast by the high roofs of the three pavilions of the decaying palace, vendors called their wares. "Oysters, fresh oysters," sang out a woman whose basket of fish smelled as if it had been many days since its contents had been pulled from the distant shores of Honfleur. "Ribbons, pretty ribbons," another younger maid yelled above the rude squalor of the crowded courtyard. An ancient hag next to her boasted of beauty potions for sale devised by the immortal Cagliostro himself.

The interior of the castle was no more serene. Generations of impoverished aristocrats, unable to afford other lodgings in Paris, had set up makeshift apartments for themselves in the great halls and former ballrooms. A royal family of France had not lived in the Tuileries for more than a hundred years; it had become a kind of poorhouse for the nobility.

It had been emptied of its squatters, but the building itself had been abused and ruined by decades of neglect. Sieur Migue, the architect inspector, had done what he could to make it livable for the royal family, but stains on the marble floors still showed where privy stalls had been, and many windows were still boarded over. To this ancient, foul, dark and evil-smelling abode had been brought the Queen who loved all things new and bright and fragrant. The National Assembly had wondrous ways of showing its esteem.

"I am sadly reduced to gracelessness and discomfort in my surroundings, as you see," the Queen said after I had been ushered into her chambers by a surly guard—no more lines of young and lovely ladies-in-waiting. Her slender white hand gestured at the sooty walls, cracked ceilings and filth-encrusted floors. "But I have not given up. Tomorrow some furnishings from Versailles arrive, and we shall see if we cannot bring some light and charm into these unfortunate rooms. If this indicates the state of mind of my people, I tremble." She laughed, as if the situation were a drawing room prank.

But there were dark circles under her eyes, and her gaity was forced. I made the three curtseys and could think of nothing to say.

"Are you well?" she asked. "Your marriage is a happy one?"

I nodded.

"It is well to be happy in marriage. I will pray for your happiness to last. Just as you once promised to pray for mine. Do you remember that and other pledges you made to your Queen?"

"I remember. I have, and will, keep all my pledges." Guards were near us; it was all I could say to assure her that the diamond was still safely hidden, and secret from all but us two. No, us three; her son, for whom I kept the Golden Ransom in trust, was part of the secret. To Charles, I had said nothing, and each time he told me of the importance of utmost trust and openness between husband and wife, which was often, I felt a pang of foreboding. It was a time of secrecy and intrigue, and a young wife should have nought to do with either.

"To business," said the Queen, reassured. "I will have some new gowns."

The commission she gave me that day was a large one, and spoken in a low voice. She would not let me write it down, but insisted I memorize it. Halfway through the whispered list of items she wished made, I realized why. The Queen was ordering a travel wardrobe. It required no great insight, no depth of knowledge, to realize that Marie-Antoinette was preparing to flee Paris. Being Marie-Antoinette, no more and certainly no less, she would escape in style.

It was one more secret I would have to keep from Charles.

Lisette and I cut and measured and sewed frantically for months before that order was completed. And while we sewed, Marie-Antoinette delayed in that foul palace, awaiting what moment, what sign, I did not know.

"Who is the countess we are making these gowns for?" Lisette asked, awed by the exquisite materials with which we worked. She stood amidst a fall of golden silk, her hand trembled with greed for it.

"It must be a secret," I said, and promptly invented a story about an unhappy marquise who wished to flee from her jealous old husband in order to join her young lover. Each day I added to the story to quiet Lisette's suspicions, and by the time the wardrobe was completed I had elaborated a plot that would have astounded even the long-winded author of *Monsieur Cleveland*.

Charles never questioned my frenetic days in the workroom, for his duties with La Fayette were keeping him busier than ever. Impromptu hanging committees had sprung up all over the city. Their citizen-members amused themselves by dragging luckless aristocrats from their coaches or beds and hanging them from lampposts. La Fayette tried to discourage such amusements, but even he, hero of two worlds, was realizing that peace and order were qualities no longer admired in Paris. There were more hangings each day than La Fayette could witness, much less prevent.

Charles increasingly crept in late at night or even dawn, exhausted and more than once with shiny patches of blood staining his clothes. Each time I saw blood I would leap from my bed or chair to determine if he be wounded, or merely carrying the evidence of a stranger's wound. The strangers were nothing to me; the thought of Charles in danger made the room dance before me.

We loved with frantic passion in those days, as if the madness around us could be allayed only in the pleasure of the bed. Our lovemaking was wordless and instinctive; indeed, our life together was becoming silent. Charles was too tired to speak overly much, and I was too filled with secrets to trust myself with light conversation.

One morning he came to me, pale and thin and heavy-lidded.

"When this is over, Julienne, we will have a life for ourselves," he said, holding me tightly to him. He rested his head on top of mine, so that when I looked up into the mirror I saw our two heads together, Charles's filled with infinite weariness and seemingly disembodied, for my gown hid the rest of him.

"Even La Fayette grows disheartened," he said. "I wait for the constitution to be passed. And then . . ." he paused to kiss my shoulder, "then I will take you to a place that is filled with peace and safety. You will have your children, and play with them on the banks of a bounteous river, where only birdsong fills the air. And there are no lampposts."

"The peace and safety will be worthless as a silver plate with no food on it, if you are not there with me," I whispered, pressing my lips to the hand which rested on my shoulder.

"I will be there," he promised. How easily promises are made. How rarely are they kept.

In May the Queen's travel wardrobe was finished. I sent it to her as we had planned, hidden under a shipment of clean linens conveyed into the Tuileries through a kitchen entrance. And then I waited for the news that the King and Queen had departed Paris. I waited. And waited. And no news of the escape came.

Finally, in June, word did come. The royal family had tried to escape, but had been captured in the town of Varennes.

Tocsins rang all day and night. The streets roared with angry mobs and I wept, as Marie-Antoinette and her family were led back to Paris like common prisoners, under guard.

Charles was part of that inglorious guard that conveyed Louis and Marie-Antoinette and her children back to Paris—and to imprisonment. He described how the Queen had disguised herself as a governess and how the King had masqueraded as a valet-de-chambre, wearing a cheap wig and plain grey coat. He didn't have to describe their costumes, I knew them well. I had sewn them.

"It was a fiasco," he reported. "First they became lost in the small streets outside of the Tuileries and so were late to meet the guard that awaited them in Varennes, to guide them to safety. The berline in which they fled was decorated with green and yellow and drawn by four horses. Didn't they know that such a carriage would attract attention? A postmaster recognized the King."

He was angry, not because they had tried to escape, but because they had made such a mess of things. He hadn't slept for two days and nights, and was limp with fatigue. Candlelight cast shadows in his hollowed cheekbones.

Numb with disappointment and new fears, I sat in front of his chair and rested my cheek against his sharp knees. He was growing so thin. How I wished to be away from all this, away safe with Charles.

"At the Barrière de l'Etoile the mob almost overturned the berline, with the King and Queen still in it. They were furious, and shouted that La Fayette had betrayed them, that he had let them escape and then brought them back to Paris only to clear his own name."

I knew that was a lie but pretended surprise. La Fayette would have known, and Charles would have been spared much danger, if I had mentioned just once the Queen's new travel wardrobe.

"I have cheese and a cold chicken. I will bring them," I said.

"La Fayette is in a very bad position now. The Queen distrusts him and calls him her gaoler. Marat and Danton accuse him of royalist sympathies." Charles continued speaking from the depths of the chair in which he was slowly sinking, so that his long legs in their muddied breeches seemed to stretch halfway across the small room.

"Perhaps, then, this is the time for us to leave Paris," I called to him from the pantry. "Charles, I want to leave. The danger will only grow worse, for all of us." I carried a tray to him, but then carried it back again. Charles was sound asleep in the chair.

He woke up later and came to our bed. I sat up crying, for I had dreamed again of the red ribbons of blood trailing down the King's marble staircase.

"Promise me we'll never be separated," I said, twining my arms around his neck.

He promised and I forced myself to believe him, forced that belief to scatter my fears like fallen leaves in an autumn breeze.

The next day Camille Desmoulins's journal carried headlines declaring "Treason! Perjury! Barnave and La Fayette abuse our confidence!" Because Manon's husband was assistant to Desmoulins, and Charles was aide to La Fayette, those headlines ended my friendship with Manon.

But if Desmoulins's rhetoric was inflammatory, the version of the flight to Varennes published by Danton was inspiration to murder. "Either you are a traitor who has betrayed his country, or you are stupid in having made yourself answerable to a person for whom you could not answer," he wrote to La Fayette in the public press. "I have said enough to demonstrate that I despise traitors, and I do not fear assassins."

"That could be construed as a threat," Charles admitted, sipping a cup of coffee and raising his eyebrows in distaste, as if we were only discussing a criticism of David's latest painting to be exhibited in the salon.

"Then he is also threatening you," I said.

"Words," my husband shrugged.

"The word treason could take you to your death," I said.

"I will never be killed for treason." He finished his coffee with a young man's confidence that the grave was never intended for one such as he.

La Fayette's unpopularity grew worse as the summer strengthened into stifling heat waves and then faded into autumn's gentler light. A mob broke into his house and threatened his wife and son, the child he had named George Washington La Fayette. They escaped unharmed, but even Charles admitted it had been a close call.

When it was time for Paris to elect a new mayor, the city ignored last year's idol, La Fayette, and elected instead Petion, a surly extremist. Powerless with the people, hated by the Queen, and distrusted by that unholy trinity, Danton, Marat and Robespierre, La Fayette decided it was time to seek occupation outside of Paris. As war seems to be the occupation of choice for ambitious men with time on their hands, he decided to lead the French troops into battle against their royalist neighbors.

"Sedan? That is far away. And there will be fighting. Stay here with me Charles," I pleaded. "Don't go with La Fayette to Sedan."

He considered for a long moment. "He, too, has asked me to stay in Paris. He will need an associate he can trust completely, to forward accurate information while he is on maneuvers."

I used to reflect often on how things would have turned out if Charles had gone to Sedan, rather than stayed behind in Paris. But time is a stern taskmaster; once it passes we can never have it back again.

In September the constitution was finally passed and Louis took an oath to support it, but the winter was no more peaceful for that progress. The revolution had a life of its own, it was being taken over by men who disdained any kind of king, even one who swore to uphold the constitutional rights of his people. Those people forced Louis of France to declare war against his wife's native land, Austria. He signed the war decree with tears in his eyes, but he signed, and the first of the long twenty-two years of war began.

The Palais Royal was a recruiting ground for the revolutionary army and was so thick with surly, pike-armed men that I could only walk about freely at midday, when they returned to whatever homes they had for a meal. I hired a fierce-looking doorman to see that no harm came to my increasingly rare customers.

"I'm pleased I remained in Paris," Charles lied soon after La Fayette had departed. "All of Paris is turning to soldiery. I could become jealous, knowing you were here alone." He had been bored and lethargic ever since La Fayette and his troops marched out of the city. To be left behind is never pleasant.

I looked past the green fluttering curtains to the exercise grounds opposite my rooms. A hundred or so men lounged there, seeking cool refuge from the heat. They looked unwashed, unschooled, and unfriendly.

"It would be as reasonable to be jealous of a pack of hunting dogs," I laughed, pleased by the indication that he could be jealous. Aside from our mutual passion in bed, he rarely showed emotion. "Look at them! So covered with filth you can't tell if God gave them fair or black hair, and so insolent they would make pigs genteel by comparison. I wish d'Orléans would take his army elsewhere. They are bad for business."

"They are a mangy lot," Charles admitted. "The best of the men are on their way to the Austrian border." Time weighed heavily for him, with his commander gone.

"The best of men is sitting here, with me," I said, smoothing his hair.

I was going to tell him then, but something stilled my tongue. I wanted the moment when I announced that I was again, finally, with child, to be perfect, to be softened with candlelight, and cheerful with the late night ease of knowing the day's work is behind. He was preoccupied and morose, as he often was those mornings.

I put my arms around him, gave him a kiss, and then went down to open the shop.

By that time Madame Fauvrette, the blowsy wife of the Montmartre deputy, had long since lost her position as my least-favored client to a Mademoiselle Maillard, an opera dancer. She was as vain and lewd as any woman who walked the earth, and perhaps even a few walking the fiery pits below.

Later in 1793, it was Mademoiselle Maillard, the illiterate prostitute and performer, who was set up on the desecrated altar of Notre Dame as the Goddess of Reason. I hope by then she had learned to hold her tongue so as not to appear as foolish and stupid as God had made her. I doubt it, though.

She possessed great beauty, but the fullness of her youth was marred by dark circles under her eyes, a twitch in her painted red lips, and an odor that suggested her overly loose social habits would soon end beauty and health.

She reminded me greatly of Yvette, and when she cast her eyes on Charles one day, I thought I would tear her hair out, so furious was I.

But Charles ignored her leering flirtations and I continued to open my shop door to her; her protectors paid well and quickly for the many gowns she ordered.

That day, while I was still glowing from Charles's suggestion of jealousy, she came to be fitted for a new costume to be worn in the drama, The Citizen Murders His Royalist Wife. There were many such revolutionary plays then, all ponderous with radical rhetoric and very light on wit and morality. They usually ended in murder, much to the delight of the foolish audiences.

On that day around which my history pivots, she was standing on the fitting stool half-naked, when the Duc d'Orléans strutted in.

Unabashed, she dropped him a deep curtsey that revealed more of her bosom than a simple nod of the head would have done, although curtseys were no longer required, indeed, were frowned upon as a royalist manner-ism. But she was an expert at displaying her charms and would lose no opportunity to do so.

"Charming," d'Orléans said, his painted lips placing a kiss in the air over her dirty palm. "Nature reveals its perfection in the female form, don't you think? And you reveal your own perfection so well, mademoiselle."

Mademoiselle, giggling, put her hands on her hips and smoothed down the strained muslin covering her loins.

"There is a reception room," I said through the pins in my mouth. "Be so kind as to wait in there, monsieur." It was a long time since d'Orléans had pestered me with his demands; I had long since hoped he had given up his design to make the Queen's seamstress a spy. The sight of him chilled me.

"Mademoiselle Maillard doesn't mind, does she?" he cooed, and he was right in that. "But leave me with your seamstress here, dear child. I would have words with her." The actress, still more naked than clothed, backed out of the room, smiling and winking at d'Orléans all the while.

"We have no business," I said, when the curtains had closed behind her. "Unless you have come to collect the rent."

"I am no insignificant landlord, madame. I have come on an errand for the nation." He puffed himself up like an overstuffed, overpainted puppet and then sat heavily in my blue brocade chair. He put his feet up on the rosewood table in front of it, and the silver buckles on his shoes etched deep scratches in the wood with every move he made.

"Alas! I have scratched your little table!" he sighed. "How clumsy of me!" He kicked the table away, breaking one of its legs as he did so.

I made no move, could only stand and wait to see where this prelude would lead.

"Monsieur de Saint Remy usually returns at this time, does he not? Such a charming, well-bred husband you have found for yourself. Such a . . . snob, I fear. All this time that my men have followed him, not once has he taken his pleasure in a brothel. You must be very good, my dear. And he must be exceedingly prudish."

The clock behind him was ready to chime the hour of seven. Charles would be home soon. The fact that d'Orléans had been watching him raised the hairs on the back of my neck.

D'Orléans followed my eyes to the clock and smiled. "Perhaps we can conclude our business before the husband returns. I hate scenes. Family discord is most unpleasant."

"We have no business," I said.

"I think otherwise. You have never been good at playacting. Your eyes tell me all I need to know." He took out a gold snuff box and took a pinch between thumb and forefinger and then carried it to his highly arched nose. His nose, I realized at this moment, was identical to that of King Louis. "It is time to stop playing games," he said a moment later. "I will have the diamond, now."

I sat in the chair opposite him to disguise the fact that my knees were trembling. "What are you talking about?" I unsuccessfully tried to match his light, insouciant tone.

"Spare me your protests. I intend to have the diamond. France needs it for her war efforts, and the Austrian whore will have no further use for it, I assure you."

It was useless to ask how he knew about the gem, useless to deny my possession of it.

"No," I said. "I will not relinquish it to you, or anyone else unless the Queen herself directs me to do so." I picked up my workbasket and began knitting at a pair of socks I was making for Charles, to keep his feet warm in the winter to come.

"Your unpatriotic attitude is most unfortunate. But I am generous. I will buy the diamond from you. And the price I will pay is this: your reputation. Or have you already told your righteous husband that before you met, you were a prostitute in the Cité?" He smiled.

"That is a lie!" I jumped to my feet, and the knitting fell to the floor.

D'Orléans picked it up. He did not hand it to me. He began unraveling the tidy rows with slow, deliberate intent. I thought of the mutilated trees and hedges of the Palais Royal gardens.

145

"I may be stretching the truth a bit," he admitted. "But your grandmother and mother were known whores. I ask you, what is a credulous husband to believe?"

"You wouldn't," I protested, knowing he would. Defeat, sour as vinegar, filled my throat and mouth.

"Of course I would. I would not let such a worthless detail as your domestic contentment interfere with my purpose. I will have that gem, madame."

I was torn in two with fear. How easy it would be to give him that accursed stone and be done with it. But each time I imagined handing it over, I would see the fear for her son's safety in the Queen's eyes, her trust in me. Why hadn't I told Charles about the Cité and Mouret? I knew why. I feared he would think me what d'Orléans would claim me to be. Too late, too late. But I could not give up the diamond, it would prove once and for all that Marie-Antoinette had been guilty in the affair of the diamond necklace. More than a reputation was at stake, it could mean her throne. Her happiness or mine. That was the choice.

What finally decided me was nothing so valiant as devotion to a Queen. The more I considered, the more I hated d'Orléans. I would do nothing to serve his purpose. I wouldn't have given him a pebble from the street.

The shadows in the room grew long as we waited. I prayed. God, let Charles not come home tonight. Don't let him return while d'Orléans is still here, let me have a moment alone with him, first. And even as I prayed, I heard my husband's footsteps coming up the stairs.

As he turned his key in the lock and swung the door open I glanced at the pretty room in which I sat, a room happily filled with Charles's books and papers, my sewing materials, a set of lace cuffs Charles had not put away. That room spoke of two people whose lives had intermingled as the waters of two joined rivers. It won't be the same after, I thought, as Charles entered.

He hesitated in the doorway. "Julienne? Why are the lamps not lit?" But his sharp eyes, even in the length of time it took for him to call for the lamp, grew accustomed to the darkness. He saw d'Orléans sitting there, still as a cat at a mousehole, and smiling evilly.

"This is a surprise," he said, his voice cold. "Julienne, you should have told me we were to have a visitor this evening." Charles hated d'Orléans, as did all constitutionalists who believed in a monarchy by contract with the people, for it was already common knowledge that d'Orléans would have Louis toppled. And there was a noxious quality in d'Orléans which precluded any sympathy and warmth even from those who were not opposed to his politics.

"I do ask your pardon," d'Orléans said in an oily voice, half-rising from his chair. His strong perfume filled the room as he moved, the rings on his fingers clicked. "Madame did not know I was coming. Please come in, monsieur."

"Of course I will. This is my home. Monsieur." I had never heard Charles's voice so icy. But because he had hesitated in the doorway and d'Orléans had remained seated, it was as though Charles obeyed the other's beckoning when he entered. He was at a disadvantage, and the crease in his forehead grew deeper, his mouth grim.

"Why are you here?" Charles asked.

"Why, my dear man, to congratulate you on your marriage, of course. It is not often a man enjoys the opportunity to pleasure himself and do a good deed at the same time." D'Orléans dabbed at his caked, rouged lips with a lace handkerchief. His eyes looked into mine. Shall I continue? they asked me. I looked away.

"What do you mean? Your words are a riddle." Charles sat next to me and took my hand.

"Come, come. No modesty is needed between friends. It is not an easy task to reform a prostitute, and yet you seem to have done so. I must admit, though, that sacrificing your name and reputation by concluding the good deed with marriage is something that most men would not have done."

I clutched at Charles's hand, but his grasp on mine was already loosening.

"Julienne seems to make an admirable wife, I admit. I would never have believed it of a former whore. Oh, I see from your expression I have spoken out of place. Alas! Don't say she herself hasn't told you of this! I believed you to have been already informed of her past history, her mother, her grandmother, her closest female companions . . . all whores." D'Orléans feigned discomfort.

"You are misinformed," Charles said.

"I think not. She was mistress to a baker. That good man offered to marry her, but she fled instead, preferring the pleasure of many companions. Until you so admirably took her from the gutter."

"If you repeat those accusations I will demand satisfaction." My husband's hand went to his sword hilt.

"Ah, well then. I come to praise you and you insult me. I will leave. I see I have overstayed my welcome." D'Orléans rose, hands on hips, and strutted to the door. At the door, he turned back to us.

"Make no mistake. You only know what she is now. But before, she was a whore."

Charles made as if to lunge at him, but I clung at his coat and pulled him

147

back. D'Orléans very quickly made his exit; we heard him laughing behind the door, and the voices of other male companions. Such as he would not come alone if there were any chance of sword play, as Charles had threatened.

"Let him go," I pleaded. "He will have cutthroats with him." I was crying then. Charles would not look at me. He slumped as if very tired, and sat in a chair.

"It wasn't like that," I said. "It wasn't like that."

"It wasn't like that?" he repeated. "Then there was a grain of truth in what he said?" Too late, I realized my mistake. I could not feign innocence. I told him, then of the rape and of Mathilde, my grandmother. He still would not look at me.

"I knew you were no virgin when we met," he said, "but I didn't guess . . ."

"What you are thinking of me. It's not true."

"You claim to guess my thoughts?" His voice was like ice.

I considered telling him everything I had kept back. If I told him of the Queen's diamond, he would then know why d'Orléans had done this, why he had lied to disgrace me. But if I told Charles of the diamond, how could I be sure he would not, in turn, tell La Fayette? The hero of two worlds was ambitious beyond his capabilities; such men are often desperate for money. He would not wish to harm the Queen, but he would want the diamond and not stop to think that every jeweler to whom he might sell it would know its origins. The Queen would be as implicated as if d'Orléans himself put it on the market.

No, I could not tell him. Not everything. Charles and I looked at each other from a great distance, considering, speculating, and most of our thoughts went unsaid.

"Why did you not tell me before?" he asked.

"I was afraid . . ."

"Afraid I would not marry you?"

"Afraid you would not love me."

"You brought me little enough," he said, and in his eyes I read the expression his father would have shown, had Charles attempted to bring me home to the Auvergne. "The one thing I expected of my wife was absolute honesty. You denied me your trust."

"If you had known . . . would things have been the same?" I asked. He did not answer. "I thought you would love me for what I am now. That the past, and the sins committed against me, for I never wished them, I did not ask for the circumstances of my birth or life, I thought they would remain

148

in the past, that our love would be all that mattered." I could barely speak through my tears.

He looked at me. With pity, not love.

"Poor Julienne," he said. "Control yourself and stop weeping. I must think."

"I cannot control myself. You are turning your back on me, and I will die without you."

"Oh, God." He moaned, his hands went to his forehead and rubbed vigorously. "Julienne, you will leave Paris. For your own safety."

"You are sending me away." Then, I did stop crying. I realized the enormity of what had happened between us. I was a disgraced wife, I would be sent to some sleepy country town, put in rented rooms, receive an allowance every quarter, spend the rest of my life as an outcast, no longer desired by husband, no longer welcomed by friends . . . away from Charles.

"You cannot send me away. I carry your child." The news I had planned to announce joyously was now a ploy to keep him with me. He paused, and then looked away from me.

"All the more reason for you to leave Paris. For your safety. And your child's."

My child. Not ours.

He came to me and put his arms around me, but did not kiss me.

"Go to bed now. We will talk more in the morning."

I went to bed, but did not sleep. I lay awake listening to Charles pace in the outer room, back and forth, back and forth, the same board creaking under his step each time, and each step called to me the end of my happiness.

At dawn we were roused from our separate thoughts by the sound of cannon fire. He came into the bedroom, still wearing the clothes of the day before.

"It sounds from the Tuileries," he told me. "I must go there immediately and see what is amiss." Instead of coming to me for a morning kiss, he went to the window and opened it wide to give us a full view of the Palais Royal.

"What news?" he called out the window, and a dozen voices greeted his inquiry.

"Danton has seized power!" they yelled. "The government is taken over by the revolution!" The voices were gleeful, even jubilant.

Later I learned that the commander of the foreign troops fighting on the French borders had sent an ultimatum to France's revolutionary army. Paris, he said, would be burnt to the ground if the King and Queen were harmed. The revolutionaries regarded the ultimatum as a challenge, and as proof of the throne's disregard of the constitution. If any one thing sealed the fate of my Queen and King, it was that very message intended to save them.

"We march to the Tuileries," the voices yelled. "Danton knows what to do with kings!"

Charles closed the window and turned to where I sat.

"Don't go," I said.

"Be reasonable. It is my duty. Help me with my boots. Or would you have me stay home out of storms so I don't catch cold?" His voice was as it had been before last night, filled with banter. Finally there was work to do, and that eased his troubled heart.

"We were going to talk this morning," I reminded him. "Stay, and talk. Go to the Tuileries later." I was filled with fear for him.

"We will talk later. I must go."

I closed my eyes and listened as his steps crossed the room, went through the door, into the hall and down the stairs. When I opened my eyes he was gone and there was less color and light in the world.

The tocsins, which had begun ringing at dawn, continued to ring louder and louder all morning, until I thought I would go mad from the din of them. Lisette did not come, and I did not open my shop, but sat in Charles's chair by the shuttered bedroom window, waiting for his return. I don't remember what I thought about. Perhaps I thought of nothing, but only sat and waited, the way souls in purgatory must wait, with a patience seared by flame.

Sometime in mid-morning the courtyard of the Palais Royal filled again with drunken revelers dragging pikes behind them the way children do when they have tired of their toys. They sang the Ça Ira and when I looked out the window I saw a fat fishwife trying to struggle into a delicate gown only half as large as the bulk of her figure required. The gown was one worn by a rank of Queen's servants; I recognized the insignia stitched on it.

How does a fishwife come to own a gown worn by the Queen's staff? I wondered, and then espied other revelers carrying armfuls of silver plate, gilt candle sconces, and decorative swords and urns, all familiar to me because they had recently been installed in the Queen's rooms in the Tuileries.

I will go there, I said to myself, striving to feel no emotion, no fear. I will go and see with my own eyes that Charles is safe.

Even if I had never before been to the Tuileries it would have been easy to find that morning. All I had to do was follow the reverse path of the looters, well marked with a stream of litter and booty fallen from hastily stuffed bundles. Just outside the Palais Royal I saw the first corpse, that of a priest. He was sprawled in the gutter, cut open from throat to belly. I stepped around him, holding my skirts and swallowing hard. I began to run.

Across from the Place du Carrousel a man, burdened with a heavy cloth sack hanging over his shoulder—and out of that sack protruded silver candlesticks embedded with garnets and pearls—stopped me. He pulled me into the circle of drunken men and slovenly women who quarreled over a gold-framed lookingglass. That mirror told me what I had tried not to think of. It was from the Queen's own dressing table.

"I know you," the man said, poking me with a grimy finger and grinning. "You're Citizenness de Saint Remy. You'll be wanted to answer some questions, aristocrat lover."

I pushed his hand away. "No, citizen. I am not. You are mistaken. Let me pass. I am on my way to meet my husband." He was drunk enough that my denial confused him. Stepping out of that dangerous circle, I forced my steps to assume a normal, unhurried pace that would not show my fear. He did not pursue me, and a few moments later I entered the Cour d'Honneur of the Tuileries.

Inside the ancient, mossy gates of the decaying palace a nauseating heat, stench and noise made me reel with fear and disgust.

The courtyard was filled with frenzied women tearing and biting at each other to claim remnants of curtains and bed linens; they screeched and cackled like witches. The men still carried their pikes, and blood dripped down them, onto their hands and the cobbled yard. Corpses were piled as high as the tall ground floor windows, and all the corpses wore the Queen's or King's livery. The guards had been massacred. There, in the palace courtyard, were funeral pyres the likes of which I hope never to see again.

Charles is not here, I told myself. Yet I pushed through the crowd, searching for him. I forced my way through to the path that led to the Queen's entrance. Over the heads of the mob I saw Charles coming toward me.

I don't remember him being so tall, I thought, puzzled. My God, he's so tall.

And then the crowd between me and my husband parted for the space of a breath and I saw it was not Charles approaching me, but his severed head carried aloft on a pike.

10

. . . the world turned upside down . . .

I . . . gazed
On this and other spots, as doth a man
Upon a volume whose contents he knows
Are memorable, but from him locked up,
Being written in a tongue he cannot read
So that he questions the mute leaves with pain
And half upbraids their silence.

—William Wordsworth

Of death, I know this: when a beloved dies, much of us dies, too. I gazed at Charles's face for the last time, knowing him to be dead, and my plans, hopes, dreams and future were all dead with him.

I fainted. And when I came to, that hellish courtyard was much quieted. The pyres of the five hundred guards that had been killed gave off evil fumes of carnage, but some of them were already no more than a smoldering pile. People came and went, but in small groups, or alone, not in threatening crowds. They talked of the prices they could fetch for stolen lace and vases, and of what they would cook that night for their dinner. They seemed like normal people, and that was the maddest thing of all. One woman even leaned over and asked if I needed help. I wondered if she had been there when Charles had been murdered, if she had cheered on the pike-armed vermin who had lifted his head from the cobbles so it could be carried as a banner.

I was tempted to laugh but an inner voice warned me I should not, or I would go as mad as the rest of them. I was such a fool, I thought. I believed that love mattered. I thought that pledges and the honor of queens mattered. It did not. None of it mattered, none of it made any difference.

I dragged myself out of that courtyard but knew I could no longer return to the Palais Royal, to the rooms where I had awaited Charles on so many long nights. There was no future there, nor a present. There was only the past. So I returned to the past. To the Cité.

On the rue des Anges, Louise opened the door to me. I walked past her, as if I had merely been gone for a long day, and was just now returning. I went to my old sewing corner in Mathilde's room, and sat.

Afterwards Louise told me I sat there for days, not speaking, moving or eating. I must have slept, for I remember wakening several times with the nightmare still in front of my eyes, a scream still sounding in the room.

I became ill. When I woke, I was in Louise's bed and she was cooling my forehead with a damp cloth.

"You've been in a fever for days. I was worried," she said, smiling at me. But then her face changed, it wasn't Louise, but Charles. I screamed.

The face changed again, it was Louise. Her hand clamped over my mouth. I was surprised by her strength.

"Please, Julie. Don't scream. No one must know you are here."

I fell against her, gasping for air.

"You called his name in your sleep," she whispered. "My poor little Julie." She put her arms around me like in earlier times, when a pretty blue ribbon could quell sorrow. But I didn't think I would ever be comforted again. Pain. I felt I would burst from the pain inside, it pushed outward from my ribs like an animal trapped in a cage, clawing and biting.

"Eat something," Louise said for lack of other words that might make sense, and she pushed a bowl of chestnut soup toward me.

I looked about then for the first time with seeing eyes. The paint was peeling from her pretty frescoes, and the splendid pink velvet curtains were soiled and ragged with age and neglect.

"Yes, I am poor again." She smiled cheerfully and dismissed the faded glories with a wave of her hand. "Monsieur de Bracy has lost everything. But he never abandoned me. His wife still has income from her properties in Austria, but she makes him beg for every sou. Because of me. He refused to give me up." Her voice was proud.

The soup tasted of autumn and poverty; it was what we had survived on in the worst times, the hunger times, Mathilde and I. I couldn't eat it.

"Where is Grandmama?" I asked.

"She died last spring. Peacefully, in her sleep."

"Did she ask for me?"

"No." Louise lowered her eyes. "The last time she talked of you was the day you left. Oh, you should have seen Monsieur Mouret!" She laughed, her old, gay laugh. "What a rage! I'm certain you did the right thing. He would have made you miserable, that fat pig of a man. He remarried, a widow from the faubourg St. Antoine. She's not meek like Adelaide was, if he gives her a black eye she doubles the favor and gives him two."

At that moment I heard a familiar, hated man's voice below in the street, yelling an obscenity to an errand boy. It was Mouret.

"Speak of the devil and he appears," Louise murmured.

Time flowed backwards as I sat in that room, listening to the baker abuse his assistant. I was a grown woman, yet my memories were those of a child, I was forgetting much of what had happened in the more recent past. Had I only dreamed of Bertin's workroom, and my own salon? Had I imagined Charles? No. There was the thin gold band on my finger, and I still wore a gown that Julie of the Cité would never have owned, not even in its torn and stained condition.

The gown had picked up a strong odor of death in the courtyard of the Tuileries; that was my reality.

I slept much. It was the closest thing to death I could think of, and it was oblivion I wished. But Louise would wake me several times a day and force me to sit up and talk with her. She feared for my sanity. I did not. It didn't matter.

"We heard about your salon," she said one afternoon after bringing my bowl of chestnut soup. "We heard it was very elegant and well-patronized. I was proud of you, Julie. Yvette was so jealous I thought she would die of it. I went to the shop once and looked in the window . . ." Her voice faltered.

"You should have come in," I murmured. But we both knew that Julienne of the Palais Royal would not have been enthusiastic about meeting her old friend from the Cité. I looked down in shame.

"I understood," she said, patting my arm gently. "I understood. It is right to try to close the door to the past sometimes."

"Where is Yvette now?" I asked, wishing to speak of other matters, for to talk of the salon meant to think of Charles, and that I could not yet do.

"In and out of prison. Soon they'll have to put in a swinging door for her.

They arrested me once, but Monsieur de Bracy arranged matters, I left after just one hour and the gaoler apologized to me. He has been good to me, Julie. So good."

"Do you hear anything of your son?" I asked. My own grief made me hard. I enjoyed seeing Louise cringe and grow pale from that wound.

"Nothing," she said simply. She smoothed the counterpane and left. I turned my face to the wall and pretended that Charles was still alive, those were his steps coming up the stairs. Later, I apologized to Louise, and we embraced and cried together.

One day, a week and a half after my return when I was able to leave the bed for hours at a time, only to stare out the window from behind the torn curtain, I did hear steps on the stairs. They paused in front of our door, we heard two men's voices speculating, conferring, in hurried whispers. Louise stood by the door, pale, with a warning finger raised to her lips. I knew I was wanted by the commune, they had searched my salon for me. My fear surprised me. I had not thought anything in the world would ever again rouse emotion in me. But I was young and whether I willed it or not that part of me which was in God's hands and not my own keeping told me I must live, and suffer, and recover to suffer again. That is what life dictates.

We listened, holding our breath, until the steps continued past our door and down the hall to where a new tenant, Mademoiselle Sartine, lived. She was receiving visitors. But those footsteps on the stairs awoke me to the danger we faced.

"You must hide," Louise said when all was quiet again. "They are looking for you. They already came here once, the day you arrived, but you weren't yet here. They will come again."

As much as I took no joy in living, I was not yet ready to die. Nor did I wish to endanger Louise.

"I will hide in the attic. In the asylum I used as a child," I said.

We lowered the old ladder. It hadn't been used in years, and creaked a protest. Some of the rungs had rotted. We pushed a cot up it and I followed. I put my mattress on the floor in front of the little window I remembered well, the window through which I had been watching my small world on the day that Louis-the-Well-Beloved had been marched through Paris in his ungracious funeral march.

Louise, with much effort, broke the ladder off its hinges and I pulled it up after me, closed the door, and was alone.

If the room had seemed cozy as a child, it was uncomfortably small for a woman. The ceiling sagged so that I could not stand without bowing my head, and I could take no more than six strides in any direction without confronting a wall. Cobwebs hung from all the corners, and a decade of autumns had littered the wooden floor with a carpet of molding leaves that had blown in through the broken windowpanes.

Without thinking, I began to scoop up handfuls of leaves and cast them back out the window, little realizing that passersby below would consider it strange to see leaves fall where there was no tree. But Paris already had more on its mind than the path of autumn leaves. Fortunately that day no one remarked the odd phenomenon. When I realized my mistake it struck me like a blow that I was now a criminal in hiding. I had kept a pledge and loved a man, and for that I was an enemy of the nation.

Days were as long as years in that asylum, and each night an eternity. I played a game, trying to pretend I was still Julie before the rape, before Bertin's, before Charles. Then, I did not have to think about those events, did not have to remember Charles. But the game never lasted long.

In my asylum I could hear women in the street sending their spouses off to work, for even in the midst of death and revolution someone must bake bread and heel boots. "Take care, Jacques. Remember to leave the pot at the tinner's," one would say, and another would curse her mate as a lazy-good-for-nothing and then send him off with a smacking kiss that sounded all the way up to my attic. I was shut out from all that, from comings and goings, from quarreling and loving, and I hated those women, I coveted their carefree poverty, their crowded beds, their many reasons for living.

To help pass the time, Louise brought me journals and papers to read. In that way I learned that the royal family was not murdered, like Charles, but imprisoned in the Temple. As long as the Queen lived, and even past that, I had a pledge to keep. There was something I must do, and the knowledge of having a task that needed tending awoke something in me that I had thought died with Charles. I made a plan, and anticipated the morrow.

I knocked softly on the floor, a signal to Louise that I needed to speak with her. She came to that attic door only once a day, to bring food and clean the pail I used as a privy.

A few moments after my knock, an answering tap sounded on the thick wooden plank that shut off my attic room from the reaches of the dangerous outer world. There were three taps, a pause, then two more. I was to open the door only to that code.

Louise's pale face appeared below.

"Yes?" she asked, as cheerfully as if she were a chamber maid being summoned to the drawing room. Her eyes were merry; she made a great point of avoiding any show of fear or sadness in her attempts to cheer me. Her blonde hair by then was tinged with grey but her blue eyes were clear as a young girl's. Age doesn't always rob a woman's beauty; sometimes it just changes it, polishes and refines it, so that the absence of youth makes the remaining beauty even more precious. With money and position to protect her, Louise would have been one of the great beauties of her time. As it was, she was just a pretty, aging woman in shabby garments.

"Louise. I must go back to the Palais Royal. Just for an hour. Will you help me?"

"No. I will not." She pouted. "You will be stopped and you'll end up in the Conciergerie. Don't be foolish, Julie."

"I know the danger. But I must do this. Help me and I will go in disguise."

"Well." She hesitated. "You are stubborn as ever. If you must. I am sure Monsieur de Bracy can get papers. And a disguise . . ." she smiled. "I will borrow clothes from old Lily. We will send you out as a ragpicker. That would be the safest disguise for a woman when the streets are filled with soldiers." This was my old Louise, who knew the lines from all the popular plays of the opera, and the details of all costumes.

I hadn't seen Monsieur de Bracy since the evening we had quarreled over my future, eight years ago. The evening he came to Louise's summon I was nervous in the old way that his large, self-confident masculine authority had made me timorous when I was still a child.

He had aged. His belly jutted out even more, so that his shirt wrinkled in despair and then stretched out over it as tightly as the skin on a cheese. His wig sat further back on his bald head. His nose was redder, his smile wistful. When I lowered the ladder and joined them he was clasping Louise to his chest, and she had to stretch on tiptoe to overcome the promontory of his stomach and plant a kiss on his mouth.

"Well," he said, looking me up and down. "Well, well." I went to him and gave him a kiss, not because of any fondness I felt, but because of the joy he put in Louise's wide blue eyes.

A smell of snuff and wine and shaving soap overwhelmed me and brought pain as I realized that Charles had used the same scented soap.

"Well. Ahem. Your plan is a bit of foolishness, young lady. No more than what I would expect from you. We shall discuss it." His fatherly tone was disapproving.

Louise arranged three chairs around a small table. She was dressed in an out-of-fashion gown of pink satin over green petticoats too lushly adorned with cloth roses to be tasteful. De Bracy wore a violet waistcoat with matching silk breeches and white stockings. Most of Paris now dressed in simple gowns or long trousers; Louise and de Bracy looked like characters from a play staged long ago. But they were happy together, cozy and familiar as husband and wife, whereas I was isolated from all that was good, all that was life. Death was a shadow always moving in the corner of my eye.

"Have you been able to get papers for me?" I asked, sitting.

"Yes. And they were expensive," de Bracy said, frowning.

"When my errand is completed, I will reimburse you," I promised.

"The cost is not my concern, Julie. I disapprove because of the danger. It would grieve Louise greatly should anything more go amiss with you. I must forbid you this scheme. I will do your task for you." His voice was exactly as it had been eight years before, filled with assurance that I would, indeed, should, obey him.

"You are kind. But only I can do this. To even tell you of what I must do would betray the trust of another." I could not endanger them by telling them of the Queen's diamond.

He snorted and began to argue, but Louise silenced him with a touch of her hand to his lips.

"If you are both determined to go through with this foolishness, then here are the papers. You are a Madame Valette, widow, born in the Cité." So far, I thought bitterly, my forged papers tell few lies. "But she was considerably older than you. You will have to do some playacting."

The next evening, when the streets were dark and concealing, Louise dressed me in a gown borrowed from Lily, the ragpicker. It was so patched and mended with odd rags and cast-off remnants that its original color and style was buried under dozens of motley additions. She scrubbed my cheeks and hair with grime from the hearth, and then draped a black shawl around my shoulders, almost completely hiding me under an ugly wealth of dirty garments.

"Remember to stoop," she said. "The uglier you are, the safer you will be. The streets are filled with ruffians and soldiers." I took a deep breath which I did not let out until Louise's door locked behind me and I was out in the street. Louise watched from a dark window, but I did not wave. A ragpicker would not have friends in even a poor building, her cohorts would be sleeping under bridges and in doorways.

There was no moon that night, aiding my disguise, and my footsteps were stifled by the red and brown leaves that had fallen early that year as if they, too, were in mourning for the past and not looking forward to the future. The rue St. Honoré was quick with shadows cast by the street lamps. A mournful autumn wind swirled dirt, leaves and bits of paper around my feet; they trapped themselves in the hems of my rags and made a sad rustling as I walked.

Few people were about, and those who were tended to be soldiers or members of the citizens' militia, armed and looking short-tempered. At the entrance to the Palais Royal I was stopped by a group of them.

"Old woman, show us your papers," a deep voice called. He was standing directly under their lamp and the tricolor in his hat shone as though it was aflame. I approached slowly, and drew the forged papers out of my pocket.

"She's not so old, from what shows beneath the filth," one of the men said, peering closely at me. "Why are you out after curfew, citizenness?" His tone was sharp.

"An errand," I whispered, trying to make my voice sound hoarse. "I have to deliver a message to a patron waiting at the Café Mécanique." Pain. That was where Charles and I had met. Why hadn't I named a different café? Now my voice trembled.

"What is the message?" He poked me in the chest. I must not strike back, I commanded myself.

"The message, citizen, is this. 'Do not come tonight. My husband is at home.' But citizen, I will not tell you the name of the sender of the message, nor he who is to receive it. I would lose my fee."

They laughed and gave me back my papers. I hobbled away, thankful that they could not see the expression on my face for the darkness. I feared them, and my fear made the hatred even stronger. Any one of them could have been the man who dealt Charles's death blow.

Inside the Palais Royal, the shadows were even stronger because of the great quantity of torches and lamps; it seemed as though all good and evil were divided there into light and dark, and the dark was winning.

I walked close to the walls, staying as much as possible away from the yellow circles of light the lamps gave off. Because my garments were dark with soot and age, I must have looked more like a lost shadow than a woman.

My salon had been sealed, as I had expected. Broken windows had been boarded up with rough slats, and my door was chained closed under a notice from the Assembly, which also claimed all the goods of the shop and warned that the proprietress, Madame de Saint Remy, was wanted for questioning. I slid through the narrow side path to the back and noticed that Madame Coulbert's marionnette theater was also boarded. I wondered what crimes against the nation this entertainer of children had committed. The boarded back windows had been pried loose by looters. Once inside, it took several moments for my eyes to grow accustomed to the greater dark. Judging by the smell of decay and damage, it was well I could not clearly see the damage done to my small salon. I wandered through those rooms, trying to capture the joy and pride they had once given me; it was gone, destroyed.

The showroom, where new gleaming cabinets and shelves of fashion dolls had once stood, was picked clean as a corpse after the feast of worms. The walls were stripped of their hangings and a pile of emptied crates and boxes rose in the middle of the floor, their contents long since looted. A small cooking fire had been built off to the side, chicken bones littered the floor.

Upstairs in my private rooms the damage was worse. The bed that Charles and I had loved in was stripped of its green covers and white linens and a long, gaping knife slash ran the length of the mattress. My wardrobe had been emptied completely. Not a shawl, fan, or slipper remained, although a carmagnole jacket I had been stitching was left in a work corner. That gave me some bitter satisfaction; the sansculottes had coveted gowns and feathers, not the utilitarian jacket.

In the closet where the Queen's diamond was hidden, empty boxes were also strewn about, but the floor boards were intact. For the first time since Charles's death I felt a moment of gratitude.

In the dark, for it was dangerous to light a candle, I felt for the board that was just a hair's breadth out of line with the others and then pried it loose with a knife I had brought. It separated with a crunching, tearing noise that forced me to sit in silence for a long time after, in case any of that noise had reached the still night outside the broken windows. When all was quiet, I plunged my hand into the gap and felt the package of muslin resting there. The Queen's diamond. My fingers moved deeper into the recess to find a second bundle—my savings, a small solid sack of coins, about five hundred livres. It was all I had to show for years of work, but it would help repay Louise for the expense of keeping me in my secret asylum. I put both packages into the deep, inner pockets of Lily's dirty petticoat. And then stood, and forced myself to go into the next room, the one I had dreaded most of all.

Charles's library. A rat had died in the walls and made the office smell of death. Bats stirred in the unused chimney. The books were gone, and the bookcases themselves toppled and broken. I tried to remember our mornings there but they seemed so distant already. I was a ghost witnessing the ruin of my own life.

The little escritoire where I had kept my ledgers and papers was also stolen and the papers thrown into a littered corner of debris. From the midst of them I was able to find the journal Charles had encouraged me to keep. It had been thumbed by dirty hands, perhaps hastily read. "It is only about me!" Charles had once complained to me. "About love," I had answered. And good thing I had not written more incriminating things. But my satisfaction was short-lived. Charles was not there to share it. The journal went into the pocket where the Queen's diamond was, and I did not know which was the most precious. It would be my keepsake of a world that no longer existed.

With the smell of mold and ruin following me, I left the shop and the Palais Royal the same way I had come, knowing I would never return.

The same group of militia stood under the same lamp on the rue St. Honoré. They were drinking and bragging of amorous exploits. "Deliver your message?" one of them called after me, laughing. I avoided the light so they would not see the tears on my cheeks and wonder why a simple message would bring forth such emotion.

rue des Anges

August 24

There were some blank pages left in the journal. I will fill them in; Charles would have wished it. What is there to say, except that I dream of him constantly? Last night he was just ahead of me in the street, but he would not stop when I called out to him. Just as I was catching up, reaching for his sleeve, a roaring crowd separated us and my husband disappeared again. No . . . not disappeared. There, behind me, over my left shoulder, in front of me, again. I whirled, trying to keep him in sight. The whirl became the graceful spin of a dance, Charles's arm was around my waist, his eyes looking into mine. With his free arm he offered me a goblet of wine, kissing the rim before holding it to my lips.

I sipped, and tasted blood. The metallic taste was still in my mouth when I awoke.

La Fayette is being called a traitor and his soldiers have threatened to jail him, according to the *Mercure*. La Fayette, I have no doubt, will soon leave Paris again, for a longer time than his battle took. I spent several hours pretending that Charles would go with him. It was a short-lived fantasy, and one that brought no ease to my heart.

That autumn, Paris was in turmoil. At the front, the Duke of Brunswick continued to menace the revolutionary army, while in France the harried leaders rounded up suspect after suspect and carted them off to any of several new prisons in the city. Convents, hospitals, hôtels . . . they were all hastily converted into prisons for antirevolutionaries. Danton saw them everywhere . . . lift a rock and he would discover some poor unfortunate who had once voiced support of the King's policies or the Queen's beauty.

161

The revolution took a new, even more sinister form. The derogatory term "aristocrat" was no longer reserved for those born of title and position. Anyone who expressed doubt about the revolution was considered an aristocrat, while anyone who agreed with the dictates of the convention was considered a democrat. Hence, lowly born chambermaids were accused of the crime of aristocracy, while former marquises and comtes who were prorevolutionary were freed of the charge.

Men went weeks without shaving and women left their hair lank and undressed to prove their innocence of aristocratic leanings. Even the revolution demanded a certain style.

In September, growing fears of counterrevolution inspired the authorities to round up the remaining "aristocrats" who had not yet been imprisoned. Yvette, who still wore the drab and sooty remains of lace at her throat, was one of these. I had seen her once, from a distance, through my asylum window. She had grown ugly with hardship and I would have pitied her, if I hadn't known she would have turned me over to the authorities for any small fee she could collect on my head. Her new title must have flattered her, but her joy was short-lived. Once imprisoned, the revolutionaries tore through those prisons with a vengeance, murdering over a thousand "aristocrats", including chambermaids of the lower class, children, and mothers with babes at breast. Armed with kitchen knives and daggers, the revolutionaries swept through the jails at their ease, cutting the throats of all they found.

My own waist was thickening, and I told Louise that I was pregnant. I had, in my grief for Charles, almost forgotten about it. I did not believe the child would allow itself to be carried full term; surely the evil and sadness of the world would destroy it, if anything as simple as a fall had ended my first pregnancy. But I determined to go through the motions as much as possible, just in case . . .

Louise was first worried, and then delighted, for it was not her nature to be pessimistic. She promised all would go well, even making light of it, saying that I would be sure to get plenty of bedrest in my asylum. With the Golden Ransom safe once again—I had hidden it in the overhead rafters, it was safe as long as I was hidden along with it—I determined to do nothing but wait. Wait to see if the thing within would truly take form and come to fruition, wait for the pain caused by the loss of Charles to diminish, wait for the evils outside my window to exhaust themselves like a hastily built funeral pyre and die away. I waited to live again, never knowing if I would or not.

Winter came with all its hardships enhanced by war. Paris again felt the talons of hunger and starvation, for the revolutionary government took no more care with the distribution of food than the monarchy before it. And for three years and more there had been more soldiers than farmers, and no nation can survive with that imbalance.

We ate chestnut soup every day and enjoyed bread only two or three times a week. I watched outside my window and there came a day when even Mouret did not open his bakery. He was fleshier than when I had last seen him, but with age, not health. The skin of his face sagged into wrinked folds as he grimaced and hung the CLOSED sign on his door.

A snaking line of gaunt citizens had already formed that morning and they did not believe that Mouret had no bread for sale. They shook their fists in his face and he quickly retreated inside, drawing the bolts on his door.

Louise cried for the first time that day.

"How are we to get bread?" she sobbed.

Her Monsieur de Bracy came to our rescue. He sent the address of a baker who knew him well and would sell bread to those buying in monsieur's name. After that, monsieur was coachless and his fine gold satin jacket was missing. The favor had cost him much.

Louise took some of my coins and bought a milk goat from a farmer who still had a few pastured on the Champs Elysées. Because the goat could not be safely left outside, we quartered the creature in Louise's boudoir, out of the reach of thieves, where it promptly ate a lace mitten and a feathered pouf before contenting itself with the pile of straw the farmer had supplied with the animal.

Louise, holding her nose against the smell, bathed it and scented it with perfume. For exercise, and to keep its milk flowing, she walked it up and down the stairs and sometimes in the street, if de Bracy were with her for protection. The rue des Anges laughed at these antics and thought Louise mad, but I had fresh milk each day.

rue des Anges

October 26

I can only write in the day, now. Louise has taken my candles. Last week Lily the ragpicker was out after curfew and saw a flashing light in my attic where no one is supposed to be living.

"Oh! It must be the poor ghost of Marie-Jeanne, the little maid who was hung there by her lover in 1746! You never heard the story? Lily, I thought you knew all about it," Louise told her.

And because Lily is old and has seen so much she has no reason to doubt any madness, she believed the story. We are safe for a while longer. But the nights are long, without my candles. There is too much time to think, to remember. . . .

Is there a way to prevent dreams? I wish I could fall into sleep and awake remembering nothing. But I sleep lightly and in my sleep visit with Mathilde, who says strange things to me and worries me. "You must polish Charles's boots," she told me last night. And I tried to tell her I couldn't, that the boots were on his feet, which were on his body, and that couldn't be found. "Foolish wife!" she laughed. "You lost your husband's body? His head is lonely, you know." I woke up screaming. Old Lily will truly believe this attic is haunted. The ghost's name is Julie, not Marie-Jeanne.

In December it was announced that Louis Capet, former King of France, was to go on trial for crimes against the nation.

Christmas was not celebrated. It was a day for God eaters, as the revolution named those who still followed the faith and, therefore, illegal and antirevolutionary. But I took half of my remaining coins and arranged for a Mass to be said for Charles.

It was a dangerous business. Louise, who helped me in this, first had to locate a certain priest who hid in the cellar of the looted Hôtel de Fiore of the rue St. Martin. I left my attic for the second time to attend the mass, disguised again in Lily's gown. It distressed me that Charles had not been laid to rest. His bones, as precious to me as any saint's relics, had either been thrown into a mass grave or lay mixed in the bloody dirt of the Tuileries' courtyard.

We said prayers for him, and when I returned to my attic that night the babe within kicked for the first time, and I took that as a sign of goodwill from both God and Charles.

The King's trial was a brief one, ending quickly in January. When there are few laws, and those arbitrary, justice is not a lengthy prospect. He was found guilty and it was put to a vote whether he should die or be exiled. A king in exile was considered dangerous to the revolution; his death was voted. Of the many who voted for death, his own cousin, Philippe Egalité, the ci-devant Duc d'Orléans, was the noisiest.

The King who had been indecisive and hesitant was brave at the end, and laid his head under the guillotine with a quiet courage that shamed Paris. His wife and children were still imprisoned.

"Now the way is open for d'Orléans to become king," I said to Louise. I lay on my cot, skirts pulled up to reveal my rounded belly so that Louise could massage the strained skin with lotion. We were out of candles and soap, but Louise still managed to find her creams. The baby kicked under her palm and Louise raised happy eyes to mine.

"She is strong and eager for life, this one," she said.

"How do you know it is a girl?"

"Because she started kicking soon and you are carrying her high. She is proud and impatient. Doesn't that sound like a woman? But d'Orléans will never be king." Louise had been to the trial, as had thousands of others. "I saw the faces of Marat and Danton and Robespierre when d'Orléans voted death for his own cousin. Those three will be pleased to be rid of all royalty, including d'Orléans. He may change his name a thousand times, but he will still be the Duc d'Orléans, and they will still hate him." Charles had said the same thing.

In the weeks that followed, Paris became a city in love with death. The guillotine set up in the Place de la Révolution was fed one head after another, so that the soil under it was constantly red with blood that dripped through the receiving basket.

"It reeks like a butcher shop," Louise complained. But she could not avoid the square; to detour around it would indicate lack of support for the revolution. Children were led there to see justice firsthand.

Neighbor feared neighbor; husband and wife accused each other. A spouse, tired of an aging mate, could denounce her and effect a quick end to a troublesome marriage; business partners seeking to become sole owners spoke against each other. We were all of us guilty. To speak against bloodshed, to doubt the outcome of the war against England and Austria, to question the zeal of our leaders . . . all such matters were crimes as deserving of death as bribery or harboring criminals.

Madame Laveau, the wife of the shoemaker down the street, complained one morning that the newly appointed section leaders were allowing farmers to charge too much for rotten eggs. She was denounced and the next morning, when the eggseller came, grinning, Madame Laveau was no longer there. Her husband disappeared the next day, and the farmer's daughter moved into the emptied house.

I missed Madame Laveau's high-pitched shrieks over the price of food. They had broken my quiet solitude, and with her gone the street grew menacingly quiet.

"Miserable house," Louise said one morning. "I'll be glad to see the last of it." She, like many, wanted to put Paris behind her. Monsieur de Bracy had decided he would take his mistress to Switzerland. First, though, he had to wrest a small fortune from his tight-fisted wife to buy false papers and a coach. Madame would go with them.

"It will be uncomfortable, being a chambermaid under the supervision of his wife," Louise sighed. I could imagine only too well the abuse the wife would heap on this long-loved mistress.

"You could come with us, Julie. Think about it." Louise would enjoy having a friend with her to dilute the wife's venom. But although I, too, was seeing the necessity of leaving Paris, I was loath to go to Berne as a servant. Charles's child would be born into servitude, and I did not believe he would forgive me that. But where to go? I had no answer, I had forgotten how to live and think past the day at hand.

The child within grew, it distended my belly and kept me awake nights with its lively kicking. I began to have faith in it, and that hope, coupled with the aching for Charles, took up all my thoughts.

Civil war erupted in the Vendée in late March when the convention attempted to conscript all young men for the wars with England and Austria. I rejoiced when I heard that there, and in all of western France, antirevolutionaries had overrun their revolutionary governments. That, of course, led the Parisian government to even greater cruelties. The Committee of Public Safety was initiated; its goal was the safety of the citizens. It took a large staff of men to keep the guillotine blades sharp, so well used were they.

About that time, one fine spring morning, I lay on my back in the attic, amused that I could no longer see my feet because of the great mound of my belly. I drummed my fingers against the taut skin. The drumming was loud and insistent. I realized it was not my fingers making the noise, but someone pounding on Louise's door.

The militia kicked it open when she was slow to answer. The footsteps went from sharp cracks to dull thuds as they moved from the bare wood floor of the hall to the worn carpet of Louise's apartment. I held my breath.

"Where is Madame de Saint Remy?" a voice demanded.

"You mean Mademoiselle Julie? Why, I haven't seen her for these eight years," Louise answered sweetly.

I heard the sound of flesh against flesh, the sound made when Mouret struck his wife for giving me bread. They struck four, five, six blows and Louise made not a sound. I stuck my fist in my mouth and bit deeply into it to keep from crying out my hatred and fear. Just when I had begun to think I might live again, because of the child, all was destroyed again. They had come for me, they would find me.

Something inside burst. I lay still, feeling my body turn limp and then stiff with spasms, and bit down harder on my fist.

For an hour I listened to the sounds of furniture being moved, drawers thrown open, angry voices yelling and threatening the sobbing Louise. But she played her part well. After a time the footsteps retreated back to the hall. Voices, angry, impatient, sounded clearly.

"You misinformed us, citizen."

"I tell you, she is here. And the diamond." It was d'Orléans. His voice shook with frustration and something else . . . fear. I grinned, forcing my teeth hard together, to keep the scream unvoiced.

"On your honor, you are charged with finding the gem. Do so, and stop wasting our time." And then they were gone.

Louise let most of the day go by before she dared give the signal. When she appeared below the trap door, her face was swollen and bruised, but she smiled.

"They have stolen the goat," she said. "And quite destroyed the room. What were they looking for, Julie?"

"Don't think about that," I said through clenched teeth. "We have another problem. The labor has started. Oh, Louise," I moaned. "It is terrible."

She smiled. "Months late to think of that, sweet. Let's see what can be done."

It is a measure of woman's resourcefulness that Louise was able to assist my accouchement all that day and night without giving away the fact that I was hidden in her rooms. She dared not ask the water carrier to bring in the tubs of water we required, so she brought in a basin of still-remaining snow from the window ledges and melted it by the hearth. When we ran out of sheets and rags she tore up a good if dated silk dress. My job was to keep as quiet as possible and bear down; she did the rest.

The attic grew fetid with my travail, and then cold as I became exhausted. When I must scream, Louise made a point of banging on her pots and yelling. If questioned, she would say that the noise was the sound of soldiers savaging her rooms; few would have paid close enough attention to know the time discrepancy. The Committee of Public Safety had inadvertantly protected me.

At dawn, my daughter was born. She was whole and rosy and perfect. Already she showed thick, black hair and a promise of great beauty, with Charles's rounded chin and high forehead.

She took the nipple quickly and with great greed, sucking with a concentration that reminded me of her father pondering one of his many maps.

167

"A good sign," Louise said proudly, wiping sweat from her bruised, fatigued face. "She will be decisive and strong. Like her mama."

But even as Aurore enjoyed her first meal, her mama fell into a soft, renewing cradle of sleep.

All other matters became of almost no importance. I nursed and held Aurore and even the attic became a kind of palace for me, a nest for just the two of us. I was particularly fascinated by her fingers; they were already long and elegant, like Charles's, and her whole, perfect, miniature fist would grasp one of my fingers with a tenacity that pulled at my heart.

And then, on the celebration of Aurore's second week of life, marked with a quiet party of chestnut soup and stale bread, we learned that d'Orléans had been arrested. It seemed to me that the Divine Being might have renewed his interest in thrusting a small amount of justice into the revolution.

I dreamed of freedom, of fresh air and sunshine for my daughter, who had already lost her rosiness and was pale as white satin. Yet each time Aurore woke and fumbled for my breast, I looked up to where I had hidden the Queen's diamond. The Queen and her son were still in prison. There could be no freedom till the diamond was returned to the Queen. I had no right to resume my life until I had fulfilled my pledge to her. But how?

I did not find the answer. It found me, in the guise of the Chevalier de Rougeville.

11

. . . a rescue attempt . . .

*"All men have not the same views about what is to be feared,
although there are some terrors which are admitted to be more
than human nature can face. What characterizes the brave
man is his unshaken courage whenever courage is humanly
possible."*

—Aristotle

He came one day bearing a token from the Queen—a small golden button decorated with seed pearls in the shape of a crescent moon. That token earned him admittance into our household, for I had designed the button myself. It was part of a set from the Queen's ill-fated traveling wardrobe.

"I have come about the Queen," he said.

The Chevalier de Rougeville was an aristocrat of the old order. The revolution existed for him only as a danger to his cherished Queen. Liberty, equality and fraternity were slogans that the canaille scribbled on walls; they had nought to do with him. His only credo was the devotion he had once sworn to Marie-Antoinette.

"We are going to rescue the Queen," he whispered to me that evening. And his eyes shone with a brave and cunning fervor.

We were in Louise's sitting room. Since the arrest of d'Orléans there had

169

been no more disturbances and we breathed easier. Monsieur de Bracy was also there, and judging by the way his nostrils flared, he took an instant dislike to the chevalier, and the chevalier to him. After the first introductions, de Rougeville ignored Louise and de Bracy as if they were servants.

"We will have to move you from here," he said. "These rooms are unsafe. If I was able to find you, so will others who have not your well-being, and that of the Queen, at heart."

They have already tried, I thought but did not say. Did he know of the diamond? No mention had been made of it, so I, too, did not refer to it.

I looked at Louise; her eyes were pleading. Tomorrow we were to put into effect our own escape plan. Disguised as a young widow traveling with child, servant and governess, we would leave France and the revolution. De Bracy had received a promise of help from the agents of Madame de Staël in Switzerland, who had been busy for two years smuggling needy friends out of France. The promise had been given because she remembered that Charles had brought me to her salon, and I had pleased her by being quiet and shy, allowing her own brilliance to shine that much more brightly.

"Tomorrow I will take you to a *petite maison*, where you will safely await your part in the Queen's rescue," de Rougeville said. "We will save her." His deep, convincing voice reminded me of Mesmer's.

Some people walk this earth cloaked in wondrous dreams; their feet never touch anything as cold and practical as the ground. The chevalier was one of those people. Later I learned that he was the man who, single-handedly, had charged the King's tumbril in an attempt to wrest him from the mob and the waiting guillotine. That attempt had failed, but it became an instant legend, a dream of courage that inspired the hundreds who did escape from France and certain death.

I could not say no to him. Not if there was any chance that his plan, which he would not reveal to me, would work. Charles, who had died trying to protect the Queen, would have wished this of me.

The next morning Louise and de Bracy packed one small bag each to take on their journey. Louise sighed, regretfully donned the drabbest of her gowns, and helped de Bracy dress in his grey, homespun jacket. Bold with the knowledge that I might never see these two again, I reached up to straighten his wig, and kissed his cheek. His arms tightened around me in a fatherly embrace. Louise tried to hum a tune to mask her emotion at this second separation between us. Aurore's birth and the dangers we had shared had bound us tightly together.

"You will be safer without us," I said. "You will travel more quickly."

"Find another goat. You need milk," she said. We embraced for a long moment, and there were no words to ease the sorrow of that parting. I watched as they went out the door, Louise going first with her hands delicately holding her skirts off the dusty floor, and de Bracy, a traveling case in each hand, following. I watched from the window as they made their way down the rue des Anges; they would have to walk to the coach awaiting them on the other side of Paris.

When they were out of sight I picked up Aurore and my own small case and left the building by a back stairwell, where the Chevalier de Rougeville awaited me.

"Permit me to carry your case," he offered with a slight bow.

I would not relinquish it; the Queen's diamond was there.

"Madame. Let me carry the case or the infant, for if burdened with both, you will surely drop one." I made a hard choice, and let him carry the case.

Once again, I left the rue des Anges.

We walked slowly, like a family taking the fresh morning air. We walked past the Conciergerie, where prisoners awaited news of their fate and where, a long time ago, the pregnant Louise had stopped to rest on that evening of Louis XV's funeral. I wondered what had become of the son born to her that night.

We walked past the Pont Neuf where street vendors still sold everything from chamber pots to love philters, except the revolution had made everything that much more expensive; past the Place du Carrousel and its stench and slums; past the Tuileries where a Queen had once lived and my husband had died.

Few people walked the streets, and many stores and houses were abandoned and boarded.

"How sad the city is become," I said, and the chevalier made no comment. His eyes darted quickly about in his otherwise composed face, searching for militia groups or other persons that might stop and question us. Often he reached up to be sure his cockade, large as a fan, stood up imposingly from his hat band.

After a long walk, but without incident, we reached our destination, a little house in the faubourg St. Honoré. Built on a hill behind the Champs Elysées, it had a full view of the Seine, which I welcomed until the river became a dumping ground for murder victims and suicides. There was a small fruit garden in the back of the house and four well-appointed rooms. The charm of the house gave me sorrow; it was just the type of home I had thought once to share with Charles.

"It doesn't please you?" the chevalier asked, seeing my face.

"Not as much as it once would have," I admitted.

"You will be safe here. It is rented under the name of Madame Brizzard, and there are identification papers for you in that name. But I suggest you keep to your rooms, rather than going out. As you said, Paris is no longer a city of gay amusements. It does not do to call attention to oneself."

In the hall he pulled a cord and a male servant, bewigged and dressed in black, quickly appeared.

"Madame has arrived. You will see to her comfort." The servant bowed.

"A meal is already prepared," he informed us stiffly. His manners were courteous but his eyes closed upon me in judgment.

"He thinks I am your mistress," I said, when he had left.

"Of course. Would you have him know the truth?" The chevalier's smile was merry. I wondered if there was a secure lock on my bedroom door.

Over dinner, a wonderful meal of fresh bread, lamb chops and the first strawberries of the season, I asked de Rougeville how he had found me, having little else to say to him.

"It was not difficult," he said, wiping a crumb from the corner of his mouth with a new and spotless damask napkin. Everything in the *maison* was new. It was a little like being asked to live in a shop, or on a stage. "I bribed one of d'Orléans's men to tell me where they had searched for you, knowing that even with correct information they would somehow bungle it. As they did. I won't ask why d'Orléans has taken such an interest in you."

"And I won't tell you."

"Where were you, by the way, the day of the search?"

"In the attic."

He laughed with sincere pleasure.

"As I have always believed. It is the obvious that fools overlook. An attic! My word!"

"Without the help and friendship of Louise, who hid me, their search might not have been in vain," I said. "I was delivered of my daughter on that day, and in that hiding place. Speaking of that, I must ask a pledge of you. I will help you in any way I can, but you must make a promise first."

His eyes grew wary.

"The nature of the pledge?" he asked, his eyebrows shooting up in an aristocratic grimace. There were moments when the chevalier reminded me of Charles.

"That if anything should happen to me, you will see to the safety of my daughter, and that she is raised in a suitable environment. She must be educated. Her father would have wished it." I watched his face as he considered this. If he replied too quickly, without reflection, I would neither believe nor trust him.

172

He hesitated, and then replied: "You have my word, madame." He had pledged to me; I decided to trust him.

Aurore and I settled quickly into the cottage. It was a charming and comfortable little house, and in better circumstances I would have preferred no other living situation to it. The rooms were airy, the garden well-tended. Its only fault was really no fault of its own, but the fact that Charles was not with us. The place was right, but the time was wrong, the circumstances were wrong.

Still, we found an oasis of serenity within the cottage fence, which was covered with creeping pink roses. Left to ourselves—the neighbors did not call, I was after all a woman of shame in their eyes—we enjoyed our new safety, the abundant meals, the clear and warm spring weather.

Outside our walls, the Terror pursued its course through the city and countryside, with so many going to the guillotine that I feared Robespierre hoped to empty the streets entirely. France was surrounded by armies and battles, and the civil war spread to Marseilles in the south and Brittany in the north.

Inside the garden walls, flowers and fruit came to fruition and I measured time by the waking and sleeping of my robust infant girl. She was the steadying gravity that held me to earth, the sun around which I orbited.

De Rougeville feared that too much serenity would bore me. "Bored women are dangerous," he maintained, and insisted I resume my studies. Under his weekly tutelage I unwillingly progressed in my knowledge of English. He was a better instructor than Charles. Or perhaps there was less to distract me from my studies. By the end of the summer I could carry on simple conversations in that foreign tongue.

Sometime in that summer, while I held my child and dozed in the long rose-scented afternoons in the garden, Marie-Antoinette was taken from her two children in the Temple and removed to the Conciergerie. She, like her husband before, was to stand trial.

"Now, she will come with us," the chevalier told me, when he had the news. He visited once a week, and only for the sake of appearances, to keep up our charade of lovers. After our initial meeting, when he had kissed my hand several times and fussed over me, he adopted a formal and polite distance that would have made the righteous housewives of the street gape with surprise, had they been able to see into our private rooms. I, who had Aurore and the living memory of Charles, was grateful for his cold distance.

"While her husband was alive, she refused to abandon him," he continued. "And while her son was in her care, she would not leave him. But now they (and because "they" always meant the sansculottes and the Jacobins, he spat

173

the word angrily) themselves have separated the Queen from her son, and she will finally agree to come with us."

The Dauphin had been put in the care of a shoemaker, a disgusting creature named Simon, who beat the royal heir and forced him to wear a carmagnole and cockade and sing the *Ça Ira*. They were educating him to be a citizen, a sansculottes. They were trying to turn him against all he stood for, all his mother wished for him. I remembered my meeting with the child; he had been intelligent and loyal and brave. I did not believe Simon would have success with his project. But at what cost would that prince cling to his own ideals, to his love for his family and royal inheritance?

We were in the dining room, feasting on fresh vegetables from the garden and a ham from the larder. Those in the city without gardens were hungry . . . hungry in August, when the fields and orchards surrounding the city were heavy with harvest. Too many laborers had been sent to the front.

"The Conciergerie is the best-guarded prison in Paris," I said, putting one finger in Aurore's mouth so she could suck peach juice from it. I tried to imagine a heavy-footed soldier taking my girl from me; how the Queen must suffer, having been separated from her son.

"I will find a way. Never doubt it," de Rougeville said. "And once the Queen is safe, we will return her son to her." After lunch he walked with me in the garden and paused to admire a patch of red carnations. "This, for instance," he said, plucking a carnation and ruffling its petals. "It is full enough that a paper, a small paper, could be hidden within. What guard would suspect a carnation?"

In my garden began what was later called the Affair of the Red Carnation: de Rougeville, assisted by a gaoler who preferred a well-lined purse to revolutionary ideals, was able to exchange several notes with Marie-Antoinette by hiding the fragments of paper in exchanged flowers. She had no pen; her messages were written by a series of pinpricks. They were tedious for her to manage, but she had much time on her hands.

"Michonis is a greedy bastard," de Rougeville told me several weeks later. The carnations in the garden were beginning to fade from bright red to a washed-out brick color. "He has been expensive to bribe. But I have seen the Queen, and spoken with her." The triumph in his voice excited me and gave me hope. I had only half-believed in his plotting. Would we really rescue the Queen?

"How does she do?" I asked.

"Well enough. She is greatly changed in appearance, but her courage and spirit are as noble as ever." The lowness of his voice, the mistiness in his eyes, suggested that the chevalier loved not only the Queen, but the woman. I had suspected it. He was probably one of the dozens who had danced with her at a ball or sat next to her at the opera, and for that one favor swore eternal devotion. The higher-placed a woman is in the world, the more likely is she to command such love. And Marie-Antoinette, before her fall, had sat at the very pinnacle of all that was lovely and desirable in women.

August heat corrupted the city with the stench that every city breeds in summer, but that year the stench turned the stomach and burned the nose for it was the stench of blood and rotting flesh coming from the Place de la Révolution. The guillotine perfumed Paris with a scent made in hell and purchased by Danton and Robespierre.

I stopped watching the flow of the Seine through my bedroom window. Corpses floated in the brown, turgid water, along with the refuse caught by the slower summer current. There were those men and women who, thinking death had chosen them, would not wait for the guillotine but instead sought a gentler repose in the river.

I waited, grateful for each day we had, each day that brought Aurore greater strength and vigor to endure whatever hardship lurked at the end of this waiting. I knew our safety, our serenity would not last, soon we would have to begin our journey again and I did not know where the next path would lead.

De Rougeville always let a full week lapse between his visits, so when he came that day in September, two days before he was expected, my oasis of safety and serenity dissolved like a mist being dried by an overly strong sun. The time had come to put to the test whatever scheme the chevalier had plotted to rescue our Queen.

He was no longer nervous or angry but instead moved and spoke with that almost jubilant self-confidence that men of action display before the hunt or the battle. His sword, that day, was polished to a blinding sheen.

"Pack just one small bag," he told me. "Only what you need. We leave tonight at ten-thirty, and you won't be returning to this house. Tonight, we travel with the Queen, north, to safety."

At sunset I repacked the same valise I had brought with me, putting in my journal, a change of linen, one other gown, garments for Aurore. At the very bottom, wedged into one of my daughter's tiny new shoes of softest lambskin—a gift from the chevalier—was the Queen's diamond, the Golden Ransom. The size of it ruined the shoe, and that caused me regret. But tonight, the Queen would be taken to safety and I could return the gem. After tonight, my pledge would be completed, and Aurore and I could find whatever future we had in store, freed of that dangerous obligation.

At the last minute, I also packed a jar of preserved plums from the garden and that silly gesture gave me strength, as if clinging to reasonable domesticity could protect me from the madness outside the garden wall. What can happen to a mother who carries pickled plums in her valise?

The chevalier arrived with the darkness of the night, in a closed carriage. After he assisted me into the carriage I did not turn for a last look at the little house where I had known peace with Aurore. I was afraid that fear would turn me into a frozen pillar, like Lot's wife, who had not been able to subdue her regret.

We spoke little, and the clopping of the horses sounded loudly in the quiet streets where no other coaches or horses could be seen and, except for the omnipresent militia, few people moved.

"They are afraid to leave their houses," de Rougeville said with a bitter tone. "For that matter, they are just as afraid to be in their houses." The Jacobins had recently passed the Law of Suspects: anyone, everyone, was eligible to be arrested and beheaded without benefit of trial or even accusation.

As we moved through the dark and quiet streets, I thought of other evenings, other night trips through the city that had once represented to me all that was life, and now was filled with death. I thought of Charles, remembering how he had pressed my hand to give me courage. I had been afraid of pickpockets and thieves, salons and society. And of truth. How foolish I had been; all that mattered was to live, to be allowed to live. I hugged Aurore so tightly to me she cried in protest.

"Are you afraid, madame?" de Rougeville asked.

"I am."

"That is a good sign. Only a fool would not feel fear at this moment." He smiled, and pressed my hand, as Charles would have done.

"You have not told me what I am to do," I said.

"You have memorized our identification papers? Good. We travel under those names tonight. When we are stopped at the barrier, say nothing. Let me say all that must be said. For the rest, you merely wait."

"Wait? We only wait?"

"We will stop the carriage outside the Conciergerie. At the correct moment, the Queen will walk out of the prison, and join us in the carriage. Then, we will be gone, and quickly. Brace yourself for a jolting ride, later." He laughed at the look of amazement I must have shown. "I told you. Fools overlook the obvious. I did the most obvious thing to do in the circumstances. I bribed the guards. They will leave the gate open and turn their backs . . . just long enough, and no longer. We wait, but we must be quick when the moment comes."

Bells chimed the hour of eleven when we reached the Conciergerie. A large cloud slid over the moon and the evening became a still-life picture in black and white, with no color or movement in it. Candles burned in many of the windows, but their glow gave no solace.

De Rougeville handed me a nurse's smock; I was to put it around the Queen's shoulders when she arrived. Marie-Antoinette of Austria, ci-devant Queen of France, would travel disguised as Aurore's wet nurse.

De Rougeville wore a timepiece in his waistcoat. As we waited, the night grew so quiet I could hear it ticking. Somewhere in the Conciergerie a door was being unlocked. I imagined the key turning in the old, rusty lock, the creak of metal as it swung ever so slightly open, as if a strong draft and not a human hand moved it. I imagined a woman, a sorrowful woman who had lost husband and country and now son, tentatively trying the handle, which moved encouragingly under her touch.

I imagined her walking out of that cell, unsteadily, perhaps confused despite her knowledge of the plan. How far she had fallen, this woman who had danced on the parquet floors of Versailles and now trod the slippery, uneven cobbles of a dark prison passageway.

In my mind's eye I saw her make her way down that long passage, moving with unsteady footsteps to the waiting carriage.

A moment later, as both de Rougeville and I sat unmoving, not daring even to breathe, the large main gate opened. A woman stood there, her too-thin figure haloed in the darkness by a lantern behind her. Her beautiful auburn hair had turned completely white, her complexion was yellowed and waxy. Her shoulders slumped forward as if she had carried too many burdens on them for too long.

Gently, with no sound, the chevalier opened the carriage door. Without taking my eyes off that woman, who exuded grief like a strange, unearthly perfume, I moved out of the carriage and in her direction, the smock already opened to enfold her. Gravel crunched under my feet. Marie-Antoinette turned to me. Her stunned, frozen face was beginning to move, to show hope and relief and fear. There were only yards between us. Her eyes were unchanged; when she recognized me and gave me that sad sweet smile that was so distinctly her own, her eyes shone clear and blue as a lake under the moon.

"Come, Madame," I whispered, reaching my arms, with the smock, to her. "Come." She was still confused, perhaps too weary to care anymore. But she took a few steps and then leaned to me with her whole being, the smile still on her lips. She was just within reach.

And then the miracle ended.

The courtyard, no longer suspended like an image in a dream, sprang to life. The concealing darkness was shredded with the lights from a dozen lanterns, and voices rent the formerly still, silent air.

"There she is! Seize her! Seize her! The Queen is escaping, you fools.!"

I heard Marie-Antoinette sigh, saw the hopeless shrug of her shoulders as a guard sprang between us; two jumped out of the darkness and took the Queen by her arms, dragging her back, back, to the interior of that dark, loathsome prison.

I screamed and did not even know that I, too, was being dragged, but by the chevalier, who then pulled me into the already-moving carriage.

Shots exploded in the night, flashing through the spinning darkness as our horse and driver gained speed. The chevalier caught my arm in the door, I thought; my arm and shoulder burned with fiery pain. No time to think, to brace myself, the carriage jolted so roughly over the cobbles we were knocked back and forth across the seats. Aurore howled with fear, when I tried to pick her up my arm, which was not after all trapped in the door, wouldn't obey the command.

"It appears, madame, you have been shot," said the chevalier, himself picking up Aurore and cushioning her against his own chest. His eyes were moist, his lips thin with anger and frustration. "And we have failed."

The pain in my arm was like that very first time I met the Queen, after Mouret's rape. Someone had tried to close the carriage door on my arm. She had saved me. I hadn't saved her. No more memories, or thoughts or even fear. I fainted.

At the barrier, de Rougeville, composed again, shook me to consciousness. He threw his black coat over me to hide the bright blood now staining the side of my gown.

"You must get out," he said. "They want to search the carriage. I will tell them you are ill, but say nothing yourself. Do you understand?"

I nodded, although the earth was spinning too fast and the ground beneath my feet was anything but stable.

Rough, angry men pushed us aside and tore through the contents of the carriage. I bit my tongue to keep from crying out as they took my bag and emptied it into the mud of the road to search it.

Aurore's new shoes were dumped into the dirt and sat there like precious pink rosebuds fallen from the branch. The right shoe swelled with a bulk the left shoe was spared, but the militia did not notice, and they did not stop me from bending to retrieve my daughter's things. I moved too quickly and almost fainted again, but de Rougeville steadied me with his arm.

His answers were as smooth and courteous as their questions were insolent.

They detained us for a quarter of an hour with their paper stamping and searches and questions and helped themselves to the food hamper the chevalier had packed. Finally, we were allowed to proceed on our way. Out of Paris. To where? I was too tired to ask de Rougeville, even when the doors slammed shut and we were in privacy again, free to speak.

"Rest now," he said. "We have a long journey this night and can't stop for a surgeon until we reach our destination." His face was a mask, but his voice trembled with emotion. "We have failed the Queen," he said, turning away and staring out at the dark, forlorn landscape.

I have had many years to consider what went wrong that night. What occurs to me is this: de Rougeville, who believed so strongly in the usefulness of the obvious, himself overlooked the obvious. He either bribed the wrong guards, or the guard had been changed.

I woke in a room that smelled pleasantly of salt air. Waves lapped not far from the windows and for the first time I heard the haunting cry of seagulls. The ocean. De Rougeville had conveyed me to the coast.

The salt air was reviving; I sat up and looked around, admiring the pretty room, which was well appointed with a sturdy oak bedstead, table and chair. The table was covered with a lace cloth, and a large vase of autumn roses was centered on it. When I tried to stretch, I could not. My arm was bound tightly in a sling. Only then did I realize that I was not alone. In a far corner, busy with her darning, was a woman. Pristine white lace capped her black curls, her modest dress was all but covered by a huge apron. Madame Grenville looked up and stared at me with an intensity that made me lower my eyes.

She put her finger to her mouth, went to the door and put her ear against it. Satisfied that no one listened outside, she came to my bedside.

"Where is my daughter?" I asked. She smiled approvingly and left the room without a word. She returned with Aurore in her arms, and placed her gently by my side.

We studied each other, Madame Grenville and I. She, only a few years older than myself, was a formidable woman. You could tell, just by looking at her, that her servants neither stole from the larder nor used unsuitable vocabulary in her presence. And what did she think of me?

"You have been playing dangerous games with my cousin." Her voice was cold. She had nursed me, taken care of my daughter, endangered herself by sheltering us; but she did not approve of me. "No," she said when I made to answer. "Tell me nothing. It's better if I know nothing. How do you feel?"

"Perhaps a little weak, but well enough. My arm . . .?"

179

"It will heal, but with a scar. The surgeon said that if it is kept clean and not used, there should be no great difficulty with it."

A distant memory, as if from an almost-forgotten dream, of a white-haired man standing over me with a red-hot cauterizing iron made me shiver.

"You are lucky it was no worse," Madame Grenville said, her voice suggesting perhaps I deserved worse. She led an orderly life, and I had disrupted it. She answered my unvoiced questions.

"It would have been more dangerous to turn you away than take you in. That idiot de Rougeville came in full daylight so I had to pretend I was receiving expected guests. Not fugitives. But don't think I approve, madame. You have a child to care for. See to her in the future, and avoid intrigues. Now, I will bring you some dinner. But you are not to leave this room, do you understand?"

With dinner, Madame Grenville also brought my garments and travel case, which she had washed. I opened it quickly, as she watched, and took out Aurore's shoes. They had been cleaned of mud; the right shoe no longer bulged with its secret.

"They are of delicate leather," Madame Grenville said admiringly. "I washed them myself. The housemaids would have ruined them. Good thing for you I did so. The item you search for is now in a jar of cream at the bottom of your case."

I found the jar and plunged my fingers into it. The diamond was there, a hard and cold lump buried in a pool of white lotion.

Madame Grenville watched and her nose twitched with distaste. She thought me a common thief. And there was nothing I could say to make her think better of me, without giving away the secret of the Golden Ransom.

"You must never, never, mention this to me," she said. "I wish to know nothing about it."

I spent all of September in that room, watching ships come and go from my window and waiting for a message from de Rougeville.

It was clear that Madame Grenville's reluctant hospitality would extend just so far; she wished to be rid of me as soon as possible. But where was I to go? The revolution was behind me, the ocean in front.

"You cannot return to Paris," she told me one afternoon. "It would be too dangerous for the child."

"Paris is the only place I know," I said. It was the place where Charles and I had loved; it was the universe out of which I did not want to be cast.

"Well, then you must learn more of the world. For your daughter's safety."

180

She cleared her throat and paced for a few minutes, her hands clasped behind her back.

"De Rougeville left money with me so I could make arrangements for you," she said. "I have done so. I have purchased places for you on an American schooner which soon sets sail for America."

Madame Grenville smiled, proud of her ingenuity, and her eyes, watching me, were as blue and unplumbed as the ocean I must now cross.

PART

The New World

Pennsylvania 1793-1814

Here will I hold: if there is a power above us,
(and that there is, all Nature cries aloud
Through all her works) He must delight in virtue
And that in which he delights must be happy.

—Cato

I have always maintained that it is necessary to prove that man
is not at present a vicious and detestable animal, and still more
to prove that good management may greatly amend him. For
the moment that all men, without exception, shall be conceived
abandoned, good people will cease efforts deemed to be hopeless,
and perhaps think of taking their share in the scramble of life,
or at least of making it comfortable principally for themselves.

—Benjamin Vaughan

12

. . . the voyage to a new life . . .

Freedom suppressed and again regained bites with keener fangs
than freedom never endangered.

—Cicero

Of the voyage to America, there is little I wish to remember. I was between two continents, two worlds, between the sad past and unknown future, and often I stared at the great rolling green sea and thought it an appropriate symbol of the flux of my own life—and of the fleet-footed transitory nature of happiness.

But I traveled under my own name, the one Charles gave me, and was free to speak openly of my life and those parts of my past that could do no harm to reveal. Only those who have lost those previous things, name and private history, can know the joy of regaining them. I was no longer in hiding, for the first time in well over a year.

Overpowering the joy of new freedom, however, was the fact that I proved a most miserable sailor. I spent most of our five-week crossing in an abject state of greensickness. There were moments when I thought the guillotine not such a cruel manner of death after all.

Adding to my discomposure was the fact that I did not wish to go to America. I was a Frenchwoman, and a Parisian; I could imagine no life that did not include the fishwives of Les Halles and the gardens of the Tuileries,

185

despite their present bloodthirsty state. But as Madame Grenville continuously reminded me, I had no choice in the matter. I could not yet return to Paris, nor could I live indefinitely hidden in her spare room. She was most firm on that point. Go forward I must, and forward meant across the ocean.

She could have sent me to England, but there were no available places on any ships going there. And, although we never talked of these matters, she knew that I had been involved in a plot with the Queen, and that I had in my possession a diamond of menacing magnitude. The farther away she could send me, the more relieved she would be; she wished only to concentrate on the fall preserving and butchering and be done with more dangerous matters.

After Madame Grenville had finished her arrangements for me, the vessel waited for two weeks past the original sailing date, rocking gently and impatiently in the waves. That displeased the efficient Madame Grenville greatly. My sailing trunk, with its large store of preserved meats, ginger comfits, vinegar waters and jugs of wine, was ready for departure long before I turned to wave farewell to my anxious hostess.

The vessel on which my passage was booked was the *Sally*, a two-masted American schooner of slender, even fragile-looking, lines. It was anchored distantly in the southern entrance of the port of Le Havre, out of sight and, therefore the captain obviously hoped, out of mind of the tribunal officials who made sport of searching and ransacking commercial vessels for their own gain.

My first meeting with that captain, a Stephen Clough of Maine, was not successful. Even the comparatively short journey in the skiff that rowed me to the *Sally*, late one October night, had left me queasy and weak-kneed. He, a full-bellied, white-bearded captain who walked the deck as easily as if it were stable land and not quaking waves beneath, eyed me with obvious disdain.

"I'll be guessing this is your first journey by sea," he said, forming the words around a large pipe stuck in his mouth.

"It is," I said, trying to steady myself after clambering up the slippery ladder.

"Well, that bloody mess you Frenchies call a revolution is making unwilling sailors of many landlubbers." He studied my thin frame, my pallor, the arm, which was still in a sling, the other arm that carried Aurore, who was certainly too young for such a crossing, and the marks of my stomach's distress on my face.

"We shall hope you make it to the other shore. Meanwhile, stay out of the way. Stick to your cabin as much as possible." His voice was not

186

encouraging. Rufus Moody, the ginger-haired first mate, who was as talkative as the captain was taciturn, led me to my cabin.

The *Sally* was used mainly as a trading vessel, he told me, conveying Maine lumber to France and then returning to America laden with French goods. Because of its commercial nature—and the fact that the revolutionary government needed the lumber—the ship was allowed to come and go with little interference. Clough, whose foul disposition and mean aspect did not reach all the way to his salty heart, took advantage of that commercial freedom to regularly convey some irregular goods to America: French émigrés.

As Mr. Moody said that, I realized with a pang that I was now an émigré. No matter how casual Captain Clough's arrangements, even he kept lists and boarding journals, and eventually my name, on one of those lists, would be given to the tribunal. And I would be an enemy of the revolution twice over, because those who left France, the émigrés, returned only with the knowledge that they would be guillotined for their homecoming. I could not return to France, having once left it. Not until the revolution was past, I told myself. In a few months, because this insanity can't go on forever, perhaps in the spring, I will return.

"It is because of the lumber, which is important to the government—if one could call a mob ruled by expediency and murderers a government—that we aren't blown out of the water," explained Rufus Moody in vivid French. It did not ease my dark mood.

I shared my cabin with one Mrs. Carmichael Willetson, also of Maine, along with her black maid, Sarah, and my own Aurore. Mrs. Willetson, aged and even more opinionated than Mr. Moody, was appalled that I traveled without a lady's maid. She was appalled that I traveled with so few trunks, that I traveled with such a small infant, that my English was so poor; Mrs. Willetson was in a constant state of appallment. I decided I would spend as much time on deck as possible to remove myself from the immediate vicinity of Mrs. Willetson, despite Captain Clough's command to stay out of the way.

Even so, I quickly and unwillingly learned Mrs. Willetson's entire life story.

"I first crossed the Atlantic in 1747, with Mr. Willetson," she started in, even before I had set my trunk on the berth and begin to unpack. "Our wedding trip. Mama insisted we go back to England, the *only* truly civilized country in the world, before taking up our position and duties in Wicasset." She stopped and peered at me to be sure I understood this sly message: England was civilized. France was not. This insult to France made me realize that henceforth, I was a foreigner and therefore open to insult, as were all other foreigners, no matter where they were from. From now on, I would be judged against the cruelest, the stupidest, the most perverse or most backward Frenchperson that my future American and English acquaintances could recall. It is the way of the traveler's memory, to recall all that is wonderful about his home, and evil about other countries.

"We were the wealthiest family in Wicasset. Papa began the first salt works there," she continued with great excitement. "Lo, how the mighty are fallen!"

That was her motto in life: Lo, how the mighty are fallen. It was appropriate. Mr. Willetson sided with the British against the Americans, bringing about the fall that his widow relived daily, sometimes hourly.

"I told him he was backing the wrong side," she repeated over and over. "The Americans were willing to pay more for salt than the British. Besides, a man of sport and breeding always bets on the underdog. Any gambler knows that. And those Americans were surely the underdog. Never saw a sorrier looking lot in my life. Didn't even have proper uniforms, I told Mr. Willetson they would win just because of the shoddy way they dressed."

Mr. Willetson, for his loyalty, had his saltworks mistakenly blown up by the most civilized country in the world, and then was irresponsible enough to be shot in a pub brawl. Mrs. Willetson was left widowed and improverished.

Since then, she had traveled back and forth across the ocean, from relative to relative, never spending more than six months in one house. She complained it was restlessness; I think no one could abide her constant chattering and fits of appallment for longer durations.

All the while Mrs. Willetson talked I sat on my berth, stunned by this avalanche of words and protestations. Sarah, the black maid, stood behind her mistress. She was a study in solemnity from the neck down, with hands meekly clasped in front, toes pointed slightly inward. Her face, however, was alive with mirth. She rolled her eyes to the ceiling, pulled down her mouth, puffed out her cheeks, and mimicked Mrs. Willetson most cleverly. Sarah, aside from her dark skin and her habit of never speaking—indeed, who could speak when her mistress was present—reminded me much of Manon in her carefree days, and caused me much homesickness.

The third passenger was a Miss Ruth Dodge of New York who was returning home because she absolutely could not, she said, face another London season. Miss Dodge was twenty-nine and still a maid. She was plain and lacked vitality; even her great fortune had not been able to procure a husband in the London marriage market.

Most interesting about Miss Dodge was the fact that she had a cabin to herself; she informed me that the cabin had originally been reserved for a different passenger, who hadn't arrived. Her own booking had been arranged at the last minute.

That information, combined with a knowledge I gained by happenstance, caused me much speculation. Aurore, who enjoyed the salty, brisk air and the rocking of the waves, had lost a little ball on deck one morning. It rolled through the iron grating of the hold and I, kneeling on the planks, peered down to see if it could be fetched. The hold was quite filled with cargo, but the boxes on top surprised me. They were of good, strong wood, not the usual cheap packing material, and they bore labels showing they had come from Versailles. Aurore's red-striped ball rested between several boxes that plainly showed the Queen's insignia.

Some of Marie-Antoinette's possessions, it seemed, were being transported to America; a cabin had been left empty until the last minute and then given over to another. De Rougeville had once said that the Queen would begin a new life in a new world. I had thought he spoke metaphorically. But perhaps not.

Heart pounding so strongly I forgot my greensickness, I sought out Captain Clough.

"Captain," I called to him, clambering over great piles of coiled rope. He was reprimanding a sailor for some fault I could not detect, and turned to me with a sour expression.

"At your service. How're your guts feeling today? I understand you've had some loosening of the bowels. Mustn't get sick, Mrs. de Saint Remy, mustn't get sick." He routinely used such coarse conversation, I think, to embarrass us, so we would stay in our cabins.

"Much better, thank you," I answered, looking him straight in the eye.

"Glad to hear that. What can I do for you?" He grinned, impressed that his sailor's vulgarity hadn't caused me to blush.

"Captain, why was our sailing delayed?" I decided to be direct with him.

"'Cause the captain wasn't on board. Or were you in such a hurry, you would have the ship sail without its captain?"

"Why weren't you on board? Where were you? In Paris? I ask because I think we might have a friend in common, and I would like to know what has become of her."

"And what friend would that be, that you are so free with your questions?"

"The Queen," I said, taking a deep breath.

"Well, God bless us." He whistled, and looked away for a moment. "You're a brazen lass, that's for sure. If I knew ought, why would I be telling you?

189

You could be a Jacobin for all I know, the world is crawling with them these days."

"I'm not. I have risked my life for the Queen. I want to know what has happened, if, indeed, she was to have sailed."

"I can tell you what can be found in any newspaper, and no more. The Queen is standing trial, even at this moment. The trial began the day we sailed." And with that, he turned and left.

I would get no more from him. He was right to be suspicious; there were eavesdroppers and agents everywhere. But I paid careful attention during that voyage, trying to fit pieces together. Rufus Moody supplied the information that the *Sally* was owned by a Mr. Swann, who was a royalist, and sympathetic to the Queen's plight. Captain Clough of Maine, when he voiced political opinion, was also considered a royalist; in fact, there was a house in Maine that had been specifically decorated to suit the tastes of France's ci-devant Queen, although she had never yet visited it. Never yet, Mr. Moody said.

Years later, when we émigrés amused ourselves with tales of the revolution, one story I heard was of a Captain Clough of Maine. He had delayed his sailing from Le Havre in the fall of 1793 in order to go to Paris. It was believed he was involved in yet another attempt to rescue the Queen. He was almost captured and just barely made it back to the *Sally*, with a good number of the Committee of Public Safety close at his heels.

I did not know that at the time of the crossing.

But the more I thought and speculated, the more convinced I became that our missing passenger was Marie-Antoinette, and the thought gave me grief and hope at the same time. Another rescue attempt must have failed; but there were agents at work for her in many places. Certainly, and soon, one of those attempts must succeed.

My days on board quickly settled into a routine but not uncomfortable monotony. In the morning I sewed, having agreed to refurbish Mrs. Willetson's aging wardrobe in exchange for instruction in English. At midday I tried to eat some soup of salted pork and old vegetables, but usually could not. In the afternoon we napped, and if the weather was good went on deck for fresh air afterward.

In the evening, I mourned.

Most days, there came an hour, just at sunset, when the sea would grow calm, and the wind and waves would gentle themselves and my greensickness would ease. It was then that I grieved for Charles, and the farther from

France I traveled, the greater was my sorrow. It was like losing him a second time, having to leave behind those scenes and places of our life together.

Aurore was my consolation. In that grieving hour I would hold her to me too tightly, peer into her tiny, frowning face and examine over and over all those details that had originated in Charles: the imperious arc of the eyebrows, the depth of the green eyes, the somewhat stern mouth and the sheen of the black hair. Aurore would stand this for just a few moments and then howl, and I would have to release her, give her freedom. I learned much of love from my baby girl. She was learning to crawl and disliked being closely confined by her Mama. She was a favorite with the sailors, who liked to see her scuttle about the deck, and they took great care to be gentle with her and keep her out of trouble.

The crossing, according to Rufus Moody, was an uneventful one. I did not ask him what he considered an eventful crossing.

Because we had delayed and sailed late in the season, we encountered a fierce storm at sea that almost toppled the *Sally*. But it did not, Moody pointed out, although for three days we were tossed and slapped about by waves almost as high as our highest mast. I lashed Aurore to the berth and prayed constantly, stopping only to relieve my heaving stomach when needed. I knew what hell was. And when the storm ended and the wind and waves calmed again, I saw the St. Elmo's fire glowing in the rigging and learned a bit of heaven.

After the storm the food supplies on board went wormy and I ate only those things that Madame Grenville had packed for me. The preserved citron was a great favorite and packed in such quantity that I shared with Miss Dodge, Mr. Moody, and even Mrs. Willetson. We were nibbling at pickled orange peel when the second memorable event of our crossing occurred. Mrs. Willetson, who had been peering out her port window, spied another ship breaking the monotony of the endless grey-green horizon of the ocean.

"How fortunate!" she exclaimed. "Perhaps they bring us mail."

We went up for news, as there was already great activity on deck. Mr. Moody joined us. It was becoming noticeable that he spent as much time near Miss Dodge as possible.

"If they catch up, it won't be to exchange gossip," he said darkly. "It's a French frigate, a privateer."

"We are not a warship," Mrs. Willetson insisted. "What would they want with us?"

"Our sailors, our provisions, our guns and our cargo, for a start. And if they've been at sea long enough, our female passengers, too." He was grinning wickedly.

"Oh, my God!" cried old Mrs. Willetson, swooning, already fearful of being ravaged. "French pirates! The worst kind!"

"No," corrected Mr. Moody. "English pirates are the worst, because I deserted from a British frigate seven years ago, and if the limeys take me I'll hang from a yardarm." At that, Miss Dodge also swooned.

For the long day we, having been sent back to our cabin by a rough order from Captain Clough, watched as the second ship approached ever nearer, until finally we could count the guns on her sides and feared we would be fired upon. But the *Sally* proved her worth a second time; her slender lines gave her greater speed. At the stilled hour of sunset the other ship began to fall back while the *Sally* continued to forge ahead.

"She takes a fierce beating in a storm, but she's one of the fastest schooners on the seven seas," Mr. Moody told us proudly. "That's because she's slim and willowlike, with plenty of top mast." He looked approvingly at Miss Dodge, who was very thin but had a full bosom and was, indeed, top-heavy like the *Sally*.

It was, I had already decided, a perfect match. Mr. Moody had rough charm but no wealth; Miss Dodge had great wealth and no charm.

We survived the storm, the pirates, and the romancing of Miss Dodge by Mr. Moody, who made her love tokens of skewered raw turtle that sent us all scurrying to the buckets. And the day came when the sea seemed almost gentle and there was a different tang to the air.

Huge flocks of seagulls circled overhead, and the big fish the sailors call grampuses swam alongside the *Sally*, as if in escort. They played tag with the *Sally* like a group of school children and their black and glistening arching dives were delightful to see.

Mr. Moody told us we had reached a sounding of thirty-six fathoms, and that we would see land on the morrow.

The next day we sighted the coast of Maine. How beautiful it looked, with its steep cliffs and swatches of green meadow! How monotonous had been the ocean.

"That's just because you haven't looked enough at it," Mr. Moody told me. "When you get to know it, you see there are dozens of shades of green, dozens of ways for waves to roll and suns to set, and they all mean something, if you look deeply enough and let the sea teach you." He spoke wistfully; this was to be his last voyage. He and his bride would reside in New York.

"I'm content to know of land," I said.

"And I," agreed Miss Dodge, slipping her arm through Mr. Moody's with an almost coy and pretty gesture.

A few days later the great, green arm of Maryland jutted out alongside the *Sally*. I had traced that peninsula on a map, with Charles standing over my shoulder, less than two years ago, a lifetime ago, a continent ago. He had put his arm around me, I clearly remembered, on the day we studied Maryland. The arm of land also turned into a welcoming embrace, as the *Sally* rounded the point into the bay, past the small nestling towns of Newcastle, Wilmington and Chester, and then into the Philadelphia harbor.

My joy was as limited as that of a bird whose cage has been opened, but is still unable to fly. I had come to safety, but without Charles. And my Queen was still a prisoner, and I still in bondage to a pledge I had made her.

Captain Clough approached me that day and spent a companionable moment at my side, puffing at his pipe and hemming and coughing as if he wished to say something to me.

"You look sad, for a lass who's been dreaming of solid ground beneath her feet for weeks now," he began.

"I think of sad things. Although I will be glad to step on ground once again."

"I return to Paris in the spring. Soon as the weather turns good. When I come back, perhaps I'll carry that friend you spoke of before. Take heart."

And then, he was gone.

13

. . . the city of brotherly love . . .

Fate leads the unwilling and drags along the reluctant.

—*Seneca*

*P*aris had been a city designed to please gods and demons. Philadelphia sought to please mortals, those poor creatures in between the highest and the lowest.

No more the darkly dangerous alleys, high-walled secret gardens, great churches and mean hovels of Paris. The city I had come to was open and modest and perfumed with goodwill. This city of brotherly love set about instantly to ingratiate itself with the stranger, like a clever hostess seeking to woo a recalcitrant guest.

The cobbled streets were wide, and the sturdy brick houses set apart from each other by green expanses of lawn. Even on busy Market Street, where new shops lined up against each other as closely as schoolboys facing a strict tutor, there was still a feeling of friendly openness; the buildings did not threaten to swoop down and suffocate you, as they did in the Cité.

I cannot claim to have noticed any of this with an unbiased eye. I had been in hiding for well over a year, and had just spent a most uncomfortable five weeks on board ship; any architecture of land would have pleased me. I do admit that the more pleasant Philadelphia promised to be, the more I missed my unpleasant Paris.

194

Upon our disembarking, Rufus Moody helped bring my trunks to the wharf. Captain Clough, that busy and secretive man, was already nowhere to be seen. All was confusion, with visitors and relatives calling loudly to the disheveled passengers, apprentice boys scrambling for trunks, and sailors squabbling. But the air was cool with autumn and heavy with the smell of fish and salt and fried pastries, perfume and sweat. I inhaled deeply and approvingly the familiar bouquet of people and commerce.

Rufus Moody, clean-shaven of his ginger beard and dressed in new broadcloth suiting, hoisted Aurore up into his arms and gave her a smacking kiss on both sides of the face. "You take care of your mama," he told her. Aurore, unimpressed, grabbed a handful of his hair and pulled. He grimaced with pain but pretended not to mind as he put her down amidst the trunks and confusion.

"Perhaps you and Miss Dodge will have children," I suggested hopefully, and in halting English. His fiancée was already on her way to New York, to make plans with the caterer and minister. "Wouldn't that be pleasing?"

"It would, if they'd be as bonny as this one of yours . . . and as strong." He grinned ruefully. "Aye. I'm in for a pack of trouble, once I say my 'I do's.' "

Tears started in my eyes. We must say farewell, Mr. Moody and I. I did not want to. His was the last familiar face I would see for . . . for I didn't know how long. True, five weeks does not constitute a long or great friendship, but in those five weeks we had faced typhoon and privateer together; he had taught Aurore how to make a fiendish face, and I had helped his fiancée plan her wedding dress. Some families who have shared the same house for decades have less in common than that.

"Well, then," he said, clearing his throat. I cleared mine.

"Well, then," he said again, and then grabbed me to him in a bear hug that took away my breath. "I know you are frightened, but do not be. There's nought can harm you here. There is sympathy for the French, and you'll be welcomed."

Nought can harm me. Was there in the whole of the wide world really such a place, where nought could harm me?

Rufus Moody tipped his cap and handed me up to a waiting carriage. Away we clattered, from the *Sally*, the wharf . . . farther yet from Paris, and into Philadelphia. Oh, the ringing of iron-rimmed wheels, the chatter of people, the sights and smells of a town! How I had missed those things aboard the eerily silent *Sally*, where the music of waves and creaking rigging and timbers was the sound that rubbed raw rather than soothed my nerves.

When I let myself hope that my Queen would herself make this same trip in the spring, I felt the closest to joy I had experienced in many a month.

I shared the carriage with a stern Quaker dressed all in black, a wide hat hovering on his head like an overly large soup saucer. He eyed me with friendly speculation and patted Aurore's head.

"Thou be French," he stated pleasantly, running his somber eyes over the lace and furbelows of my gown and hat. I had thought them simple, even drab when Madame Grenville presented them to me for the voyage; in Philadelphia my French garments stood out like a peacock's plumage in a dovecot.

"I am Mr. Samuelson of Church Street," he announced gravely. This, I would never get over . . . the instant ease with which Americans exchanged names and even intimate details of digestion. "Thou be going to Azilum?" he asked.

I nodded, thinking he referred simply to refuge. I had not yet heard of the French town that was being built in the wilderness of Pennsylvania to shelter the great numbers of émigrés arriving in Philadelphia.

"I wish thee good fortune and a peaceful life. For thy little one, too." Aurore, newly shy with thumb stuck in mouth, watched him with equally serious green eyes and squirmed deeper into my lap. I nodded, wordless.

From the carriage window the murky waters of the harbor soon disappeared and, rounding a corner, the orderly, red brick city came into view. I stared out the carriage window, intrigued by my new and temporary home. Many of the people wore the plain black-and-white clothing of the Society of Friends. The women walked proudly in clothes that the poorest Parisian shopgirl would have disdained for their plainness. They walked in small groups, and some even alone, busy with errands. Charles had told me that the American women enjoyed greater freedom than the French, and would even stop and talk to men on the street, if they so desired.

Children played, fearless of traffic and strangers alike, on a wide expanse of paved brick surface between the houses and the cobbled roads.

"Sidewalks," said Mr. Samuelson with pride. "They protect us from the rudities of traffic. I have never traveled in thy Papist land, but I understand thou have no such thing there, and pedestrians must trod alongside carts and carriages and suffer whatever fate, and horses, put in thy path." He laughed at his joke, and the black hat bobbed up and down over his uncurled hair.

The carriage turned off Market Street into the section of Philadelphia known as the French quarter. The streets here were narrower and the more modest houses made of wood, not brick. The salty, sulfuric smell of the river was strong. Some of the houses were boarded and abandoned, their gardens as overgrown as those on the rue de Sèvres.

"The yellow fever," said my companion. "It struck hardest here, near the river. August, it was the worst. The fever always seems to come in the hottest part of the year, with the fetid air. No house was safe. There were so many deaths there weren't enough carts to transport the bodies. There are those who say the fever came in the ships that brought in the French from the plantations of Cap Français." He nodded sagely.

The revolution, by then, had spread to the West Indies and the French colony of Saint Domingue. Rich beyond compare with cotton and coffee, sugar and indigo, the colony was the envy of Europe. But the slaves, who outnumbered the freeborn French and Creoles by ten to one, rose in bloody rebellion when the revolution, with its cry of liberty, reached them. The islands blazed with fire and blood. Those French and Creole citizens who did not die, fled. Many of them had come to Philadelphia, where they were much in demand, socially, for their gracious manners and ghastly stories. But like anything imported in excess, they would soon lose their novelty and be nuisances rather than amusements.

"You think the Creoles brought illness?" I asked. If such belief was common, I couldn't think that French people in general would be overly welcomed, despite what Mr. Moody said.

"I think nothing. Some mysteries are penetrable only by the Spirit." He leaned closer to be heard clearly over the clopping of the horses. "Thou will want to leave the city in the spring, and not spend the summer here. The surgeons believe the illness will return this summer. Have thou means?"

Of this, too, Charles had warned me: "They think it is nothing to speak as openly of wealth, or lack of it, as we speak of titles and positions. They mean no offense."

"A little," I said. "But I had thought to stay in Philadelphia." I wanted to be near the harbor, to see the ships come and go and await the time when one would carry me back to France.

"Well, God will guide thee," he said complacently. I envied his conviction.

The carriage stopped in front of the Pension Rose Noir, a small, wooden house painted white and blue. But the paint was so old it was peeling in large flakes and the little house tilted towards its more substantial brick neighbor, as if seeking consolation. Pots of withered marigolds lined the four steps of the front entrance, their brown heads gone to seed and lightly coated with frost.

The driver, in a hurry to find other fares for his day's wages, tossed my trunks quickly to the sidewalk and then hurriedly handed me down from the carriage.

"God keep thee," yelled Mr. Samuelson as the carriage careered down the narrow street, the sound of his strange American accent growing fainter by the second. I turned and, balancing Aurore on one hip, lifted the brass knocker of the pension.

The door opened after a long while, revealing a rosy-cheeked girl of ample proportions who wiped her greasy hands on her apron before inviting me to enter. This was Beth McCrory, the upstairs maid, downstairs serving girl, cook, scullery and floor sweeper—in all, the only help that the proprietoress, Madame La Roche, could afford. She was only fifteen, but had a scowl on her forehead and glint to the eyes that suggested a matron of greater age.

She was mean, our Beth, but only by reason of her too-demanding chores. The pensioners, rather than be lashed by her sharp tongue, carried their own soiled plates from the dining room and did not fuss over bed linens that were washed on an irregular schedule, if at all.

"Lordy, lordy," she said that first day, glaring at me. "Another Frenchie. I'll fetch the missus. I suppose you'd better come in from the cold 'fore you take a chill and expect nursing."

More tentative and shy than I had ever been with the imperious Madame Bertin, I stepped into the narrow hallway, meekly and with flushed cheeks.

Madame La Roche appeared a moment later.

"French?" she asked, her own voice revealing an accent that brought homesickness. She was of small stature, and her pear-shaped figure was accentuated by the dated cut of her gown, with its wide panniers and tight, flattened bodice. She wore gilt timepieces criss-crossed over her bosom, as had Louise twenty years before.

I nodded.

"Two dollars a week for room and no board. And don't think to find cheaper. You won't. The French Welcoming and Charity Society takes up some of my costs." She nodded her head vigorously. Her birdlike voice was surprisingly businesslike.

"Agreed," I said. "But how much extra for one meal a day, to be taken at noon?"

She hesitated. And then: "Would the meal be sweet or bitter if the wine glasses were raised to the Queen?" Her strong accent left no doubt as to which Queen she meant.

"A toast to the Queen would sweeten any repast," I said. "I follow no political persuasion, but I am loyal to her." It felt as good as sunshine in winter to be able to say those treasonous words aloud. Mr. Moody had told me that in America all people were free to speak their minds. While history has exposed some limits to that freedom, I have always appreciated the principle.

"Then make yourself at home, for home you are, dear," said Madame La Roche, crushing me, with Aurore still in my arms, to her tightly strapped bosom. "The noon meal is included with the cost of the room, for royalists."

Thus, I made my entrance into the royalist society of Philadelphia. With freedom of speech comes the requirement to speak. I had never named myself a royalist, but only a friend of the Queen, but I could no longer avoid declaring one way or the other. I declared for Marie-Antoinette, and I would discover many others who had done the same.

Of course, there were as many Jacobins as there were royalists in Philadelphia, perhaps more. The revolution had not been left behind; it was there with me, in America, in Philadelphia, in the Pension Rose Noir. There was no escape, no absolute safety. But for the moment, I was safer.

A moment later Beth was grudgingly pulling and heaving my trunk into an upstairs bedroom. This small chamber was filled with mementos of Madame La Roche; dusty fans, dried nosegays, miniatures of small, smiling faces with resemblance to hers, opera programs and menus of festivities, all of which had taken place in Paris many years before. She clung to memories the way shipwrecked voyagers cling to driftwood, for such was Madame La Roche.

She had followed her husband to Philadelphia three decades before, to visit a grown son who had settled in the United States. It had been a more leisurely time when women could pack at ease, bringing chests of love letters, first fancy gowns, satin-lined boxes of children's outgrown garments, family silver, and sentimental sketches of sunsets over the Seine. The husband had lingered in Philadelphia, dabbling in gun powder manufactories, while his slender wife grew increasingly corpulent and homesick.

Madame outlived both husband and son, and found herself alone in Philadelphia, and then outcast from her native home by the revolution. Needing both income and companionship, she threw open her home to those more destitute than herself. The French quarter was filled with similar homes, similar stories.

"Coffee and bread is set out in the dining room at eight o'clock prompt," said Beth. "It's cleared even prompter at eight-thirty. If you sleep in or want coffee at any other time—I know how you Frenchies love your cup of coffee—you're to go around the corner to Fontaine's and buy a cup. Excepting the possibility of fever or childbirthing, there is no carrying of trays to the room," she continued in her young-old voice. "I've got too much to do to cater to ladyships."

"I understand."

Beth turned to leave and did not hold out her hand for a "consideration" as the coachman had. She knew better than to expect tips from the impoverished French émigrés.

"I do like young'uns, though," she added over her shoulder as an afterthought. "I've got four brothers and sisters in Germantown and I do miss 'em sometimes. You can leave yours with me in the kitchen some afternoons, if you need, and I'll see she don't eat gravel or scald herself." Distressed by her own softness, she then glared harshly at me and stomped out of the room. I was hungry, but terrified to ask for the forbidden tray.

Aurore and I chewed the last of our hard biscuits from the sea chest as I unpacked our few belongings. I hung my three gowns against the wall, put my journal on the night stand, and draped a crystal rosary—a farewell gift from Louise—over the dressing table mirror. Even though the room was exceedingly small, my few possessions gave little notice of my presence.

My first excitement at arriving had already passed. I was weary of being a stranger, of occupying other people's rooms, other people's homes.

But there was one more chore to do before I could rest on that soft-looking bed, close my eyes, and forget for a time all that I wished to forget, while remembering in dreams all I wished to remember.

I took the Queen's diamond out of my sewing case and stitched it into a corner of Madame La Roche's stained, yellowed quilt. The condition of the bedcover spoke of much time passing between washings, between being handled by Beth or anyone else other than myself; it would be safe there. The lump it made was only slightly higher than other lumps where the cotton padding had wadded up, creating hills and valleys of aged cloth.

That done, I lay down with Aurore in my arms and as we fell asleep I could still feel the rocking of the *Sally* beneath me. I dreamed it was carrying me back, in time and place, to France, to Charles.

My days in Philadelphia soon settled into a comforting regularity. Mornings began with a gathering of the pensioners of the Rose Noir in the dusty, lackluster dining room, for coffee and stale bread.

Phlegmatic Monsieur Debocco was always the first downstairs, pinching the rolls to find the least stale, and pouring half of the communal pitcher of cream into his coffee bowl before the others arrived. He was an elderly bachelor with grey, fuzzy whiskers lining his fat, pink cheeks and an absentminded air that was sometimes endearing, sometimes infuriating.

Next arrived Madame Brisset, full of spleen and announcing to Monsieur Debocco that he had failed to pay his wine bill. White-haired, tall and regal, Madame Brisset never let us forget that she had once been companion to Madame du Barry, mistress to the old King Louis. She was overly proud and addressed us as one would address servants, and was not much liked.

Beth, who soon knew almost all our secrets, once hinted to me that one of the pensioners of the Rose Noir was not as fond of Marie-Antoinette as was pretended. I always wondered if she referred to Madame Brisset. In the evenings, when our glasses were raised to the Queen, I would watch her sniff and wonder if it was dust or disdain that made her nose twitch.

I habitually arrived third in the morning order, in time to mediate the regular quarrels between Madame Brisset and Monsieur Debocco, who liked to dispute who had been richest before the revolution.

Last to arrive was dreamy-eyed Mademoiselle de Monquet, a pale blonde Creole of great beauty who, in her six months in Philadelphia, had already been the subject of two duels and one article in the *Courrier Politique*. The journalist had called her "Fair Queen of the Black Rose," but he had overlooked one other perhaps minor truth: Mademoiselle de Monquet was quite mad. She came to breakfast dressed in a ball gown, the huge, swaying skirt of which could touch two walls of the little dining room at the same time. And each morning she showed the same surprised consternation that the musicians had not yet arrived. Disappointed, she would glide back up the stairs and repeat her entrance three or four times to give the unordered orchestra time to arrive. Finally, weary and hungry, she would join us with a patient smile and sip from her coffee bowl as if it were a champagne glass.

Despite her constant disappointment, she was unfailingly gay and well-mannered. As her madness was a harmless one, we grew to love this strange and beautiful woman who believed life should be filled with morning dance parties.

After breakfast we cleared the table and straightened our rooms, even Mademoiselle de Monquet, who always worked with an ear cocked for the musicians who never arrived.

In the afternoon, I roamed the French quarter for hours on end, peering into shops and cafés where French was the accepted language, taking a quick cup of tea in dingy parlors where the conversation revolved around fondly remembered Parisian balls and theater parties.

And then, still not weary, I would carry Aurore beyond the safety of the French quarter into American Philadelphia, to Market Place which ran from the harbor to the River Schuylkill, or to the produce sheds of Front and Second Streets.

Here, the old fisherman, Benjamin, sat with his one-eyed orange cat, nodding in front of a small warming fire lit inside a bucket. The cat would rise and rub against my ankles in greeting and Benjamin, always eager for companionship, opened oyster after oyster for me, and took rock candy from his pocket for Aurore.

One day, feeling particularly energetic and not eager to return to the pension, I walked the length of the harbor, all the way to the northern liberties. There, rolling gently in the swell, lay the strange-looking ship that Benjamin told me was to be powered by steam, not wind.

"New fangled," he had hissed in a toothless snarl. "Steam is for teapots, not ships."

I eyed the eccentric, sailless vessel, thinking how much Charles, the student of mechanics, would have enjoyed exploring her works.

"Mama, Mama, the woman is crying" a young boy jeered behind me.

"Hush," said his mother. "She must be French."

As close as I was with my expenditures, there came a day when Beth, collecting the rent, saw me reach to the very bottom of my purse and search frantically for the needed coins.

"In a bad way, are ya?" she asked, no surprise in her voice. "Better have a talk with the missus." I purposely carried Aurore with me when we went to find Madame La Roche in the kitchen. I was terrified of being thrown out onto the street, and she had a soft spot for Aurore.

Her grey head was enveloped with steam from the canning pot. I heard her loud sigh over the bubbling of the water.

"Last year, I would have told you to go to the charities for assistance, but they aren't as open-handed as they used to be. There's too many, too many," said Madame La Roche, meaning us émigrés. "Normally, I'm a great respecter of privacy but, my dear, you must tell me about yourself, so we can find a solution to this problem. Have you property in France? We could find a speculator willing to buy it, although it takes years now to clear a title."

"I owned no property," I said.

"Family?"

"None."

She looked at me with great weariness.

"Your husband's family, then."

"They were against the marriage. I could not write to them."

"Explain, my dear."

"Charles's father was already on the verge of disinheriting him for joining in the American forces under La Fayette. When Charles returned and married me, his family made that estrangement final."

She looked at me with renewed curiosity. And then a glimmer of hope opened her eyes a bit wider.

"With La Fayette, you say? There is hope, then. I've heard that some of the French who fought here are being granted pensions. Perhaps you could apply for one in your husband's name."

"Senator Morris would be the man to apply to," said Beth with that bottomless information that canny servants often have. "Me mum's sister married a Frenchie back in 1777. He got blown to pieces in Massachusetts and she got a widow's pension, even though he weren't American. Senator Morris fixed it for her."

"Then Senator Morris you must see," confirmed Madame La Roche.

"I'll see him on Friday," I promised, newly fearful. It was Monday.

"You'll go tomorrow," Madame La Roche insisted. "There's no need to fear. He is a gentleman, and fond of the French. Besides, he is at home Wednesday evenings. If you call on Tuesday, perhaps he'll invite you. My dear," she exlaimed, "this is no time to be timorous. Senator Morris is second in importance only to Washington himself. It would be a great advantage to have him as a friend. You must do it. For Aurore. Dress in your finest. And wear plenty of rouge. You're far too pale."

And so on the morn, dressed in my finest and wearing plenty of rouge, I left Aurore with Beth and set out to ask charity of Senator Morris.

I had dressed with as much care as if I were once again setting out for an audience with the Queen. America allowed no royalty. But when Robert Morris walked down the street, people all but bowed. He was, at that time, the largest private landholder in the United States, owning properties in New York, Philadelphia, Virginia and Washington. He was also a member of the Azilum landholding company, although I had not yet learned of that.

The previous evening the Pension Rose Noir had been filled with stories, told for my benefit, of how this English-born American patriot had single-handedly supervised the financing of the American revolution. Power flowed to and from him the way lightning coursed up and down the strings of Franklin's kites.

Morris was quick to take offense, and slow to forgive, and won many enemies that way. He was greatly disliked by the Hamiltonians, who favored closer ties with Britain. And the French Jacobins accused him of royalist sympathies.

But he was steadfast in his loyalties, and in his deep affection for the

French, to whom he felt indebted for their help in the American revolution. More important, he simply liked the French, while he disliked his country of birth. Going against custom, he even sent his sons to school in Paris rather than London, and encouraged others to do the same.

In spite of having learned all that, I walked slowly. The first snow, pretty as confectioner's sugar, was drifting lightly over the city. My coat was not thick enough, but I was warm with nervousness. Inevitably, I reached my goal.

The Morris residence, at the corner of Market and Sixth, was just a stone's throw from President Washington's house. Washington himself had requested that his friend live in easy consulting and visiting distance. The houses here were of imposing size and grandeur. Dubiously, I knocked at the huge door. A black porter opened it and quickly showed me into a waiting room, without asking my errand. He must have seen a steady stream of visitors such as myself, whose need and despair showed in the too-bright patches of rouge painted over wan cheeks.

The waiting room was rich with Gobelin tapestries, a mahogany sideboard and French marquetry tables. It smelled of beeswax polish and last summer's flowers, preserved in bowls of potpourri. I had plenty of time to examine that room, to admire the portrait of the Morris family painted by Stuart himself, which hung over the hearth. The waiting area was filled when I arrived; it was emptied and the sun was low in the sky, when my name was announced.

"Forgive me, my dear, but I am rude enough to save the most pleasant interview for the last of my day," Senator Morris said, rising from behind his desk when I had finally gained admittance to that office. I had not expected gallantry, but was grateful that he tried to put me at my ease.

He looked much as Stuart had painted him, vigorous and virile and determined. Rigorously straight rows of powdered curls framed his stern face. It was not an elegant face; the nose was too large, the brow too deeply furrowed. But the mouth was sensual and the eyes piercing; they must have discomfited many a man who spoke words not in agreement with Morris's thoughts.

He looked like a man who has worked hard for many a long hour. His lace was loosened at the throat, his hands moved slowly, he only half-rose from his chair. His eyes quickened when they finally met mine, though, and I took pleasure in thinking that I awakened his curiosity. I moved with more confidence to the chair opposite his huge, paper-strewn desk.

"Madame de Saint Remy?" he asked gently. I nodded and smiled, resisting an urge to straighten his lace jabot. There are some people who, when we meet them for the first time, already seem familiar, even beloved, to us. Charles was one. Senator Morris was another.

"Tea," he said, not waiting for an answer. The tray was already there, on a Louis XVI sidetable. He poured from a huge silver urn enameled with portraits of Marie-Antoinette and King Louis.

"You have come for a pension," he said finally, after our tea cups were almost emptied. He was said to have the second sight; some even attributed his financial success to this inner vision of his. "Tell me, how did your husband die? I should mention that I remember him well. The Marquis de La Fayette was a frequent visitor to my household, and he often brought your husband with him. A most sincere and intelligent man."

"The Tuileries massacre," I said, putting down my cup, for my hand trembled.

Morris fidgeted with a small metal object I couldn't identify. Like Charles, he enjoyed mechanics.

"Ah, yes. That disaster. If only the king hadn't ordered his guard to put down their weapons . . ." He cleared his throat as if in apology for even that mild criticism of Louis. "I am sorry for your loss. I count it as my loss, too. Monsieur de Saint Remy was a brave man, and a friend." He touched the tips of his forefingers together, pressed them to the bridge of his long nose, and peered at me. "He married you after returning to France, did he not? You are young."

The late sun slanted through the window and brushed a hunt tapestry behind him. The drops of blood that fell from the deer's side glowed jewel-like and mournful. I nodded, thinking there was no knowledge of importance this unusual man could not discern.

"We—Charles and I—have a daughter," I did finally think to say.

"Children compensate for many griefs. We must see what can be done for you and your child." He rose then and, standing behind my chair, put both his hands on my shoulders. Such strength flowed from him to me that Mesmer himself would have envied this power. Without thinking, I reached up to grasp the hand of this man I had first met only minutes before. I wept, and he gave me his handkerchief.

"Come to dinner. Tomorrow, at four," he said. "We must cheer you. I will send my phaeton." He cleared his throat. The interview was over.

Madame Brisset was mortally offended. "A former seamstress! Invited to the most important salon in America!" A salon in which she, former member of Versailles and wealthy abbess of Notre Dame de l'Assomption, had never set aristocratic foot. "What is he thinking of?" she bristled in great agitation.

"My husband fought with La Fayette," I informed her cooly, newly aware of an importance I acquired through deeds with which I had nought to do.

"How lovely. There is sure to be dancing," said Mademoiselle de Monquet hopefully. She rose from her chair in the drab parlor and twirled. Monsieur Debocco watched her and heaved a sigh.

"You must wear your finest, and plenty of rouge," said a triumphant Madame la Roche, carrying in the evening lamp. We were only allowed one; oil was expensive.

"Perhaps not quite as much as today," I said. "I ruined the senator's handkerchief, and the American ladies seem more reserved in their use of cosmetics."

"Tch! What do they know! You must look your best!"

"I must," I agreed, determined to have my own way at least in this matter of rouge. I wished to do honor to Senator Morris's drawing room. French-women, especially young and handsome ones, were popular additions to American dinner parties. I wished to shine for him. Now, when the best that can be said of me is that I am remarkably well-preserved, rather like well-cured ham, now I can admit my vanity without apology. It was more than Charles's reputation that earned my first invitation into American society.

The next day witnessed an extraordinary amount of flurry in the Pension Rose Noir. Petticoats were newly starched, feathers steamed, the curling iron kept hot and to the ready all day. Midday dinner, for the first time since my arrival, was late and no one noticed. I was pushed and tugged and fussed over like a young girl about to be presented to the Queen. Mademoiselle de Monquet herself fitted her best ball gown to my more slender figure, sighing all the while over the dancing she would miss.

And at four o'clock promptly the tarnished brass knocker summoned us all to the hall, and the door was opened for the awaited escort.

My escort entered, stooping to avoid hitting his exceedingly tall head.

"Madame de Saint Remy?" he asked, looking back and forth a little wildly at the over-eager group that greeted him.

My escort, Henri Arraché, was a mere youth, with red hair and freckled face and arms grown newly long beyond his coat cuffs. He stared disconcertingly at the vast expanse of bosom that showed above the blue silk of my borrowed gown.

I offered my hand. He took it in a viselike grasp and gave it a wrenching handshake in the American manner, not the expected kiss. Yet, there was a French accent in his voice, an accent as tenuous as summer's memory of winter.

Turning away to kiss Aurore, who squirmed in Beth's firm hold, I felt

Henri Arraché's wide blue eyes linger on me. Aurore, filled with the unhappy knowledge that her *maman* was leaving, set up a plaintive wail.

"Little one," cooed the flaming-haired youth, trying to placate her, and he placed his huge hand on her small head. She stared at him and released such a shriek that he stepped back, intimidated.

"Better that we leave quickly," I said, smiling at his awkwardness.

With Senator Morris, that imposing, powerful person, I was quickly at my ease; with this raw, overgrown youth I was not. We rode in silence, each listening to the crunching of snow under the phaeton wheels, and thinking of nothing to say. Snowflakes fell onto Monsieur Arraché's beaver hat and the reddish queue tied at the back of his neck. His hair was unusual, combining palest blonde, fiery red and hints of darker brown, so that it seemed to always be changing hue, as the light on it changed. Louise's hair had been of similar color.

"Your daughter is a pretty infant," he said finally and with some effort, as if it had taken him the past fifteen minutes to prepare that simple statement. I hoped fervently that Henri Arraché would not be seated next to me as my dinner companion. As lacking in wit as his attempt at conversation was, I could make none better.

"She's much prettier when she's not crying," I said.

"Ah, well, that's the way with women." My young escort smiled and affected all the world-weariness and ennui of a jaded rake.

He drove like a madman, as seems to be the custom with young men. Rounding one corner I slid across the seat and thudded against his side. He reached out an arm to steady me. I was trembling with cold and with fear that the phaeton would overturn. He mistook my fear.

"There's nothing to be frightened of," he said kindly. "Senator Morris will see to it that you are comfortable. He and his wife are very kind, and genuinely concerned about the welfare of the émigrés in Philadelphia. He can be mean as a bear when he needs to, but nobody crosses Mary, or the guests under her roof. You may want to avoid mention of Genêt, or course," he added as an afterthought.

I had already been warned by Madame La Roche to avoid any mention of the Genêt affair. Feelings ran too high about it, and many of those feelings, at least in this matter, were decidedly anti-French.

By then, I had been long enough in the city of brotherly love to learn that its citizens were as vehemently opinionated as any other city's. And opinions were divided between two camps—the pro-British and the pro-French. Loyalties were shown in many ways other than political votes. The pro-French favored bright clothes and complicated sauces on their meats.

They used French interjections in their conversation, and boasted of the great help the French had given the Americans. And of the great assistance the French needed to achieve their own revolution for democracy.

The pro-British dressed in somber riding habits as often as polite manners allowed, disdained sauced food, and complained bitterly that American trade was being ruined by granting too many favors to the French and not enough to the British. Still recovering from their own war with Britain, they saw no reason why the United States should join in the French war against Britain.

The opinions, the year before, had broken out into violent civil unrest. There had been street riots and threats of lynchings. More than a few gentlemen of Philadelphia wore newly crooked noses or had gaps in their teeth for expressing the wrong opinion at the wrong time, and the fierceness of the battles had forced President Washington to take measures: the hurriedly passed Neutrality Proclamation had been intended to please both sides by favoring neither.

Unfortunately, at the same time that President Washington was signing the Neutrality Proclamation, a certain Minister Genêt, envoy of the French revolution, arrived in America. Ambitious and fast-talking, Genêt was not interested in neutrality or peace. He expected Washington to send money, arms and soldiers. Immediately. And in great quantity.

To prove his point, he went to Louisiana, recruited his own army, and then tried to take that territory for France, not caring at all that his rabble army had made people testy and suspicious. When that project failed, he captured and sailed an American frigate, flying the tricolor from her mast and pirating in the name of France.

He quickly did more harm in one year than a handful of wiser ministers could have undone in a hundred. But by the time he realized his methods lacked subtlety, it was too late. He was ordered back to Paris.

With excellent reason to believe that his head would be separated from his shoulders if he returned home, he instead stayed in America. He retired to a country house which was said to have two dozen bolts on each door. Out of sight, he was far from out of mind and his very name made tempers flare.

"I will not mention Minister Genêt," I promised Henri Arraché.

Light and music streamed from the Morris house. Someone was playing a polonaise on the harpsichord and the notes echoed in the still night. The tune was well-played but it increased my sense of separateness, made me feel like a playactor who had not learned her lines. It was a tune I had once heard with Charles, in a different city, on a different winter evening.

Mrs. Robert Morris, elegant, formidable, looking very deserving of her sobriquet of "Queen of Philadelphia," greeted me at the door. I recognized her from the portrait I had studied so long in her husband's receiving room; she knew me from whatever description Senator Morris had provided.

"My dear. Welcome to Philadelphia, and to our home." She kissed me on the cheek, and there was sympathy in her eyes. But underneath their warmth was a harder glint. I had no doubt that should I mention Genêt, or any other disaster, I would never again set foot in her popular parlor.

The house was bright with candlelight that illuminated rich tapestries, elaborate enameled silver urns, and crystal liquor decanters. Gentlemen in brocade jackets and powdered wigs leaned against the hearth in each room. Women with elaborate curls and old-fashioned panniered skirts clustered in whispering conversation broken occasionally by a gentle laugh. All was shining, elegant luxury.

Abandoned by our hostess, who had other guests to greet, I wandered the rooms with restless curiosity. Had Charles sat on that sofa, leaned against that mantelpiece? I, younger, would have been sewing for Mathilde in the rue des Anges when he was a visitor to this household. If some playful angel had spoken to me of all that was to come, that I would love and lose a man such as Charles, and then cross the sea and be welcomed in the second most important home of America, I would have been incredulous, to say the least.

Henri Arraché, taking his role as escort too seriously, hovered over me, tall, awkward and silent in these small pilgrimages to the scenes of Charles's own visitations. To be rid of him, I joined a group of ladies clustered on a yellow sofa. They had, I noticed, been closely examining my own gown and their looks of admiration gave me courage.

"It is French silk," one of them said, after we introduced ourselves. "French silk is impossible to get these days. And what an unusual style." Mademoiselle de Monquet's ball gown had a hoop, but no panniers. "Is it Parisian?"

"It was made in Saint Domingue, I believe." I accepted a crystal punch cup from a servant who carried a silver tray as large as a table top.

"You are Creole, then?"

"No, Parisian. The gown is loaned to me." They tittered.

"Ah, how sad!" they exclaimed, looking quite gay and satisfied. "To have lost title and all that goes with it!"

"No, I was not titled. I was a seamstress." They drew back in alarm, but I smiled. There were far too many Frenchwomen in exile who claimed titles and positions they had never enjoyed in France; I would not be one of them.

"A French seamstress!" the prettiest of them finally said. "How fortunate! Will you take orders? Are you in custom?"

I remembered the empty purse back in my room, the thinness of my winter coat.

"Of course. You may come to me at the Pension Rose Noir to be fitted." Their coldness disappeared. They all chatted at once with great animation. A seamstress with knowledge of Parisian styles, it seemed, was more interesting than a former marquise with dusty tales of court life.

Senator Morris spent much of his evening to-ing and fro-ing between his study and the parlor in serious conversation with small groups of somber faced men. Not until just before dinner was announced did he have time to greet me. He, too, eyed the gown with appreciation.

"Charming. You do us great honor, and I am pleased you join us. I only hope you don't find the company tedious. Many of the gentlemen are of an ungallant mind to discuss business, including your host, I'm afraid."

"I, too, have discussed business," I admitted. "Forgive me, but many of your guests will soon be customers of mine, as my skills as a seamstress have been made known."

He laughed with sincere pleasure. "It is the American way. We combine business and pleasure to further both. But now you must think only of amusement . . . I, too, will put away other concerns, if you will join me, madame."

He bowed and invited me to dance. Soon, troubles would pursue this man to distraction. But that winter, after the riots that had threatened him in 1793, and before the collapsing land deals that would eat his tremendous fortune in 1795, he was vigorous and successful and joyous.

It was the first time I had danced since Charles's death. At first it felt very strange, but the senator guided my steps and soon we were dancing so heartily that his queue swung over his back like a pendulum, and my skirts swirled. We pounded our heels on the fine parquet floor until Mrs. Morris's face darkened, but by then the music was finished, and her parquet was saved from further harm.

Only slightly breathless and smiling happily, Senator Morris took my arm and pointed me in the direction of the dining room. He handed me over to Henri Arraché, who was to be my dinner partner.

Dinner began with four cream soups. It ended three hours later when the remains of six roasts, a salmon en croûte, an acre of vegetables and enough pastries to satisfy all of the Cité were cleared from the table. Madame La Roche had warned me that the Americans were of formidable appetite. But the incredible amount of food proffered us had destroyed my appetite, not whetted it. Henri Arraché ate heartily of all the dishes and between mouthfuls he talked of horses, farming, blacksmithing and other topics of which I knew little and desired to know less.

I fell to daydreaming and moving chunks of apple clafouti in chocolate sauce from one side of my plate to the next. The ladies fanned themselves vigorously; men belched behind damask serviettes. Mrs. Morris rose grandly.

"Punch and toast will be served in the drawing room," she announced. "The President and his lady will join us."

If Napoleon, in a later year, had been able to announce a victory at Waterloo, his voice would not have been more triumphant. President Washington was a frequent visitor to the Morris home, but Mrs. Morris did not let routine obscure her sense of drawing room success. The élan of her voice impressed us all with the honor she was able to bestow on us. There was a slow scraping of chairs over the polished floor as we rose and made our stupefied way to the parlor.

The ladies, taking shallow breaths to protect already strained seams, regrouped around the yellow sofa. Henri, leaning against the mantel, his face flushed with wine, smiled and raised his glass to me. I, wearied of talk of horse breeding and wheat fields, tapped my closed fan on the side of my cheek. He did not know I was telling him his attentions to me were wasted. He winked.

Moments later George Washington, splendid in mustard silk breeches and crimson waistcoat, entered with Martha Washington on his arm. He towered over her, a tall, stern-faced man grown stout, sad and not easily won by the mercurial public. Thick-waisted Martha had to take two steps for his every one, yet they moved smoothly together in unison.

The cares of public office seemed to weigh heavily on the president. It was easy to speculate that even as he sipped punch and tapped his toe to a lively rendition of "The Fair Flower of Northumberland" he was deep in thought, scheming a way to reconcile his feuding ministers, Hamilton and Jefferson. He smiled only infrequently.

Mrs. Washington's round, double-chinned face echoed her husband's solemnity. Through war, revolution and the grief of a childless marriage, she had kept her place by his side. So tightly did she cling to his arm, with such devotion did she shield his large figure with her own smaller one, that when I was presented to him they bowed together over my hand.

"Madame de Saint Remy," said Senator Morris as the president made his awkward progress down the reception line. "Widow of our late friend, Charles de Saint Remy."

"I am grieved to hear of your loss," said President Washington, and indeed, his eyes, framed as they were by the deep, gouged lines of age, looked sad.

I wondered if he truly remembered Charles, or if he had learned to disguise distraction as sympathy. I curtseyed. Washington took my hand and pressed it gallantly to his dry lips.

Then, surprisingly, he asked me to step a reel with him. He took my arm in his, led me to the dance area, and guided me though the lively steps without speaking a word. He was a very nimble dancer, but his face never lost its grave expression. Only his eyes grew merry. And when the dance ended he kissed my hand a second time, and with greater warmth, before rejoining the patient Mrs. Washington in the reception line.

That is the story that my grandchildren beg to hear over and over. How the great George Washington, made even greater through the transformation of history into legend, danced with a French seamstress.

He and Martha left just moments later to return to the peaceful solitude of their own hearth. The room, which had been quiet, burst into conversation and Mary Morris shone like a beacon, so pleased was she that the President had interrupted his evening at home to honor her parlor.

I, however, grew nervous. Senator Morris hadn't said a word about my pension, and I was afraid that he had forgotten his promise. The amber-hued punch bowl was almost empty when he finally invited me to join him in his study.

No candles had been lit in that room, which smelled reassuringly of tobacco and leather-bound volumes. Only moonlight illuminated it with a gentle sheen that was most welcome after the frantic blazing of candles in the salon. We sat for some moments in silence, I afraid to speak, he not wanting to. He seemed to be breathing in the night, letting the stillness renew and refresh him for the task ahead. I was filled with foreboding.

"Madame," he finally spoke, pressing his hands together and touching forefingers to his nose, as he had the afternoon before. "Your pension will be granted. but I must tell you, it is not a large one. Not sufficient for your needs, I fear. Unless. . . ."

"Unless what? Tell me everything, the bad with the good." I smiled encouragement. It was impossible to feel fear with this man's intelligent, strong gaze on me.

"Would you accept guidance from one who has your best interests at heart? I will suggest a plan of action with which your husband would have approved."

"I will listen, and with gratitude."

"The pension, as I said, is not large. I recommend you invest it in land and a house. We have not much wealth, but we have much land, and it would be better to accept land, which remains, rather than money, which all too

212

quickly disappears." Morris was famous for his faith in real estate as the true fortune of America. His daring manipulation of land values was eyed askance by even his own partners. But when others questioned, Morris bellowed "Am I a man or a mouse?" and relentlessly pursued his goal of acquiring as much land as possible.

"Will I have enough, then, to buy a house in Philadelphia?" I asked, pleased.

He cleared his throat. "It was not Philadelphia I had in mind. It is becoming too difficult, too expensive here. I was thinking of the countryside . . ." He lit a candle then, and smoothed a map already laid out on his desk. "Here. We are building a colony . . ." and his finger traced a curving black line on the map, "on the Susquehanna. It already shelters many French exiles. The land is inexpensive and fertile, the countryside hospitable. We have named it Azilum."

I hesitated. I had not planned to leave Philadelphia and its harbor where, some day, a ship would carry me back to France. But his plan made sense. It would provide a cheaper means of living than expensive Philadelphia could, and Aurore would be safe from the threat of yellow fever.

My hesitation was short-lived. There are times when destiny holds out her hand to us and we must take it. The night I left Mathilde's room for Bertin's workshop was such a time; another was when Charles entered that shop for the first time. Senator Morris extended his hand to me, and we clasped fingers over the map of Pennsylvania.

"Azilum. When I was a child, I played a game of hiding in asylum. Now it seems a reality."

He smiled and kindly patted my shoulder as reassurance.

I did not know that the green crescent meadow on that map would become one of the great loves of my life. Yes, we can love noisy cities and nestling villages and quiet forest as much as we sometimes cherish the beloved who may inhabit those places. This life is rich with the possibility of love.

And danger.

When I returned to the Pension Rose Noir late that evening—early morning, really—I realized another reason to flee to the wilds. I, and the Queen's diamond, would never be secure in a city as crowded with strangers and varying loyalties as was Philadelphia.

When I returned that night, the stained ochre coverlet into which I had sewn the diamond was gone.

14

. . . the journey continues . . .

Hope, deceitful as it is, serves at least to lead us to the end of our lives by an agreeable route.

—La Rochefoucauld

I undressed and washed in darkness so as to disturb sleeping Aurore as little as possible. My head spun with wine and the honor done me by the president, and the plans made for me by Senator Morris. In darkness I climbed into the high four-poster and pulled the coverlet to my chin.

It felt smooth and cold beneath my fingertips. The ochre coverlet had been rough and thick.

Startled, I fumbled for the tinder box on my nightstand and lit a candle. Spread over me was not the old, ochre coverlet but a new blue damask one.

I jumped out of bed and flew into the hall, ready to accost and accuse a thief who by then, sense told me, was already leagues away. Turning in a circle with frustration and not knowing what to do, I spied light seeping under Madame Brisset's door. Age had robbed her of the ability to sleep long or deeply. But was she awake for another reason? She had never liked Marie-Antoinette. And she sorely regretted her own lost wealth.

How had she known? The important question, though, was not how or why the diamond had been stolen, but how I would retrieve it.

Eyes narrowed, I knocked loudly at her door. Too loudly. I heard other

214

sleepers rouse, other doors open, long before Madame Brisset's. She had stopped to don wig and rouge.

"Where is my coverlet?" I demanded with loud voice.

She looked at me as if I were a madwoman. "Your coverlet? Why ask me such a ridiculous question?" Her nose twitched and she looked down the length of it with cold, grey eyes.

"Because you have it." I tried to force my way into her room. She blocked my entry with a surprisingly strong arm.

"Nay, she don't," Beth called querulously up the dark stairwell. A stub of candle lit her red, sleep-swollen face and her white nightcap was crooked, but she looked anything but childish. She was furious at this midnight disturbance. I felt the first twinge of doubt.

"If you don't have it, I'm . . ." I started to apologize to Madame Brisset. She muttered "canaille" and slammed the door in my face.

"What do you want with that old rag?" Beth asked.

"I . . . I'm fond of it."

She snorted. "It's old enough that Methusaleh would laugh at it. I sold it to the ragman tonight. Didn't know you was so attached to it."

First came relief. It hadn't been stolen after all. Then, despair. There must be as many ragpickers in Philadelphia as there were in the Cité.

"Which ragman? Do you know?"

" 'Course I know, I got eyes in my head. Old Charlie Jones, he who has a shack down by the fishing wharf." She frowned deeply. "Frenchies. All lunatics, far as I can tell." She stumbled back to her quarters and left me alone on the stairs.

I found Charlie Jones's shack long before the sun found the horizon, long before the early-rising fishermen guided their gaily painted boats into the grey harbor. The door was not locked; indeed, it was so flimsy it would not have supported the weight of a bolt.

"Charlies Jones?" I called, pushing it open. "Are you here?"

"I'm here," a voice called from a dark corner. "I live here. But you don't, lessen I've died in my sleep and gone to heaven." The voice was old and mean.

The ochre coverlet was easy to describe, and almost as easy to find among the piles of rags and used clothing. But the price was hard to agree upon. I forgot my lessons of Les Halles and the Fair of the Holy Ghost market; I grabbed at it and let greed show in my eyes. I paid five times what he had paid Beth for it, but was content; the little bulge in the right hand corner indicated the diamond hadn't been removed.

215

After that escapade, I installed an extra lock on my door and would give the key to no one, not even Beth.

That, of course, caused many a raised eyebrow in the Pension Rose Noir. "She's probably hiding a varlet in her room," I head Madame Brisset say one morning as I was entering for breakfast. I flushed, but said nothing. They must think whatever they wanted to think . . . as long as it was not too close to the truth.

There was, at that time, considerable gossip among the exiles of a fortune in jewels smuggled abroad for Marie-Antoinette's later use. I realized that some, believing in fairy tales, might inadvertently trip over the truth. The diamond was rehidden in a bowl of potpourri put high on a shelf of the wardrobe, out of sight.

Still, I slept only fitfully and felt anxious whenever I was out of the room. Not for the first or last time, I wished that the Queen had consigned this gem to someone else's guardianship. But it was mine, and would have to be, until the Queen joined us.

Until the Queen joined us . . . lovely sounding words. I repeated them often, and feasted on hope that winter.

In early December Senator Morris sent his phaeton for me again, and spent a long afternoon giving me closer details of my new home. He spoke warmly of the perfections of the new colony, of its fertile fields, the gentle river that would provide both transport and communication with the more distant world, and the beauty of the setting.

He made it sound like a rustic idyll, a perfect place for the raising of Aurore. And while I could not imagine the delights of quiet country life for myself, I wished them for my daughter. Even Philadelphia, as distant as it was from the revolution, was not serene enough for my purposes. Opinions were too vehement, trouble too near the surface. It was too crowded, too volatile. Every so often we would hear of a French émigré who had been shot by a Jacobin, or of an American Jacobin beat by a former aristocrat.

I, known as a royalist, no longer felt secure. And, there was always the fear of yellow fever hanging over us. In the country, Aurore would be safe . . . and so would the diamond, and my pledge to the Queen.

I did not tell Senator Morris about the diamond or the pledge. He, in turn, did not inform me that French Azilum was intended to house more than fleeing royalists. Marie-Antoinette herself was to come there, once her escape, or release, was effected.

This I learned from hearsay. And the more I discussed my own plans with my Philadelphia acquaintances for removal to the new colony, the stronger did those rumors become that the Queen herself had agreed to the same plan many months before, when the colony was just beginning. In fact, it was speculated that the Queen planned this last-resort exile many years earlier, when the turmoil had just begun in Paris. There had been much commerce and friendship between these two countries, and the Queen had surrounded herself with young and adventurous men, many of whom had visited America and spoken well of it.

She, poised precariously between the old and the new, had chosen the new and put her faith in it.

Knowing this, I began to take a keener interest in the affairs of the émigrés and the attitudes of the Americans. Marie-Antoinette would need to have about her women who could inform and guide her in this new world. A sense of purpose filled my time with greater significance, and helped push aside my continuing grief over the loss of Charles. There was more to do now than just wait.

"How do the Americans receive news of the revolution?" I asked at dinner one evening. "Are they for the émigrés, or the revolutionaries?"

"Both," answered Monsieur Debocco, pouring himself more wine. "They are a confused nation."

"It is not confusion," said Mademoiselle de Monquet, smiling. "It is that they so delight in anything French that they like all French people, good and bad alike." We stopped our chewing to look at this singular young woman who believed good of all. With her golden curls, porcelain complexion and china-blue eyes, she was as unself-conscious as a child, in the way that mad people often are. Our gazes upon her brought a flush to those fair cheeks.

One morning I had thought to do the obvious, something that all the others had overlooked. I asked the young mademoiselle why she dressed for the morning in a ball gown.

"Why, it is a morning's journey to Bellevista, where the ball is to be held," she informed me sweetly. "Mama said I might wear my gown for the trip, if I promise to keep my shoulders covered against the sun. It is my first ball," she announced with great pride. And then she had leaned closer to me and whispered her great secret. "My first ball. But I already have a suitor. Alexandre has promised to speak with my father tonight. But you must tell no one." I promised, and then pieced together the rest of the story. She had never arrived at that ball; instead she had been put aboard a ship for America. Bellevista, one of the first plantations of Saint Domingue to be burned, was already in flames as she dressed for the ball that would not take place. I do not know what had become of her family, or of the Alexandre who was to speak to her father that night.

"It is as Monsieur de Crevecoeur said, 'There is room in America for everyone,' " said Madame La Roche, slicing a bowl of winter apples for our dessert.

"No, it is like the French proverb, 'Between two stools one sits on the ground,' " said Madame Brisset in a frosty voice. "Americans can't decide even a simple issue."

"They sit at the table with all of us, out of the largesse of their hearts," insisted Mademoiselle de Monquet petulantly.

"Don't talk nonsense, and don't confuse politics with gallantry," Madame Brisset reprimanded the girl. She was always as harsh with her as we were soft, having no room in her heart for youth, beauty and that childishness of thought that was part of the mademoiselle's madness. We glared at the older woman and Madame Brisset left the table shortly after.

"Off with her head!" Mademoiselle de Monquet remarked gaily. We laughed. Perhaps a bit of her madness touched us all. To stare down death, as many of us had before coming to the new world, is to invite madness. We were all desperate, and desperation is a stone's throw from that greater chaos of the mind.

"Well, well," clucked Madame La Roche. "I go to the cobbler this afternoon. Does anyone have heels that need mending?" Our young mademoiselle skipped from the room to fetch a pair of torn dancing slippers. She had, in the weeks since my arrival, found an outlet for her passion for dancing. She went nightly to the Hotel Oeller, much to Monsieur Debocco's dismay.

"That means she will be out again tonight," he sighed. "She dances indiscriminately with all who ask, whether she has been introduced or not."

"She is out of funds, monsieur. She wishes to find a protector." Madame La Roche was realistic in these matters.

"If we don't guard her, she'll end up in the third tier." He poured more wine and heaved a great sigh. The third tier was a special section of the Philadelphia opera house, where women of low reputation sat. The good wives of the city called it "the guilty third tier," and it was not uncommon for the harlots who occupied that tier to be taken to the harbor and dunked in the cold saltwater. Monsieur Debocco, who rather enjoyed mademoiselle's childishness of thought, was right to be worried.

I, too, began to frequent the Hotel Oeller, not for amusement, but to recruit more customers in need of a good, French seamstress. This hotel, located near the French consulate and St. Mary's Catholic Church, was a favorite gathering place of the émigrés.

Ladies who had once danced at the Bal d'Opéra of Paris, gentlemen who had played whist in the game rooms of the Palais Royal, found the Hotel

Oeller a gay, if unsophisticated substitute, and a respite from the drudgery of life in exile. There were punches made from French wine, music and blazing chandeliers, and a promise of gaity. All of us who attended mourned one or more loved ones and the Oeller ballroom was crowded not just with the French who did escape, but with the brooding remembrance of the many who did not. We all felt as if we should cast two shadows, not one.

On one of my last evenings there, I remember the conversation I had with the famous Nina Marchand, regarding those ghosts that followed us everywhere.

Monsieur Debocco had escorted Mademoiselle de Monquet and myself, for even in the midst of a world turned upside down Madame La Roche would not let two women wander alone into the evening. Mademoiselle quickly joined a reel gathering full force on the ball floor; Monsieur Debocco took up his station at the buffet, surreptitiously filling his own glass when the servants weren't watching.

I, counting myself as one of the older matrons who wished to hear the music only from a comfortable distance, took a table at the opposite end of the hall, where it was possible to converse or daydream, as one wished.

Nina Marchand invited me to join her. She, too, sat alone. Her husband, a wealthy farmer-general of Burgundy, had been guillotined and all their property confiscated. She escaped France in a rosewood trunk aboard a merchant schooner bound for the Bahamas Islands.

Sixty years old, she was yet one of the most astoundingly beautiful women I have ever met. Age suited her as well as youth suits most other women. Her naturally white hair was dressed simply, drawing attention to the marble clarity of her cheeks and jaw and full, rosy mouth. She always smiled, but it was a quixotic expression, inviting one to share her amusement. More impressive than her beauty, however, was her intelligence. She had read all the works Charles had required me to read. Unlike me, she had understood and enjoyed them.

"Time," she said that evening, turning her smile upon me. "We seem to have stopped time in its tracks. Or perhaps we just ignore it. It's as if a clock inside us had stopped ticking at one particular moment, and we will stay forever locked in that moment. Madame d'Arboisville, for instance," she said, nodding toward a table distant from ours. "See how she sits there knitting one warm woolen stocking after another for her son, Hébert. She goes nowhere without her knitting."

"That seems determined, but not necessarily strange," I protested.

"My dear. Her son died three years ago. And Madame Sallier. She wears that dingy gown not because she has no other, but because it was the gown

219

she wore when Monsieur Sallier was taken away. Hiding within it, she can pretend that he will return, that it is the same evening, the same place, the mistake will be rectified, and her husband quickly returned to her. And you . . . " She paused, not wanting to offend.

"Continue. What of me?"

"You talk of Charles as if he is still alive. His likes, his dislikes . . . you won't touch the punch if it contains giniver, as he did not approve of strong spirits. You express guilt for not having finished the volume of *Emile* he required you to read." She paused again, considering if she should say more. She did.

"Do you not consider the possibility of giving your heart again? You are too young to spend the rest of your life in mourning. You cannot stop the clock for long, you cannot hold time in one place. Consider, if you will, that crossing the sea was but one step in your journey. To live is to venture."

I was not ready to bestow on others what had once been Charles's. As far as my heart was concerned, I still found the memory of my husband more persistent, more vital than the promise of another alliance. But Nina Marchand was of different mettle. Ten years later she published her memoirs, which many critics likened to a female Don Juan's. She wrote in delicious detail of her many liaisons, in both Paris and Philadelphia, and made it clear that her heart did not dwell on past griefs. Too clear, perhaps, for some of the gentlemen mentioned. When the book first appeared in the Philadelphia bookshops there was a flurry of departures as aging patriarchs and young officials quickly decided in favor of a country retreat until the dust should settle. Ah, how we virtuous housewives smiled as we read those detailed, luscious memoirs behind locked bedroom doors!

I pretended to be unaffected by her words, but I was not. It was more than Charles I mourned. We had known great pleasure together, and I missed that physical intimacy that consisted of so much more than lovemaking. The hasty morning kiss, a touch of the hands over the dinner table, the sight of a man's naked loins as he bathed himself . . . the more I ached for those pleasant familiarities, the more I denied my need of them. I felt myself shrinking within my own skin, as if life were slowly draining out of me.

I busied myself with work, taking enough orders to keep me sewing from sun up to sun down. Once again I was a prisoner within four walls, this time bound by financial need and the duty to guard the Queen's diamond. But by Christmas I had enough money to splurge on a suckling pig for the pension, and new clothes for Aurore. That cheered me.

The holidays were a blithesome time. We spent precious pennies on boughs of evergreen to trim the parlor, and filled huge glass bowls with strong rum punch for visitors. Carolers livened the narrow, snowy streets of the French quarter with pleasant music, and in the evening we walked to St. Mary's to hear Christmas Mass. It was Aurore's first Christmas celebration, and we made it as gay as we could. She was taking her first, hopeful steps, preparing some day to walk away from her devoted *maman*, as all children must.

The second time that Henri Arraché came to the pension, Aurore walked to him on unsteady feet, laughing rather than shrieking. This pleased him greatly.

"I have brought the papers," he told me, shaking the snow from his hat and stamping his feet to warm them. I took his coat and hung it near the fire, to dry it. "For your homestead in French Azilum. Senator Morris sends them, and a list of supplies you will need. He asks if you will approve the list, and the expenses. I am to assist you. Ah. Thank you."

The last was addressed to Monsieur Debocco who had brought him a cup of spiced wine from the bowl. Monsieur mistakenly thought the young man was calling on me.

Henri Arraché accepted the cup and took a seat near the hearth, watching me with evident pleasure; I stared back at him in dismay. He seemed overly young to be put in charge of this venture. But I had no choice other than to trust Senator Morris's plans. I sat in a chair near Henri Arraché, and peered at the lists. They were incomprehensible to me. However, I pretended to study the papers for a long while, frowning over such unfamiliar concepts as seed potatoes and team oxen. I was to take up farming, it seemed, to provide an income, for my pension provided only land and house, and no annuity.

"I admit I know little of these matters," I said finally. "Do the charges seem correct to you?"

"They are fair enough. Senator Morris and I have already approved these. You just need to put your signature to them, and I'll arrange for the shipment."

A hint of masculine superiority in his voice irked me.

"I will go over these more carefully. And then send them back to Senator Morris," I insisted.

"Then I will go over them with you," Henri Arraché insisted, smiling. "Springs seems a long way off to you, probably, but there's no time to waste." Aurore clambered onto his lap and smiled up at me.

We spent many long evenings poring over house plans and seed lists. Henri Arraché was methodical and determined that nothing be wasted, no extravagance permitted.

"Roses?" he asked one evening, raising sandy eyebrows. "You have ordered rose bushes?" He sternly crossed them off the list and scratched over them, "two pear trees."

"Put the roses back on the list," I demanded. We eyed each other over the table. His eyes lowered first.

"One pear, one rose bush, de Brabant variety. It produces hips that will make a good winter tea," he compromised. Charles and I had not had time to learn together the gentle art of compromise. With this youth I learned to argue and bargain, to settle for less to gain more.

Even so, I learned little about Henri Arraché. His voice said he was of French birth. Yet he was American in all other things.

"Yes, I was born in France," he admitted unwillingly one night. "But America is my adopted home; my loyalty is to her. I have lived here a long time, and hope never to return to France."

"You hate France so much?" His voice had been hard with vehemence. But he looked up in surprise.

"Hate? France? What is there to hate in hills and roads and towns and those parts that make a land? No, it is not the country I hate but the people. And only a few of them. The revolution will rid the land of their vileness."

"The revolution has rid the land of many things," I said bitterly.

"Your husband. Forgive my thoughtlessness . . ." He was all hasty apology and reached for my hand, but I would not let him take it.

"You are a Jacobin, then?" I rose from the table where we had worked. Was Marie-Antoinette one of those vile people he wished Franch to be rid of? If so, Henri Arraché was one of the many people I could not trust.

"I am an American," he insisted. "France and its problems are nothing to me." He rose, too, and we glared at each other.

"I am tired," I said. He left, pale and thin-lipped.

I went to bed early, but did not sleep. Aurore was fretful and Madame La Roche, kissing her goodnight, had called her a poor, fatherless child, filling me with pity for Aurore . . . and myself. I tossed and turned, trying to concentrate on the instructions for setting in rows of berry bushes or the proper feed for a team of oxen. But my fevered mind saw Charles, his long limbs tangled in mine, the sheets roiled as whitecaps washing over our mutual pleasure.

Senator Morris and his wife invited me to a New Year's celebration and to several afternoon teas, and I was glad for their friendship. Madame Brisset had long since ceased speaking to me, but I enjoyed meeting those Americans who were friends of the senator. Also, I longed for news of home and thought that that distinguished parlor might have fresh reports of Paris and the Queen. But the *Sally* had been one of the last ships to cross the ocean that year; all the news I heard was stale. The Terror continued; the Queen and her children were still imprisoned. That was all I knew of Paris.

There were more pressing matters afoot in Philadelphia. The city was grown too crowded with émigrés and some of the Americans were less than good natured about it.

Monsieur Debocco was attacked by a gang one night and relieved of his purse and winter coat. When he applied to the Philadelphia charities for assistance, he was informed that the funds were exhausted. The subsidy for the Pension Rose Noir was halved, and our expenses thereby doubled, and that at a time when all prices in the city were severely inflated. At Fontaine's café more and more of us just sat and talked without ordering coffee or the proprietor's *coupe fantaisie d'Austria*.

I worked constantly but had made the mistake of accepting too many orders from those French who followed the old custom of ordering on credit, and paying as little as possible. I determined in the future to take only American customers who paid cash on the spot, and did not win many friends among the exiles because of that.

On top of all those other troubles, my room was broken into and ransacked by an unknown intruder.

It happened one night when I had been invited again to Senator Morris's. Henri Arraché was not at the senator's that evening. It was also the first time that all the other members of the Pension Rose Noir had also been out at the same time. My room was the only one searched. While the others were surprised by this, I was not. It was evident that the diamond was not as much a secret as I had hoped. D'Orléans had known of it, and spoken of it, and now someone was searching for it.

They had not found it. The out-of-sight bowl of potpourri still hid the gem high on the shelf. I wondered why Henri Arraché had not been at the senator's salon that evening. My distrust of him grew.

I realized that winter, my winter of hope, how much of our time is spent in waiting. I waited, then, for spring, for the season of deliverance, for the safe arrival of the Queen.

For Aurore, though, the present was a sugarplum already in the hand, the future a word she did not comprehend. All was new to her; snow, children carrying ice skates over their shoulders, the smell of baking gingerbread, the rose silk of Mademoiselle de Monquet's gown. The days when I tried to greet life on Aurore's terms, as a cause of immediate pleasure or distress and not a far-distant prospect, were the days I came closest to living as I had once lived with Charles, when life would again creep all the way to the ends of my fingertips and not rest in a twisted knot close to a wearied heart.

I grew fond of Madame La Roche and grateful for her devotion to Aurore. Months before I even began to pack, we quarreled emotionally over when I would return to Philadelphia from my country retreat.

"Not in winter," she said. "It's too cold and the roads too dangerous with ice. Aurore would take a chill."

"In spring, then."

"Impossible. The rivers will be high, the roads deep with mud. You will get swept away." She sniffed and dabbed at her eyes with the handkerchief I had embroidered for her Christmas gift.

"Summer," I suggested.

"No. It is too busy a time. You will disappoint me and not come."

Autumn, we agreed, would be the rendezvous time, after harvest but before the first snows fell. She went back to her kitchen to begin a new baking of gingerbread men for Aurore.

The snowfalls eased in March. My lists and orders were complete, and Henri Arraché made a quick journey to French Azilum and back to see how the colonists already there had fared over the winter.

"You will be pleased," was all he told me, and I did not question him. My immediate future was to be in that township, it was inevitable. Knowing I could not change my mind, I did not wish to know much about this place in advance. Let the fact of it be a sugarplum in the hand, not another distant worry.

In April, one fine morning when the sun was hot enough to make the dew on the roof steam toward heaven, my sea trunk was once again packed and I dressed in travel clothes. Aurore, sensing my nervousness, was fretful and I put my hand to her forehead constantly, to see if it was fever that distressed her, not just nerves. A dock hand who lived in one of the squalid sheds close to the harbor had collapsed in a burning fever the day before. It was not the feared yellow fever, but the scare made me eager to be away with my daughter to the safety of our country retreat.

I envisioned that retreat as a small and gentle village made of winding, cobbled roads, rose-bordered paths, pleasant little cottages and flowering fields where tame deer pranced. I would wear a straw hat and carry an ivory-tipped walking cane during langorous afternoons of picking wild berries. In the evening Aurore and I would read together, so that when we returned to Paris in a year or two, or three at the most, her native tongue would not sound strange to her ears. It would be a time of leisure and peace.

I forgot that wild berries have stout thorns, that deer are hunted creatures fearful of men, that the simpler a life is, the harder its work can be. All I knew of the wilderness I had learned from Rousseau's speculations. Thank God for the ignorance that gave me false courage.

Henri Arraché, dressed in sturdy homespun, arrived in a coach already overflowing with trunks and chests. He beamed with joy, showing a young man's delight with journeys and adventures. Madame La Roche snapped at him for bringing mud onto her carpets, but he gave her a big, friendly hug. The gesture, instead of easing her distress, set her to wailing and Henri, afraid of women's tears, retreated quickly back to the street with my trunk swung easily over his shoulder.

"In the autumn," I promised her, shedding a few tears myself. I had not wept on the day of Charles's murder; indeed, tears are most comforting when we least need them. She continued to weep and wail as my boxes were loaded, and when it came time to kiss Aurore farewell her white, round face was the very mask of tragedy.

Mademoiselle de Monquet and Monsieur Debocco stood side by side on the sidewalk. The mademoiselle was thinner in the face and thicker in the waist, the merriment in her eyes had changed to a desperate glint. She had found a dancing partner and a lover, but not a protector. Her conversation was increasingly disjointed, her madness more prominent.

"She was jilted by the soldier who promised to marry her," Madame La Roche's first letter to arrive in the winter would read. "The child is doing well and will probably survive, but mademoiselle has been taken to the asylum." Instead, the baby died and it was the mother who lived for many years, chained to the walls of the Philadelphia madhouse in a much less kind asylum than I would find.

Monsieur Debocco died the summer after my departure, of yellow fever.

But all that was in the future, and I bless the providence that keeps such foreknowledge hidden from us.

Two other women were already in the coach, a Mademoiselle de Rélevé, from Saint Domingue, and a Madame Guillemard of Poitiers. Mademoiselle de Rélevé was blonde and sixteen, and as silent as one of the stone nymphs of Versailles.

Madame Guillemard, thirtyish, was accompanied by three young sons, Jacques-Pierre, Louis and Antoine. Preoccupied as she was by those three, she presented no discernible qualities, either good or bad, except the constant desire to restrain her unrestrainable children. They were a storm of boyish restlessness and they crawled over their mother and the boxes on the floor like a litter of puppies.

"A pleasure to meet you," she said in a high, harried voice, but could not extend a hand to me for her round arms were each wrapped around a squirming dirty-faced child and the third was wedged between her knees.

"Henri, Henri! Will there be Indians?" ten-year old Jacques-Pierre wished to know. "We want to see Indians." His mother blanched.

We had been repeatedly reassured that the only Indians remaining in Pennsylvania were peaceful creatures who cared only about trade and hunting. "They pose no threat," we were told so many times that we became dubious. When men constantly seek to reassure, it is not reassuring. The three boys awoke our first fears with their clamor for great and bloody battles on the meadow of Azilum, and we laughed nervously.

"Jacques-Pierre, you will frighten your mother," Henri reprimanded him.

"Oh, no, no, I have no fear," said that frantic woman, making a quick sign of the cross over her bosom.

"Are the ladies ready?" Henri called back to us from his seat next to the driver. There was dubious silence; he took that for assent. The driver flicked his whip high over the horses' backs and our journey began.

I leaned dangerously far out the window, waving adieu to Madame La Roche. Mademoiselle de Rélevé broke her silence. "How the woman carried on, with that weeping and wailing!" was her dry comment. "You'd think we were going to the ends of the earth, not upper Pennsylvania!" She looked at me with eyes cold and blue.

Madame Guillemard, soon to be known as the peacemaker, nodded vigorously.

"If Jacques-Pierre, Louis and Antoine are to live there, it will be a wilderness soon enough," she said. "They have been too long without their father's guidance."

To prove their mother a liar, the three boys immediately stopped squirming and sat docilely on their seats, their faces filled with angelic patience. We were not deceived.

"Monsieur Guillemard will be joining us directly, when he leaves France." The unspoken "if" hung in the air thick as the smell of April rain. If he is still alive, we all thought. The thoughts and unspoken sentiments of the exiles almost always contained one "if."

"My mother and father are also arriving soon," Mademoiselle de Rélevé said. "My brother is not. He returns to school in Paris." Madame Guillemard and I lowered our eyes. Henri had already told us that this young woman's family had perished in the slave revolt, and she herself suffered a memory lapse, having no recall of the events immediate to her departure from Saint Domingue.

"Of course they will," Madame Guillemard said with such warmth that de Rélevé looked at her with suspicion.

We sat in silence for some moments. Mademoiselle de Rélevé soon brightened again. "I've heard that the Queen herself will be coming to Azilum," she said.

Madame Guillemard and I both cleared our throats and peered out the window without comment. The Queen's journey to Azilum had been spoken of before, but only in hushed voices. Never in loud voice, in full daylight among strangers.

"It would be lovely to be presented to the Queen," persisted the young woman. "My mother was presented to her before she wed Papa and followed him to Saint Domingue. I have the fan she received, somewhere here in my cases . . ." Her voice trailed off, her clear forehead creased as a memory tried to rise from some inner darkness and could not. She spent the rest of the morning staring out the window in meditative silence.

Aurore soon fell asleep on my lap and I, too, grew silent and meditative.

The first part of our journey was a trip of several days overland to Wilkes-Barre. All too quickly the paved roads of Philadelphia turned to rustic lanes and then to muddy paths cutting through forest and marsh. Houses and farms became one hour apart from each other, then two and three, appearing in the wilds like small oases of civilization in a world that still belonged to primal forest.

In Paris, one could travel hours out of the city and still admire well-built and heavily traveled roads, and small cottages flanking luxurious châteaux at regular intervals. In Pennsylvania, civilization ended so quickly it seemed to be a temporary truth in a universe of doubt.

Madame Guillemard and I agreed to pass the long hours usefully, by taking turns reading aloud. By convincing Jacques-Pierre, Louis and Antoine that they had been pierced by invisible Indian arrows, we could coerce them into playing dead, and remaining silent, for ten minutes at a time to accomplish this reading.

Madame began with a long passage from a collection of sermons. I followed with a scandalous passage from Les Liaisons Dangereuses. Paine's Rights of Man rested between us on the seat, unopened. Madame had need of spiritual enlightenment, I wished to be distracted; neither of us wished to contemplate politics.

After a very short time this reading plan was abandoned, along with Jacques-Pierre's, Louis's and Antoine's enthusiasm for playing mortally wounded and remaining silent. We squirmed and sighed and lapsed into private thought, for even heavily quilted petticoats are no protection against the rigors of long days of travel.

Then, trunks and boxes were transferred to carts, the coach was left at a farmhouse where we were served a rough meal, and we resumed the journey on horseback. It was my first experience with this mode of travel, and it quickly laid to rest my dreams of graceful canters through the forest paths of Azilum. I was nervous and uncomfortable on a horse; we arrived at no mutual understanding, that poor beast and I.

The greater my discomfort became, the more at ease was Henri Arraché. With each league we journeyed from Philadelphia, the young man became more self-assured. The wilderness suited him better than a drawing room. Aurore rode with him, and although there was little conversation between us, he seemed always at my side.

We entered a forest of extreme and savage beauty. It was a silent landscape of black and white, for here the spring had not yet reached and patches of snow still dotted the forest floor. Birds of every size, color and song winged overhead in noisy patterns. Marshes striped with last year's cattails led into giant groups of pine and oak, and the thin light that filtered down had a cold and frightening quality.

Our progress was hushed by a thick carpet of needles. No flowers yet bloomed and the world grew as quiet as the first days of creation, before the earth was graced with those things which delight and reassure the senses. I had never felt so distant from Paris, not even on the ocean during those misty days when water and sky met in an indiscernible horizon and we seemed to cross infinity.

All but Henri and the three boys grew heavy-hearted. When we reached Wilkes-Barre and saw the crude wooden houses and how quickly the forest and wild meadow infringed on the world of man, we grew yet more heavy-hearted.

There, we left behind the rented horses and hired a Durham boat and a guide, to take us upriver.

This guide was the most singular man I had yet met. His name was Alors Smith. His mother had been a Delaware who knew only one word of French, and it was her single comment when she was delivered of the son begotten by a French soldier. Smithy was bandy-legged from years of riding, and carried about him a stench that was even more singular than his name. His long hair of unrecognizable color was smoothed back with bear grease, his buckskin trousers and shirt seemed to be absolutely unfamiliar with soap and water. His vocabulary was such that I was thankful Aurore was still too young to understand much of what was said.

"He is the best guide on the river," Henri said apologetically.

I soon overcame my distaste for our guide. The wilderness sets different standards than a drawing room, and Smithy more than met those standards. We had to progress upriver against strong spring currents, and more than once I feared our flatboat would be forced against the destructive boulders of the riverbanks. Smithy, as strong as he was smelly, kept us on a steady course. With much cursing.

The ladies sat stiffly on the flatboat, handkerchiefs to noses, fearful of death by water. Jacques-Pierre, Louis and Antoine were delighted with this watery change of scenery, so much so that we spent many anxious moments catching them by their coattails to keep them from falling headlong into the swirling waters.

"Can't they sit still?" I asked in exasperation, exhausted and sodden with the recent effort of keeping Louis, who had been fishing with one of his mother's brooches tied to a string, out of the river.

Madame Guillemard shook her sad face and raised her eyes to heaven.

Smithy turned and leered at the three boys.

"See them trees up ahead, just past the curve?" he asked in a threatening voice.

The boys nodded, awed by Smithy's ragged raccoon cap and torn sleeves.

"If you three don't shut yer traps and stay on yer arses, quietlike, for the rest of the day, I'm gonna hang ya from them trees, and use ya for target practice. When yer half-dead I'll cut ya down and take those nice Frenchie curls of yers. Fetch about a sack of grain for each of 'em. Grain's more important than noisy boy children, any day." He tipped his hat to their shocked mother.

After that, the boys sat wide-eyed and quiet.

The river grew gentler, the afternoon warm, and the trip began to take on a dreamlike quality. Thick sun made me drowsy. Black flies buzzed overhead, and when I closed my eyes I thought I heard music. A gentle breeze made the new leaves of budding trees whisper, the water whispered past the boat. Henri's voice, low, deep, murmured things I couldn't hear. He was questioning Smithy, making lines, curves, on the map he was sketching. Aurore lay asleep in my lap, and I drifted.

"Are you happy?" Charles asked softly. He caught a flounce of my neck lace in his lips and worried it gently, it was night and his skin gleamed like an ivory idol in a darkened temple. His arms were around me. "Yes," I said, but I heard the sound of crystal being shattered, and it was my heart. A large piece of crystal flew out of my chest, leaving a bloody gap, but there was no pain. Aurore stood before me, tall and beautiful with her father's eloquent green eyes. She held the piece of crystal in her hand. Charles stood next to her, his arm around her shoulders. They turned away from me, they were leaving.

Henri leaned over me, concern showing in his young, sunburned face.

"Just a dream," I mumbled, still half-asleep.

"You cried out." He raised a hand to brush a wisp of hair from my cheek. I pulled away. Rebuffed, he returned to his seat near Smithy.

Madame Guillemard silently took my hand. She had been in Paris in 1793 and had seen the Terror with her own eyes; nightmares and dreams were something we all lived with.

After many days of wearying travel we entered that blue curve of the Susquehanna that I had first traced on Senator Morris's map.

My life has been circumscribed by water. In the Cité, the narrow dark streets had marked the earth like wide planks on a ship forging through the Seine. My journey to safety, to America, had been over water. This new home was arrived at by water, by the river I had first heard named by Charles. I was excited and hopeful.

We stood to see better, so that Smithy began cursing our impetuousness, but just when he swore we would all rock headlong into the river, the flatboat scrubbed against the shallow riverbed, and we came to a halt. There was an uncertain moment of silence. We had reached the end of our journey.

I saw a marshy field dotted with crude log cabins. The smoke from their chimneys rose only three feet above the roofs and then snaked back to earth, swathing the colony in sooty smoke. The wharf was a narrow plank walk thrusting into the river.

Everywhere were signs of recent construction which, to the uneducated eye, looked more like destruction. Tree stumps still sticky with resin, piles of logs, sacks of unloaded supplies littered the meadow. A half-finished tall fence leaned in the strong spring wind. The town of our deliverance, our safety, was no more than a muddy, trampled meadow on the edge of nowhere, a mere outpost, littered with the roughest of shelters.

"Where is the French town?" I asked, thinking this must be where the laborers lived.

"This is it," Henri said with pride. "It has grown tremendously since last summer."

"Indeed." It was all I could think of to say. I was holding Aurore tightly and had to be careful of each movement.

Madame Guillemard, however, acting on our group sentiment, did what any well-bred Frenchwoman of refined sensibility would do upon such a dismal arrival. She swooned. In a dead faint, she had to be carried from the flatboat to her residence, much to the crowing delight of Jacques-Pierre, Louis and Antoine.

15

. . . a new loss . . .

Console thyself, thou wouldst not seek Me, if thou hadst not found Me.

—Pascal

*I*t quickly grew dark. An orange disc of sun slipped behind the hills, and the colors of the day . . . the green of the landscape, the violet of Madame Guillemard's gown, the red glints of Henri Arraché's hair . . . turned to shades of grey as we unloaded the Durham boat.

Later, when my eyes grew more appreciative of the subtle colors of nature, I would admire the progression of green, purple and darkest blue mixed with black that the hills and forest would undergo at twilight. That night, my first, I saw only grey, and then darkness. I had never before known such overwhelming darkness. In the Cité there had been the candles of Monsieur Mouret's windows to help light the night. In the Palais Royal, midnight had blazed almost as brightly as noon. But in Azilum only small campfires and a handful of candles were lit one by one as night claimed the land. Their brightness seemed fragile and not reassuring.

We worked in silence. Our task might have been easier if I hadn't had to stop every few minutes and hold the salts to Madame Guillemard's nose. But her swooning, demonstrating as it did my own feelings, which I had not expressed as well, did not make me impatient.

However, the inhabitants of the Great House, hearing the commotion of our arrival, soon arrived with lanterns and helping hands.

Those two dozen people who greeted us had been there over the winter and their thinness, the desperation with which they greeted us, added to my terror. Most of them were aristocrats, and they approached with absurdly graceful steps, the women holding their gowns delicately out of the mud, the men posing with hand on hip . . . but their eyes, their eyes . . . I thought they would devour us alive with those hungry eyes.

Then I realized they were anxiously looking for one particular personage. They, too, had heard the rumor that Marie-Antoinette was to come to Azilum. Perhaps the boyish yells of Jacques-Pierre, who was of an age with the Dauphin, or a glint in the darkness of Mademoiselle de Réleve's reddish-blonde hair, which was not dissimilar to the Queen's, had awakened hope of the royal family's arrival.

To want something with that kind of desperation makes us too vulnerable, it leaves us open to all the evil, all the foolishness, of the world. When they silently ascertained that the Queen was not among us, their eyes thankfully changed. The somber mood lightened; some men even jested and women laughed lightly, as if carrying heavy travel cases through muddy paths in the darkness of a wilderness night was something they had always looked forward to with delight.

We were led in scraggly parade from the small wharf, which threatened to collapse back into the mud from whence it rose, to the Great House. This, in low whisper, was also known as the Queen's House. It had been built to shelter Marie-Antoinette and her children.

It was a log cabin an imposing eighty-four feet long. Indeed, it was reputed to be the largest log cabin in the country, and it occupied the center of Azilum in the way a queen presides over a court. Its wood-shingled walls and roof gleamed brown as fur in the darkness. The double front doors were so wide a team of oxen could march through them. Omer Talon, manager of Azilum, impressed a group of visitors later that year by hitching his horse team to a huge tree stump and pulling the stump through the wide doors into the huge central hearth, where entire trees could be burnt.

Four red brick chimneys rose from the roof. The moon had risen by then, and the chimneys cast large and eerie shadows on the meadow. The American laborers who helped build Azilum were most impressed by those chimneys, and by the very size of a house needing four huge hearths to warm it. They were also awed by the many large windows, all glazed with real glass. Most of the neighboring houses, I would learn, had open casements that were protected only by waxed paper or hides, or no windows at all, to make them easier to heat.

Inside, there were two floors with a large, wide hall running the length of each, with rooms opening off the hallway. Staircases leading up and down the higher floors were of polished rosewood, rubbed to such a sheen they reflected the fleur-de-lis wallpaper imported from France. But the bumps of the hewn logs underneath distorted the patterns of the paper.

The rooms were large and cold. They were bare by Parisian standards, but the furniture they did contain, the plush chairs, carved sofas, paintings and vases, were of the highest quality. Some of the furnishings had come from Versailles itself; I wondered if Marie-Antoinette had selected them for her exile.

My overall impression was not a positive one. The cabin, large as it was, was crude and ungracious compared to the homes of Paris. The setting was terrifying. Just as I forced myself to smile, to accept my own exile with good grace, I heard a bloodcurdling howl outside, and almost dropped the travel case I carried.

"Only a catamount," said a woman near me. "They don't come closer than the orchard. Usually. Still, it's better not to go abroad after dark." She smiled wistfully. "Of course, there's not much to go abroad for. After dark, or before."

I forced myself to return her smile and said, indeed, one could catch up on much reading, here.

"Something to eat?" she offered. "Perhaps you are hungry?"

No. I wished only to sleep.

Bertin's bell rang in my ears, loud and insistent. "Manon, what time is it?" I called, not wishing to rise. Manon didn't answer. I opened my eyes. The bell was still ringing, but she wasn't there, I wasn't at Bertin's. I was in a room I didn't know. Aurore, nestled next to me, was still asleep, thumb in mouth and cheeks flushed. The bell, whatever it announced, soon stopped, but I was wide-awake and a sense of misgiving would not let me return to sleep. Daylight flooded the chamber.

It cannot be as bad as it seemed last night, I told myself. Those dingy cabins, the hungry eyes of the colonists . . . surely that must have been part of a bad dream. I stretched sleepily and turned toward an open window. A lace curtain fluttered in the breeze, and that pleasant domesticity buoyed my courage.

The air certainly seemed good, sweet enough to taste and invigorating. The sun coming in the window was as thick and yellow as honey. The window itself was a good strong one, glazed with eight little panes set into a wood frame. Somewhat reassured, I rose from bed to look tentatively out that window.

Color had returned to the world. The blackness of the night was over and the sky was a blaze of blue streaked with violet. The river, which reflected a newly risen sun, was a golden ribbon meandering between green fields, and even the grey-brown cabins seemed more cheerful in the morning light. Dawn has a way of renewing whatever promises life has made us. I took a deep breath and even smiled, made braver by the new day. It will be an adventure, I told myself. Something to talk of when I return to Paris.

Aurore stirred. I dressed both of us quickly, and went downstairs, following my nose, to a long room where coffee and bread and huge platters of ham were laid on a highly polished but clothless table. Henri and a couple were already sitting there.

"An early riser. Excellent," said a woman I might have met the night before, but did not remember. Her hair was coiffed and powdered, she wore a formal gown of violet silk. She was thin, middle-aged, and even on the rare occasion of her smile her eyes showed rage, never joy. This was Madame Euphonie Marie-Hélene Farquet, once a duchess. She stiffly poured coffee into a chipped cup for me, and then tried to take Aurore from my arms.

"There is a nursery upstairs, madame. Surely you don't bring your child to table?" she asked coldly. Her eyebrows shot up to meet formal, white curls.

I protested and Monsieur Farquet, the woman's husband, put down a yellowish, dry-looking biscuit to speak in my defense.

"Rousseau didn't approve of many of our harsher practices. And they are both frightened, Euphonie. Let the child stay. This is Azilum, not Versailles."

"I know that all too well," said his Euphonie, but she gave up her struggle to ban Aurore from the table.

"Did you rest well?" asked Henri, when that small battle was over and won and Aurore was seated happily on my lap, messily sipping milk from my coffee saucer. "Madame Guillemard and Mademoiselle de Rélevé are still asleep."

"Well enough." I avoided his eyes. The boyish pleasure in them displeased me. In fact, I was angry with Henri Arraché. It was, I reasoned, his fault I was there in Azilum, and I did not wish to be there. Catamounts, muddy paths and unfriendly Madame Farquet had not warmed my feelings for my new home, and last night's sense of desolation had already returned.

"If you like, I will show you around this morning. You could not have seen much last night, as tired as you were."

"As you will." I refused to smile.

"I seem to have fallen from grace once again," he said, frowning.

"Whatever do you mean?" I frowned back at him, refusing to understand, to even speak the same language, for he spoke in English and I answered in French. More reasonably, Senator Morris, who made these arrangements for me, should have borne this anger, but he was not at hand.

"Perhaps later you will tell me why you are angry," said Henri Arraché, rising. "I will come back for you in an hour." And he skulked out in a most satisfying manner.

But the coffee was good, the milk for Aurore plentiful, and the morning still had a pleasant freshness to it that lessened anger and awoke curiosity. My anger with Henri was superficial at best.

After breakfast I returned to my room upstairs and shoved my traveling case under the bed, not knowing where else to hide it. Its false bottom shielded the Queen's diamond. I studied the arrangement with misgiving and many sighs, but reassured myself with one thought: the Queen would soon be with us, and the diamond returned to her own hand.

When Henri returned at the appointed time, I smiled and let him take my hand. My anger had passed, and was replaced by curiosity. I was here, and I must stay here, for the time being. Better to make the best of it as, it seemed, the Queen would have to do.

The tour of Azilum could have been accomplished in five minutes; Henri took several hours and would not relinquish my hand, once it was given.

My new home was, indeed, a frontier town. If I'd had any doubts the evening before, the clear light of day dispelled them. And we were to be colonists, bringing civilization to an area that before had been nothing but hunting ground or farmers' distant fields. Schufeldt's Flats it was called before Senator Morris and the Azilum Land Company bought up the acreage, thinking the locale would suit a queen in exile.

I plodded through the mud alongside Henri, smelling the piles of droppings left by the horses and oxen teams, listening to the crude songs of the laborers.

Most of the work songs were unfamiliar American ones, or even less familiar German or Irish ones. At that time, Americans and earlier immigrants greatly outnumbered Frenchmen in our so-called French town, and the handful of Frenchmen we had were not known for their industriousness. Many of them had hired laborers to perform the hard work of settlement.

At that early hour of the morning it was mostly servants and hired laborers who were about, not the French colonists themselves.

I thought of how foreign this place was, of how far we were from anywhere, and found it preposterous to believe that the Queen would willingly venture into this wilderness.

"The Queen will not be happy here," I mused aloud.

"Is she happy imprisoned in the Conciergerie?" Henri asked, watching me through narrowed eyes. "This is not Versailles, and that is in its favor. Nor is it a death chamber, as any room in France must be right now for the former queen. Here, she will be a mortal being, equal with all mortals."

"No. Here, she will be a queen in exile, awaiting, as we all do, the time when we may return to France. You speak like a Jacobin," I said.

"I am an American. I told you. Come. There is more to see."

At that time, there were some sixteen roughly built cabins lined on wide paths, which marked the meadow and met in a center market square. That square, like much of the town, was more dream than reality, a mere mark put on paper, not an actual achievement. It revealed itself as the town center because the mud there was stamped smoother than in the other parts of the colony.

Senator Morris's map of Azilum had shown streets, the central market, orchards, and other amenities. The actual village, as revealed by Henri, offered unpaved wide paths with mud so deep we sank into it up to our ankles. The paths were laid on straight lines, though, and crisscrossed each other in promising fashion, as if they might actually some day be avenues.

"The streets will be named after trees, as they are in Philadelphia," said Henri. "Oak, Walnut, Pine."

"Just like Philadelphia," I agreed, and he ignored the sarcasm in my voice.

The orchard was a field littered with the stumps of freshly felled trees, and only a few knee-high seedlings gave promise of apples and plums to come in any reasonable future. Where the mill was to be stood a grouping of straggly white pine. Where the chapel was to be was a dense thicket of briars. And all about us were burned-out campfires, lean-to's and other evidence of the gypsy-like existence of the laborers, and some of the families of Azilum.

The site was surrounded by dense forest and hills on three sides; the river made the fourth natural wall of our township. Immediately on the other side of that river stood a granite cliff of immense height. In the narrower parts of Azilum, standing between hill and cliff, you could imagine that you had fallen between a crack in the planks of the universe floor and would never be heard from again.

"Parts of the river must be dredged, to allow for river trade," Henri said. "Then, we expect the population to grow as high as five thousand."

"You expect much," I said.

Twenty-three French families were in residence. Some had had the foresight to rescue some of their fortune along with their lives, and so there were also a number of American and Dutch servants, and even a few slaves, although slavery was supposedly illegal. The families lived in their own rough cabins or in the Great House, if their cabin was not finished. The servants had rooms in the houses, or small sheds unattached and placed at the back of the lot. The slaves had been put in a row of shanties at the river's edge.

"Many are still unused to American ways. They will change when they realize the necessity for change." But even Henri's normally overly confident voice expressed some doubt. We were, by then, finished with the tour and on our way back to the Great House, where I had slept the night before.

"But where is my house?" I asked.

Henri pointed behind us. I saw a stone foundation. Nothing else.

"It requires further work." Henri laughed. So did Aurore, who had acquired a new habit of laughing when he did. I did not.

"You will stay in the Great House until yours is finished. It's comfortable, isn't it?" he asked.

"Very, if still a bit rustic."

"It is the most elegant house in this part of Pennsylvania," he said, irked by my indifference to the glory of the Great House. It came into view as we struggled through a patch of mud in front of a half-completed cabin.

"It is large," I admitted, pausing to consider it and not finding other words in its favor.

However, the Queen's House became the heart of Azilum, our goal, our dream, our pulse. The pianoforte in the music room, the dinner china, the silk curtains with their pale blue stripes, all had been selected for our Queen, to please her. There was even a schoolroom for her son, and a shelf of toys that included several balloons with gaily-painted baskets, for they were known to be the Dauphin's favorite toy.

Looking at the Queen's House, examining its still public rooms, for its rightful owner was not yet in residence, I could feel reassured. Something this large, this filled with hope, could not be disappointed. The Queen would come to us.

"And now, I must attend to other matters. But I would be honored to be seated next to you at dinner." He spoke formally, as if we were in a drawing room, not ankle-deep in mud. He seemed shy again and I forgot that we had quarreled just a moment before.

"If you don't lecture me about feeding oxen," I qualified.

He laughed. And then frowned. "I should warn you. Dinner in Azilum is more formal than you might have anticipated."

"I think I can manage suitable attire," I said.

I did. But barely. At four o'clock, when the inhabitants of the Queen's House gathered, there was enough lace, powder, pomade, silk and perfume to outfit half of Paris, I thought. The women wore low gowns with squared necklines, gloves, fans, curls and even beauty patches; the men were no simpler in their attire.

Outside was wilderness. Inside, there was French china and an assembly that would have been adequately dressed for a royal reception. Monsieur Farquet, I estimated, had over six yards of lace in his cuffs and jabot.

Twenty people gathered in the dining room for dinner, where French wine was poured into French crystal, in celebration of our arrival. I had brought Aurore with me and Madame Farquet again was disquieted by this. No matter how philosophers may paint us, not all women have a natural love for children.

"Ah! It is the devoted mother," Monsieur Farquet greeted me. "What a lovely vision, a madonna and child!" Madame Farquet's handsome head turned stiffly to regard her husband. Her eyes were the cold ones of a woman who has forgotten what love is. Not all love is lost through death; sometimes time itself is the thief that steals it.

I saw the way this haughty woman regarded her husband, the way she cringed whenever a night sound—a cricket, an owl, an unknown stirring—entered the formal dining room, and I pitied her.

Henri, as an official envoy from Senator Morris, made the introductions that night, both at dinner and after, when the other inhabitants of Azilum gathered in the music room, as was the nightly custom. The names blurred at first; I was conscious that Azilum held more erstwhile aristocrats than any wilderness colony should be blessed with.

Many of them were haughty in the extreme and held their crystal punch cups delicately between thumb and forefinger with the little finger pointed straight up to God, He who made them in all their glory. I thought the Queen, who had not liked stiff pretension, might find some of our company boring.

Monsieur Farquet, however, was amusing. Despite his six yards of lace at the wrists, he seemed truly to enjoy the challenge of the wilderness, and showed considerable enthusiasm. He spoke passionately of the joys of felling trees, clearing land, hewing logs and reading Rousseau by the clear light of dawn.

239

Judging by Henri's grin, however, I soon guessed that Monsieur Farquet knew little if any of those projects, despite his enthusiasm.

A Monsieur Moreau ate enthusiastically and silently, his eyes never lifting from his plate. He, a priest who had refused to pledge to the Nation first and the Divine Being second, had been forced to flee France when a more politically compliant priest had been sent to replace him. Monsieur Moreau was so silent, so preoccupied, I could only imagine he was busy conversing with the God who allowed those catastrophes. Judging by monsieur's expression, God was not explaining himself well at all.

Monsieur de St. Christophe, like Mademoiselle de Rélevé, was from Saint Domingue and this young man, with his watchful brown eyes, immediately took upon himself the role of mademoiselle's guardian. She spoke little and usually did not finish her sentences. Her eyes had grown even more vague since our arrival in Azilum.

"My brother relishes ham," she said during that dinner, delicately toying with a slice. "He will be . . ." Was she going to say pleased? We who knew her brother to be dead, said nothing. Monsieur de St. Christophe pressed her hand and urged her to try to eat.

There was also a Monsieur and Madame Gatereau from Lyons at table that night. He had been a silk merchant and was enthusiastic to learn that I had been a couturière and knew his goods. His had been the first silk factory to be burned in that city. If the quality of his relations with his workers matched the quality of the silk he had produced, the factory, in my opinion, deserved to be burned. That, I did not say. I let him boast of his brocades, although I had disdained to use them.

There was a Mr. John Keating, an Irishman of French sympathies and remarkable high spirits, also from Saint Domingue. He was a friend of Senator Morris who had whispered a warning about him in my ear: "Be cautious, my dear. The man appreciates beauty as much as the next, but never for more than a few days." Keating had lively green eyes, black hair that fell in spikes over a high and white forehead, and a keen wit that was the salvation of the dinner table; too many of us were prone to brooding. He made much of me and complimented me so often that Henri began to flush and drum his fingertips on the table.

Monsieur Talon, our colony manager and the builder of the Queen's House, was not with us that evening. I had looked forward to meeting him. As head of the King's secret police, he had spent many hectic years in Paris and Versailles and had treated with Danton himself to secure deportation papers for the royal family. The papers were not granted, and when his plans to take the King from France to safety were discovered, he himself had been forced to flee the country. He who had once been a governor of the Châtelet with an income of 100,000 francs a year, now was manager of a wilderness colony. There was said to be no man in the world who felt greater loyalty to the Queen and her children.

"Monsieur Talon is not with us," sniffed Madame Farquet. "He travels much. Not that I blame him. This is no place for a civilized person. I believe he is in New York this time."

"Yes, and when he returns I shall tell him that you criticized the gown the Queen wore for the New Year's feast of 1790. You know how he detests any slight of the Queen's taste." Mr. Keating, I saw, was teasing our haughty lady, but she, having no humor in her person, became quite enraged.

"I merely meant that the gown was not as suitable as it could have been. All those pink bows over simple gauze, when she could have worn lace . . ." She rose from table in her determination to defend herself. I searched my memory.

"Pink bows? Was the underskirt also white, trimmed with gold flounce?" I asked.

"I believe it was," sniffed Madame Farquet. "You, too, remember the unsuitability of such a garment?"

"I sewed the gown," I said. "It was made to the Queen's own specifications. Lace was already out of style by then." I stared pointedly at the lace overskirt and bodice Madame Farquet wore. I disliked her greatly.

"A seamstress! At table! This is the last straw! And one who does not know the correct tone of voice to use to her betters!"

"Sit down, Euphonie," her husband ordered. "The soup is getting cold."

John Keating, having started all this trouble, laughed merrily and winked at me. His good humor was infectious. I smiled back.

"And you, lass. You'll not be using that pert tone with our good manager, when he returns. He is no democrat."

I was humbled. And so John Keating achieved what he was excellent at, he raised my spirits and dashed them. Under his merriment was the dark melancholy of his race and all his wit and humor were tainted by it. He rode his horses at breakneck pace and delighted in long and hard trips so that we all feared that his moods and sporadic melancholy would put a quick end to his life. I am old now. But John Keating is older yet, and still driving people to distraction with worry.

He gave me fair warning, though. Talon was not a democrat. He was to be the most conservative of our colony, a man who would hear no evil of the King, Queen, or throne itself, a man who held infinite regard for the aristocracy and its outlawed privileges.

It is, I have noticed, often so with people who were themselves of low birth, as was Talon. Was not half my love for the Queen due to my own inability to achieve even a fraction of her greatness? We must have dreams, a chance to spy a little paradise on earth; little people must sometimes peer through tall, separating windows into the lives of the great.

It was Talon who had purchased and hand-carried to Azilum the toys for the Dauphin, hoping to amuse the royal boy during his exile and make up for past unhappiness. Talon who had chosen the French wallpaper and china and gilded mirrors of the Queen's House to charm Marie-Antoinette. I looked forward to meeting him. He would be, I believed, someone I could trust. Even so, I resolved not to tell him of the diamond and my own purpose for awaiting the Queen. I had been sworn to silence; I could keep my vow a few more short months.

Over dinner we talked of the opera, of Mozart, of fashions, and of cutting trees. We avoided discussing revolution, war, death and finances. We talked only of trivia, keeping silent about the things most on our minds and in our hearts. That is the essence of dinner conversation, even in the wilderness. We dined on thick potato soup, ham, and last summer's wrinkled apples.

When dinner ended we gathered in the music room. If the Great House, which was more commonly called the Queen's House, was the heart of French Azilum, then the music room was the heart of that house, and the pulse that would course through our world for the next decade. It was there we met, in joy and in sorrow, to receive news and gossip, to mourn and celebrate, to talk of thrones and crops.

By wilderness standards it was a glorious room, with a ten foot ceiling and a fireplace at either end of the long room. The floors were polished parquet, the walls papered in blue-and-white floral, the long windows draped with silk curtains. Sofas and chairs and love seats were arranged in small groups, and against one wall, between two windows overlooking the silver Susquehanna, stood the pianoforte, waiting for the Queen's own touch.

In this room, one could almost forget the dark wilderness that brooded outside the curtained windows.

We were of good cheer, that night, and hopeful. When Talon returned he would have news of Paris, for with the spring came the increase of communications, of ships and letters once again crossing the sea. Perhaps, we all silently hoped but did not say aloud, perhaps the Queen herself would return with him.

Madame Farquet sat down to play, her aristocratic back as straight as a rod, her fingers light and skillful on the keys, moving like a butterfly searching for nectar in the notes of the music. She played, "Oh My King, the

Universe Has Abandoned You!" from Grétry's *Richard the Lion-Hearted*, and when the last tremulous note died away there were few dry eyes left in the music room.

Madame Guillemard, in a paroxysm of emotion, fled the room. We knew she wept for her own missing spouse as well as our dead king. I followed her upstairs, and scratched rather than knocked at her door, as had been the custom of Versailles. We cried in each other's arms for several moments, and then laughed at our foolishness. Why despair? The Queen would come to us.

The days that followed suffered that same course—tears and laughter were in great abundance, we were as children who stumble and know not if they should pout or chortle. So much was novel to us, there was so much we must learn. If we were to succeed as a colony, if we were to make Azilum all that it could be for the Queen, and for ourselves, we must put aside grief and accept wholeheartedly the tasks before us. There was bread to bake, wool to be washed and carded, there were clothes to be mended, cows to be milked.

Those of us who found comfort in work—and not all of us preferred work to sullen laziness, I admit—rose with the sun and labored through the day. Idleness was treason. Each chore accomplished, each skill mastered, or at least attempted, was a paean of love for our Queen, who would join us.

And as the women learned to confront ill-tempered cows, pecking chickens and hours upon hours of straight-stitching to produce the needed linens, so did many of the men learn hard labor, clearing fields, raising fences, hauling stones.

That month was filled with the sound of progress, of hammers driving in pegs, of saws rasping through wood, of trees being felled and hewn into logs. For the Queen, we thought, each time we kneaded the sticky, uncooperative batters that would become bread. For the Queen, we thought, each time one more field was plowed, one more cabin completed.

Voices—English, American, French, German—wafted on the fresh breezes that brought the sweet scent of pine into the rooms of the Queen's House. The German farmers who surrounded Azilum came first out of curiosity, and then stayed to help. Not without pay, of course. Their labor rates were high, but we needed their assistance, and their knowledge.

Indeed, there was more we didn't know about our new life than we did. That was proven when Monsieur Farquet announced his tree felling contest one evening in the music room.

"Tree felling?" I look up from my sewing, grateful that Madame Guillemard's concert had been interrupted. She was a very enthusiastic, and equally unskilled, musician. She had been playing the same piece over and over, trying to perfect it, so she could play for the Queen.

"Monsieur Farquet is ambitious. He wants to clear another field before it is too late for the spring planting. Best way to do that is announce a contest. The first man to fell his tree wins all the rum he can drink."

"And the losers?" I asked.

"They win the same prize. That's why the contests are popular." Henri leaned closer and whispered in my ear. "If Monsieur Farquet wins, I will personally eat the tree he fells. He knows Rousseau, I admit. But he knows nothing of forestry."

The day of the contest was only two days later. Word spread fast and far, and many of our American neighbors came to share in the work and the later feasting and dancing to fiddle music. The morning air was acrid with the smell of sand and vinegar used to sharpen thick axes, and much betting was made on the outcome.

The ladies of the colony rose early and gathered in the huge kitchen of the Queen's House to supervise the cold meal that would be carried to the tree-filled Lot 17 in the southern pasture. We had an unspoken contest of our own to see whose voice could carry the loudest, and whose commands would carry the most weight.

Madame Farquet, as usual, gave promise of ruling the kitchen, but gentle-spoken, harried Madame Guillemard surprised us with a loud and vehement, "Do not, I tell you, spread the maple syrup on the biscuits! They will become soggy! What would the Queen think of soggy biscuits?"

By midmorning, when the sun showed through green treetops, the chickens, biscuits, preserves and cheeses had been packed and the ladies laced into their best gowns. The American women wore practical homespun and white aprons. We French stubbornly wore satin and silk in every color of the rainbow. They tittered about our foreign finery, but we held heads . . . and hems . . . high.

The meadow adjoining Lot 17 was embroidered with white-and-yellow wildflowers and the air was warm and sweet. It was a day beautiful enough to erase the memories of the unpleasant journey and my first disappointment with the colony. My hopes were new again, like the spring itself.

Henri, rule keeper of the contest, tipped his hat with a broad grin and explained the regulations. There was some good-natured quarreling among the French and American men who stood clumped about him, axes in hand. But a few moments later they all strode off in different directions, their axes gleaming, their faces determined.

Smithy appeared, grinning and hopping with pleasure. "There's danger and excitement in store when the Frenchie men take to the woods. Never know what'll happen." He punctuated his comment with a spit at either end and a chuckle in the middle. "All this, and rum, too. Damn."

Henri fired a pistol and soon the morning thudded with the sound of men hacking and slashing at huge trees. The trees began to creak and groan. When Delilah later told me that all living things had sacred spirits, I remembered the almost human moans of those trees.

The American men stood in one spot and aimed repeated blows into one area that soon developed into a pale, resin-weeping wedge. Monsieur Farquet aimed a blow here, removed a chip there, and hopped all the while around the tree in a kind of dance, lace cuffs flapping madly. There was, I saw, little science to the French method of felling trees.

Soon the Americans had hatched out large wedges. They gracefully stepped aside, gave a mighty push of their experienced arms, and three oaks fell in the forest of Azilum. Monsieur Farquet and the other Frenchmen were still doing their hopping dance. When a considerable girth had been opened and the tree started to sway, they dropped their axes and tried to assess which direction the falling tree would take. There was a long, mad moment as they realized they had guessed wrong and, zigzagging through the forest, made it to safety just seconds before the trees crashed down.

Monsieur Farquet, sweaty but gracious, added another keg of rum to the celebration from his own store and shook hands with the winners. Our picnic lasted until late afternoon, for we extended it with races for the children and then an hour of dancing to the fiddler's music. John Keating taught us a lively dance of hops and skips, popular in Dublin, and then sang a song that made the ladies blush. By then the barrels were emptied, the men were in great need of sleep, and they collapsed together in heaps, snoring and muttering with the ease of men who have worked hard and drunk well. The ladies, too, napped in the open, content as heathens.

I rested with my face pressed against the cool, sweet grass, breathing in the green scent. Madame Farquet, her long, pale nose jutting into the air like some exotic flower, condescended to ease onto her back, the blanket securely under her to protect her from contact with anything as lowly as earth. "Disgusting," she murmured just before she fell asleep.

I woke with a red nose and burning cheeks, which Madame Farquet deemed a great sin. She herself had preserved her lily complexion by resting under a beribboned parasol.

We returned to the Great House in trailing, disheveled groups with armfuls of tired and fretful children. There was a guilty air of conspiracy

245

about us; we had done the unthinkable. We had enjoyed ourselves, while the Queen was still suffering the trials of travel or worse, was still imprisoned.

And then, we became hopeful. Talon had returned from his journey. Dusk had fallen and all the windows of the Queen's House glowed golden with candlelight; Talon's horse, recognizable to others, was tethered in front, still lathered from a long ride.

Surely, finally, there was news. News of the Queen. Good news. Our waiting was over, or soon to be.

182 We rushed toward the music room, knowing that Talon awaited us there. But why hadn't he joined our celebration? He is tired from his long ride, I reassured myself. He was just about to come out to us, to tell us.

The double doors with their imported lace curtains were swung open. Talon rose from his chair facing the fire, and turned to us. His face was pale and lined. Weariness exuded from his eyes, his slumped back, the curious way in which he lifted his hands in greeting, and then let them drop limply at his side. He hesitated. Then he spoke simply and briefly.

"The Queen has gone to trial, and been found guilty. She was guillotined."

Our waiting was, indeed, at an end. And with it, our hope.

16

. . . a new goal . . .

*I had friends. The idea of being separated from them forever,
and of their grief, is one of my greatest regrets in dying. May
they know at least that my thoughts are with them until the
last moment.*

Marie-Antoinette

O ver the years I became a collector of details of the death of Marie-
Antoinette, once Queen of France. I was not there. But I feel as though
I was, so well have I pieced together and imagined that nightmare scene.

She passed her last evening on earth by writing a long letter to those she
was leaving behind. Were those hours long or short? What pace does time
use when we know it is coming to an end?

She addressed it to her sister-in-law, Madame Elizabeth, whom she trusted
above all other women. The Queen's thoughts were for the two children
she was leaving behind, and how they should be prepared for their futures.
She never once gave up hope that Louis-Charles would claim the throne
from which his father fell.

"My son must not forget his father's last words, which I expressly repeat
to him here: he must never seek to avenge our deaths," she penned quickly
and without blotting the paper. She faced eternity; she forgave her murderers and required her son to do the same. "May my daughter remember that

in view of her age she should always help her brother with advice . . . let them both remember that they will never be truly happy unless united."

That, too, must have been painful to write. Her own brother and all other members of her family had abandoned her to the bloodlust of the revolution. They could have rescued her a hundred times over. They did not.

She wrote through that long night, pausing perhaps to remember a yellow diamond, and a seamstress pledged to keep it in trust for that son and his future. She might have thought of that foreign land she had heard of, Pennsylvania, where it was said they had built a refuge for her. She would never see it.

Nor would Madame Elizabeth and the two children ever read Marie-Antoinette's last words. The letter was intercepted by her enemies and found under Robespierre's mattress at the time of his arrest, along with other personal papers of the Queen's.

Did she sleep? I think not. She would have lain awake, remembering her trial, the leering, cruel faces of her people, pointing, joking, making obscene gestures at their former Queen. She would have thought of her prosecutor, Fouquier-Tinville, and his one-and-forty witnesses, who repeated endless lies they had been paid to list in public, to defame her. Scullery maids who had never been higher than the kitchen cellar reported of intimate and treason-ous conversation between the King and Queen. Noblemen of dubious background and false credentials, who had never even met the Queen, reported seeing little pistols hidden in her garters, for use against revolution-aries.

Some of the fabricated charges would have made her smile. But only briefly. The charges, as patently false as they were, were a matter of life and death . . . her life, her death.

The last charge made by Fouquier-Tinville made her tremble in real anger and outrage. Until then her courage and her calmness had won her more than a few admiring friends in the gallery. The prosecutor was desperate for one last blow that would completely, irrevocably destroy her. He accused her of forcing her son into having incestuous relations with her. The Dauphin had signed a paper stating this to be a fact.

Serene, even detached, until that moment, she rose to her feet and turned to face the spectators in the gallery, who grew still. To be accused of such a hideous crime was more than she could stand. And he had signed that paper . . . she realized all too quickly what that meant. Her son had been forced to turn against his own mother.

Even the slatterns in the gallery thought that the prosecutor had gone too far with that charge: they hissed and threw things at Fouquier-Tinville's head.

The trial was brought to a quick conclusion. The outcome had already been known for many months. Robespierre wished to be rid of the Queen.

Those would have been her most recent memories, that last night. Perhaps she anticipated dawn with a heart that lightens when the end of a terrible journey is in sight. Her strength was almost at an end. But she had just one more chore she must do. She must die.

There were no candles in her cell. She waited in the dark and then rose when the small, barred window revealed the first grey light of dawn.

She dressed in unadorned white, keeping her back modestly to the door. She had been allowed no dressing screen, no privacy, to shield her most intimate actions from the view of her guards. She combed her hair, which had turned completely white although she was not yet forty years old, and placed a simple white cap on her head.

Samson, the executioner, entered her cell and brutally forced her hands behind her back, as if she were a common criminal. That was the only time she protested. "Louis XVI did not have his hands tied!" she reminded him, but uselessly. He bound her, and tore the white cap off her head. With long, gleaming scissors, the executioner slashed her hair away to bare the neck.

The King had been conveyed to his death in a closed carriage. They had allowed him that final reverence. The Queen was put in an open tumbril that had been used to cart manure. All could see her, and jeer at her. She kept her head high, as her mother, Queen Marie-Theresa of Austria, had taught her when she, still a young daughter, had been sent from home to be Queen of the greatest nation in the world. When she closed her eyes, did she imagine those jeers sounded similar to the yells of joy that had greeted her first entry into Paris? They had loved her once. Now they hated her. She had not changed. The world had. On the rue St. Honoré someone threw a rotten tomato at her white gown and it splattered, red as blood and odiferous, against her thigh.

The artist, David, saw her pass, and stopped to make a sketch. It is unflattering. He captured all the misery, but none of her grandeur.

The Place de la Révolution was filled with screaming, blood-crazed spectators and a large body of mounted troops surrounded the scaffold. The Queen was pulled from the tumbril and pushed up the steps to the guillotine. It was their haste, not her clumsiness, that made her trip and bump into the executioner. She politely begged his pardon.

The plank was pulled vertical in front of her; she was lashed onto it, the leather bindings cutting through her thin dress into her skin. The pain reminded her that though she was already in hell, she still lived, the nightmare was not yet ended. The plank was lowered into a horizontal position; the Queen looked down and saw the bloody receiving basket where her own head would soon fall.

The blade falls onto the white, graceful neck that had been kissed by a King and one other, her Count Fersen. Memory ends. Feeling ends. Life ends. A silence; the crowd is hushed. The Queen is dead.

The executioner, as he has been instructed, picks up the head to show it to the people. Cruel and excited by this deed of a lifetime—how many executioners get to remove a queen's head?—he slaps it. The head of Marie-Antoinette, severed from its queenly body, blushes with shame for her people.

Such was the death of Marie-Antoinette.

After Talon's announcement, there was little to say. We left the music room.

Aurore was asleep in my arms. I carried her up to our room and put her to bed. Then, I went to my sewing case.

I had grown careless in my safekeeping of the diamond. I had not even bothered to remove it from the false bottom of the case. I had felt safe in Azilum. It was not like a city, where alleys could turn into ambuscades, rooms easily ransacked by any of ten thousand thieves. And I had hoped, had believed, that soon the diamond would be returned to the Queen, and I would be free of it.

The yellow gem sparkled and flared in the dark room. It is difficult to hate something that beautiful. But I did. The diamond still existed. The Queen did not. Charles did not. How dare a mere stone count for more than life, more than love? For more than truth? I had deceived Charles with my many secrets, and the diamond had been one of them. How I wished to be free of that stone, and its burden of memory.

But what to do with it, now that the Queen was dead? What would have been her instructions?

I went to the sleeping Aurore and sat next to her, watching the delicate flicker of her blue-veined eyelids as she slept. Her hair was already as black as Charles's had been, her skin as fair. Every time I looked at her I saw him, and it was as if something warm and life-giving newly burned in my chest, like dawning love. She was my past, she was the love incarnate of my life with Charles. And she was my present, the thought that filled my days, and most assuredly she was my future.

The Queen had felt this for her son, I was certain. I had seen them together, seen the way the mother searched the son's face to see if he was well that day, if he was happy, or in some childish difficulty.

I knew then what I must do. The diamond had been given me in safekeeping for that son, not the mother. My pledge was intact, my vigil not yet over. My waiting was just begun.

I tucked Aurore securely into the bed, put the diamond in my pocket, and tiptoed down the staircase of the quiet, somber Queen's House, out into a dark and cold spring night. The diamond must be kept safe, and safe perhaps for a very long time. The river sang lightly on one side of me; I walked in the opposite direction, away from its music, toward the forest behind us. Owls called back and forth in the night and the yip-yips and howls of wolves sounded from a great distance. My skin began to prickle. I had never before been alone in such a vast and dark night, where wilderness is the cruel womb that casts us forth, frightened and solitary, into a world that is never truly safe.

Yet, I did not feel the fear I had often felt on midnight Parisian streets where, although there were plenty of lamps, there were as many dangers. The darkness, I told myself, is not a threat, only the things that are hidden within it. I walked on.

I found the tree that Smithy had once pointed out. It stood a hundred feet high and was called the Old Man of the Forest. The Indians considered it sacred; the French settlers considered it lovely, in a Rousseauish way. This tree would not be felled, it was safe. I dug a hole between its gnarled roots and put the diamond there, sheltered in a little wooden box.

A catamount growled from the next hilltop. I heard the crackling of twigs underfoot and, hurriedly replacing the soil over the box, ran back to the Queen's House.

The next day, all the mirrors and portraits in the Queen's House were draped in black. The lid of the pianoforte was closed and we spoke only infrequently, in whispers. We went into mourning for our Queen, and even the sun shared our grief. Thick black clouds had gathered overhead and the spring rains began that morning. Music and laughter fled like winged hope which will not be held in the hand.

I arose even earlier than usual, hoping to avoid companionship at breakfast, for my spirits were very low. The death of the Queen reminded me of all I had sought to forget: the bloody terror of Paris, the impossibility of returning there in the foreseeable future. I had been merry the day before. Now, I was disconsolate.

But there was one who rose even earlier than myself. Talon, looking only slightly rested from his journey, stopped me in the long hall and asked for a private interview, away from the others, as soon as I had taken my coffee.

There were deep shadows around his eyes and his mouth was grim. But even at that very early hour his hair was powdered and his coat newly pressed and brushed.

"I like to meet with all the new colonists," he explained. "Join me as soon as you are able." But I suspected he had purposes other than social ones for seeking me out. The former head of the secret police could not suffer mystery, and I presented him with one. Excusing himself, he made his way down the hall, limping in obvious pain. That handicap he had acquired during his escape from France, wherein he had been forced to hide within an empty rum cask for the entire sea voyage.

I dressed with care and applied rouge in preparation for this interview, dreading it, knowing he would ask questions I could not answer. I remembered to scratch rather than knock at his door, and curtseyed meekly when I entered, keeping my eyes downcast.

His modest office adjoined the music room downstairs, but thick walls and lack of windows made it a very private place. Talon did not offer tea and try to put me at ease as Senator Morris had.

"I understand you were in the Queen's confidence?" he began, as soon as I was self-consciously seated in his presence, a half-hour later. He frowned and looked very put out.

"No. I was merely one of many seamstresses fortunate enough to win her favor," I lied, keeping my eyes on the carpet.

"That is not how I understand the situation."

"Then your understanding is based on false assumptions."

I looked at him then, and we stared at each other for a long while, both accustomed to displaying stubbornness and falseness, in the name of Marie-Antoinette. I could tell him nothing, for she had sworn me to secrecy. And because he knew I was false with him, distrust showed in his face.

"You are not in a safe position. You need protection, and it would be better if you trust me," he tried again.

"I do trust you. But my relationship with the Queen was a simple one involving no confidences."

"I see. It is coincidence then, that the traveling wardrobe found in the carriage at Varennes was your work? Coincidence that the agents of the Duc d'Orléans were known to be searching for you, immediately after the Queen was imprisoned? Coincidence that the Chevalier de Rougeville established you in a *petite maison* while he planned an escape for the Queen?" There was triumph and challenge in his voice.

His face was close to mine, inviting me to unburden myself to him. I was amazed at the amount of information he had. But I could not speak. I stared again at the carpet.

He tried a new strategy.

"Your husband was a constitutionalist, was he not?" His tone changed from conspiratorial to hostile and dangerous.

I bristled, sensing what was to come. Talon was the staunchest royalist in France, the most conservative of the many conservatives. There would be nothing good he could say about Charles, who, though he had died in the Queen's service, had campaigned for the constitution.

"He was. But he never wished harm to the royal family."

Talon snorted and clapped his hands once, very loudly.

"Never wished harm? A Jacobin? You are ingenuous, madame. But be warned. There will be many that wish you harm. Some, because you are loyal to the Queen. Others, because they think you are not."

"I understand. And what of you? Is there now ill will between us?"

He smiled then, for the first time, and sat down across from me. The interview was tiring him and I felt a sudden burst of sympathy for him.

"Ill will? No. I don't think so. But I fear for you. And let me warn you. I have plans for this colony . . . plans that did not cease with the Queen's death . . . and if I discover reason to think you will impede those plans . . . you will rue the day I gave you opportunity to speak, and you did not."

He looked at me sternly.

"If you fear disloyalty to the Queen and her children, look elsewhere," I said, rising to leave. I felt very alone.

Grief is better borne in activity than in idleness. We continued our work, our chores. There was still much to do, if we were to survive the summer and the coming winter. And even beyond survival, we dared hope. Again. Marie-Antoinette's son lived. Talon had told us that the room set aside in the Queen's House for him would be kept intact. We could hope that someday the house would shelter the son, if not the mother.

Henri was everywhere. I could not turn down a stairwell, open a door, walk a forest path, without bumping into him. He pursued me, and I found it amusing, and sometimes irritating. With Charles, I had been the hunter. Now, I was the prey, the fox being run to ground. But I had no intention of being captured. He was only a youth, still gangly from too much quick growth, often shy, untaught in the subtleties of society. He was, in fact, only five or six years younger than myself, but he seemed younger to me because

Charles had been ten years older . . . and Charles was still the standard by which I judged all men.

In fact, there was something other than his youth, his lack of sophistication, that made me grimace whenever he presented himself too often in one day. He reminded me of someone, but I couldn't think who, and I, too, was losing patience with mysteries.

One early morning, when I was sitting in my bedroom with Aurore and remembering a different early morn, the day of her birth, I caught myself missing Louise. We hadn't corresponded since our parting in Paris. She didn't know where I was, nor did I know her whereabouts. I could only hope that she had made it safely out of France with her Monsieur de Bracy. At that moment, Henri happened to pass beneath my window. I knew then who he reminded me of. Louise. It was her red-gold hair, her white skin that tended to freckles, her high-arched nose, that his own features resembled.

Now this is what comes of too much grief, and too much change, I told myself. You are inventing phantoms, you are wishing for things that cannot be. But I could not put the idea out of my head that this Henri was my own lost Henri, son of Louise. I wished it to be so, because it made France seem a little closer, to think that lost child was so near.

I wished it to be so, and no one and no thing could prove it was not so. Henri himself had admitted a certain lack of certainty about his birth and family.

Even so, I still felt an instinctive distrust of him. Much had happened since this young man had been a babe-in-arms, and he was as much a mystery to me as I was to Talon.

"You don't smile as much as you should," he told me one day, trying to take my chin in his hand. I stepped back from this young man who spoke so vehemently against the old order in favor of the new. In his presence I felt torn between my loyalty to the Queen and my even older love for Louise and her infant.

"There is much on my mind," I answered, and quickly chose one topic I thought would be safe. "My cabin, for one thing. When will it be finished?"

"Soon. Will that please you? I want you to be content in Azilum, so you won't leave."

"Leave?" I stared at him incredulously. "Where would I go?"

It was an oft-thought, little voiced question in the days following the news of the Queen's death. We had come to join her in exile, but having come, found we could not leave. Philadelphia was swollen with émigrés from France and Saint Domingue and the original warm welcomes for the exiled French were quickly cooling. There were bitter political feuds, and the expense of caring for the many impoverished émigrés was become too costly. The poorhouses of the city were newly filled with a population that spoke a foreign language, had foreign manners, and talked too much of the past while thinking too little of the future. The charity funds were exhausted and so was much of America's sympathy.

News from France was worse. The guillotine fell more frequently, not less. Those of us who had property when we departed our homeland found we owned it no longer. Titles and funds were confiscated. And to return home would, for almost all of us, mean quick death, for even just leaving the country was a great crime against the new nation.

There was nothing to do but wait it out in Azilum. And bear, as well we could, the little news we received from the outside world. We devoured month-old reports and newspapers that were sometimes three months old, and counted our dead. Madame Guillemard's husband was guillotined; her sons were now fatherless. This caused the whole community concern, for the little, always-distracted woman was well-liked by all of us, and we feared losing her. She would, we thought, return to Philadelphia, now that there was no prospect of her husband coming to share and ease her wilderness life. But Madame Guillemard, despite her frequent fits of vapors, was made of sturdy fabric.

"He would have wished us to stay. Our sons will be better off here," she said. "Here will we stay." Here will we stay, agreed many other members of the community, awed by Madame Guillemard's stoic determination.

My friend, Manon, also went to the guillotine. She had committed the treasonous act of being wed to a printer who fell out of Robespierre's favor. Manon. So filled with love, so eager to embrace life. Now, dust.

When I learned of Manon's death, I tore the little decorative frill of lace off my brown workgown. It was a gesture of anger, of mourning. I stared at my image through the black gauze draped over the mirror. I could almost hear Manon's gentle, mocking voice. "You look like a starved mouse," she would have said. "Brown is not your color at all. And the fit! Alas!"

But the fates tease us. They offer just enough justice to make us hope for more. Manon died. But so did d'Orléans. Also guillotined for treason. I sincerely hoped that his failure to find the Golden Ransom had something to do with his fatal disfavor. Then I could feel I had had a hand in ridding France of that demon.

"My only fear is that the devil himself won't keep d'Orléans, but will return him to us in another guise," said Madame Farquet, when we heard this news.

And once we accepted all these things, the good with the bad, nature itself attempted to console us.

Blithe spring that knows no modesty nor restraint descended upon us in all her glory. Tethered bulls bellowed for the shy, lazy cows in the pasture; feather-light, half-wild kittens appeared from the dark recesses of sheds and barns to play in the honeyed sun. Life was renewing itself.

The dreary hills, inspired with fresh vanity, decked themselves in tiers of white mountain laurel, and stars-of-Bethlehem bloomed in the paths of the cathedral-dark forests.

In Azilum, where nature still held sway over man and his folly, spring was not a mere time of year, it was an event. We could no more resist her call than we could those other instincts that bid us eat when hungry, sleep when tired. Nature bid us be glad, as she was, and song was heard again in Azilum. The lid of the pianoforte was again raised and grief was put aside like an ill-fitting coat.

My cabin, as Henri had promised, was completed in that bittersweet spring which brought us so much sorrow, so much promise. I was thankful. The Queen's House, despite its size, was growing crowded—not just with visitors, but with the ghosts we all carried about with us. If I was to bide in Azilum for a while, I wished my life to begin. I was tired of being a guest in other people's homes.

When the cabin was done, and Henri sent over several American work-men to fetch my trunks from the Queen's House to my cabin, I had a feeling that came close to joy, despite my brown dress of mourning.

I carried Aurore in both arms, not lightly in one, for she had grown heavier and longer with the wholesome air and plain, nourishing foods. She was no longer a baby but a small girl. That, too, gave me a sense of joy, that my daughter was safe and prospering. Henri proudly led the way, that day of my homecoming, as if he had built the cabin singlehandedly. Smithy, muttering and cursing under the weight of one of my trunks, directed the two Americans who carried all my other worldly goods easily under their arms.

Smithy, intimidated by the grandeur of our parade, paused at the front step to scrape the dung from his boots before entering; my glance warned him he should do so. He spied the rose bush planted by my front door.

"Bejesus! Crops to be got in, and the Frenchies are planting bouquets!" he hooted.

But I didn't mind his jeers. The first red tips of growth were already showing; I would have roses soon.

I swung the door open and we entered. We toured the cabin slowly, with

Henri pausing often to explain dovetail joints and the importance of grading the land to slope downhill, and other such pieces of information to which I paid scant attention.

The cabin was simple and plain. If I told my grandchildren they had to live in such a house they would blush with shame, for they were born after we had grown richer with the years and were spoiled. They must have their drawing rooms and sitting rooms and two different parlors, one for Sunday and one for weekdays. But the new cabin, which still smelled strongly of sawdust, seemed a mansion to me, for it was mine, and mine alone. The first house, like a first love, is a significant event. Other loves, other houses, may follow, indeed be better, but they never have the poignancy of the first.

There were two rooms downstairs, and two rooms above, with a cook-house and pantry in back, separate from the house. The bare wood floors had a pleasant golden sheen. The chinks between the logs of the walls had been filled in with mortar and the walls whitewashed. There were four windows in front, four in back, each set with eight small panes of glass. The Americans, impressed, tapped tentatively on those luxuries.

Furniture ordered from Wilkes-Barre had arrived, so my home already contained an oak four-poster in the bedroom, dining table and chairs, a bureau and some small tables and chests. I touched each piece lovingly, with possessive pleasure.

In the back, between the main house and the cookhouse, was my garden, complete with a small wooden pavilion, herb beds, and stone paths meandering between them. It was planted with lavender and thyme, bee balm and iris, and other flowers which, while useful, are best when enjoyed solely for their colors and scents. Even the Queen's House did not have such a lovely garden, a garden to please the eye and nose and mock the frightening wilderness with its sweet orderliness.

Aurore, having struggled free of my restraining arms, tottered to a clump of chives that was already showing round, purple blossoms. She plucked at them with abandon, flinging them gleefully in the air and in her hair.

I closed my eyes, overcome with the sweetness born with the sight of my daughter, safe and healthy and crooning to herself under a shower of purple petals. The sun was warm and soothing, the air fresh, and Henri's clasp of my hand as firm as the life force that sends up the green shoots in springtime.

"Are you pleased?" he asked, knowing already I was.

"Very."

"A kiss for thanks, then," he said, grinning. He leaned down . . . he was tall, taller than Charles . . . and pursed his mouth, but I kissed his warm, sunburnt cheek. He returned the kiss, but his to me was full on the mouth, lingering and filled with an intent I did not share. It was troubling; it stirred emotions I would prefer to keep aslumber. I stepped back and broke off the embrace. He ducked his head to hide emotion he no longer wished to reveal and continued our tour.

We walked to the cookhouse behind the garden. There, I admired the hearth, which was large enough to hold four pots at once, and a small brick oven where bread could be baked. In a separate room a few steps down was the pantry, built over and around a running stream so I could keep milk and butter without spoilage. The stream made a gentle music that I could hear from my bed if the night was quiet and I did not move. I spent many nights listening to that crystal murmuring of water that would flow soon to the Susquehanna, later to the Atlantic ocean and then, I thought, would lap at the shores of France.

"How does this work?" I asked Henri, tentatively touching a metal cage of sorts that swung over the central hearth.

"It is a meat turner. You see, there is a handle there, off to the side. Turn that and an entire side of beef will turn, and cook evenly."

"I see." There was misgiving in my voice. Helping to knead bread in the huge and servant-busy kitchen of the Queen's House was one matter; running affairs in this smaller kitchen where I would work alone—and uninstructed— was another matter all together.

"I have found help for you," Henri said, smiling to reassure me.

"Do I have the means to afford a servant?"

"You must. Unless you plan to plough your own fields and brew your own tonics."

"I will have no slaves." I knew that a slave could be purchased for less than a year's salary for a freeman-servant; but Charles and I had agreed that slavery was a great evil that harmed both individuals and society. Other colonists had no such scruples, and found easy and numerous ways to circumvent the inconvenient law that made slavery in Pennsylvania illegal. Hovels—slave quarters—cut a jagged line against the riverfront of Azilum, growing apace as our colony grew.

"I am not a slave," said a strong voice behind me. "I am a free woman. And my man Joshua is a free man."

I turned to that voice and beheld the tallest woman I had ever seen. She had entered the cookhouse without making a sound. Indeed, when she wished, this woman was quieter than a downy-footed kitten. When angry, though, she could be noisy as thunder.

Her skin was the color of creamed coffee tinged with a russet hue; her thick black hair was shiny with bear grease. She wore an indigo cotton print dress over leather hose, and around her neck a leather thong supported a beaded purse. The purse jingled pleasantly when she walked (she could also keep it silent, when she wished to pass unnoticed) for this medicine bag of hers was heavy with secret talismans. Her nose and lips were as handsome as those of a Roman statue, her deerskin jacket was cunningly embroidered with porcupine quills. She could have been thirty years of age; she could have been sixty.

"I am Delilah," she said, and her voice could not have been prouder had she said, "I am the Queen of France." The man behind her, who was dark as a moonless night, without her russet tint, said nothing, but only glared fiercely at me. He was three heads taller than myself and thick as a tree. He wore no shirt and I could see his back had been scarred by the whip.

"You like rabbit stew for dinner?" Delilah asked. I was speechless. She took this for assent. Even so, I would have rabbit stew whether I wished it or not, her posture said. She and her man were so tall they had to stoop when they left the cookhouse.

Henri stared intently at the low-beamed ceiling. His hands played nervously behind his back. "She's three-quarters Indian, one-quarter African," he said, not looking at my face.

"Indian!" I had a sudden vision of being murdered in my sleep and scalped.

"Delaware. It's a peaceful tribe." He was still studying the low-beamed ceiling, avoiding my eyes. "She and her man will work for you in exchange for land to build their own cabin and a share of the harvest. Joshua will do the field work, Delilah the cooking.

"My God, woman!" he exclaimed, finally losing patience with the expression on my wary, frightened face. "Did you expect a powdered fop in silk breeches? Joshua can do the work of five Frenchmen, and Delilah, you'll find, is more intelligent than Voltaire and Rousseau combined. You'll thank your fortune for her, come this winter."

And so Delilah entered my life just when so many other guiding presences had left it. I would, as Henri said, realize my good fortune in the years to come. Delilah was no mere servant, no meek half-breed. She was a woman of the Lenni-Lenape, the tribe the French called "Delaware." They called themselves the Original People, and viewed all others as inferiors.

This tribe was famed for two things: its great knowledge of agriculture, and the even greater pride of its women. The women in this society owned everything, land and cabin, and if a woman separated from her husband she kept the children, not he.

When Delilah told me that she lowered her eyes, not out of modesty but out of pity for me. My husband had been a European. With me, it was just the opposite. Indeed, if Charles had lived, and if he proved vindictive rather than forgiving, he could have taken Aurore from me. It was an unsettling thought, this picture of Charles grown cruel enough to separate mother and child because of a mother's past crimes.

Delilah followed the White Path of the medicine woman, and the sound of her chants soon became a familiar, welcome part of each day. Her path was disciplined and serene. All objects had a soul, all objects had a name. Tobacco, the scent of which soon filled our home, for it was great medicine, was known as Grandfather, as was fire. Water was Our Mother, and all the different winds, which were caused by spirits, had names, so that for Delilah even thin air was filled with life.

It was Delilah who taught me that the corn must be planted when dogwood leaves are the size of a squirrel's ear; that children must go to bed when the whippoorwill calls in the evening; that to dream of snow means a long life; that visitors will come when the cat washes her face; that angelica cures a child's stomachache from eating green apples. It was Delilah who taught me to collect the medicinal water that gathers in tree hollows, and to listen to the secret song that the Great Spirit sends to all his children when he is pleased with them. I have heard this secret song. It is made of the sounds of the wind in the tree-tops, the murmur of clear water, the rhythm of a sleeping child's breath, the beat of your own heart. And once I lost my fear of the wolf, even his comfortless howling could become a part of that song.

With Delilah, I prospered. Aurore, unlike the other French children of our settlement, never suffered the whooping cough, and our cabin and table acquired a rustic comfort missing from many of the other cabins.

We settled in together quickly and easily, with Delilah soon taking control of the kitchen and pantry and silent Joshua doing the heavy work of the fields. He smiled only when fearless Aurore clamored to be lifted to his broad shoulders. He spoke only to Delilah, who had herself purchased his freedom from the Pennsylvania farmer who had beat him with the whip. His dark glowing eyes followed her every movement with a jealous devotion.

It was the look in his eyes I thought of at night, when all was quiet and I was alone in the great bed. Charles had once looked at me in that way, and the memory of it made those spring nights feverish with need and desire. It was as if my husband were merely absent, not dead. Perhaps if I had been able to mourn him, to bury him properly, it would have been different with me. But I could not let go of him.

Henri was certainly ready to console me, but I was not ready for him. He spent many evenings with me, helping me put Aurore to sleep in her own little cot, and then sitting with his chair close to mine, in front of the hearth. We sat in silence till the urge to speak came, much as did the Friends in their Philadelphia meeting halls. It was comforting to sit in front of my own hearth, in my own home, even though it be no more than a cabin in a rough clearing. I knitted thick hose; he whittled wooden animals, a whole Noah's ark of them, for Aurore.

One mild spring night, as we so sat, I came to know his history, and the knowledge of it only served to increase my belief that this youth was Louise's lost child, newly restored to me.

His foster father, a Monsieur Arraché of Bourges, was a cabinetmaker. Henri said little of this man. And all he did not say led me to believe that his master had not been kind; taking in foster children was a lucrative enterprise that often had much to do with profit and little to do with concern for the children. Their mothers paid fees for their upkeep and the children themselves could literally be worked to death, if a master so inclined.

Henri had been set to work in the shop as soon as he could walk, and by the time he was nine or so had learned much of the art of cabinetry. So well, in fact, that his master's three sons grew jealous of his skills, and tormented him. Between the master's cruelty and the sons' jealousy, life became difficult enough that Henri ran away. That was a dangerous affair; if captured, he would have been beaten, bound, perhaps even thrown in prison.

"But luck was with me," he recalled that night. His face was half in shadow and the reflection of angry flame showed in his pale blue eyes, eyes the same color as Louise's. "I ran to Paris, and begged for my bread. I dined better as a beggar than I had in the Arraché household. And one day, a finely dressed servant offered to take me to his master's house for a meal, if I would do some work for them.

"I told him in no uncertain terms to jump in the Seine. I knew what kind of work two older men could have in mind for a young boy. But he took great offense and claimed so strongly that I misjudged him that I apologized, and followed him home. His master turned out to be Dr. Edward Bancroft."

"Bancroft?" I asked, putting down my knitting for a moment to concentrate the better.

"He was a part of the American mission to Versailles in 1783. He was wealthy and influential. And also of an amorous disposition, but without the taste for youths I had first imagined. My 'work' turned out to be no more than caring for his mistress's many pet dogs."

Henri laughed, remembering faces, voices, moments that could not be expressed in words, and the first flush of revelation that comes when a child learns that life can be pleasant, it need not be all misery and hard work.

"There were a dozen dogs, and they each had to be bathed daily, and perfumed, and tied up with ribbons and bows. They were walked in a private garden that was mown four times a week and planted with roses for the dog's pleasure. Bancroft's mistress was batty. But very beautiful and as soft with me as she was with her dogs. I was happy with my new 'work.'

"When the mission ended and Bancroft had to leave Paris, he pitied me, and arranged for me to return to Philadelphia with him. The price of my passage was secrecy and an ability to think up alibis on the spot. He was grieved at parting from his Parisian mistress and sought to console himself with some of the prettier passengers who sailed with us. Mrs. Bancroft was a rightly suspicious wife, but the fact that her husband traveled with a rehabilitated runaway softened her feelings. I'm pleased to say I was useful to Dr. Bancroft. And then, in Philadelphia, I met Senator Morris. He trained me as a surveyor and mapmaker. End of story." He poked his boot into the hearth, pushing into place a log that had rolled out of the flames. Sparks shot up into the darkness.

"Maybe. Maybe not," I said. That evening my yearning for company, for memories of Paris, overcame my distrust of him. I decided to speak to him of Louise. "You were raised in Bourges, but where were you born? And what year?"

"Paris, I believe. They sometimes called me the city bastard. But I don't know the year. Little effort was made to celebrate my birthday and nothing was said of my mother. I was, of course, the product of some illicit relationship; she wished to be free of me."

It wasn't like that, I wanted to tell him. I remembered the day of Henri's departure, how the soup had tasted of dust and Louise had cried into hers.

"I would guess you were born in 1774," I said.

"Could be. Why does it matter? Why this interest?" He leaned closer to me, a newly hopeful and amorous look in his eye. I pushed away the hand he tried to place on my knee.

"I think, Henri, I knew your mother. Yes, yes, it is a great shock, I know, but listen. Her name was Louise, and she gave birth to a child she named Henri, in Paris in 1774. And then, that child was taken from her, and she lost him, she did not know what had become of him, because he ran away from his foster parents."

"I did not realize how greatly you missed France," he said, looking at me with pity. "Julienne, there must have been hundreds of male infants born in Paris and named Henri in that year."

"Yes, Henri." But at that moment I claimed him as that long-lost child. As much as he continued to deny the mathematical possibility of such a reunion, the more convinced I became, over the years. His nose had the same aquiline curve as Louise's, his red-gold hair grew white and silky at the temples and nape, as hers did. His smile, the tilt of his head, the springiness of his walk, as if gravity did not affect him as much as it affected the rest of us, all reminded me of Louise.

Henri, that evening, grew silent. He rose to put a new log on the hearth long before the others had been consumed by the red, devouring flames.

"Where is she, this woman you think is my mother?" he asked in a low voice.

"I don't know. When we parted, she was to go to Austria. I have not heard from her since."

"Did she travel alone? In such times?" He plucked at a thread on his jacket sleeve.

"No. Her protector traveled with her. I knew him also. He was kind and generous." He heard the unsaid message: he was your father.

"Very generous. If he was who you suggest, he appears to be in the habit of giving his sons away. But these are past matters. I have more concern for the future."

He left then, bowed with deep thoughts. I had given him nothing but doubts, I had poured salt over old wounds, all in the name of truth seeking. I was angry with myself. With Charles, I had told half-truths and caused pain, with Henri I was pushing to make a possibility as certain as the whereabouts of the north star, and had caused pain. Was there no middle ground to be walked, in this matter of truth telling? But beneath the anger, rising to the surface, was pleasure. Henri was restored to me, my brother, my friend. I only wished I could trust him.

As pleasant as the evenings in my own home were, I made a point of spending many evenings in the music room of the Queen's House. It was expected. Not to do so, in such a small community, would have been considered very unfriendly; and I grew lonely, even with Aurore and Delilah and Henri and my memories.

So three or four times a week, after the evening meal, I would don my best dress, smooth my hair, and walk the short space of brown road between my cabin and the Queen's House. Monsieur Talon encouraged us all in this; he wished to keep our spirits as high as they could be, to avoid dour and bitter loneliness, to refresh ourselves with music.

"We must learn to live again, not to dwell on old memories," he instructed

263

us with solemn eyes. "Enjoy the hospitality of the Queen's House." When he was with us, which was only half the time and sometimes less, he would don his best silk breeches and white hose, powdered wig and take up his ivory-handled walking stick, and himself ladle our after-dinner punch.

We sipped rum, and listened to Madame Farquet's perfect but cold performances of Bach, and Madame Guillemard's impassioned but faulty versions of Mozart, and all the while wolves would be howling in the hills behind us and sometimes in the very paths of Azilum, for they were cunning at broaching our barricades. We pretended not to hear them. We drew the curtains tight and pretended that we were not a mere pinprick of candlelight intruding into the universe of infinite darkness outside those windows.

We talked of farming and bread baking and those quickly exhausted subjects gave way to gossip. There was much speculation about the rumored fortune in jewels and money that the King and Queen had had smuggled to America before their imprisonment. I listened, and of course did not say that part of that treasure was buried in our west wood, under the Old Man of the Forest.

After the more interesting rumors, we discussed the less interesting ones.

"I understand Monsieur Arraché spends his evenings with you. Alone," said Madame Farquet one Sunday evening, her back stiff with outrage. "In the dark," she added through thin lips.

"It is true," I admitted, and her outrage was so exquisite her powdered hair fairly prickled and stood up with it. "But madame, as Senator Morris's agent, certainly you would allow him access to our homes. And as for the darkness, well, it does seem to follow the sunset. There is little I can do about it."

Her eyes bulged at my flippancy.

"You are a widow. And he is a man," she protested.

"Now there is useful information," I said, wearying of her and rising to leave. In Paris, people were being guillotined daily by the cartload. America, if our scant information was correct, was at the brink of war with France. Aside from the political turmoil and dangers, we faced hunger, isolation, poverty. And Madame Farquet worried about the lack of chaperones.

"It is her way of forgetting her problems," Henri said later. "Don't fret about her."

"You are right. But perhaps we could arrange an elopement or some other scandal so that she will concentrate on another victim."

My wish was granted. During one of our Saturday night musicals, amidst the ringing of already-chipped crystal punch glasses and the rustling of the women's silk gowns, and the heartier, deep voices of the men talking of felled trees and cellar depths, the first engagement was announced in Azilum.

Monsieur de Blaçons, a good-natured and energetic young man, a marquis and Abbé de Sévigné, had arrived in Azilum just days after myself. Not one to let grass grow under his feet, he had already gone into partnership with a Monsieur Collier and opened Azilum's first haberdasher shop. His bride-to-be was Mademoiselle de Maulde, former Canoness of Bonbourg. Both were personable and likable and aristocratic, both had narrowly escaped death in France, only to flee to Pennsylvania and find there the love they had never known in Paris. It was most romantic, most enjoyable; it was better than one of Beaumarchais's plots.

We had watched them eyeing each other for several weeks. It was with advance knowledge that we waited patiently as a group for Monsieur de Blaçons to make his announcement.

"Ahem!" he called, standing on a footstool in our midst. "Most kind ladies and gentlemen. Be it known you are all invited to a feast at this time and place, three weeks hence. Before the feast you may want to assemble in the chapel, where Mademoiselle de Maulde will there do me the honor of becoming my wife!"

Mademoiselle, standing next to him, blushed pink as a wild rose and fanned herself in a mild frenzy as the ladies of Azilum rushed to offer congratulations. "A wedding!" cried young Madame Homet, who had herself been wed less than a year. "It is a good sign for our colony!"

We all shared this sentiment. There had been too much death, too many partings. Now, there would be a joining together, with a new generation that comes of it. Why, then, did I feel pain, not happiness? Because I thought of Charles.

Charles never looked so joyful when he spoke of our wedding, I thought, watching Monsieur Blaçons's face, which was even more glowing than that of his bride. Don't think such things, I commanded myself. Charles was different. He was more serious by nature. But I had to admit I was jealous . . . of their joy, of the coming years together they would enjoy, of the way he looked at her.

I forced myself to go to Mademoiselle de Maulde and give her my congratulations.

"Thank you," she said with gladness. "But it troubles me that I wish to ask more of you than your goodwill . . . " She hesitated prettily, waiting for me to say she should continue.

"Ask whatever it is that troubles you. Who could refuse such a lovely bride anything?" I asked. Henri looked at me in a strange manner. Only he had noticed the tautness of my voice.

"I have heard of your talent with the needle. Indeed, we all have, and that the Queen herself boasted of your work, and was pleased to wear it. And I . . . I have not a single gown that would be half good enough for a wedding . . . " She hesitated again and the room grew silent with waiting.

"Nothing would give me greater pleasure than to make the gown myself." I broke the silence with a light, high voice that spoke of great merriment with this prospect. Inwardly, I shivered. Didn't the woman know how much work must go into such a dress, and she getting married in three weeks time? And we didn't even have the stuffs we would need, the tissue fabrics and laces; they would now have to be ordered and brought upriver. "No greater pleasure," I repeated with a little laugh.

Ah, well. There is nothing better to do with the long evenings, I told myself with some bitterness and a great deal of self-pity.

It was surprising that the fairer the weather became, and the sweeter our days, the greater grew a resurrected unhappiness. It was as if the newly refreshed beauty of the world contrasted with my old, drab sorrows that would not go away. I ached for Charles, for the feel of his arms around me, for the sense of that larger male presence that does not really make life easier but does make our hours more pleasant in their passing.

Henri and I were spending more of each day in each other's company and it distressed me that I could not fully trust him. It preyed on my mind that he had not been at Senator Morris's home on the evening that my room at the Pension Rose Noir had been broken into and searched. The more I grew to know him, the more I sensed that he was an honorable person. But my promise to the Queen forbade me relying on my own instincts.

My unhappiness, though, was but a spring puddle compared to the ocean of Madame Farquet's misery. She and monsieur finally left the Queen's House and moved, most reluctantly, into their own cabin, next to mine.

"It is . . . ungracious," said madame that first day, standing in the middle of a barren and rough room, her face as stony and cold as one of the grey boulders the farmers rolled from the fields.

Her eyes went up to the low-beamed ceiling, looking for the crystal chandelier that would never hang there, and to the wide-planked bare floor, which would never know the warmth of a Persian carpet. Seeing her at that moment, her haughty face free of every emotion except regret for all that had been lost, I pitied her. Indeed, her cabin was smaller and darker than mine and had not been white-washed, and no curtains hung at the windows.

Monsieur Farquet had said they could afford no servants, she must learn to do for herself.

"If only I could continue my residence in the Queen's House," she sighed wistfully.

"I will ask Delilah to come later and help you," I offered. "We will make the curtains." She clutched gratefully at my hand.

By early summer Azilum had grown greatly. We had become somewhat famous by then and had many visitors, so that the guest rooms in the Queen's House were in constant demand and a Monsieur Beaulier opened Azilum's first inn. There were two other colonies, similar in intent and hardship, north of us in New York, and it became the fashion, for a few years, to travel northwest of Philadelphia and gawk at the "Frenchie settlements." We were almost as popular as a trip to the great Falls of Niagara.

Mostly we enjoyed the novelty of being a novelty and the superficial companionship it brought; there were many feasts in the Queen's House but we never saw the same visitors' faces twice at that table. Henri said we must be patient. The visitors would disappear with the autumn, and by January even the most reclusive of us would be hungry again for visitors.

Our settlement also established a smithy and several shops, and we began building our own gristmill and theater. The Americans had assumed we would all become farmers and spend our days in the fields, but many of our colonists found commerce preferable to farming. By early summer many of our best fields were rented to the nearby American farmers who better appreciated their value.

"Bejesus," Smithy spat one day. "Give 'em the best farmland in the world, and they want to become damn clerks. Can't say as I understand the Frenchies. Not at all."

As in other places, other times, my days took on a comforting regularity. At dawn Aurore and I would wake and go to the cookhouse, where Delilah would already be waiting for us. There we would eat oat gruel sweetened with maple syrup, and stern Delilah and her silent Joshua would eat with us, so that I remembered what it felt like to be a child amidst adults.

After breakfast, Delilah would take Aurore to the kitchen garden with her, where they weeded rows of beets or picked the green, small peas for our stew. Joshua and I would walk the long, rutted street that led to the market square of Azilum, and past that to the green and beige fields bordering the south side of the river.

Together, we would examine the small shoots that would lengthen into rows of wheat and corn. Joshua had plowed the furrows straight and wide so we could walk the rows and pluck the weeds that grew faster and thicker than the crops.

My afternoons were spent in the cabin sitting room, which had become my new sewing room. It was arranged in Bertin fashion, with a large work table pushed against one wall—her tables had been of carved rosewood, mine were rough pine slabs—and the rest of the floor and wall space taken up by falls of lace, muslin, cotton and silk cloths, and boxes of scraps and ribbons, all purchased at Hollenback's trading post. The last of my money went into that stock; if the crops failed or other disaster struck we would be penniless.

But I felt confident. I had started anew three times by then, and it became less frightening each time. The plain wilderness cabin took on a luxurious, chaotic appearance that pleased me greatly, for it reminded me of the extravagance of my Paris life. Lengths of pink silk fluttered from pegs on the whitewashed walls and green grosgrain ribbons dangled like vines from pewter candle sconces. White lace hung over chair backs in frothing waterfalls. Under those, little Aurore would hide and wait for me to pass so she could leap out, growling like a catamount. I was never surprised but always pretended to be.

Because Mademoiselle de Maulde had no money for fine cloths, the materials for her wedding dress had been donated by various ladies of the community, inspired to generosity because I was sewing the gown without charge. A pink silk overdress was cut down from one of Madame Guillemard's gowns. "I won't wear pink again," said the black-garbed widow but there was no self-pity in her voice, only acceptance. The delicate Brussels lace of the neckline and cuffs was supplied by handsome John Keating, who had removed it from his own shirt to adorn our bride. Hence began a style of appearing at the Saturday musicals in the Queen's House in homespun, rather than fancy dress. Lack of frills made Mr. Keating even more dashing and added greatly to his popularity.

The green petticoat and matching ribbons were supplied by Madame Homet. She and her husband, a former steward of King Louis, had been building a second home for the Queen some distance from Azilum, so that the Queen and her children could have a home both in town and country. In those early days we had no—well few—doubts that Azilum would grow into a thriving town. With the news of the Queen's death, however, work on that second home ceased.

"The green cloth was to have been worked into a coverlet for the Queen's bed," she explained, handing over the fabric. "If it cannot be used to please the Queen, then a wedding gown is the second best fate for it."

And so, Mademoiselle de Maulde's wedding gown became a patchwork of our hopes to come and those dreams that had already failed us.

When my rose bush was aflame with a second bursting of carmine blooms, the wedding gown was completed. I was pleased enough with my work that I tried it on before presenting it to our bride. I considered it in the mirror, trying to see it and myself the way Charles would. I was wed in golden silk; he had liked the way it made my dark hair even darker. And we had quarreled that day. It was bad luck to quarrel on the wedding day. Someone should warn Mademoiselle de Maulde, I thought, but my misgivings were for myself, who would go alone to a wedding and return home alone with only memories for warmth.

On the great day of Azilum's first wedding, we were led in procession by Monsieur Carles, former canon of Guernsey and now priest to our colony. The chapel, newly finished and still smelling of green wood and sawdust, was awash with wild blossoms, their mingling perfume was the scent of summer itself.

One hundred of us gathered in the chapel and knelt in the rough interior to ask blessings for the couple's union. Many of our American neighbors had been invited, but they would not enter the chapel. They waited outside, eager to partake of the feast and dancing that would follow.

"Papist foolery!" had exclaimed Colonel Jamison, whose farm bordered the newly planted orchard in the southwest pasture. It was many years since he had worn a military uniform but the Americans, proud of the outcome of their war with England, clung to military titles the way vain women cling to the compliments of their youth.

His daughter, Sarah, waited outside with him, but her neck promised to be longer by several inches when the day was over, so high did she stretch her head to peer into the chapel. "Look at those gowns!" she sighed.

"Can't be an American and a Catholic, too," Frau Schillinger told me.

"Why not?" I asked, more curious than affronted.

"Just can't. Presbyterians make the best Americans, and Methodists second to them, and then the Quakers and Lutherans. But Catholics? Doesn't wash." She nodded her head so vigorously that her stiff poke bonnet fell forward, completely obscuring her face. And with a face like that, good riddance, Manon would have said.

In the chapel, sun slanted through our glass-paned windows and fell beneficently on the couple who stood before the altar. They made their vows until death, and we bowed our heads in a brief spasm of mutual grief, for many of us had already suffered that parting. Abbé Carles raised his arms in benediction. "Go in peace," he said at the end of the ceremony.

Monsieur Talon provided the wedding feast at the Queen's House, of wine, roasted chickens and wild berry tarts. We toasted Madame and Monsieur de Blaçons frequently, hoping that Talon would continue to pour the wine, which was French and very good. Madame Farquet played minuets and rondelets on the pianoforte. The hills of Azilum echoed with good will and music.

Late in the afternoon, when some of the ladies were already weepy and their spouses sloppy from an excess of wine and merriment, Talon announced a special surprise for the couple. He had to yell to be heard, and when he had our attention he made his way through the wedding party and extended to madame a plain, brown parcel. She took it with a pretty curtsey, probably thinking it was a set of linens.

"All gifts are welcome," she laughed. "I have not a pot of my own."

"I think you will find this more precious than a pot," Talon said in a momentous voice. We watched with curiosity as he helped her tear the strings. He stepped back as the brown paper fluttered to the floor, leaving in Madame's trembling hands a clutch of envelopes.

"Letters. From Paris," she said in a hollow, disbelieving voice, reading one and then another. Her voice grew excited. "From Paris. And New York. And Philadelphia. Letters!"

"There is a large sack of them," Talon told us, smiling. "News and letters for the entire community. This is my gift. We have begun a weekly post between Wilkes-Barre amd Azilum."

Only a person who has had to flee home, country and loved ones to settle in an isolated wilderness community could appreciate the significance of Talon's gift. We were still isolated, but no longer shut off. No longer quite as alone as we had been. It was as if a window appeared where once there had been only a wall.

But for me, the window opened onto nothingness.

Madame Guillemard and I, two widows of Azilum, stood back while others who still had the greatest gift of all, hope, flew forward to claim their mail. There was much weeping that night, both for joy and sorrow, as the colony read of more deaths in France, and happier news of births and recoveries from illness. Even in the midst of hell's flames there must be some little joy to lighten the heart, else the flames would no longer matter.

My correspondence consisted of a single letter from Madame La Roche. There was no news of Louise; and the others . . . Charles, Manon, even Mathilde . . . were dead.

"I fear for her sanity," Madame La Roche wrote of Mademoiselle de Monquet's seduction and pregnancy. "Monsieur Debocco offered to wed her, but she laughed and tried to scratch his face."

"Bad news?" Henri asked, sitting next to me. He was dressed more formally than usual for the wedding, in a blue satin jacket with snowy lace at the throat and wrists. He looked splendid. Louise's child is a winning young man, I thought. I was very aware of blonde Sarah Jamison, who stood across the room with her father and watched Henri the way a cat watches a mouse, cooly but with serious intent.

"Yes," I said. "Bad news. Mademoiselle de Monquet in Philadelphia is ill." He went to get me a glass of wine, and I continued reading.

But that was not the only news. "A man with whom I am not familiar was asking after you," Madame La Roche's letter finished. "I am afraid he was not a gentleman. He pretended to be a close friend of yours, but was surprised when I told him you had removed to Azilum. I hope I have not erred in giving him that information."

Someone asking after me? I had no friends, certainly no relatives, to make inquiries. It was not a friend, then. I felt cold, despite the warmth of the afternoon.

"I do not like to see you distressed." Henri, at my side again, whispered and leaned closer, putting his hand over mine. I looked at him long and hard. Henri knew where I was at all times. Henri would not need to make inquiries, nor would he have someone else make inquiries about me.

"Henri, where were you the night of Senator Morris's Twelfth Night party?" I asked him, finally.

He looked startled, and took a long moment to think. "That was the night I dined with Charles Boulogne, at Senator Morris's request. He was in Philadelphia for a brief time and we had business to conclude before he returned to Albany. Why do you ask?"

"My room was broken into that evening."

His eyes narrowed, as he considered. "And all this time you have suspected me? Why did you not ask sooner?"

"I feared your answer," I answered truthfully.

"Well, then, you may write to Senator Morris and confirm what I have said." He was angry.

At that moment Miss Sarah Jamison glided between us, sensing her opportunity.

"It grows warm in here," she said, smiling at Henri in a very inviting manner.

"Very," Henri said stiffly.

271

"I believe I do feel faint. Lead me outside, Henri," she said, and her blonde curls bobbed up and down. Madame La Roche had warned us of the boldness of American girls, who scorn chaperones and are as at ease with young men as with their own sex. And the parents encourage them in this.

Too young and inexperienced with such matters to know how to reject her offer without appearing rude, Henri let himself be led away.

Suddenly weary, I left the music room and walked alone to my cabin. The day, once outside the noise of the Queen's House, was as still as the Garden of Eden before God placed man there.

I realized why God had created man, as troublesome as he was. It was not good, being alone.

17

. . . new love and a small revolution . . .

If a man should importune me to give a reason why I loved
him, I find it could not otherwise be expressed, than by making
answer: because it was he, because it was I.

—Montaigne

When a wolf howls, she is remembering her other life, when she was human and loved; she grieves for it. So Delilah said.

That evening a wolf howled from the river side of Azilum. She must have crept through the colony from the forest, drawn by some unknown need, to share our flickering candlelight, our music and laughter. I walked warily, listening for soft padded steps, but felt no fear. I felt pity for the need that had driven the animal to this environment, which for her was both foreign and hostile. Here, in this place we had made, she was the exiled one, the stranger, the lonely one, cut off from her own.

The sun had set and the moon not yet risen. My cabin was in darkness. Even the downstairs fire had been allowed to burn down to black soot with no remnant glow. Aurore slept peacefully upstairs, but for me there was no peace, only the unremitting loneliness that cut me off from life, from the time when I was still human, and loved.

I lit a candle and opened my work ledger, hoping to find some distraction there in the columns of figures. Senator Morris had sent the ledger a week earlier; it was a summary of my accounts and pension, which was already exhausted. That did not distress me greatly; I had my home, Aurore was safe, and I would work again as a seamstress to provide for us. As for the poverty I would surely know . . . I was no stranger to it. Those other times, when my clothespress had been filled with gowns and I sipped creamed coffee out of fine porcelain, those had been the strange times. When I was still human, and loved.

Senator Morris had sent a letter with the ledger. Bored by the stern columns of figures, I picked up the letter and reread it for perhaps the twentieth time.

He wished me well. He hoped Aurore was growing fat and happy in the Azilum sunshine. And wasn't it a pity beyond bearing that the Queen's son fared so badly.

Little Louis-Charles, that intelligent and sweet-faced boy with the brownish-gold curls, still languished in prison, according to all reports. It had been hoped that with the monarchy destroyed, his royal parents dead, Louis-Charles would be set free and exiled to one of the many royalist groups waiting to welcome him . . . to ourselves. But Robespierre was holding the child as hostage, apparently, in his Paris prison. "The conditions of his imprisonment are of the worst," Morris had written. "He is starved and regularly beaten by men, who in earlier years, would not have been allowed to wipe his shoes. He receives inadequate fresh air and sunshine, is given little medical care."

I mourned for the Queen's son . . . and in my heart of hearts was relieved that Aurore was safely asleep upstairs, and it was Marie-Antoinette's child who received such abuse, not mine, even though her child was royal and mine was not.

There were already many claiming that Louis-Charles was no longer heir to the throne. Many, other than the revolutionaries, that is. The nobility of France was turning its collective back on him, just as it had turned its back on his mother. He had, upon the death of his father, become Louis XVII, three years before. Albeit, only his mother and aunt and sister had performed the ritual obeisance within the prison rooms they still shared. To all others he was still known as the Dauphin and there were already some who hoped he would remain a prince who would never be king.

Marie-Antoinette's brother-in-law, the Comte de Provence, for one, had no desire to see Louis-Charles restored to his father's throne. Why should he? In luxurious exile, hiding and traveling between the many courts of Europe friendly to the émigrés, he had assumed for himself the power and respect due his nephew. He had, in effect, become Louis XVIII, as though the Dauphin were already dead and buried. Many exiled royalists assumed Provence would be king, once the revolution ended.

Not we, in Azilum. We recognized only Louis-Charles. And we feared for him.

Was all to my satisfaction? Morris's letter went on. Was not the Great House (the Queen's House—he never referred to it as such, though), admirable? How it must steady the soul and fill it with pride, to know you are taking part in such a noble and great experiment, he said. To create a town out of nothing. Surely Charles would have been most proud of my decision to become one of the community of French Azilum. They needed people of my character, my strength.

I listened to the wolf howl and wondered if she was impressed by my character, my strength. I was not. I longed for Charles, or at least for what we had once had; I feared for Louis-Charles and his inheritance which might, in the end, come to nothing more than a single diamond buried under a tree in Pennsylvania. I feared for myself, remembering the interview with Talon, his warning of secret Jacobins even in the royalist womb of Azilum. And I wondered if Henri was still angry because of my suspicions of him.

The wolf howled again, closer this time. The loneliness inside me was like the darkness outside, all-powerful, all-encroaching, creeping into every corner, unable to be defeated, until the night was in me and my loneliness was in the night and there were no boundaries between my misery and the darkness. I put my head in my hands and cried.

Delilah, with silent cat steps, moved behind my chair.

"You have trouble," she said. Her voice was like the sound of wind moving through the highest treetops. Her strong hands went to my forehead, pulling my head off my arms, massaging my temples. "Tell Delilah," she said gently.

"I can't," I said, closing my eyes. How could I say it? I was jealous of the way her Joshua looked at her, jealous of the way that Monsieur de Blançons's bride would be carried to bed that evening, jealous even of the way the wind teased and taunted the honeysuckle vines.

"Dead husband makes trouble," Delilah said. "He won't let go of you."

"I don't want him to let go . . . I don't want him to go away."

"That is why you weep? Then he is ready to leave, but you won't let him go." The Delawares believed that dead spirits linger on earth for a time, putting things in order and saying farewell. If the proper ceremonies aren't performed for them, they stay overly long, and cause hauntings.

"Come," she said. "It is time." She relit the fire, fanning and blowing it into tall red flames that warmed the room and gave good light. Then, she fetched her store of tobacco, which was kept in a round wooden box decorated with porcupine quill designs and a bit of lace I had given her from the wedding gown. Delilah was fond of lace; it was the only vanity she possessed.

She opened the box and knelt before the fire, signaling that I should kneel beside her. I did so, more out of curiosity than anything else.

"Grandfather," she called, throwing a pinch of tobacco on the fire. "This woman here has trouble. Her man is dead, but his Heart Soul still walks behind her. She must be left in peace." I remembered my dreams, of Charles walking in front of me, behind me, but never beside me.

Delilah sat back on her heels, reached for the pipe next to her, and lit it. She took a long draw of the smoke, and then gave it to me. This, I knew, was a great honor which must not be refused. The ceremony was for me; I would share the tobacco. I did as she had done, imitating all her movements, but the smoke burned my lungs and I coughed. She smiled patiently and told me to try again. The second time the smoke warmed rather than burned. It was a pleasant feeling, it seemed to drive out some of the dark night that had filled me before.

"You. Dead husband." Delilah called. The room was thick and yellow with tobacco smoke. The familiar objects in it grew hazy, as if I saw them through a curtain. "You know your time is past. Listen to me," she instructed him.

A breeze stirred the curtain, the night wind sighed.

I felt dizzy. Charles was there, behind me, if I turned I would see him. Delilah put her hands on my face so that I could not turn, could not look about. But I felt him, his breath on my neck, his skin on mine, warming me, pressing into me, and I was loved and human again. I knew, in that moment, that Charles had forgiven my lies and half-truths.

That was what haunted me most. He had left in the midst of our quarrel, and it was the uncertainty of his forgiveness, of his continuing love, that had tormented me even more than his death. We had not said farewell, nor kissed in parting. A sudden draught brushed the back of my neck, gentle as a kiss.

I believed, finally, that he had died loving me, and the knowledge drove the rest of the darkness out of my heart.

"You must leave this woman now," Delilah said. "Follow the White Path to your rest."

The wind sighed again, and then the room was empty. I was still there, Delilah was still there, the fire was still there. But the room was empty. It was as if Charles had just walked out of the room as in the old days. But my heart was no longer heavy.

"Pass your hand over the flames three times, and say farewell," Delilah told me. "It won't hurt. Do as I say."

I passed my hand over the flames. They were cool as stream water. I said farewell to Charles, who was already gone, walking the White Path, freed finally of his earthly burdens.

The next morning, when dawn stippled the room with gold, I awoke feeling better than I had in many a week. My heart and my steps were lighter; I woke Aurore with a nonsense song that made her laugh and twine her little arms about my neck with joy. She still looked like her dead father, but the raven sheen of her hair, the deep green of her eyes, stirred my heart to joy and admiration, not sorrow. Sorrow was fled like last night's shadows. The wolf that was sorrow had returned to her lair, she no longer followed me.

"Picnic," I told Aurore. "Today we will have a picnic. Yes?"

She squealed and we danced together, she with her chubby legs wrapped around my waist, before dressing and going down for Delilah's oatmeal gruel.

"Did you sleep well?" Delilah asked. Just that. But her eyes were filled with unasked questions.

"Very well," I said. Just that. But I answered all those questions.

"Good. Now eat."

"Delilah. Tell me one thing. About Monsieur Henri." It was his face I thought of that morning, before I opened my eyes to the day.

She looked up from her bowl, her black eyes large and luminous. She waited, spoon halfway to her mouth.

"Is he trustworthy?" I put it as simply as I could, not wanting to explain about the diamond . . . or Miss Sarah Jamison. In this new, clearer light of dawn, I remembered what I had felt when the blonde American had stepped between Henri and me, leading him away. Jealousy.

Delilah smiled, and there was victory in that smile. "You can trust him," she told me.

Aurore and I both bolted down our bowls of gruel, eager to be out. It was Sunday, fair and mild already, and a day of pleasure, not of chores. Talon had promised a picnic. I had not been excited about it before last night; now I was. Henri would be there.

Madame Guillemard and I walked together to Table Rock, with her Jacques-Pierre, Louis and Antoine and my Aurore following us, leading us, playing in and out of our legs, like puppies. This place we walked to was a favorite piece of our wilderness landscape, consisting of a huge, flat rock

277

large enough to accommodate a dozen people, and situated in a sylvan glade of such beauty it seemed to be a corner of the Elysian Fields.

Last year's leaves crackled under foot and chickadees sang overhead; the day was gladsome.

"You had good news in your mail, last evening?" Victoire Guillemard asked. We had recently begun addressing each other in familiar terms. We sought and found a sisterly companionship in each other.

"No. A friend has become ill." I kicked at a stone in my path. Antoine kicked it back to me, but I missed it on my second try and was hence out of their game.

"But you look happy," she commented. "Much more so than usual."

"Perhaps it is just the fineness of the day," I suggested.

We walked in silence for some time, and then . . .

"Victoire," I asked. "Do you think you will wed again?"

She squinted her fine brown eyes into the distance, as if the purple mountains to our west held secret omens.

"I don't know. My marriage to Emile was arranged by my family when I was but a child. We didn't choose each other, and did not meet until the day of our formal betrothal. But he was kind and we did well together. We had peace and serenity. But the idea of loving where I pleased . . . " She giggled. "It sounds adventurous, doesn't it? To fall in love?" And then her voice grew shrill. "Antoine! Come down from there! Now!" He was halfway up a very tall oak and when he half-climbed, half-tumbled down and landed on his backside in the mud, his mother sighed and rolled her eyes to heaven.

"Of course," she added. "A second marriage could not reflect my wishes only. The first time, my parents choose. The second time, if there is one, who knows but that my sons will choose for me."

"Or at least frighten away fainthearted suitors," I admitted.

When we arrived at Table Rock, Monsieur Talon's private cook had already set out the fresh fruit pies, piles of pancakes with jugs of maple syrup next to them, slices of ham, biscuits, cheeses, cold roasted quails and rabbits. The food was plain but abundant. There were so many dishes that the grey of the huge stone barely showed through. And in the midst of all was a cake, cut and frosted to look like the Queen's House, with little pebbles and springs of greenery placed around it to resemble the topography of Azilum.

"Oh! A tableau!" Mademoiselle de Réleté cried with delight, clapping her hands.

"A fête, to cheer you!" announced Monsier Talon, coming to greet us and limping in obvious pain. The damp of the morning increased his suffering. But he smiled broadly.

The ladies rushed forward to admire the cake; the gentlemen gathered at a table, where a half-barrel of rum was ready to be broached.

Our newlyweds, Monsieur and Madame de Blaçons, blushing at the usual morning-after jests at their expense, cut the splendid cake and Henri poured the rum.

I waved and smiled at him, and something in my chest gave a little lurch when he smiled back. He was certainly a handsome youth, with that waving red-gold hair and high-bridged nose. And it was plain he adored me. Why not try, just a little, to please him? The thought made me smile. It opened up endless possibilities.

I took two plates of cake from Madame de Blaçons, thinking to give one of them to Henri. But by the time I sidled through the crowd to the rum table, Miss Sarah Jamison was already at his side.

Hurriedly, I gave the second plate to Jacques-Pierre, who had just finished a large piece of cake fetched on his own; he was a greedy child.

"I can't," he groaned, refusing the plate and rubbing his belly.

"Take this," I hissed at him, "or I'll tell your mother who put the dead skunk under her window last week."

He accepted the slice of cake with a greenish grin.

Confident that Henri and Miss Sarah, now sitting under a tall pine, hadn't seen that telltale second plate, I joined Victoire under our own pine tree. Jacques-Pierre, who was cramming cake into his mouth at alarming speed, gave me an agonized look, fearing that I would tell his *maman* of the skunk. I smiled reassuringly at him, and then turned my sweetest smile on Henri and Miss Sarah. The hussy was breaking off bits of cake and putting them into Henri's mouth with ungloved fingers.

"Monsieur Arraché has found an admirer," Victoire said. "Or perhaps two?"

"Don't be silly. He reminds me of a friend from Paris. That is all." I jabbed at my cake but had no appetite for it. Just yards away, under the tall pine, Henri meekly accepted another piece of cake from Miss Sarah's rosy fingers.

Jacques-Pierre, finished with the second piece of cake, was looking ghastly. Victoire jumped up to hurry him behind a patch of bushes, leaving me alone and unhappy. Aristide du Petit-Thouars, known affectionately as the "little admiral" among the two dozen ladies residing in Azilum, came and sat at my side.

This young man was a great favorite with the settlers, especially those of the fair sex, for he was handsome in the dark, Gallic manner, gallant and famous for his daring exploits at a time when even children and old women had been forced to engage in daring exploits to stay alive. Fans fluttered in hopeful frenzy whenever this bachelor was near. He had lost one hand while fighting for the Americans. When their war was over he had been captured and imprisoned in Lisbon for several years by the Portuguese, and then had journeyed to Philadelphia, out of reach of the guillotine at work in his homeland. Such a life could not have been invented, it was beyond the reaches of mundane imagination.

His missing hand only served to increase his appeal by making women even more solicitious of his comfort and well-being than manners would otherwise have allowed. We all enjoyed fussing over him. The truth is that he achieved more with one hand than other men achieved with two. He was the overseer of the laborers in Azilum, and a stern but fair taskmaster he was . . . and an inspiring one, for no proud and whole man could let himself be outdone by a one-handed master. Half of the week he lived in the Queen's House with Talon and other guests; the other half he abided alone in his own cabin, seventeen leagues deeper into the western wilderness bordering Azilum. His sisters, whom he loved dearly, were still in France.

"Some punch?" he asked, bowing before me. The arm that ended in a hook rather than a hand was tucked into his waistcoat; his black eyes were merry and flirtatious.

"Please," I said, grateful for his attention.

He made a great show of fetching two cups and carrying them pressed between his good arm and chest so they would not spill, and then sitting close, very close, at my side. Miss Sarah Jamison held another piece of cake to Henri's mouth but he was watching du Petit-Thouars and was slower to rise to the bait. That was what he looked like, I decided, a great stupid trout surfacing for horseflies. I smiled at the little admiral and leaned closely into his black waistcoat. He knew the game I was playing at, and played his part nobly and with good cheer.

"Is there any word from your sisters?" I asked. I smiled again, and fluttered my fan. Any observer would think we were speaking of more intimate topics. That was our intention.

"None." He picked up my hand and kissed it. Henri was frowning. "But I have not given up hope. We must none of us lose hope. It is our most precious possession."

"All our hope did the Queen no good," I said, playfully tapping his mouth with my fan, lightly as a butterfly landing on a flower. Now we had Miss Sarah Jamison's attention. I was, thanks to Manon's instructions, particularly skillful with mannerisms employing a fan. Sarah was not. She could not have made that playful little tap without making a fool of herself.

"Nor did it do her any harm," he countered. "It is too pleasant a day to think unhappy thoughts. I am enjoying myself." He leaned closer, putting his weight on his good arm and holding the injured one a little behind his back. "I saw the second cake plate," he whispered, grinning.

"I thought you might have. It was foolish of me."

"It was charming. I more than half-wished I was to be the recipient." Ah, how gallant was our little admiral! Men are not so charming anymore, they have lost the skill. "But given the fact that the cake was not for me, could I ask another favor?" he whispered, leaning ever closer. Henri, straining to hear, was tilting to us and away from Miss Sarah like a tree in a storm.

"Anything," I said, almost meaning it. The petit admiral took my hand and again raised it to his lips, looking into my eyes all the while, and then whispered into my ear. I smiled. I laughed lightly. I tried to blush as I nodded "yes," and whether I blushed or not no longer mattered, for Henri was on his feet and making toward us.

But before he could reach us, the little admiral had also risen to his feet and had moved to the center of our small party.

"Mesdames and messieurs," he called. "Your attention please, for a moment." The sound of forks clattering against plates, the soft murmur of voices heavy with food and sun, even the clamoring of the children softened, as all faces turned to the handsome Frenchman whose left sleeve was tucked into his waistcoat.

"This morning we finished building Azilum's own gristmill," he announced. "We shall grind our own flour and prosper more for our independence!" His voice rose on a note of triumph and cheers rose around him.

"There is a problem, however," he continued. "We have neither sifting cloth nor grind wheel. The first difficulty has already been solved, thanks to the noble generosity of one of the fairest ladies of our privileged colony, Madame de Saint Remy." He paused for effect. "This beautiful and virtuous woman has generously offered to endow us with her finest silk petticoat, to use as a sifting cloth."

"Petticoats! In a public announcement! This is what comes of settling in the wilderness with savages and peasants for neighbors," snorted Madame Farquet. Her husband hushed her.

"Euphonie, there is nothing unseemly in this," he said, stepping forward and looking ridiculous enough to prove there was some truth in his wife's declamation. He wore his best powdered wig on top, but on bottom a pair of stained buckskin trousers.

"In honor of our gristmill, and to show my devotion to Azilum . . . and the beloved child whom we all await, may God protect him"—we bowed our heads in brief prayer for Louis-Charles—"I will personally contribute two dollars toward the purchase of the grinding stone," Monsieur Farquet called in a proud voice. His wife threatened to swoon with dismay, but he continued staunchly. "This is a community in which Rousseau himself would have been proud to participate; here, soothed by nature's gentle purpose will we begin to forge a new life, a life built on harmony and reason, a life—"

"That is unnecessary, Monsieur Farquet . . ." said Sarah Jamison, herself stepping from the listening circle to become a participant. "Just in time," said Smithy, who had crept in next to me, silent as a cat walking in snow. "When Mister Farquet gets wound up, he do go on."

" . . . Unnecessary in that my family will be pleased to donate the stone for your new mill. It would please us to make this gesture of friendship toward our new neighbors. " She blushed prettily, bobbing her blonde curls a few times. She smiled sweetly at Henri. And not as sweetly as me.

"Never has a man before me had the honor of living with more excellent friends and neighbors," said the little admiral, hand on heart. "Never has the spirit of generosity been clothed in such beauty!" He bent and kissed Sarah Jamison's hand, and then mine. Each time he bobbed down that young woman and myself were eye to eye and as wary as two hawks circling the same rabbit. Henri, with an innate intelligence about some things but innocent about others, stood off to the side, looking perplexed. Sarah calmly accepted the applause and cheers and then moved as if she would go to Henri's side.

"Wait. I have more I would say." I put my hand on her arm. I had used a loud voice; the attentive circle turned to me again and waited as I had commanded.

"Our community will have bread with which to feed herself." I smiled at several of the gentlemen, letting my eyes rest longest on Henri. "But we do not live by bread alone. We are a proud race and a civilized one, despite our present circumstances. In addition to a mill, we are building a theater, are we not? If the world were just, our beloved Queen herself would have appeared on that stage. She would have wanted us to complete this theater. We must do it, for her, and for that royal son who is in our thoughts and prayers. And for that purpose I will sponsor a lottery. Two weeks from now a ball gown, designed and sewn by myself of French silk and Belgian lace, will be drawn for. Tickets are one dollar each, and the money will be used to purchase a velvet cloth curtain for the stage."

I knew the French better than Sarah; I was one of them. And my gift of the theater curtain drew much more applause than her gift of a grindstone.

I won the duel, although only Sarah and myself knew of this contest, and the right to take Henri's arm and let him lead me home that day.

"Whatever possessed you?" Victoire asked later, as we sat darning hose. "How can you afford such a project?"

"I will find a way. Somehow. It will be worth it, just for the look on Miss Jamison's face. And I bet she won't sit for a week when she tells her father he has to buy a millstone for the Frenchies!"

Victoire giggled and I smiled, remembering the look of delight and gratitude on the little admiral's face. It was Henri I now wanted, but I was not completely indifferent to the handsome du Petit-Thouars. His gaze had been tender and flattering. Henri's had been perplexed at first, and then later in the afternoon the first glow of triumph began to appear in his eyes. He knew I was no longer indifferent to him, no longer insistent on treating him only as friend or brother.

My skin seemed on fire. Even touching needle to forefinger to darn hose awoke sensations long asleep. When that chore was accomplished and Victoire had gone to her own cabin to fix a supper for Jacques-Pierre, Louis and Antoine, I told Delilah to set an extra plate at our own table.

"Henri will come tonight," I said. She nodded and was not surprised.

Upstairs in my sleeping room I brushed my hair and tied it back so that it fell in black waves to my waist. My sunburnt face reminded me of Mathilde, who had always threatened to sell me to the gypsies because I looked like one of them. Where was that child I had been? Somewhere, inside, she still lurked. My looking glass told me I looked not much older than when I had first met Charles. I felt so much older; much had happened since then.

I sat on the bed and then swung my legs up for a quick rest. I closed my eyes. "Charles," I whispered. Again, "Charles." I waited for that change in atmosphere, that almost tactile sense of memory that made the dead more alive than the living.

But the room remained empty.

"You have been dead for two years," I whispered. "And now, I must live again." A gladness rose in me, that I could say this aloud and finally mean it. Not just survive, not just struggle through. Live.

Henri arrived just as Delilah's rabbit stew was bubbling and browning in its heavy iron kettle and the candles were lit on the dining table. I opened the door to his familiar knock and saw him leaning against the doorframe, his red-gold hair slightly disheveled, a lace jabot poorly tied at his throat. He looked as if he wasn't quite certain why he had come, or knowing why, feared the evening ahead. Pursuing the prey is one thing; catching it another.

"Are you alone, or did you bring Miss Jamison with you?" I asked, smiling.

"Julienne, don't," he pleaded, suffering a real agony.

Once he was in my house, however, I could tease no longer. I sighed and leaned into his arms. They went around me without hesitation, I felt his mouth on the top of my head and breathed in his smell of leather and sun and meadow. His first kiss was tentative and shy; not so his second and third. Delilah's stew went untasted. We were busy elsewhere.

Upstairs, behind the tightly closed bed curtains, Henri pulled and struggled with the lacings on my gown. I could have been of greater assistance but I lay back lazily, enjoying his travail. There was a wildness in his eyes that pleased me, and made me feel calm . . . until the last lacing was undone and I felt his breath and hair trail over my skin, seeking those places that provided the greatest pleasure.

He repeated my name over and over, making a kind of song of it, and held back from taking what I wished to give for a very long time, until my confidence and calm were burned with desire and I writhed in his arms. He was skilled, my Henri. I, the elder, had thought to condescend to him with my greater knowledge of such sport; his talent humbled me. The hours of that night passed quickly.

He called me his love before we fell asleep, twined tightly together.

I awoke to the sound of Delilah knocking at the door. Henri rolled over and reached for me as I slipped out of the curtained bed. Aurore was deep in childish dreams in her little cot.

"What is it?"

Delilah had no need for candles to guide her at night. But she held one for me, and I knew I was called for some errand.

"Smithy is here. Asking for Mister Henri. Big trouble."

"What trouble?"

"Smithy is shot." Her eyes narrowed as she peered over my shoulder to where Henri lay sleeping, visible through the parted bed curtain. She looked at him then at me, and smiled approval.

"Shot. Oh my god. Henri! Henri! Wake up!" I shouted, and then reminded him in a whisper not to awaken Aurore. "Smithy is downstairs. Delilah says he's been shot."

Henri was out of bed and into his trousers with amazing speed. I helped with his shirt and boots, thinking of the countless times I had helped my husband with that simple chore, and how pleasant it was to have a large, strapping man fumbling with buttons and laces and cursing at his cuffs and bootstraps atop a mussed bed. This hurried dressing was, in its way, even more intimate than our lovemaking of the hours before.

Downstairs, we found Smithy where Delilah had left him at the back door, half in and half out and looking about to faint and undecided about whether he should faint into the cabin or out of it. He pressed his hands over his thigh, and when Henri forced away the bloodied fingers we saw a gaping hole in his filthy buckskin trousers, burnt at the edges and opening onto a red mass of flesh.

"Delilah, get hot water. And clean rags. And your cooking tongs," Henri said. "Better bring a sharp knife, too." She brought those things, and we watched as Henri gingerly extracted several small pellets from Smithy's thigh and then washed and bound the wound. I was proud of Henri's skill, proud of the way the knowing Delilah nodded approval.

Smithy grimaced and cursed all the while. Once the urge to faint had left, he spluttered with rage.

"Old man Jamison shot me!" he said, half in anger, half in disbelief. "I never t'would've believed it of 'em. He shot me. And me and him such good hunting friends. Didn't I give him half of that venison last week, knowing damn well his shots had missed the buck by a mile? Didn't I?" He was hurt and offended by Jamison's breach of manners.

"Tell it from the beginning, Smithy," Henri insisted, washing his hands in the now pink-tinted water of the basin Delilah had brought.

"Jamison came to collect his taxes today," Smithy growled. "I told him plenty a' times I wouldn't be paying no excise tax on my still. Even Gov'ner Mifflin says the tax is an illegal one and no good republican should have to pay it. But does Jamison listen? No better'n a coon hound that's gone deaf.

"He comes around, all dandied up in a Sunday suit to collect his damned whiskey tax. I told him, 'Jamison, you'll get no tax money from this freeman. Retreat, now, before I fill you with lead.'"

"And?" said Henri, looking grim.

To the French, the affair that would soon be called the Whiskey Rebellion was a strange, even laughable matter. But Henri, as Senator Morris's envoy to the colony, took it seriously, as did all clear-thinking men. A few years before, Congress, needing funds, had levied a tax on distilleries. But few had paid this tax, calling it as unjust as the earlier British Stamp Act, which had inspired the colonies to revolution. Some mountainmen and other citizens were so outraged at being required to pay tax on their whiskey that they signed secret covenants, vowing to resist the law to the death. Old Herman Husband had almost convinced Bradford County and other parts of eastern

285

Pennsylvania—including French Azilum—to secede from the state, rather than pay the tax.

What was at stake was Washington's authority, as president of the land. And Senator Morris's financial investment in Azilum, which was great.

"And . . . " Henri said again.

"And I shot at him. Over the head, like, so as not to injure him, but only scare him off. And the damn fool fired back. He probably aimed over my head, too, which is why he hit my leg, being the kind of shot he is. So I fired again. I was riled. And bejesus, I think I've killed Colonel Jamison."

"Christ. You damned fool," Henri said. "I'd better get over to Jamison's farm and see how bad the damage is. If he's dead . . . well, Smithy, I'll have to take you to the sheriff in Wyalusing. It's that, or let the other farmers lynch you, which is a lot more deadly than a time in jail." Smithy sobbed now in pain and grief.

"I told him to retreat," he said, over and over.

"I'm coming with you," I said.

The night was black as molasses and smelled that sweet, too, as Henri and I rode over the north pasture of Azilum on his grey mare. I sat in front and tried to remember the seriousness of our errand, but mostly I leaned back against Henri and enjoyed the ride. At the Susquehanna his horse, Ceres, gave a pretty neigh as she picked her delicate hooves through the rock-strewn river bed and crossed over to the eastern shore. The water was shallow enough to ford on foot, although it was not yet mid-summer. It crossed my mind, but only for a second, that that part of the Susquehanna was too shallow to support a trading community and the boats that would need to come and go. Much of what had been planned for us was more hope than reasonable expectation.

Lights shone through the windows of the Jamison farmhouse where it sat at the top of a little hill, with the river running like liquid silver in front of it. Henri jumped from Ceres, helped me down, and then we walked hesitantly to the house, fearing what we would find. It was ominously quiet. Only the crickets and frogs broke the stillness.

Sarah, dressed in a white nightgown, robe, and saucy beribboned cap on her blonde curls, answered Henri's knock. She looked us both up and down for a good while before asking us in. I forgot. I, too was in a nightgown under my mantle.

"It's late to be paying calls, isn't it?" she asked, raising her eyebrows. "And dressed so formally, at that." Her voice was like honey that has had pebbles stirred into it, harsh and cold but all sweet around the hard lines and angles.

"Miss Jamison," said Henri, trying to use an authoritative voice. "I believe you well know this is no social call. Is your father here?"

"He is," she said, smiling. Henri and I sighed with relief. If he made it back from Smithy's camp he might be wounded, but he was most certainly not dead, as Smithy had claimed. "But he's fit to be tied. He and Smithy have been at it again over the whiskey tax, and this time the fools shot at each other. Pa is wounded."

"Badly?" we asked as one.

"Ask him yourself," said daughter Jamison, leading us down a narrow hall to a dimly lit room that was filled with hunting traps, nets, skinning knives, and a shelf of pistols and rifles. "Papa's treasure room," she said, and her honey voice was heavy with sarcasm.

"Colonel Jamison! Are you all right?" Tall Henri bowed his head and shoulders through the doorway.

"Look for yourself. Do I look harmed? You think that smelly goat of a backwoodsman could get the better of me?"

Colonel Jamison roared at us. He was red in the face and sweating. He sat on a stool, knees wide apart, jamming a cleaning rod up and down a stout, powerful looking rifle. His grey hair had come untied and fell in lank clumps over his face and shoulders; his staring angry eyes had something of the madman in them.

"Now, Papa. Don't take on so," soothed Sarah Jamison. "You two have quarreled before and always made it up."

"This is no quarrel. He fired on me. He broke the law of this land by refusing to pay his owed taxes, and then he fired on me. That's not a quarrel. It's a revolt. I'd be dead now, except he used his rabbit rifle, not his deer musket, fool that he is." He pulled out a small, leather-bound book from his breast pocket and exhibited it proudly in his huge hand. There, imbedded deep in the cover, were five small pellets.

"He ruined my New Testament," said Colonel Jamison gloomily.

"I'd be pleased to buy you a new one," said Henri, sensing that peace of a sort might yet be arranged.

Jamison kept silent and cleaned his rifle with yet more vigor, his thick grey brows knitted over his eyes.

"One with real gold lettering, and etchings inside," Henri said.

"He insulted me personally, but that I can take," sighed Colonel Jamison. "But he also insulted a tax collector for the great government of this land, as it is written by President Washington."

"You know Smithy doesn't recognize any government larger than an

Indian campfire," said Henri. "He never has, and never will. If it's the tax money you want, I'll pay it for him. On condition you never tell him."

"What's your interest in this, boy?" Jamison's face was filled with suspicion.

Henri bridled at the open insult. He drew himself up to his full height, which was considerable, before answering.

"My interest is this. If everyone who upholds a law starts to shoot at everyone who disagrees with the same law, it seems to me we'll soon have nothing but chaos. There are plenty who would agree with you, that Smithy deserved to be fired upon. And there are just as many who would agree with Smithy, that you, excuse me, sir, deserved to be fired upon. When too many people start taking sides like that, it turns into a war. Now, I don't want Bradford County, or any other part of the country, seceding just because of a tax. As Senator Morris's personal envoy, I intend to keep the peace in French Azilum and its environs. There's no harm so far. But if you persist, and Smithy persists, then we'll be in a hell of a mess."

Henri was breathless by the time he finished.

"There's some truth in all that, though you came to it by a roundabout way," Jamison said, putting down his rifle. "Tell you what. You give me three dollars for a new New Testament. And another six dollars in owed taxes." He squinted as Henri opened a cloth wallet and began counting out coins. "Make it an even ten," Jamison said.

"Don't tell Smithy. Just never bring up the matter again," Henri said. "You know how he feels about this excise tax."

"I know, but the government is government and taxes are to be paid." His voice changed from anger to concern. "How is he? Did I hit him?"

"In the thigh. But he'll probably heal good as new."

"Smithy wasn't good as new even when he was born," grumbled Colonel Jamison.

Our business peacefully concluded, Sarah led us out of the dark, rifle-cluttered room back to the hall. The cabin smelled foully of the cabbage they had eaten for dinner; the Americans, unlike the French, did not believe in detaching the cookhouse from the main house. But the cabin was tidy and clean and I could see Sarah took pride in her housekeeping.

"Do visit again," she smirked. "But next time you might consider something more suitable than a nightrobe." She smiled at Henri and then slammed the door.

"Don't worry, Julienne," said my new lover. "I already knew she's almost betrothed to a downriver farmer. Her pride's been stung, is all."

"What makes you think I was worried about Sarah?" I asked. (Indeed, Sarah did quite well with her downriver farmer and grew quite wealthy—

and fat—with the years. But she never smiled at me again, and she never stopped smiling at Henri.)

Smithy healed, as Henri predicted, but he kept his leg stiffly bound and his temper at high ebb so that he hobbled, step, hop, bejesus, step, hop, bejesus, until the feastday of the Virgin's Nativity in September, and all the small boys of the settlement mimicked him.

That was the extent of French Azilum's involvement with the great Whiskey Rebellion of 1794. Elsewhere, armies of backwoodsmen surrounded cities and towns, threatening to burn them to the ground. Townspeople organized "committees of safety," something that reminded us French of the revolutionary tribunals we had fled. Washington, faced with a situation that could easily turn into civil war, gathered together an army and the rebels, intimidated, slunk back to their homes. The rebellion was over before the fall harvest was ripe.

The country was far from peaceful, though. There was talk of war with England again, this time on the side of France. The British were stirring trouble by promising hostile Indians they would drive the "Yankees" back across the Ohio for them.

None of this was of much concern to me. I ignored the troubles with the Indians just as years before, I had ignored the new Jacobin clubs. I had closed myself within that smaller world that is love. Procuring bottles of Henri's favorite port for after supper, searching for the prettiest wildflowers to put in my sleeping room, so their perfume would fill our dreams . . . those were the things that concerned me.

And Azilum, now seemingly of its own will, continued to build and expand. The days were filled with the constant noise of hammering and sawing. Our chapel and gristmill were completed, as was the little theater.

That summer we received one of our most important and most controversial visitors, Charles Maurice de Talleyrand-Périgord.

Although he had long since been excommunicated by the Church, I still thought of him as the Bishop of Autun, the powerful, revolutionary ecclesiastic and politician who had celebrated the huge, disastrous, open-air Mass in honor of the revolution in 1790 . . . where I was pushed, so that I later lost Charles's first child. The Feast of the Federation had been a sorrowful event for me; because of those associations I was not overly eager to meet Talleyrand.

Others were even less enthusiastic than I. Most royalists considered Talleyrand to be a traitor, and nothing less, for his role in the revolution, which was not insignificant. It was his suggestion that they confiscate church property to obtain funds; his rhetoric had fanned the flames of the revolutionaries. He had tried to remove the royal family from France, it is true. And like all the others, he failed. And then, like the others, the revolution turned on him. He had been living in exile in England since 1793, but when the war between France and England grew hotter, he was expelled from that country, too. And now he had come to the United States, and wished to see the colony of Azilum.

Talleyrand did not ask to visit my wilderness home, so he never knew he had been banned from it. He had known Charles, and would have condescended to offer words of sympathy to his widow. That, I did not want. Not with Henri always hovering over me, jealous, attentive, easily wounded Henri. My lover, Henri. He had carried me from the past to the present, we were happy in each other's arms. I was free of the past and of the mourning for Charles. No. I would have no conversation with Talleyrand, who would praise Charles and look at Henri with all the haughty disdain an older, experienced man saves for the young.

I did attend several dinners given at the Queen's House while he was a guest. I remember him as a man whose eyes never ceased moving in his alert, somewhat smug face. He took in everything with those eyes and had a way of talking with one hand in front of his mouth, as if he would obscure the truth even as he tried to state it. He survived three—or is it four?—governments, Charles Maurice de Talleyrand-Périgord. He helped to make and then break three of the most important men in my lifetime: Louis XVI, Napoleon, and Louis XVIII. Who would have thought that such a man would live a long life and die peacefully, of simple old age?

Poor Abbé Carles was frantic all the while Talleyrand was in Azilum, and spilled the communion wine during one of his Masses. Henri, too, was intimidated by the great man, although he took great care not to show it. Talon send him this way and that over the roads and mountains of Pennsylvania, securing special French wines, German hams, and other delicacies.

But once the single candle in neighboring Madame Farquet's cabin was extinquished and the dark night promised secrecy, not even an order from Talleyrand could keep Henri from appearing at my door, grinning and eager.

"I wake up and am afraid it's a dream," he said one night in September. "I have to touch you, hold you, to know you're there." The darkness was alive with the sound of chirping crickets and the deep bass love songs of the river frogs. His voice was like a child's, or like a man that still carried within a little boy who had awoken often to find he was alone. His fair hair was damp on his forehead. I pushed it back out of his eyes, loving the man and the child within.

"Hold me," I whispered to him. "We will dream together."

290

18

. . . the departures of summer's end . . .

Loss is nothing else but change, and change is Nature's delight.

—Marcus Aurelius

Sometime in that raw, beautiful Azilum summer Aurore left her infancy behind and grew into a wild, splendid creature, separate from me. She had no more patience with my ministrations but would sup only with her own spoon and from her own bowl of hominy, sweetened with amber honey. Her eyes filled with resigned scorn when I minced her meat and vegetables for her.

Even during the intimidating thunderstorms of summer that swept over our colony as swiftly as birdflight, she disdained my bed and would cower in her own, green eyes wide with awe and new independence.

She trotted through the muddy paths and fragrant wildflower fields with a determined avidity that promised trouble in the years to come. Her displays of childish arrogance had more to do with her father's aristocratic origins than my own humble ones.

"'Fin" she would demand haughtily, pointing to a tray of Delilah's muffins. Delilah, patiently waiting for the "please" that was too long in coming, would shake her head so vigorously that her medicine bag would sway back and forth across her chest. Delilah always gave in to the command in those sea-green eyes, as did we all, and began to call her Queen Esther. This pleased

Aurore tremendously. Queen Esther was a Delaware squaw who had massacred land-greedy Europeans in bloody and famous battles.

"She's a changeling," I complained to Henri one day as I pulled her, muddy and squirming, back over the cabin threshold into the safety of my sewing room. She had run out the door without looking and had almost been knocked over by a passing mule. It was the beginning of the early harvest and the paths of Azilum were rutted and busy. The German farmer riding the startled animal jerked hard on the reins and himself toppled off the animal into dust-swirls and dung pats. I didn't understand his language, and the anger in his voice made me glad we spoke separate tongues.

"I was never so much trouble, nor so regardless," I said, wiping and fussing over the child after apologizing to the farmer.

"Mothers' memories are short," Henri laughed. "No harm has been done, and if you never caused more grief than this you must have been perfection itself."

"You spoil her!" I said, angry because his words recalled the many times I had been exiled to my attic asylum to avoid Mathilde's curses and cuffs.

He pulled on his ear, grinned and strode off in the direction of the gristmill to examine the timbers, which had swelled in the summer heat and humidity. It was Henri's way to avoid quarrels rather than rush headlong into them as I was wont to do. He sidestepped disagreements the way others sidestepped mud puddles in their path, with an easy elegance that was, in itself, the last word.

Aurore, however, delighted in trouble. She would be hungry only when there was no food prepared; during meals she sat glassy-eyed and miserable, her mouth as tightly shut as a sewn-over button hole. She wanted to play with her rag doll and wooden animals all night, even when the adults of the colony dropped with fatigue from the lateness of the hour. And then in the morning, when I encouraged her to sit and watch me sew since it was not too soon to accustom her to the craft, she would wilt with sleepiness. When I wanted to hug her she squirmed away; when I was busy she would clamber onto my lap, spilling the peas I shelled or the chicken I plucked.

Her growing independence was part of nature's purpose, but no less hurtful for that. Already, I anticipated the years to come when she would be a grown woman who rolled her eyes at her *maman*'s advice and feared that her *maman*'s visits would be overly long, and I sighed.

But the heart seeks always to be full, so I consoled myself with my young swain's adoration and sought closer friendships with the women of our rustic colony. My sewing room was often filled with gossips who passed long hours there. We sewed and talked and talked and sewed, sharing old and fresh news, dreams and speculation, so that sometimes I was reminded of Bertin's workshop and the seamstresses, whom I missed. Many of these newer friends were former countesses and abbesses of noble blood; they would not have enjoyed the comparison.

Nor were they as well-informed as Bertin's seamstresses had been. Our thoughts that summer were much on Louis-Charles, still in his prison. Bertin's girls would have known what foods the little king was served at each meal, and in what quantity. They would have known when he suffered poor digestion, when he had a cold in the chest, when he had enjoyed some small kindness at the hands of his guards.

We in Azilum knew none of this. We could only speculate, and move from hope to fear and back again, as we waited for his anticipated liberation.

I suspect that many of my visitors enjoyed my humble salon because their own pasts shown so much more brilliantly there than did my own history. Or what they knew of it. Once I laughed aloud thinking of what their expressions would be, should I appear to tea wearing the Queen's diamond around my neck. But that thought also brought more worries. They would, of course, assume I had come by it dishonestly.

I also overlooked the possibility that they were lured there more by Delilah's excellent biscuits and teas than my chatter.

Only one woman disdained to visit, and that was Mademoiselle Adelaide de Rélevé.

"She can't abide to have blacks near her," Victoire told me. "She dislikes the freedoms you permit Delilah." Delilah had an African grandmother and was darker complexioned than the other Indians of the area.

"The freedom Delilah has is hers by birth, not by my tolerance," I answered, irritated by such pretensions. "This is not Saint Domingue, where the de Rélevé's and the other rich families of the north plain decided that liberty was a condition reserved for the whites of the island. And Delilah is more Indian than black, anyway. We should live at peace with each other." That is always easier said than done.

It was Mademoiselle de Rélevé who won the lottery for the gown, but it brought her no happiness. Her memory, long confined to a darkness we couldn't reach, broke free that August and blazed fiercely, and much damage was done by the time we cooled the flames.

She, with her hair the color of daffodils and eyes blue as wild forget-me-nots, spent most of that summer in a cool daze, smiling and dancing gracefully in the music room, and accompanying Victoire's faulty but spirited piano-forte recitals with her high, trembling voice. Monsieur de St. Christophe was her constant companion, except at those moments when courtesy required her to abandon his attendance on her for modesty's sake. He was a most courteous man, Monsieur de St. Christophe, careful never to overstep the bounds of good manners, never to impose, never to demand, and perhaps that was part of his undoing. His eyes never left her face; she never once, that I can recall, looked at him.

But their relationship was of little interest to me. She was cold and unfriendly and, in a manner I came to identify with Creoles, treated her superiors as her equals, her equals as her servants, her servants as slaves, and slaves as animals. If all whites in the island shared her attitude, I was not surprised that the blacks, promised liberty and given chains, murdered these Creoles in their beds.

I was busy with other matters. My new gown salon opened in July, in my downstairs sewing room. It was small, but it began well, despite the many difficulties. We had no talented sign painters yet in Azilum, and the lettering on my shingle displeased me because of its crookedness. I acquired the habit of looking up and frowning everytime I entered my doorway, and so acquired a permanent wrinkle between my brows.

Even more troublesome and momentous was the question of stocking my supplies. I was, as the merchants of the Susquehanna trading posts constantly reminded me, quite a way from Paris, and there would be no guarantee that French silks and Belgian laces would always be available. And if they were, how could I afford them? Mister Hollenback, manager of the trading post closest to Azilum, agreed to give me a quantity discount on goods after much haggling and arguing, but even so the cost of the goods I wished were very, very dear for me and my customers. Not for us the crude, cheap baize that the American women wore; we wanted bombazine for our gowns. The American women could wear pigeon feathers in their aigrettes; we must have peacock.

"I shall do what we did in Paris," I said to Delilah, as I arranged a display of blue-and-white calico—French calico, the best. "I will charge more of those who can afford to pay more, and try to make up profits that way." That meant charging my wealthy American farmwives more, and my French exiles less.

"And unlike Paris, there will be no credit," I mused aloud. "They will have to wait until the harvest is sold before giving their orders."

Delilah stood, stern and solemn, arms crossed over her chest. But she eyed a buff colored lace buffont on the table. She tried it tentatively on top of her thick, black hair. I took it from her and pinned it over her bosom, where it was supposed to be worn. The thick rows of cascading lace made her chest curve like a pouter pigeon's; she laughed with delight, but then put it back on the table, saying that Frenchwomen lacked sense. That was the Delaware way of saying she thought we were mad.

Aurore, jealous of the attention Delilah was receiving, crawled into a large open trunk filled with laces and ribbons arranged in wild confusion. The American shopkeepers hadn't learned that trick yet; lined-up goods in neat and strict order look unfriendly and less desirable; let them be slightly disheveled, temptingly out of order, and they sell much more quickly. Women want what other women have not been able to obtain. Didn't Madame Lamotte act on that, when she assumed that Marie-Antoinette wished to buy Madame du Barry's famous diamond necklace?

Aurore sat in the trunk, gleeful and as pretty as Pandora about to open her box of troubles. Red, blue and yellow ribbons cascaded over her dark hair.

"And you, poppet, shall have all the scraps, and I will sew you the most colorful gowns a girl ever wore," I promised, scooping her up and dancing around the room.

Delilah, unsmiling, danced a few steps too, and her leather moccasins made a hissing sound as they slid over the bare wood floor. Her beaded necklace clicked gently.

Our dance halted at the wooden frame supporting the gown I had newly finished for the lottery. The arms of the dress stuck out at harsh right angles over the scarecrow form, and a painted cloth face rested precariously atop it in a foolish manner, but even so the gown was magnificent, and I was proud of my work. Wild iris had been blooming in the marsh when I first sketched the gown onto paper. Their forms and colors were repeated in the paneled skirt which was made of a series of deep blue petals over a white petticoat. The lighter blue bodice had been trimmed with white edging and a golden silk fichu.

The gown had cost me a considerable sum and Henri had shaken his head many times over this foolishness. It was, he said, worth the cost of a good, sturdy plow. But it was worth it when the doors to my shop opened and Sarah Jamison entered.

"I will trade you Bessie, my milk-goat, for this dress," she said and her eyes were big with covetousness.

"No. It is for the lottery," I said. "Buy another ticket and hope for the outcome."

But it was not Sarah's lucky day. After Delilah cleared away the tea cups and plates, served at my own expense to those who came for the lottery and to see my shop, she carried in a bowl containing stubs from the thirty purchased tickets.

The twenty ladies in the room moved eagerly forward, as cats do at feeding time, and the men stepped back, sensing that they were in the way, at best. Talon had come, too, and I was honored by this although he eyed me askance and did not smile. Ever since our interview, which had ended with his frowning at what he took to be my lack of cooperation, he had continued to frown at me.

"Folderol," complained Colonel Jamison, his purse three dollars lighter for three lottery tickets. "All this fuss over a dress."

"Hush, Papa!" came Sarah's sharp voice from across the room, and the farmer hushed, cowed by the authority in his maiden daughter's voice.

The lingering August twilight was reflected in the hopeful faces of the women who gathered round my table. They held their breath as Aurore, blindfolded even though she was years from reading her alphabet, reached one chubby hand into the crystal bowl borrowed from the Queen's House and pulled out a piece of paper.

She shrieked, delighted with the attention, and then clapped her hands. Her own dress was a miniature replica of the Iris gown. Even then it pleased Aurore to dress finely and be the center of attention. Even then she was beautiful, with her hair dark as the fleeting night and her face radiant as the new day. Victoire's middle son, Louis, leaned his six-year old frame against the hearth mantel, and stuck out his tongue at her.

"The winner . . . " I read slowly, to heighten the drama, " . . . is Mademoiselle Adelaide de Rélevé!" I smiled and clapped to hide my disappointment; I had hoped Victoire would be the winner. It irked me that she who had disdained my house and hospitality should now wear the gown I had sewn with such care and pride. We were all foreigners in a strange land, but de Rélevé had firmly remained an outsider even to us.

She accepted prettily and with modesty so that the men at least applauded enthusiastically for her, although many women were tight-lipped.

"Thank you," she said with a curtsey, and Monsieur de St. Christophe clapped as though she had just made a speech declaring the end of all evil in the world.

"Monsieur Talon invites you all to the Queen's House," Henri then announced over the high voices of the women and the mumble of the men as they circled each other to tell whatever tales men tell when the rum is free and the evening long.

Most events of worth in the settlement were concluded in the Queen's House; it was Talon's attempt to make a community of us, to keep us from being a random collection of exiles thrown together by chance. But already there was dissension among us, in the form of a proposed letter of recognition to the Comte de Provence, who was calling himself King Louis XVIII. Some men of Azilum felt that Louis-Charles could no longer be considered our rightful king. He was too young and too powerless. He, like his royal mother and father, had been abandoned.

Others, including myself, insisted there was no rightful king but the son of Marie-Antoinette, and refused to acknowledge the claims of the Comte de Provence. Talon was of this opinion. But he could not force his opinion on others. Sides were being taken, lines drawn. It did not make for an atmosphere of good will. It had not occurred to us that it is possible to live and breathe without declaring allegiance to any king; the thought was as heretical as atheism.

The French men broke into two groups, those who favored Provence and those who remained steadfast in their love for Louis-Charles. But both made their way to Talon's drawing room in a peaceful manner. The American men shuffled their feet uneasily. They did not enjoy those evenings in the Great House. With their nankeen jackets and muddy boots, they felt as out of place in the French drawing room as most of the French men, with their lace cuffs and powdered queues, looked in the wild forests of Azilum.

But Sarah would go, hence her father would too, whether he wished it or not, and he dragged along a few of his cronies and we made a party of sorts that evening. I would rather have spent the evening alone with Henri but went along to accept compliments on the Iris gown and create some new business.

"Exquisite!" exclaimed Madame Farquet. "The gown personifies all the beauty that was France, before." She took my arm as we walked.

"You are too kind. But that gown would not suit you," I protested. "I have not yet created the design that would compare to your own elegance." What I meant was that since Madame Farquet was a pauper, she and I had no business to discuss. I thought of Aurore and the things she would need in the years to come. Charity would be a luxury I could not afford.

"I must have a copy of that gown," Sarah Jamison hissed as I passed by.

"Agreed. But in pink, don't you think?" She had silver coins with which to pay. I made her pink gown, and a yellow-and-white Iris gown for others, and even heard a few years after that a lavender imitation of the Iris gown had shown up in Mr. Bingham's parlor in Philadelphia. I now consider the style to be overblown, but it satisfied the longings of the women of Azilum who dreamed of Paris operas, not chicken coops.

It was hot that evening in the Queen's House. The warmth of the August day did not dissipate with the night, but hung over us like a heavy blanket, bearing down, slowing our movements, making us lethargic. Even with the long windows and double doors thrown open to catch the stray breezes, the foreheads of the women grew dewy and the men puffed and grew red in the face.

Despite the heat, Mademoiselle de Rélevé changed into the Iris gown and entertained us with an aria from a Gluck opera, a lengthy song filled with trilling pathos and sadness. She missed not a word, and it struck me as strange that the young woman could remember lyrics so well, and so little of her own life. She talked of her mother and father and brother as if they still lived, and would arrive any day. Many in Philadelphia had done that also, but it was rarer in Azilum. The harsher reality of wildnerness life burst those fragile and worthless illusions. Where there is loss, there must be mourning if the heart is to heal. Yet she danced and sang as if she hadn't a care in the world. Monsieur de St. Christophe watched her as if he could die for love.

Shadows played about the room, flickering around the carved porcelain vases and delicate tables that had been purchased by Talon with an eye to pleasing Marie-Antoinette. Mingled with our own music we could hear the sound of drums coming from the shanties by the edge of the river, where the slaves were housed.

The blacks there were underfed and overworked, many bound for life to contracts that took much of them and gave them only the barest essentials for survival. The children were thin and listless and their mothers had black eyes that looked through their white owners.

Delilah, part black herself, scorned such inferior people, but spent many evenings there, mixing potions and medicines and binding wounds caused by field accidents and owners who favored whips.

The drums played loudly that night, overpowering the thin music of the pianoforte as easily as night overcomes a single candle, reminding us that we were strangers to this land.

At one point Mademoiselle de Rélevé stopped in the middle of a dance and pressed her hands to her temples. "They are so loud," she complained, frowning. "Papa has told them they must not play so loudly. It is forbidden."

Monsieur de St. Christophe led her to a chair and pressed her hands between his. She was agitated and wild-eyed. Her feet tapped under the blue-petaled gown as if she must run. Dr. Buzard, separating himself from a circle of men who surrounded the punch bowl, came over and laid his palm over her forehead.

"She's overheated and distracted. It's the heat," he said. "Perhaps it is reminding her of Saint Domingue. Keep watch over her tonight."

But as soon as we showed concern, she smiled again, and protested that we were making a fuss over nothing. The dancing continued.

It was at midnight that Henri noticed that the night was growing lighter and warmer, not darker and cooler. The drums stopped suddenly and the night was ominously silent. Then we heard screams. Henri stepped out through the double doors, was swallowed by the grey light, and then returned, pale and tense.

"Fire," he said, and his face was ashen. "The shanties are ablaze."

There was mad confusion as we ran to the door. The billowing skirts of the women crushed against each other fighting for the right of way, and so many men tried to go through the door at the same time that the wooden frame shuddered and threatened to break. Henri shouted commands.

"Bring the buckets. Form a line from the river to the shanties." Almost all of us had seen this process before, in the Auvergne or the Cité, or the sections of Philadelphia where householders had been too poor to pay for the protection of Franklin's Union Fire Company.

We grabbed buckets from the storeroom and ran to the river, shedding whatever finery could be removed without scandal to keep our garments from scorching. Trees and bushes leading to the shanties soon wore shawls and lace bows and feather headpieces. On one branch a man's wig swayed in the hot, cinder-filled breeze, startling us with a cruel imitation of a head on a pike.

The shanties were not far from the cabins; if the strong wind carried a spark to just one of our wooden roofs the whole settlement could be ashes by morning. We had grieved and jested and complained about the difficulties of our lot in Azilum. Faced with losing it, though, we worked with a frenzied determination to preserve what we had created.

Henri, striding about and giving orders to confused men and women, stole one brief moment to hug me for courage and gave me a distracted kiss, forgetting that we had, until this moment, managed to keep our alliance discreet, if not secret.

"You must pass the bucket faster," I yelled at Madame Farquet to keep her from offering one of her vexing comments on wilderness morality.

Adelaide de Rélevé, still dressed in her Iris gown, was on my left side on the line. She passed the buckets quickly and with no show of emotion, but her hands trembled. I don't know when she disappeared. There were too many other tragedies to keep her in mind. The first shanty burned to the ground and Adelaide was there beside me when the black woman who had lived in it dropped to her knees and wailed. A second shanty burned, but we stopped the fire before it destroyed a third. When I finally passed the fire bucket for the last time, Adelaide was gone.

We trailed back to the Queen's House in an exhausted, disheveled line of men and women, our faces black with soot and grime, our hearts heavy with the sense of our own fragility. Even Henri, who normally was strong and cheerful as the noon sun, was made subdued and solemn by this near-disaster.

Only then, when I thought our evening's hard travail was over, did I remember Mademoiselle Adelaide de Rélevé, who was nowhere to be seen. The night felt newly ominous. I walked faster, remembering her wild eyes and her confusion when the drums, which had been silent for hours, began to play. Henri, without asking why, quickened his pace to match mine.

The Queen's House was just as we had left it, with doors and windows flung wide. Victoire's sheet music was still open on the pianoforte, Monsieur Talon's snuff box open upon a table. Half-emptied cups of punch rested on side tables, rivulets of condensation running down their sides and onto the delicate wood.

But from upstairs I heard a wailing such as I had never heard before. Henri, taking the stairs two at a time, reached the room first and tried to block my way through the door. I twisted under his arm and forced my way through.

We found Delilah, proud, stern Delilah, cowering on her hands and knees in a corner of Adelaide de Rélevé's bedroom. Adelaide stood over her, arms raised high, ready to strike again with a riding whip. Aurore sat on the floor next to Delilah, unmoving, her eyes wide with fear. She did not move or call out when she saw me; I was terrified she had been beaten too, although we saw no immediate injury.

Adelaide, seeing us, froze, and there was great confusion and cruelty in her eyes.

I ran and scooped up Aurore as Henri crossed the room in three strides. He grabbed the whip from Adelaide and raised his hand as if he would strike her in exchange for the blows she had given Delilah. But he did not. Adelaide screamed and went limp; her eyes rolled up before closing and her lips were white.

"Delilah," I said. "Run and get Dr. Buzard. Please."

She did not move, but looked at me with a steady, burning hate. Her dress was torn, red blood seeped through the blue homespun. Adelaide, pretty, delicate Adelaide, had done this. But Delilah, dark-skinned woman of the Delaware, hated all French at that moment.

"Please," I said again. "She has a sickness of the mind, Delilah. She lacks sense." I used the Delaware phrase for insanity.

Delilah nodded then. She went for Dr. Buzard, and Henri and I carried Adelaide to her bed. Despite the continuing heat of the evening, her hands were cold as ice.

"Shock," pronounced Dr. Buzard, feeling for the weak, fluttering pulse in the slender wrist. "Her memory must have returned tonight and it was more than she could bear."

Monsieur de St. Christophe came in and clasped the unconscious woman in his arms. After some moments her eyes opened and some of her color returned, but she could neither see nor hear us. She began to shiver, and cry out.

"Papa! Papa! Don't leave me! It's dark, Papa. I smell smoke. Papa, what is the smoke?"

Monsieur de St. Christophe crushed her to him, but as much as he wanted to, he could not erase the visions and memories that flooded her disturbed mind. She cried out and struggled with unseen demons for the length of that long summer night, and as we pieced together her cries to make a story of them, we, too, began to shiver.

Other plantations of Saint Domingue's rich north plain had been burned first, there were months and months of burnings. The nights had been evil and yellow with the fires. Her father had believed the killings and burnings to be a momentary aberration and would not flee; any moment sanity would return to their island. It did not. Their turn came. Ogé, the runaway slave, led his army to them, surrounded the plantation house, and then circled closer and closer.

Adelaide and her family waited, smelling the sickening sweet smell of burning sugar cane that came to them on the tropical wind. It was too late to leave. They waited, trapped in the huge, wooden house with its delicate balconies and the vine-covered trellised windows, and the night grew light and hot as the fields around them burned.

Her mother played a slow aria on the pianoforte. Her father stood behind her mother, his hands on her shoulders. Adelaide sang the accompaniment to her mother's music, proud that her voice did not tremble.

The dog, Moumou, took fright and ran to the dark coolness of the root cellar. Adelaide ran through the spark-strewn darkness after the beribboned dog, meaning to save Moumou rather than abandon her family. But by then the drunken, blood-smeared army was there, outside the door, and she could not return to the main house.

She could still hear her mother playing at the pianoforte, above the sound of the wooden doors of the house being axed and splintered open. She found a loose board in the cellar door and pried it further loose so she could peer out. Some of the faces that rushed past were familiar. They had been cane cutters and fire feeders and even house servants, and now they were breaking down the doors of her home to murder her family. Some of the ex-slaves still wore the steel neck rings of servitude but their chains were broken. The faces were black or brown or the pale color of coffee with cream, every hue but the lightest, the color of privilege. They beat on drums, hollowed tree trunks covered with taut goatskin that her father had forbidden the slaves to own because they were part of the secret voodoo.

They laughed as they threw flaming torches onto the paper-dry roof. They called upon Damballah and the other gods to witness the blood sacrifice, and poured rum on the ground. One of them, the one who played John the Baptist in the rites Adelaide had once secretly witnessed, had a snake coiled around his neck.

Her six-year-old brother did not comprehend why his mother sat so calmly at the pianoforte, oblivious to all but the black-and-white ivory keys under her fingers. The white keys are the important ones she had told him, the black keys are nothing without the white. Frightened by the sight of High John, who was once their liveried footman but who was now a stranger, he ran.

Adelaide, still peering through the crack in the door, saw him rush headlong into the night, into the black army. Her brother, a small patch of white, was swallowed whole by the rioting blacks, and then was spewed forth again, a flailing white banner atop a tall pike. Her mother was dragged away from the pianoforte and the music stopped. The screams started. The raping lasted for half an hour before she died, and long before those screams ended Adelaide's father was slashed open from the throat to groin, bloody and pulpy as a side of beef.

The house, already dried and tortured by the hot winds and the rain of sticking, burning sugar cane, took fire easily. Adelaide crouched in the dank cellar, clinging to Moumou, forcing him to stay silent. She knew she was being cowardly, her mother would not have approved, but there was no other way to be. She did not want to die, not if she would have to scream and thrash under body after body, like her mother. The fire roared overhead, the revolting slaves danced and sang in front of the cellar door, and she survived.

This was the revolution in Saint Domingue, this was the night she relived. We watched by her, wiping her forehead, moistening her cracked lips, holding her arms down when we feared she would injure herself.

"It would have been better had the Assembly declared the blacks to be free and equal, as they promised," Henri remarked once under his breath. "And you wonder that I have no love for France, and French law."

"Is your chosen home without sin? There are slaves here in Pennsylvania," I reminded him.

Monsieur de St. Christophe held Adelaide until she finally fell asleep in his arms. Henri and I left them like that, Adelaide finally resting, her face composed again but looking vulnerable and alive so that we knew the healing would begin now, and his face, pale and masklike, as if he had taken her grief into himself.

We were all so concerned about Adelaide that no one thought to worry about Monsieur de St. Christophe. He looked so strong, seemed so capable. Now, all these years later, I recall the look on his face as he held his beloved and know that it was not strength we saw, but a misery so deep, a despair so complete, that a decade of sunshine, a cathedral of candles, could not reach the dark corners of his suffering.

At dawn, with no sleep to strengthen me, I went to Delilah in the cookhouse, to discover her part in the evening before.

"We smelled the smoke and saw the fire," she told me, grim and angry. "Aurore was afraid, she wanted to go to the Great House and be with you. When we got there you were gone to the river. But the Frenchwoman from Saint Domingue was there. She started to yell that I killed her brother, that she would kill me. She got a whip. I was holding Aurore, I was afraid Aurore would be hit, so I ran upstairs. She ran after us. Then you came."

I checked the wounds on Delilah's arm and face. They were not dangerously deep, but her pride was greatly wounded. She had never been struck before. "That woman better stay away from me. I can fix her," and she shook her medicine bag in warning.

Many of us were relieved to learn the next day that Adelaide was to return to Philadelphia. None of us truly fit into that wilderness home, but Adelaide was the least likely of us to find any kind of peace or comfort there. While her memory was restored, there was a hard glint to her eyes that still made us uncomfortable. No, we were glad to see her go, as soon as her fever was gone and she could travel. She reminded us all of too many things, too much suffering, that must be forgotten or at least pushed aside. For the first time in many months I had my old nightmare about the drums in the Place de la Guillotine and Charles's head before me on the bloody pike.

Eventually, Adelaide found work in Monsieur de Mery's new French bookstore in Philadelphia, and was content there, according to her infrequent letters. "I loathed Azilum," she wrote me. "Loathed the cabins and the shanties and even the fields. I prefer my little rented room on Market Street. It is very different from Saint Domingue, and that is all that I wish."

She never asked for news of Monsieur de St. Christophe, and as far as I know no one ever informed her that we found him one day in late

September, hanging from a thornbush tree. Silent Joshua cut him down and carried his body to the Queen's House, to be readied for burial.

This young man was the first to be laid to rest in the small cemetery next to our log chapel. We ignored the fact that he had died by his own hand, and buried him in consecrated ground.

Delilah, for twelve nights after the funeral, set a place for him at our table, and put on his plate the largest pieces of meat, the sweetest berries, the whitest bread.

"For twelve nights he will stay here before beginning his journey on the Sky Path," she said. "He needs food. No one in the Great House will have sense to set a plate for him. We must do it." I hope his journey to the other world was kindlier than his path through this life.

These tragedies, coming so close together, helped change my feelings for Henri and what had begun as passion, as physical craving, took on deeper dimensions. I turned to him for comfort and companionship. I spoke as freely to him as I did to Victoire, and he became my friend and my solace, in addition to being my love. That first joyful passion turned to a softer, more constant need that only quieted when he was with me. I anticipated his company with the same hunger with which I anticipated Delilah's sustaining meals, and felt as though I would never have my fill of either. He grew more confident, more authoritative; before my eyes, within my arms, the boy was becoming the man.

We avoided discussion of political theories because such doomed conversation resulted in quarrels. And I did not tell him of the Queen's diamond. Something still held my tongue. But we were open and loving in all other things and I forgot Talon's warning that the agents of revolution could reach even Azilum.

In September our little wooden theater was completed, and the gold curtain raised for the first time. There were as many people on stage as in the audience. Henri and I were invited to read a scene from Shakespeare's *Romeo and Juliet*, an invitation which led me to believe that our liaison had become common knowledge.

Henri, looking more than a little foolish in garb meant to resemble that of an Italian Renaissance youth, tripped over the wooden scenery and showed no talent whatsoever for playacting. But love gave a certain sincerity to his voice. When he spoke the lines, "Hence banished is banished from the world, and world's exile is death; then 'banished' is death mis-termed," only the most hardened men in the resin-smelling, shadowy theater did not reach for their handkerchiefs.

My line was: "My husband is on earth, my faith in heaven." I grew aware again of the largeness of the human heart, which can yet love a dead husband while making room for a new love. The human heart, I'm told, is made of chambers that lead back and forth into each other and love, like blood, must flow in a constant and circular pattern.

We were soundly applauded for our performance, and Madame Farquet even admitted, somewhat grudgingly, that the Queen herself would have enjoyed it, although she had not cared much for the English author. We were invited to the Queen's House after, but by unspoken agreement Henri and I, newly afire, went to my cabin instead, and quickly, quickly, made our way up the narrow stairs to the bedroom.

"Wherefore art thou?" I asked, and Henri's red-haired head appeared from under the blanket cover. "Thou art the dawn," he whispered, misquoting but filling me with delight for his intent, not his literary accuracy.

But in the heat of ecstasy, I called out Charles's name, so that both Henri and I felt forlorn afterward.

The heat of August grew strongest at the end of the month, as if summer were struggling with the new season to come and boasting of its strength. Mosquitoes swarmed in thick clouds over the river, and the marshes hummed day and night with the drone of insects. Our clothes were constantly damp with perspiration and the relentless sun felt more like enemy than friend. I wrapped a wet turban round my hair to do my chores, à la Franklin, and let Aurore wade in the low, heat-gentled river with Antoine.

Summer was fierce with us, it burned our skins, cracked the soil in our gardens and fields, made tempers touchy. But it was worse in Philadelphia, and I was glad we were away from there.

"The city has emptied of all who can afford to go elsewhere," wrote Madame la Roche during the midst of another yellow fever epidemic. She could not afford to leave the city, and so kept her pension open over the summer months. "I no longer receive guests or new boarders, however, fearing the contagion. I would be bored if I were not frightened. Mademoiselle de Monquet had to be locked in her room yesterday. She had gone into the street dressed only in her petticoat and chemise. Her pregnancy is beginning to show. And that other thing." That other thing. Her madness.

Delilah showed me the Delaware way of preventing pregnancy, but the poultice was so revolting I continued to use the vinegar-soaked sponge that Manon had taught me about. As much as I cared for Henri, it would not do to return to France with an illegitimate child. It had not yet occurred to me that the wars that were supposed to be over in two years would last for twenty.

305

Nor did it occur to me that my faithful, adoring Henri would leave me.

In September, summer began to lose its contest, and the nights became chill.

"What will winter be like?" I asked Henri one very early morning when we embraced under the weight of all the coverlets I had, yet were still cold.

"I won't lie," he said, holding me closer. "It will be difficult. In January the snow will be so high it won't be safe to leave the cabin and go any distance greater than the cookhouse, especially if the snow is falling. The snow falls so thickly sometimes you could become lost in the storm even though you're just an arm's length from your own door. The roads and river will be too dangerous for travel and for a time the settlement will be shut off from the outer world."

"Like a cloister," I said, thinking it might be pleasant to spend a few months in peace and quiet . . . and pleasure, with Henri.

"If you like, like a cloister. It would ease my spirits to know you are cloistered. But have no fear, I shall see that all is in order before I leave."

"Leave?" I sat up and the cold air struck my naked shoulders.

"I must be gone over the winter. Senator Morris has other work for me to do. Didn't I mention it? Didn't you know?" His face was stricken. I could tell by the guilt in his eyes he had purposely avoided mentioning it until this moment.

"You did not. I did not," I said, standing now, cold both inside and out. He rose, too, and tried to take me in his arms again, but I pushed him away.

"I hope this anger means you care more than I hoped," he said, but his voice was dubious. "Perhaps when I come back, this spring, not such a long time, really . . . we will be wed." He mumbled the last word.

"Wed? When you come back?" I realized I was sounding like a parrot, but my shock and anger prevented more stylish communication. Aurore moved inside her own little curtained bed and I worried that she was having another nightmare, but her struggle for sleep ceased after just one word escaped her. "Henri" she had called out.

"It is to Ohio I must go," he said, as if those details would make a difference, would ease the pain of parting. God, how tired I was of farewells, of partings, of waiting and of false hope. "Senator Morris needs a surveyor for properties there," Henri continued.

"Senator Morris needs you," I said, climbing back into bed and pulling the covers up tightly to my chin, like armor, so Henri could not get back in. The bed felt too large already.

"Julienne, my contract ends in the spring. In April I will be free to come and go as I please. As you please. We will be married." He sat on the bed and tried to take my hands but I would not let him.

"I won't be here," I said. "The schooners will begin to cross again in April. I will be in Philadelphia, or already at sea. On my way home, back to France. I won't stay here. I hate Azilum." I meant that I hated him; Azilum and Henri were much the same thing in my mind.

"We will talk of this in the spring," he said, showing the stubbornness that would become more prominent as he aged. "You will be here, Julienne, if it is a safe homecoming you await. You could grow old waiting for Paris to be safe." He was angry then, angrier than when I had lain in his arms and called out Charles's name. I had insulted Azilum, which meant more to him than his own pride. He kissed me as if we had never quarreled, and left the cabin to begin his day's work.

The silk tassels on the corn turned brown, and small, sharp-tasting apples fell from the trees planted by the earlier Dutch settlers as Henri began to conclude his work in Azilum and prepare for his journey west. Henri was finished with us, and so was summer.

The large sky was like a blue-and-white silk mantua that grew lighter and finer as the days grew shorter and cooler. The trees embroidering the hemline of the sky-cloak turned a more delicate shade of green, and then blazed red and gold. Crops in the fields, the great golden squashes, rippling rows of grain, speckled beans and red-topped beets were ready for harvest. The pastured cows, sleek and lazy with summer's heat, grew noisy with appetite and put on weight for the winter. Canny sows grew sad-eyed and wary, sensing the coming slaughter.

Grey, muddy spring had passed, and now golden, royal summer was passing too, and all the world prepared for farewell.

But I could not say farewell to Henri.

I could pretend and say that it was a great love that made me suffer so at the thought of his leaving. But love is based on need, and I will be honest. Henri was the lover who kept me warm and pleasured at night. He was the farm manager who helped Joshua plant the fields, the man of business who introduced me to the sometimes not-so-subtle differences between French and American commerce. He was indispensable, amusing, and no laggard at love.

"Who will help me when you are gone, Henri?" I asked him.

"You are not alone." He put down his ax and rubbed his blistered palms together. The pile of wood he had chopped for our winter hearth rose six feet in the air; I teased him and said the wood would last for five years, at least. It was gone by March. "Delilah and Joshua, Monsieur Farquet, Colonel

307

Jamison, du Petit-Thouars . . . there's a good thirty people you can turn to in trouble, Julienne. Though I'd prefer you didn't turn to du Petit-Thouars." He still remembered the picnic, and was jealous.

"Then you stay here with me," I said, putting my arms around his waist and leaning my cheek against his strong back.

"I cannot," he said, and that seems to be the way of the world. The woman says "stay." The man says, "I cannot."

The sun was behind Henri, it turned his hair to a golden cloud that circled his head. His dark summer color was already fading. He looked young and irritatingly attractive.

"Will you miss me, woman?" he asked, grinning and turning to face me. "Then begin sewing what you will need for your wedding day, and keep out of trouble with that work."

"No, I will begin to sew my travel clothes to return to Paris. I will sell my property to Colonel Jamison and be gone."

"I would not sign deeds so quickly." He no longer smiled. "You will find yourself homeless again. Paris boils with revolution still, and you, from what you have told me, are a known and dangerous criminal, wanted by Madame Guillotine." He was angry, and hid his anger by teasing. He knew that my shop had been sealed, and I was wanted for questioning. Of the diamond, he knew nothing.

We quarreled frequently, those last few weeks and days. At least, I tried to quarrel. Henri would only smile and leave the room if I badgered him too severely. "You will be a shrew when you are older," he warned. "Your tongue grows sharper than the ends of the thornbush." But he would be pushed no further out of my life than the downstairs sitting room on those evenings when, hands over ears, he deserted the bedroom.

To make matters worse, Aurore seemed of a mind to quarrel, too, and was frequently fretful and sulky and then high-spirited by turns. She pushed me away and then trailed after me, not knowing her own mind, just as I pushed Henri away and then pleaded with him to stay. Delilah took to sprinkling the corners of the cabin with special herbs and water to drive away bad spirits.

How will I say farewell? I asked myself over and over, knowing I did not have the strength, that I had said more than a lifetime's share of farewells already. Henri's presence in my home, even as he prepared to leave, grew stronger so that no corner or cubbyhole was free of his touch and the memory of him.

How will I say farewell? Azilum without Henri would be like Paris without Notre Dame, like Notre Dame without its altar . . . empty and purposeless.

And in the end, I didn't say farewell. I hid in my bedroom, blankets pulled over my ears but still hearing Henri give last minute instructions to Delilah and Joshua, and Smithy instructing Aurore in the fine art of spitting.

It was very early morning. The air was cold and damp and grey. The rest of Azilum still slept, even the birds were still quiet.

"Give this to Madame de Saint Remy," I heard him say. I heard the tone of his voice, the almost-covered hurt that I had not come down.

At the very last moment, just as the clop-clopping of Henri's and Smithy's horses threatened to fade away into the greater distance, I ran to the window to wave. Henri was too far away to see, and he hadn't looked back.

I sat at the window, stricken, newly alone.

Delilah came later, and brought his gift. It was a skirt hoop, the traditional gift that an American man gives to his betrothed.

Aurore crept in behind Delilah, her eyes red with weeping, the pain of loss mottling her pink cheeks.

" 'Ri gone," she sobbed. No longer independent, she reached her arms up to me and clambered onto my lap. I hugged her and kissed her eyes where the tears still started, and consoled her as best I could, and found some measure of consolation myself.

19

. . . the hunger moon . . .

*It would not be better if things happened to men just as
they wished.*

—Heraclitus

After Henri left, the rhythm of life in Azilum slowed. Dawn dragged
its feet across a sky that stayed reluctantly grey longer and longer
into the morning, and evening was increasingly fast to arrive. The wind grew
noisy with the southern flight of traitor geese who would not winter with
us, but instead sought warmer lands. We must now prepare for winter,
Delilah said.

The last fruits and vegetables of the gardens were harvested and lined up
in neat, prosperous-looking alcoves in the earthen celler. "The apples must
not touch each other," Delilah cautioned, so I arranged them carefully apart,
small red globes of September sweetness shining against the rough brown
slats on which they rested. Carrots were buried in sand-filled casks, potatoes
hidden from light in thick, burlap bags. Dried herbs filled the ceiling of the
cookhouse, scenting it with thyme and mint.

Lazy-eyed calves and bleating lambs were herded back to the shelter of
barns and sheds, and half their numbers were slaughtered. The days were
mournful with the lowing of animals who were not so insensitive they
couldn't smell their own approaching death. Madame Farquet gloated over
her blood puddings and Aurore cried for Mazie, one of the slaughtered.

The cookhouse filled with sacks of dried corn and pendants of cured ham and salted beef. It seemed to me a veritable wealth of food had been accumulated, but Delilah frowned.

"The hunger moon comes in February," she warned. "The cookhouse could be empty by then, if we're greedy now." It would not be like winter in Paris or Philadelphia, her black eyes said. If we run out of food, there is no market to trot to, there is only our own cellar to depend upon. I respected her solemnity and when it was my turn to bury eggs in pots of grease for winter storage, I broke not a one and was pleased.

Days grew bleak, our breath frosted in the grey light as we made our way to the chicken coops and wood sheds. Like the milk cows and oxen who ruminated with bovine contentedness in the dark confines of barns, we of the colony kept more and more to our own cabins, loath to stray from the genial flames of the hearth.

The summer work of Azilum had been like child's play compared to the coming season and its anticipated hardships. The Queen herself had milked cows and weeded a little garden in her Petit Hameau, and we, in similar manner, had feasted in the cordial forest and danced in the blithe meadows like children on holiday. But the sly approach of winter ended the holiday. We were no longer city people cavorting in the provinces, but wilderness folk facing a harsher verity. The Azilum winter would be like a brigand who forces his way in to loot our lives of comfort, and I was glad for the busyness of this time, which kept me from thinking overly much of Henri.

And of Louis-Charles. Winter would close the roads. There would be no post, no news, from Philadelphia or Paris. All we knew of the Dauphin was that he was still imprisoned, and he was growing weak and dispirited. Certainly, he would not be coming to us in the next few months.

I resigned myself to the fact that the Golden Ransom would have to sleep many more months at the gnarled, woody feet of the Old Man of the Forest. I visited it once, that autumn. But instead of clearing away the fallen leaves and cleaning the resting place, as dutiful daughters do at family memorials, I scattered more leaves over it, hiding the place even more thoroughly.

As the days shortened and the nights grew colder, the world grew smaller and lonelier. My life seemed filled with people who were gone from me . . . Manon, Louise, Charles, Henri. I remembered even old Mathilde with sadness, although she had not loved me. I ached for them all and was comforted only when Aurore would let me take her on my lap and hold her for a long while.

Our colony, which had been so busy and filled with people in the summer, grew quiet. The visitors we had left, and no new ones came. Almost no new ones, that is.

In early October the brothers Darnton, formerly of New York and Paris, arrived with the first snowfall. Both events were unexpected: it was too late for visitors, too soon for snow.

Even so, we of the colony awoke one Saturday morning to find our world hushed by a thick blanket of pristine white. Determined to be jovial, we celebrated with a last outdoor dinner served in the trellised dancing pavilion of the Queen's House.

The children caught lacy snowflakes on their tongues and plunged through snow drifts that reached to their waists. Their shivering, mittened *mamans* served a congealing stew of rabbit and sweet potatoes and talked of ball gowns and dried berries, until the cold drove us back to our hearths like a scolding nurse.

And that evening two young men appeared at Azilum, covered with ice and snow and in such disrepair we feared greatly for their health and recovery.

Monsieur Farquet, who had been hunting all day, discovered our new winter visitors prostrate in the snow outside the Azilum barricade. A fox had dispatched Monsieur Farquet's best laying chicken and he, in fury, had gone alone into the woods with his musket. Madame Farquet had wailed as if he were marching off to cross the river Styx. As bitter as their relationship was, she had no desire to be widowed and left to her own devices in the perilous wilderness winter. But to catch the fox monsieur would go.

To our great and unflattering surprise he returned safely the same day, just as we were gathering for a musical soirée to lift our spirits. Renard was still free, but Monsieur Farquet's leather hunt bag was swollen with game and Monsieur himself more than a little puffed with pride. Now it will not be felling trees but hunting quail and turkey that will fill his conversation, I thought without enthusiasm. But I was wrong.

"Two men. Gentlemen, by the looks of them. Need help," he panted as rivulets of melting snow streamed from his now much-torn scarlet brocade coat onto the floor of the Queen's drawing room.

"Gentlemen? At this time of year?" Talon showed immediate suspicion.

"The snow was unexpected. I would guess many travelers have been caught unaware," John Keating mused aloud.

"They are even now perishing of cold," Monsieur Farquet, still puffing, reminded us as we exchanged puzzled glances. "They are too weak to walk in by themselves. Their horses have gone lame from the ice."

"Then we must fetch them," Talon decided and the men in the room, eager for excitement, rushed for their coats. The ladies, still thawing from the picnic, remained in the drawing room, content that these visitors be brought to us, rather than that we rush headlong into the cold to them.

"Maybe it is the post coming with news that we might now return to France," Madame Farquet guessed. She had become more optimistic ever since Renard ate many of the chickens monsieur had purchased for her to tend.

"Maybe they bring news of Henri," I guessed, and so we each voiced the desire of our hearts. It was many minutes before the men were led into the drawing room, their sodden coats removed and warm blankets wrapped around them, and cups of hot wine placed in their white, shaking hands.

"I present Armand Darnton, and his brother, Louis-Marie," Talon announced formally, after the two were huddled, trembling and sneezing, before the hearth.

One, the elder who was perhaps thirty years of age, looked up from his mug of wine and smiled genially, although his ears and nose looked painfully red. His hair and eyes were brown, his form tall and slender and straight. He glanced at all of us gathered there, but it seemed his eyes stayed longest on me.

His brother, Louis-Marie, looked up not at all but continued to gulp his wine in large, noisy slurps. He was round-shouldered and fair-haired.

"Why have you come here?" Talon asked them. His tone was magisterial and not friendly. I looked at our manager in annoyance, wishing his innate distrust and suspicions would rest momentarily at least.

"Why, to visit Azilum!" gaily exclaimed Armand Darnton. "I have heard much of this community."

"In this storm?" Talon said. "Only a fool would travel in such weather."

Armand Darnton reddened with the insult, but continued to smile. "To be sure, it was fair and mild when we began the journey," he said. "But if our presence is unwelcome, we will leave immediately . . . " Darnton the elder made to rise. Madame Farquet, closest to him, put her hands on his shoulders and pressed him back into the chair.

"You will not leave," she announced. "Give us the news of Philadelphia." Several others echoed this demand, and more wine was poured into Armand's mug. He leaned back, grateful, and told of the tea parties and balls, operas and plays that had occupied the Philadelphia autumn. He was, it seemed, a welcome visitor in every drawing room in the city, and in New York, too, and his cheerful gossip filled the entire evening. He was an excellent conversationalist and told many witty jests at the expense of the

American hostesses of Philadelphia, and we listened and laughed long into the evening.

There were visitors in the Queen's House again, and we were glad for their company. They, Armand at least, seemed equally pleased with us. That first snowfall melted and disappeared, but not our visitors. The brothers Darnton lingered.

In November the playful, teasing snowfalls became as earnest as a priest administering the last rites, and as chilling. Our bravado was gone; we bowed meekly into the wind. The wide avenues of Azilum, which had been muddy rivers in spring and dusty lanes in summer, became broad ribbons of white which led into brown, leafless forests. Our little world was washed clean of color, all about us was white and grey and brown except for the defiant garden colors of our gowns. The wind clattered at our doors and windows and slapped ice and snow in our numbed faces whenever we stepped outside, and the children, grown pale and thinner, whispered of the ghosts of the Indians murdered by Sullivan.

Without Henri to warm me, the cold nights grew long and frightening. I lay awake through many lonely hours, listening to the night birds hooting in the snow-laden pines, and the whistling of the wind. Sometimes I would hear a shrill scream in the dark distance and know that an owl had trapped a rabbit in its fearsome talons.

As the winter snows deepened, the forest animals, emboldened by hunger, crept closer to our village, filling the night with the stealthy shadows of wolves, the delicate steps of deer, and the raucous maurading of raccoons who broke into the root cellars and feasted on our precious stores. Foxes preyed on the chickens, and weasels stole the eggs. The world reverted to a savagery we had been too naive to notice in the more pleasant summertime.

I worried about Henri, knowing that the winter where he was was even more hostile, even more filled with danger and hardship. I thought of Azilum as the wilderness, but it was not. It was Ohio where our world ended and the terrible unknown began, and it was there that Henri had gone, to ride with Major General Anthony Wayne, to determine how quickly that western land could be safely approached by settlers. Senator Morris had an eye to increasing his landholdings again.

Ohio, at that time, was still dangerous with British soldiers, and resentful Indians who had been pushed westward by encroaching whites. Wayne, who was known as Mad Anthony—a title that did not reassure me—had winter headquarters in a place called Greenville. While his mission was to establish peace with the Shawnee, Iroquois and Chippewa, from all accounts he spent more time shooting at them than talking with them. And the English had provided the Indians with muskets, and powder and ball so they could shoot back.

Such was the dangerous situation into which Henri had gone. Smithy had once jested that if they made it through the Indian war parties they would probably be court-martialed by Mad Anthony for not wearing Injun scalps on their belts. Henri had said that was foolish; Ohio was peaceful enough, and there was nothing to fear. But it seemed to me that men were most liable to say there was nothing to fear when, indeed, there was much to fear.

So, in addition to my loneliness, my own fear, I must worry about Henri, too, and pass the long months not knowing if he was well, injured or even dead. My appetite died under this burden and soon Delilah was pressing me to eat, not to conserve food.

But the winter, in a way, was also a blessing. It burned away what was frivolous in our nature to reveal the true flame within. The whiteness, the cold, the whistling wind . . . it all seemed of a purity so great it humbled me. I became more serene and less restless, less filled with needs, constant needs, always clamoring for something to be done, something to be fulfilled. I was being tempered, like a fine metal that learns to flex without breaking. I determined anew to survive and to prosper.

Madame Farquet profited from her husband's fascination with felling trees and was able to trade a cord of wood for a side of pork, which she then traded to me for a new gown. She greedily selected creamy lace and my finest blue brocade. While I measured the length and breadth of her she read to me from *Tanguy's Journal*, which was printed in Philadelphia and carried news of the revolution. A fur trader, passing through, had delivered an issue that was only four weeks old.

It was an especially cherished issue. It described Robespierre's last festival, and his downfall. The Reign of Terror was over in France. But not the revolution.

"He had held a Festival of the Supreme Being," Madame Farquet sniffed, turning a page. The hiss in her voice told me instantly she spoke of that devil in human disguise, Robespierre. Hungry for news of home, we devoured the details of the festival, trying to imagine ourselves there, and then finally admitting we were, for the time being, better off where we were.

At that festival, Robespierre had caused Paris to be decorated with blue, red and white flags hung from every lintel and lamppost. They were, to be sure, a decor preferable to their former adornment: the swinging, lifeless bodies of aristocrats. All of Paris ("Can't be a great many people left there," commented Madame Farquet) marched to the Tuileries, where Robespierre

315

delivered a speech and then a spectacle. Wood and wax statues of Atheism, Ambition, Egotism, False Simplicity and Discord were set ablaze. From under the carnage of the statue of melting Atheism appeared another statue representing Wisdom.

Wisdom, having come through the flames was, of course, somewhat scorched and charred that day, but the crowd cheered despite the cinders marring the new deity. Perhaps they were afraid not to applaud. More than a few had already been guillotined for no other reason than a lack of enthusiasm.

After the conflagration, "liberty trees" were planted all over Paris. Had Monsieur Mouret planted one outside the door of his bakery, I wondered? I could imagine him grumbling and cursing as he tried to shovel into the ancient dirt packed hard as stone by centuries of trodding feet while the potted "liberty tree" waved in the currents of heat that always emanated from the windows of his bakery. It occurred to me that perhaps Mouret had been guillotined. To my great surprise, the thought grieved me. Hatred must eventually be surrendered to mercy. My hatred of Mouret was part of the past, part of an old life that had no more to do with me, nor I with it.

Robespierre's last, ill-begotten celebration ended with a bizarre ritual in the desecrated church of Notre Dame. My former customer, the lewd opera dancer Mademoiselle Maillard, postured atop the stripped altar in a costume that revealed more than it concealed. I did not understand how even the mad inmates of Charenton could have confused Mademoiselle Maillard with any kind of divinity.

The festival was a charade, a parody. Robespierre was pulling at straws to amuse a crowd which was no longer entertained or entertaining. He had lost his touch, his power, his control. A month later he himself was arrested by the Convention, the journal article announced. He tried to shoot himself but only succeeded in disfiguring his face, so that he went to the guillotine bound in bloody bandages. The crowd bayed with glee like bloodhounds scenting a wounded rabbit. This was the death of the great Robespierre the Incorruptible.

"What were their names again?" Madame Farquet asked, for I had taken the journal from her to stop her fidgeting.

"Barras, Tallien and Fouché are the ones who overthrew Robespierre," I said. "Now stand still, or I shall never get the hem straight."

"Barras," she murmured. "I once had a stable boy by that name. Do you think it could be the same? Imagine, a stable boy in control! It doesn't bear thinking about."

"A pity they had to guillotine poor old Madame du Barry. When I was a child I saw Louis XV's funeral procession and was very disappointed that she was not part of it. I very much wanted to see what a royal mistress looked like."

"Her beauty was greatly exaggerated," madame sniffed. "I found her rather plain, in fact. Of course, with her wealth she could purchase the most flattering gowns and jewels. Wealth does much for helping a plain woman create the illusion of beauty."

"And for feeding children," I said. It was not yet Christmas, yet even my inexperienced eye could judge the speed with which our food stores were being diminished. It was discomfiting to worry about hunger while being in possession of the Golden Ransom, which could have fed all of us for many years to come. But that was not its purpose. Nor could I have sold or bartered the gem, even if my conscience allowed such a treason. Who in Azilum could have afforded such a rich bauble? The jewel rested at the feet of the Old Man of the Forest, waiting, as I waited, for news of the Dauphin.

"Have you heard from Monsieur Arraché?" madame asked, pulling and straightening her gown. The chemise under it had been patched so many times I turned my head away in shame for her.

"One letter. From Ohio. He suggested I buy a Franklin stove if the hearth doesn't provide enough warmth. He said I should not pay more than six dollars for it."

He had also written, "Don't sign any papers with Jamison, or leave before my return. I love you." That, I did not tell madame.

"I want 'Ri," Aurore pouted. She pushed aside the ribbons she had been playing with, and cradled the husk doll Delilah had made for her.

"Henri is gone," I said for the hundredth time. "But go ask Delilah if we might have dinner. Maybe she'll let you stir the johnny-cakes." I lifted her down from the table and she tottered from the room on chubby, still uncertain legs, glad to have an errand. It had snowed for days on end and she was tired of being indoors.

"Delilah makes the best biscuits in Azilum," Madame Farquet said, her nose twitching in hunger. "You are lucky to have her."

"I think it's more that she has me. I can't even touch a frying pan without first asking permission. She thinks it is her kitchen, not mine. But I am thankful." More than thankful, I was finding Delilah to be an intelligent and canny friend who had much to offer beyond her domestic and medicinal skills.

To save wood, she and Joshua had moved out of their own cabin and into mine for the winter. We had become close in those long months, not close as Manon and I had been, in a young and frivolous manner, but close as

317

women who have both faced hardships can be. We did not need to chat or amuse each other. It was enough to share a fire in the evening. And sometimes we taught each other things from the two very different worlds of our pasts. I taught her to make simple bobbin lace to help satisfy her taste for that luxury and to cook some French sauces, which she promptly improved with her dried herbs.

She taught me bits of Lenni-Lenape orderliness: to slice loaves of bread into twelve pieces and to close jackets with twelve buttons, so that the home would be in harmony with the twelve moons of the year; that the sun is a great medicine we shouldn't hide from to keep our complexions pale, as Europeans did; and that if you lie very still at night and wait with great patience, you will feel the gentle motion of the earth as it is carried along on the back of the giant turtle that supports it.

The earth moved on the turtle, but this morning Madame Farquet was not about to. Her eyes were fixed on the dining room table.

"Please stay to eat," I said, prompted by her longing gaze.

"Only if you insist," she replied with alacrity. "Do you think Delilah will let us have some of her blackberry preserves to go with the cakes?"

Delilah did not. She did not care for Madame Farquet, and would waste no good preserves on her. But the cakes were good on their own. Over that meal I watched, mildly distracted, as my guest's golden citrine ring flashed on her thin finger. It was, she said, her last jewel, the others having been sold, bartered, or left behind in a wall safe in the faubourg St. Germain. Its color and size reminded me of the Queen's diamond, although it lacked the fiery brilliance of that stone.

"What is the news of the Queen's son?" I asked her in a low voice. Lately, when we spoke of Louis-Charles, it was in a half-whisper, the voice people use when they speak of the dead. Even with Robespierre gone we feared greatly for the Dauphin. And there had been more prorepublican riots in Philadelphia that autumn. By unspoken agreement we grew more cautious about mentioning the Dauphin. There were too many who preferred he would die in his prison.

Madame Farquet looked up from her heavily buttered cakes, her small face under her white wig—which was now showing evidence of moth damage—distorted by the large bite she had just taken.

"My husband still insists that the Dauphin will be brought to Azilum. Of course, monsieur is often wrong in such matters. He predicted the revolution would be over in 1790, and now it is five years past and no end in sight."

"None of us foresaw how long it would last," I said, only half-eager to defend her husband. I had long since learned why her eyes became dark beads of antipathy on those rare occasions when she actually looked at him. Not only had she married to please her family, which was common enough, she had been in love with another man at the time, and had never ceased loving him. Monsieur, locked out of the marital bed after the birth of their first and only child, promptly established a *petite maison* in the faubourg St. Honoré, complete with mistress of course, and spent most of his twenty years of marriage there. There was, as the saying goes, little love lost between monsieur and madame.

"It was an accident that when he fled France his wife was with him and not his little mademoiselle," Victoire had whispered to me one night in the Queen's House. "He had his trunk packed and papers ready, but madame showed up and, fearful for her life, insisted on departing with him. He could not refuse, of course. She is his wife."

And so Madame and Monsieur Farquet, who had lived apart, separated by the Seine and half of Paris for more than two decades, now spent their days and nights together in a small cabin in the wilderness. I did not envy them their situation.

"When will he be brought?" I asked.

"My dear, who can say? First he must be fetched from prison. Then from France. It may be years. Please pass the cakes."

Years. Of waiting, of guarding the Golden Ransom, of knowing that my life would never truly be my own until that pledge was fulfilled. Suddenly Madame Farquet's high, imperious voice set my teeth on edge and I wished she would leave. I wanted to walk in the forest, to hear the ancient whisper of falling snow that has nothing to do with the madness of human politics.

I could not. Immediately after she left I received a message summoning me to the Queen's House for an interview with Talon. I should have been curious, for such messages from our chief administrator were rare. Indeed, we had not had private conversation since that first interview, after the news of the Queen's death. But I was dull with cold and weariness, and my only thought was that I would have to change my gown, which was a nuisance. Talon still insisted on formal attire and manners; in fact grew more insistent, as if newly washed lace, pressed gowns and powdered hair would save us from the darkness that lurked outside the Azilum barricade and inside our own hearts.

The day was still and silent with cold. Even on the most biting days of winter in Paris, there had been life and activity in the streets. Pierre with his flute, Lily with her dragging cloth bag of scraps, the opera dancers in gay costumes on their way to rehearsal . . . many such had defied the winter either from need or bravado. But in Azilum all was still, except for the rustle of dead leaves hanging listlessly from black branches, jostled by a wind which, Henri said, originated in a far north land where people wore furs all year round.

The Queen's House was covered with a clean powdering of snow on its steep, shingled roof, and its sides rested in drifts that crept up toward the first floor windows. The slumbering river was a curving silver ribbon that waited in icy sleep.

The scene looked like a child's dream created in marzipan and set into a powdered sugar base. It was the stuff of fairy tales and legends, a plaything brought to life and greater size by some mischievous magic for Marie-Antoinette, the Queen who did not survive to see this bagatelle.

The wind began to blow again, biting at my face like a living, angry thing, whipping the snow and moaning through the trees; the house lost its playfulness and became a brown, wooden arc floating on a white, wrathful sea of snow and politics. I huddled deeper into my cloak and pounded with a numb fist on the huge wooden door.

Monsieur Talon himself opened it; again, I should have guessed something was afoot.

"You arrived promptly. Thank you," he said sternly. His wig was slightly askew and the cold had worsened his limp. I followed him down the winter-dark halls of the great house to his private office into which, not too gently taking my elbow, he ushered me.

Monsieur Talon's office revealed more of himself than he may have suspected. A velvet waistcoat freshly steamed and brushed hung from a peg, a wig stand bore an elaborate formal peruke. Contradicting those evidences of aristocratic habits were the leather leggings and the fur cap of a woodsman, set to dry before the hearth. He lived, of necessity, in two worlds. A portrait of his wife, who was still in France, hung on the wall over the hearth. But a woman's lacy handkerchief lay crumpled in a corner, left there by a "visiting niece" whom we all accepted as his mistress. The nights were long in Azilum.

"Tea?" His face wore a troubled frown.

"No, I have just had some," I said, rubbing my chapped hands together and knowing this was not a social visit.

"Then I will get to the point. What do you make of this, Madame de Saint Remy?" He handed me a worn and soiled scrap of paper. The writing was barely legible. *Mme. de S.R. in Azilum. Find, and return with it. Price is agreed.* There was no signature at the bottom, but only a crude cipher.

"It means nothing to me," I said handing it back, but I was already feeling colder than I had a moment before. My hand was not as steady as I wished it to be. They were my initials. And the only thing of value I possessed, the only thing worth finding, was the Queen's diamond.

Talon's frown deepened. I had no doubt that had we been in Paris, and he my master, he would have struck me at that moment, so great was his impatience.

"I was hoping you could tell us something about this. The initials would seem to refer to you. This message was . . . ummm . . . intercepted, shall we say, but we needn't go into those details. We do not know who was to have received the message."

"I know nothing of this mystery," I repeated.

"What was your relationship with the queen?" He fired the question at me.

"I have said before. I was her seamstress. One of many seamstresses."

"That is all?"

"That is all."

He paced for some moments and then turned to me again, hands behind his back, a cold smile on his face. "You sewed the travel wardrobe found in the carriage in Varennes, where the King and Queen were betrayed when they tried to flee France. You left Madame Bertin's establishment under a cloud of suspicion. You were seen in frequent conversation with the Queen's enemy, the Duc d'Orléans. You were involved in the badly planned scheme to bring the Queen out of the Conciergerie, which brought the Queen to a worse condition of imprisonment."

Talon leaned back on his desk, folded his arms over his chest, and glared accusingly.

"Those facts are twisted. I was the Queen's friend and never wished her harm," I protested.

He smiled. I had made a mistake. A mere seamstress would never claim friendship with a queen.

"Perhaps your husband, the constitutionalist, wished her harm."

I refrained from pointing out that Talon himself might once have qualified for the title of constitutionalist, in the very early days of the revolution. "My husband died defending the Queen," I said again. I was close to tears, being attacked so fiercely and unable to defend myself except but weakly.

Talon, unmoved by my distress, continued to glare.

"There is a mystery here," he said. "And I will unearth it. Beware. If I discover that you are not a friend of the Queen, and of her son, then you will have much to fear from me. If you are a friend of the Queen, and of that unfortunate child who will soon be our rightful king, then it seems you

321

must beware of one other than myself. I maintain those are your initials in this message. Do not take this warning lightly."

I handed back to him the scrap of paper.

He took it, and cast it into the flames. Then, he sighed and tapped his fingers on the desk. "Sometimes," he began with a pained voice, "sometimes I think we did our countrymen a disfavor by naming this place Azilum. It is misleading. From some evils there is no asylum. Surely you have learned that by now. With whatever ease or difficulties we ourselves crossed the sea, so too may others, bringing with them much of what we wished to flee. I would be surprised if there were no Jacobins here. They seem to be everywhere else. Rather like silverfish. No matter how well one cleans the cupboard, they always appear sooner or later."

I sat, silent and frightened, wishing that Henri were not so far away.

"Since you are unable to communicate any knowledge of this to me, there is not much more I can say." He was angry, in the way protective men become angry with women who refuse their protection. "But I will tell you this. The cipher at the bottom causes us to believe that this message originated in Paris, and is connected with Philippe Egalité."

"D'Orléans is dead," I said. Wasn't he? And didn't death end his power?

"Yes. D'Orléans is dead. And his faction broken. But many of his former followers still live. You can be sure that whatever knowledge d'Orléans had, he shared with others. He was not well-known for discretion."

I remembered the night in the Cité, the night Aurore's birth began, when d'Orléans and three men had searched Louise's room. I had heard him promise those others that they would have the diamond that night. There were others who knew, who wanted the Golden Ransom.

I rose to leave and then sat back down. My old suspicions and fears returned, replacing my longing for Henri.

"Monsieur Talon," I began, and hesitated. "Monsieur Talon," I tried again. "What do you know of Henri Arraché?"

"He is immoderate in his political views. Like many young men, he favors change simply because it is change."

"Yes. That I know. But his character. What do you think of his character?" I stared guiltily at the lace handkerchief in the corner and blushed, knowing that this was not the kind of question a woman should be asking about a man who has already shared her bed for some months.

Talon, too, stared at the lace handkerchief, and then bent to pick it up.

"His character is not yet fully formed. I could not hazard a guess," he admitted finally.

It is easier to detect stealthy footsteps during a quiet snowfall than during a spring in the Palais Royal. I trudged back to my cabin, listening all the while for such footsteps behind me, but heard none.

Jacobin agents were not all I had to fear and anticipate that winter. In February, just as Delilah had said, came the hunger moon, the time when all stores had to be carefully measured against the remaining weeks of winter.

"Cornmeal mush for breakfast and dinner," she informed me after inventorying the cellar and cookhouse. "Ham only for Sunday." In Paris, during the hungry years, I had hated the smell of old and rotting chestnuts which permeated the poor houses of the Cité. In Azilum, I learned to dread the smell of cornmeal mush. "Hunger is the best seasoning," Mathilde used to mutter when I pushed away a bowl of chestnut soup; Delilah had only to mention hunger moon to make me reconsider cornmeal.

"Mister Van der Zorn, now there was a man who paid no attention to hunger moon," she told me one morning when I had no appetite for mush. "He saw that big yellow moon and counted how many times his kine mooed to be milked in the morning, but he disregarded all the signs. He made his wife feed the family like there was no day to follow the next. And by March, all his ham and peas and cornmeal were gone, and there was not so much as a blade of grass growing in the fields."

"What did he do?" I asked, pausing with a spoonful of mush at my mouth.

"Killed his missus and ate her," she said, nodding. "I was a very small child then, but I remember how hard we had to work to get rid of her ghost. She was very angry."

"I don't think we'll have to stew anybody, Delilah. Just make smaller portions."

"And keep that Farquet woman away from the cookhouse," added Delilah.

"Easier said than done." But as much as we complained about Madame Farquet's appetite, which was dainty in her home and bestial in mine, I enjoyed her company and could not turn her away. Loneliness is a beggar when it comes to company, and I was lonely. The little cabin with its huge hearth was too big and too cold. I listened at night for the heavy sound of a man's footsteps coming up the stairs, and during the day for the cheerful noises of a man attending to chores, and all the while wondered if by longing for those noises I was being disloyal to the Queen by loving her enemy.

My dreams were taken over by a new personage, half-Charles and half-Henri, who danced with me in the Palais Royal and then pulled me, stumbling with giddiness, through the southern pastures of Azilum where the wild purple asters bloomed in August. In the morning there were dark circles under my eyes and the sharp edge of solitude turning in my ribs.

Delilah gave me strong teas made from the bark that grows on the east side of trees, and from the ginseng root. She made me tell her my dreams, and the recurring one about the half-Charles, half-Henri man made her frown and reach up to touch her medicine bag for better luck.

"I'll fix it in the spring when the flower-that-hangs-down comes," she said.

But there were many weeks to get through before the secretive May apple would blossom.

Snow fell and fell from the sky until it was as deep as the height of a man in some places. Wolves howled in the hills and ventured closer each night, drawn by the innocent bleating of the lambs in the sheds. Talon warned that some of the more daring wolves might leap the barricade, so none of the children were to go outside alone. The howling of the great grey wolves sounded almost human, as if they would have us pity their cold and hunger.

"Don't listen," Delilah told me when the wolf songs were especially plaintive. "Maybe a *loup-garou* is with them, a wolf spirit."

I knitted fiercely and forced myself to think of things other than howling wolves and the ever-falling snow, and how very far away from us was the rest of the world. I thought of Versailles in the spring, when all the orange trees were brought out of the glass conservatory and lined up in formal rows in the Queen's private garden. And of the smell of strong coffee and powdered sugar cakes that wafted from the cafés of the Palais Royal. I thought of sunshine filtered by tall chestnut trees, and of glittering silk gowns and women promenading along the flowerbeds of the Tuileries, and of how perfect Marie-Antoinette's complexion had been.

Such thoughts brought homesickness. But the Terror was over in France, buried with the corrupt body and soul of Robespierre. The Revolutionary Tribunal no longer existed and the guillotine, it was said, would soon rust from disuse. Soon, I would be able to return to Paris.

Until then, I suffered that thing that Henri had warned me of, cabin fever.

Cure came in the form of increasing attention from our visitor, Armand Darnton, who had stayed with us through the winter.

In the summer, I admitted to myself, he and his brother would have been unremarkable. In the winter, when the roads were impassable and our stories so oft-repeated amongst ourselves that we preferred silence to another telling, they seemed the height of charm and novelty. We fussed shamelessly over Armand Darnton. To my great delight, Armand Darnton often chose me as his dinner companion, when we all gathered in the Queen's House.

The brothers paid for this hospitality with novel stories and gossip of the best salons in Philadelphia. Armand, the elder, was the spokesman for the two, as Louis-Marie stuttered when he spoke and preferred to sit in the shadows. Armand had an eloquent and dramatic manner that enhanced his stories and gave them monumental qualities. Of course, I suspected immediately that he altered his tales to make himself seem braver and more cunning than he really was. But exaggeration is a gentleman's perogative.

The story of hunting and killing a wolf when he was but seven was stolen from the childhood of La Fayette. The humorous tale of how his father, dressed only in small clothes, prowled the château gardens at night to shoot at stray cats was taken from a story told about King Louis XVI . . . except the King, of course, wore a blue-and-gold overcoat over his small clothes.

Armand Darnton told lies. But they were charming lies, to gladden us and make the long winter hours pass on gilded wings. The days and nights of Azilum flowed again at a quickened pace. Now I know that the days and nights were merely responding to the first pulses of spring, which we were too uninitiated to detect amidst the lingering snow and cruel winds. But then I was younger. And very lonely.

When Armand began to woo me, I did not close my door to him.

He made it clear that he would like to stay in Azilum as long as we would tolerate him; he was in no hurry to be elsewhere. I was in no hurry for him to leave. We spent long hours together, and those hours were flirtatious ones. Delilah's usually soundless footsteps became heavy with disapproval whenever Armand was in the house, which became more and more frequent.

"I think your servant does not care for me," he commented one evening. "Nor your friend, Madame Guillemard. The one won't leave us alone, and the other won't come near me. But how charming an idea, to have an Indian as a servant. I congratulate your originality, my dear." He was sitting in a chair whose cushion was still flattened and creased from the weight of Henri. We faced the fire but out of the corners of our eyes we could see Delilah hovering about in the darkness, where the fire did not reach.

"Delilah, I won't be needing you anymore this evening," I said, using a tone of voice I had learned from Madame Bertin. Delilah did not move. "Go," I said. She cast me a look that made the blood rise to my cheeks, and then stalked away. I knew I would have to apologize on the morrow, but it was worth it. Alone with Armand, I spent a long hour listening to his praises of my originality, my sense of adventure, my spirit, my bravery . . . and more personal things. He was a flatterer of great skill, but he knew the right phrases to make a lonely and fretting woman feel like a queen, a Venus among mortals.

325

When he left he kissed my fingertips, but his eyes spoke of more ambitious desires. I hadn't played this game in a very long time. It was quite pleasant.

After that, we spent our evenings alone, after attending an hour or two at the Queen's House for courtesy's sake. Armand would drink from my usually decorative bottle of French brandy . . . I tried not to think of the expense . . . and tell amusing tales as I knitted or sewed, and the warmth of the hearth was little compared to the heat of the compliments he paid me.

He was interested in all facets of my life. Charles, I reflected, had little interest in what my life had been before I met him. That is why, I think, when he learned a half-truth from d'Orléans he could not conceive of the whole truth. And Henri was interested in all to do with my life in Azilum, but my history in France held no charm for him. It was as if, with those two, I existed in isolated fragments, like a book with chapters cut out of it.

Armand wished to read the entire book. He was most impressed by my relationship with the Queen, and would have me talk about her and the commissions I completed for her for hours on end. He was well acquainted with all the details of fashion and could even tell a Brunswick coat from a Joseph's coat, a feat usually unknown to the male of the species.

"You designed the lavender Polonaise she wore for the New Year's Ball of 1788? That marvelous confection? Ah, yes, I remember it most distinctly. It was easily the most wonderful gown there. Of course, the Lamballe's was lovely too, but no match for the Queen's costume."

"You were at the ball?" I asked. Then he was higher placed even than he claimed.

"Yes, I attended. I was tolerated at court because of the financial services my father had provided to Louis XV," he answered with grave modesty. He is rich, too, I thought. Or was.

"Your father may have been of service, but I'm certain you were held in no less esteem than he," I said. Armand smiled and kissed my hand.

"I would be happy to think you hold me in esteem," he said.

When we finished discussing the Queen's wardrobe, he insisted I tell him all about my "original" life in Azilum. He asked to be shown everything, the root cellar, the snowy pastures, the cookhouse, the upstairs and downstairs of the small cabin.

"What a cunning bureau," he said, when we finished the tour where we had started, in my sitting room. He opened the drawers and tapped the sides. "Well made of strong oak. You have taste and discernment, madame."

He was most taken by my sewing table, fresh from Hollenback's trading post and still smelling of a heavy coating of beeswax polished to a fine shine.

326

It had been made in the Prevan manufactory in the faubourg St. Antoine, a workshop famous for its intricate designs. Many wealthy, jewel-loving women of Paris had favored Prevan's bureaus and desks and armoires, for they were equipped with secret drawers and false bottoms for concealing small and precious possessions.

It had been an extravagant purchase for me, although I had paid only a fraction of its real value. Such French furniture, thanks to the mass beheadings and insolvency of the aristocrats, had been imported by the shipload and could be bought quite reasonably . . . if one could own such a piece and not dwell on the probable fate of its previous owner. I had intended to hide the Golden Ransom in it. It had, however, occurred to me that if I was familiar with Prevan's false bottoms and secret drawers, others would be too. I left the Queen's diamond buried at the base of the Old Man of the Forest.

Armand tapped delicately at the side of this table, his knuckles rubbing against the wings of a cupid painted in misted pastels over the gleaming rosewood.

"You have secrets in here, my dear?" he asked, his dark eyes narrowing with the teasing smile he gave me. "A journal, perhaps, or a love token?"

"If I answered that question, it would no longer be a secret," I said. I held knitting in my hands—a warm pair of stockings for Aurore—and for a moment forgot I was a widow, a mother, a frontier woman who dined on corn mush and could judge the strength of a wolf by its midnight howl. I waved the half-finished stocking in front of my face as if it were a fan, and I a young coquette.

"Would you care to dine with me tonight?"

"I would be honored," he said. "Also afraid . . . that your servant might add arsenicum to my portion."

"Ah, how you jest!" I laughed, but the thought had crossed my mind that Delilah knew as much about the noxious herbs as the beneficial ones. "I shall prepare the meal myself. Delilah is indisposed today," I reassured him.

According to Lenni-Lenape law, when women have their monthlies they can prepare food for no one but themselves; Delilah had stayed away from the cookhouse for the past two days, she would surely stay away today, too.

"In that case, I can think of no greater pleasure than sharing your table. It will be not food, but ambrosia." He took my hand and kissed it.

"It will be not ambrosia, but cornmeal mush," I warned him.

But I was determined to do my best with that meal. The thought of a good feast, after weeks, months even, of counting each pea and filling up on mush before enjoying two bites of bacon, made me tingle with joy. This was to be my rebellion. Against the winter. Against Delilah. Against hardships themselves.

I had learned some cookery from Delilah, and the hard winter had taught me a fine appreciation of food. Shameless, I raided the cookhouse and the cellar for the best of what I could find, sawing off huge hunks from our last ham and selecting the whitest, plumpest potatoes for a ragout, and the least shriveled apples for a tart. I traded my second-best petticoat to Madame Farquet for a bottle of her husband's port. This had to be removed from his house to mine somewhat surreptitiously, while he was enjoying a mug of ale in Monsieur Lefevre's public room near the settlement square. The last of the cheddar went on my yellow crockery cheeseplate, the spring strawberries preserved in wine were decanted for dessert.

By the time the table was set and another hunger moon had risen my sense of guilt and anticipation was as thick as the cream that rises to the top of the milk pail.

"You never took such care with Henri's meals," was the sharp rebuke of my conscience. But it seemed years, not months, since I had seen Henri, and an even longer time since I had enjoyed the luxury of insouciance.

Aurore trotted after me all afternoon during those preparations, a speculative look on her small face making her seem older than she was. I made a little tart just for her to ease my guilt, and then sent her to bed early with a promise that we would go sledding on the morrow.

And then I brushed my hair and left it loose on my back, smoothed my gown and waited. Armand came fashionably late and the glow in his eyes told me my preparations had not been for nought.

But whatever I was planning, and I still will not give a name to it, was not to be.

Delilah, appearing from nowhere, pulled her chair up to the supper table and would not abdicate. Startled, Armand and I exchanged anxious glances over the candles; she ignored us and smacked her lips noisily over the ham ragout. I cleared my throat so many times it grew raw and Armand shot her looks that would have frozen the Medusa. But Delilah, stern with intent, chewed solemnly and stayed. When she finally spoke, it was to tell Armand that Henri was a very good shot with the musket.

Armand, after his color returned, kept up a steady rain of chatter that was meant to be amusing. It only resulted in giving me a throbbing headache. Delilah mentioned Henri's name every time she opened her mouth. I was torn between doubt and longing for Henri, and realized that I missed him tremendously. The meal and the evening were ruined.

I began to wish that both Delilah and Armand would go away. I had forgotten to put cinnamon in the apple tart, so that it looked pretty but was actually quite bland. It occurred to me that Armand, chatting on and on about the Bal d'Opéra he attended in 1789 and who wore what, could be described as the same.

After dinner, courtesy required me to invite Armand to the sitting room, although my appetite for flirtation was extinguished. Delilah followed, placing her chair in the corner where we couldn't see her, but she could see us. She tugged incessantly at the medicine bag hanging around her neck and the jingle of her talismans so unnerved me that after one very long hour I rose from my chair and extended my hand to Armand, who was still talking about the Bal d'Opéra.

"It grows late and I am weary."

He raised his eyebrows. "How original you are," he said, taking his leave.

As soon as the door closed behind him, Delilah disappeared as stealthily as a black cat merging into the shadows. As I crept up the stairs, quietly so as not to awaken Aurore, I was surprised to feel no anger. I smiled, remembering Delilah's unprecedented but timely rudeness, and Armand's shock.

In the morning, as we shivered at the cookhouse table and forced down mouthfuls of hot hominy sweetened with molasses, Delilah made no mention of the night before, nor did I. She was smiling, though, and seemed even taller than usual.

"I saw the white stag last night," she said. "The men will hunt now, and come home with game to feed us for the rest of the hunger moon."

"What is the white stag?" I asked.

"An omen of good hunting," she said, as if I hadn't paid close enough attention the first time. "But the Darnton men will come home with empty bags."

"More magic, Delilah?" She ignored the acid in my voice.

"No magic. I looked at their horses in the stables. They have sores and bruises. The Darntons don't ride well. They will have to spend all their time staying mounted, no time to aim gun." She was pleased.

That afternoon, as Delilah had prophesied, Talon and Monsieur Farquet announced that there would be a great hunt to augment our dwindling supplies. Invitations to this affair were sent to farmers and settlers all the way up to Wyalusing. It would be a ring hunt, and the more hunters, the more game would be caught in the ring.

The next day dozens of men gathered in front of the Queen's House, dressed in riding leather and armed with bows, rifles, shotguns and sling shots. I sat sewing, listening to Victoire's son, Jacques-Pierre, beat the huge drum used to frighten the wolves, deer and fox in the distant woods. The animals, made incautious by so much noise and commotion, would be herded into an ever-shrinking circle of armed men, and then slaughtered. It was an unpleasant day. The drum reminded me of the Place de la Guillotine, and the slaughter of the animals in such a calculated, inevitable manner seemed cruel.

But by the end of that afternoon a dozen deer had been felled, and just as many wolves, so that the hunt was deemed a great success. The men returned tired and bloodstained, but triumphantly bearing more than enough venison to feed us in the last months of winter, and fur skins for new boots and cloak-linings. The colony smelled of roasting meat that night; the smoke soared up the dark sky and made the pale yellow hunger moon look sooty and tired. Each door in the colony was covered with a new fur pelt hung to be cured.

But Armand had come back empty-handed.

20

. . . the homecoming . . .

*Let us lay it down as an incontrovertible rule that the first
impulses of nature are always right. There is no original sin in
the human heart.*

—Jean-Jacques Rousseau

The same exuberant geese that had so ungallantly abandoned us eight months before now honked and called back and forth in Azilum's fields and pastures. Occasional groups of them, as if in dispute with the others, would take wing and embroider the pale blue sky with brown chevrons. Winter was memory. Spring was come home again to our doorstep, filling the sky and fields with joyous noise and new streaks of green growth and pastel flowers, where only days before it had been grey and white.

I crouched in the dank mire of my herb garden, my apron filled with clumps of chives and garlic, and compared the bird's freedom to my own rooted-to-earthness, another of Delilah's phrases. It meant my steps were too heavy.

"You need sun, get strength from the Father," she told me, and so I was put out of doors like a child, with my apron and hat and thick garden gloves, away from sewing room work that kept me pale and gave me backaches. I was set the task of turning the soil with a wooden trowel around the green

331

swords of iris and tender stems of yarrow and catnip. "No metal," said Delilah. "Metal offends plants."

Delilah was voluble with cautions that season. The medicine bag around her neck grew constantly heavier and rounder with the weight of her talismans. She had the same dream over and over again of water turned muddy and frothing, a dream the Lenni-Lenape said predicted disaster. She'd also had a vision, and while she wouldn't tell me what the vision was, she insisted that Aurore have a dog. "All children need a dog," she decreed. "Dogs draw bad luck to themselves, protect the child." And so she had brought home a squirming little thing that was all soft tan-and-black fur and with a rounded, but distinctly wolfish-looking face that prevented me from asking too many questions about the dog's lineage.

Finished with weeding the iris, I dug a neat row of small craters for a first planting of sweet onion. Sachema, the puppy, worried the hem of my skirt, taking it in her sharp little teeth and tossing her head to and fro as if the ragged flounces were an intruder. Sachema meant a kind of king in Delilah's first tongue; Aurore had named her after Delilah's grandfather, who had been a great leader of the Delawares. It didn't matter to her that Sachema was female. Nor did it matter overly much to me. I hoped that Marie-Antoinette's son would be with us sometime before Sachema grew old and feeble because I meant to give the Dauphin one of her puppies as a gift. Boys, I knew, like rough and tumble play. But then, so did Aurore.

"Go away, Sachema," I said, pulling my muddied skirt out of her reach. But her round, black eyes looked so hurt at the rebuke I laughed. "Go ahead, then, if you must," I said, fanning the hem in invitation. But by then she, like I, was distracted by the raucous calling of the geese. In almost human fashion Sachema was most intrigued by those geese that flew overhead and were unobtainable, rather than those that waddled in the approachable field. She trotted back and forth, clamoring passionately at the unreachable sky and its tempting cargo of noisy flight.

Aurore, who followed behind me on muddy hands and knees, scooped up Sachema and admonished her with a pointed finger. "Bad," she said. "Make Mama angry."

The winter had been difficult for my daughter, that much beloved child who sometimes required more patience than I had. Her groping hands had acquired the strength to rip fragile clothes and shatter expensive china dishes, and the admonition she gave her puppy was one she had learned firsthand from me.

"Here, Aurore, sweeting, put the onion in the hole," I said, wishing to make up for past hours when I had been less than sympathetic to her childish

332

ways. Every time I looked at her I felt an urge to crush her to my chest but had learned not to, as she was more liable to squirm away than to put up with such coddling. She grew taller and stronger every day and sometimes I was angry with her for that which she could not help, indeed, had nothing to do with. I yearned for a babe-in-arms, for the sweet, milky smell of a new infant who would coo and grasp my finger and stare back with slightly crossed blue eyes.

The loneliness of winter had been replaced by this deeper yearning that was aggravated each time I found a new bird's nest in the garden, each night the bold tom cats of Azilum howled under a window for a house-bound tabby. All about me was new life, but I was barren with old dreams.

Aurore took the small green sheath and planted it root up. Quickly, I set it to rights and then my hand, large and sunburnt, and hers, small and still pink, patted the moist dark earth over it.

We finished the row like that, in contented silence, moving slowly forward on hands and knees to arrive at the trunk of the honey locust tree where the aromatic herb bed ended. The lemon-colored sun did not reach that spot. It was cold, the earth under us still remembered winter. I reached for Aurore and pulled her onto my lap, and then Sachema, too.

"When 'Ri coming?" she asked plaintively.

"I don't know," I said. "Don't you like Armand?" Her wordless answer was easy to read in the little honest face. The few times that Armand had attempted to take Aurore on his lap she had jumped down as quickly as her inherent sense of politeness had allowed. He bought her a cloth doll with a prettily painted ceramic head and hands, but she put it in the bottom of her trunk and continued to play with the corn-husk doll Delilah had made for her.

Her dislike was obvious. Mine was more subtle. I had wearied of him, of his profligate exaggerations, his all-too-predictable gallantries. The first novelty of attraction had disappeared. More and more, rather than admiring his taste in garments or his appetite for gossip, I resented the quickness with which he emptied the costly contents of the brandy decanter. When Armand looked at me, I knew I was being compared, often unfavorably, to every woman he had ever met. When Henri had looked at me, I felt like I was the only woman in the world, and immeasurably precious.

There were no more extravagant dinners or long evenings for Armand and myself. I missed Henri and was more content to drink the lonely dregs of his absence than the cloyingly sweet cup of Armand's presence. Still, Armand lingered in the colony, even after the roads opened again for spring travel. Talon asked several times if he had it in mind to purchase a lot and become a permanent member of our township. Armand waved his hand and smiled, but never made answer.

I hadn't heard from Henri for many months. There had been no more letters from Ohio, and my loneliness was nothing compared to the fear I hid from Aurore. I knew it was only the snow and the winter-tedious roads and trails that had kept Henri from sending word. Wasn't it? I asked myself countless times. Then why no word from him in the spring?

In the winter I imagined him unconscious in a snow drift, his leg twisted under him in unnatural fashion, and Ceres, turned mean from the cold, running away, abandoning him. Or bound and gagged inside a tent, a Shawnee war party holding him hostage. But in the spring I imagined him seated at a candle-lit dinner table in Greenville, some daughter of the regiment feeding him sweetmeats and his Julienne of Azilum forgotten. I don't know which vision tortured me the most, Henri on the verge of death, or Henri on the verge of life without me.

Still with Aurore and Sachema on my lap, I shifted my weight and twisted until we were in the sun again, outside of the chill shade of the honey locust. I lay back in the dirt and closed my eyes. The sun turned the colors under my closed lids into a golden haze, a mist through which any vision might enter, and I tried to will myself to see something of the future, as Delilah sometimes did, to receive a message of reassurance or warning.

"Julienne, you are ruining that gown." It was Victoire, her voice motherly and scolding. "Rolling in the mud like that, you're as heedless as my unruly sons."

"That's as good a message as any, I suppose," I said, opening my eyes and sitting up on my elbows.

"What are you talking about, Julienne? And do get up out of that mud."

"Pity, good friend. Who's to care if I ruin a gown or not? Aurore doesn't mind, and there's no one else to please in this large world." I opened my eyes wider to see her frowning face haloed by the noon sun at her back. From my vantage on the ground her small, black-covered shoulders held up the velvety blue sky.

"Self-pity? And in front of your daughter, too. Julienne, you surprise me. You should remarry. You need a firm hand and less leisure."

I picked up a handful of pebbles and tossed them lightly at her feet.

"Bad Mama, bad Mama," Aurore shrieked, delighted.

"Get out of the mud," Victoire said one more time, losing patience with us. "I come with serious news." I noticed then that her mouth, with its usually full, soft lips, was thin and tense. She was knitting at a furious pace even as she stood in the garden, and I could see she was agitated. I stood,

334

shooing away Aurore and Sachema. If it was news of Henri, Aurore must not hear it, not like this.

"Talon has heard that the Dauphin is dead," Victoire said when Aurore had run off to join Delilah in the cookhouse. Victoire stopped knitting and blew her nose into a stained, torn handkerchief that had no lace or embroidery adornment.

For one moment, I felt a warm tide of relief. It is not news of Henri. She has heard no bad news of Henri.

Then, came shock. The meaning of her message fell on me like a weight, crushing that first relief. A second time, then, we must see the end of our hopes and ambitions. This one simple statement: Talon has heard that the Dauphin is dead, killed them anew. Was it true, then? Marie-Antoinette's son, the royal child of France, the future of France, the king of France, was already turning to dust and corruption, as did all men?

"Louis-Charles. Dead. How?" I said finally. I sat back down, heedless of the mud, and Victoire, overcome with grief, sat next to me in the mire.

"Neglect, it is said. Neglect so pernicious as to be deemed murder." She wept.

Beyond the cookhouse and the knee-high stone fence where the garden snakes sunbathed, I could see the brown-shingled wall of the Queen's House. Even in the traveling season when our colony was so filled with visitors and émigrés that many cabins slept four to a bed, a room had been kept empty and waiting in that house . . . for the Dauphin, and his sister. It was the traveling season now (where is Henri? a voice called at the back of my thoughts) and the colony and house were strained with visitors, newcomers, curiosity seekers, yet that room, again, had been kept empty. For nought.

We wept together a few moments. After the death of our Queen I had thought few things would matter to me as much as they once had. I had been wrong. The death of her son was even more painful. She, after all, had lived a good deal of her life, even if she hadn't been allowed to reach the span of years she might have had.

He had been a child, no more than ten years of age and the last three years of that short span he had spent imprisoned, buried alive in a dark and damp dungeon with neither decent food, air nor companionship to sustain him. His father had been killed, and then his mother, and then he had been separated from his sister. He had been beaten and forced to wear the carmagnole of the revolutionaries and learn the words of the Ça Ira; he, royal child of France, had been instructed and whipped by an illiterate shoemaker. And he had died. Death is that much more unjust when it takes those who have not had the opportunity to live.

After a while Victoire rose again . . . her backside was as muddy as mine, now . . . and said she must return to her cabin to see her sons were up to no mischief. I wiped at her gown, but the mud clung to it persistently.

"It's ruined," she said. "Everything is ruined. Come to the Queen's House tonight. Talon will make the formal announcement."

"Yes. We must bring out the black crêpe for mourning again. I'll come." I watched her go and my thoughts and mood were dark. Not just with grief for Louis-Charles.

There was still the matter of the diamond. What must be done with the Golden Ransom now? I had kept it for the Queen, and then for her son. And they were both dead.

I couldn't give the diamond to another, say Talon, for safekeeping. He, or whomever I selected, would think me a thief. How could I honestly have come by such an extravagant gem? Nor could I sell it, for the same reason.

Worse than the accusation of theft, though, was the knowledge that when the diamond came to light, Marie-Antoinette's guilt in the affair of the diamond necklace would be assumed. That final risk of falsely proven guilt would have been worth only the price of seeing her son on the throne, nothing less. And that, now, was impossible.

I thought about this problem for the rest of the afternoon and came up with no solution. The priceless gem had become a terrible burden to me. I wished again that Marie-Antoinette had not favored me, had not saved me from Mouret's beating that night so long ago, just to hold hostage my own life in this manner. I was growing weary of queens and thrones and diamonds. And where was Henri?

We dressed in black and twined black ribbons in our new short curls for the evening at the Queen's House. It was the style that year for the Frenchwomen of Azilum to shear their hair and wear it short and tousled; it was in memory of all those beloved ones who had had their own hair cut at the neck to make the guillotine's work easier. And, it was to make the summer heat more bearable. We had suffered greatly the summer before.

We gathered in silence in the music room, prepared to weep and mourn. But to our surprise, Talon entered dressed in a bright red waistcoat and yellow brocade breeches. He smiled as he descended the main staircase.

We, gathered before him, hesitated and looked back and forth at each other, not knowing how to react. Armand caught my eye and raised one arched, black eyebrow as if to say, "What is this madness?" He made, as if he would come to my side, so I quickly looked away from him, back at Talon.

This was the appearance we had expected the summer before, when we awaited news of the arrival of our Queen, and he had, instead, worn black and a frown to announce her death. Now that we awaited the announcement of the death of the heir to the throne, he had dressed gaily and smiled.

"My friends," he said, pausing midway down the stairs as if he could not wait. "I have received other information, a message that indicates that the Dauphin is not dead. We must rejoice." A gasp went up from us and then we all began talking at once, asking questions that still have no answers.

I listened carefully to every word that night, and could make little sense of the matter. All these decades later it is still a great mystery.

Some child imprisoned in the Temple had died, Talon and all subsequent reports informed us. That much was certain. On June 8 a child's-sized coffin had been carried out from the cell where the Dauphin had been led in.

But that dead child was not the Dauphin. I am as convinced of it now as I was then, as are many others. Including some who wish it had been LouisCharles. There were too many mysteries surrounding the death of the Dauphin, too many bits of fact and speculation that did not add up to a simple death and burial.

His sister, still alive and imprisoned just doors away from her brother, had not been allowed to see the body. She, who would recognize him beyond doubt, had been denied that right to say farewell. No one, in fact, who had known the Dauphin while he lived had been called in to identify the dead boy. And immediately before that child's death, all others had also been refused permission to visit him. In the past year his guards had been changed frequently and there were few, if any, guards left in the Temple who could with accuracy identify the royal child. Surely that was not coincidence, but purpose. A switch had been made, a child posing as the Dauphin had taken the Dauphin's place in that cell, and in the Dauphin's coffin.

There were the reports of the varying condition of the child prisoner that further hinted at a switch of prisoners. In 1794, visitors were able to report that the Dauphin, despite his hardships, was in relative good health for the circumstances; he was intelligent and articulate. Two months later, those who visited saw a child in monstrous health, confined to bed, louse-ridden, and incapable of saying a single word. Could those two have been the same?

One child in the Temple had rickets; the second had scrofula. And three doctors who were called in to treat the prisoner with scrofula were imprudent enough to suggest it was not the same boy they had visited earlier. All three physicians died shortly after, and in strange circumstances. After the coffin was secretly buried, four men involved in the burial also died sudden and unnatural deaths. Years later I heard it whispered that Josephine, divorced wife of Napoleon, died prematurely because she knew the whereabouts of the living Louis-Charles, son of Louis XVI and heir to the throne.

"Some contend that this death means nothing, that the young child is full of life, that it is a very long time since he was at the Temple," Talon read aloud from the *Courrier Universel*. And we agreed. Gathered to hear of our King's death, we rejoiced to hear he had escaped his prison . . . and was still in this life.

Did the Convention free Louis-Charles, or did the royalists rescue him? This was one of the questions we could not answer.

The Convention, for reasons of its own, could have decided to decree the Dauphin dead and bury a pauper in his place. Their reasons for doing this would be complicated, but obvious. With the royal son still alive, they held an important hostage. They could use this boy as a pawn against other possible heirs to the throne, including the Dauphin's ambitious uncle, Louis XVI's brother the Comte de Provence, who had already accumulated a great party of followers and was ready to be crowned Louis XVIII when the revolution failed.

Or perhaps royalists, having failed to rescue the Queen, had finally rescued the Queen's son.

This is the story we pieced together that night. An unknown child was pronounced dead in the King's name. Louis-Charles was secreted out of the Temple, hidden in some unsuspected conveyance . . . perhaps a laundry basket. The unknown child was buried quickly and secretly. The casket, perhaps, had fallen during its journey and jarred opened so that those carrying it noted—with startled and frightened eyes—that the dead child they carried was older and taller than the Dauphin, and that was why they, too, died.

Talon, rejoicing that night, also announced reason to believe that the child would soon be conveyed to America, if he was not already on his way. Ministers in charge of the child before the so-called death had been journeying to the West Indies; surely they were an advance mission to America, to pave the way for the removal of Marie-Antoinette's son to America?

He did not say the child would be brought to Azilum. But that was taken for granted by all of us there. The Queen had not come to us. Her son, who still lived and was free of the Temple, would.

That night, still dressed in black, we danced until early morning, and drank more wine than we should have, and were happier than we had been in many months. But where is Henri? the voice in my head kept asking.

338

The next day, instead of draping the Queen's House in black mourning, we gave the house a momentous cleaning and freshening, finding in that most domestic of activities the expression required by our renewed joy and anticipation. The Dauphin's room was opened and cleared of boxes and building materials and decorated in the lively greens and blues thought to appeal to a young boy. This would be the child's schoolroom. He would need much time to be instructed in those things a king must know and a prisoner cannot learn. Talon ordered books by the crateful from Philadelphia, a globe, a desk and shelves. And toys. The child must have time to play, to regain some of that carefree aspect that is so precious to the child in living it, and to the grown man in remembering it.

The ceiling was painted with a cream background adorned with rows of golden fleur-de-lis, and a tester bed, huge and elaborately carved, was purchased for his bedroom. Victoire and I elected to embroider a coverlet for the royal youth. Over our stitching we wove together those details and speculations that wafted to us on the spring air along with the scent of pipes from the open windows of Talon's drawing room. There were constant meetings in Talon's office and a sense of plans being made, things afoot, in the spring air.

"I've heard the switch was made before Hébert was guillotined." Victoire said one day, bending her rosy-cheeked face over the blue satin. Her plump fingers darted back and forth over the cloth with all the skill of a gentlewoman bred for fine needlework. But her hands were calloused and work-stained.

I shifted in my hard chair, remembering the cushions that Bertin's seamstresses had sewn into their petticoats, and the blue cloth whispered an echo to her own soft voice.

"Why would Hébert spirit the Dauphin out of prison?"

"For the same reason some suspect Barras of the scheme. To keep the child alive, for use as a pawn. If the war failed, he could trade the Dauphin to the English to assure an easier truce for the French."

"An easier truce for himself, I think. Hébert would have used the child as ransom for his safety with no thought of France's well-being. But surely Hébert would not deliver the child to the safety of a royalist colony. To us." Doubt. More doubt. Always doubt.

"No, he would not," Victoire agreed. We grew silent.

"More likely, the royalists in France have managed to free him," she said a moment later, determined to be an optimist in this matter. "And so, the Dauphin will soon be with us, in the safety of Azilum. I've never met the

Queen's children. What an honor!" Her fingers moved up and down, in and out, leaving in their wake a trail of silver fleur-de-lis.

"I saw him twice." I jabbed my needle in and out. "Once when he was but a few months old, and again when he was about five. He was a beautiful child. He had his mother's eyes and mouth." I did not add that it was on that day Marie-Antoinette entrusted me with the Golden Ransom—the day she foresaw her future, and his.

I still have that coverlet, stowed away in one of the many trunks that accumulated in the course of a long life. I can judge which are Victoire's confident stitches and which are my own clumsier ones, for I was nervous during the making of that coverlet. I thought of the Dauphin, who would soon come to Azilum, and of my two interviews with Talon, when he had warned me that he feared Jacobins even in Azilum. I feared that royal child would never reach a place of safety. And I thought of Henri who had not yet returned to Azilum, although the wild dogwood had already ceased blooming and he had promised to return in the spring.

It was a difficult season. The weather constantly shifted from wet to dry, with days of strong sun followed by nights of thunder and storm. It was a time of contradiction. We rejoiced in our hearts, but must wear long faces in front of visitors as if in agreement with the official verdict that the Dauphin was dead. It must not be known that he was anticipated in Azilum; such knowledge would increase one hundredfold the dangers of his journey.

A good deal of my peace of mind, however, returned in July riding a horse named Ceres.

It was early afternoon and I was fetching from my bedroom a piece of wool that needed mending, when I looked down to see whose horse was so weary that the clop-clop steps sounded like a sad tattoo. Below in the street Henri and Smithy passed. They and their horses were covered with mud and travel fatigue. But Henri was whole of limb and straight in the saddle.

My heart paused for a moment and then beat faster. I waved through the window, but Henri did not look up. Nor did he stop at my door, but continued down Walnut Street to the Queen's House. Of course, I thought, arguing against disappointment. He will want to bathe. To see Talon and finish with business. And then . . . he will come tonight. But the evening was a long way away yet and I longed to feel his arms about me in the embrace that would end my loneliness.

Preoccupied, I attended to the mending, and helped Delilah chop vegetables for stew, and even cut out a new gown ordered by one of the wealthy German farmwives, and still time seemed stuck in its course, forbidding the evening to come. Aurore knew Henri was returned but quickly absorbed herself in play with Sachema, and I admired the innocence of childhood, which can yearn for one thing yet be content with another.

It was our custom to eat our largest meal of the day at noon, but when work was finished and the day over Delilah set out the plates again. That day our supper was not leftovers but fricasee of chicken, salad of wild herbs, and corn muffins marbled with berries. Delilah set a vase of black-eyed Susans on the table and dressed her black hair with a heavy coating of bear grease, after donning her best cotton dress and cleanest leather leggings.

Her medicine bag had mysteriously shrunk during the day. When I went upstairs to dress my hair I found a wilted stem of May apple in my ribbon box. There was a rabbit's foot planted under the bed, and a perfectly round, black stone under the pillow; the bed linens were pungent with the sweet smell of tobacco, the herb that Delilah deemed the most potent.

I left those charms in place and added a few of own: rosewater on my neck and hands, a clean lace fichu, a row of curls over a powdered forehead.

Henri and the first evening star arrived simultaneously. The night air was warm and musky with summer as I opened the door to him. He had dressed in his black suit, which was still creased from its months of storage in the Queen's House, his red hair had been brushed severely back into a queue at his neck and tied with a black ribbon.

He carried wildflowers and hung his head a little before entering, a suitor not knowing what to expect. But the man who came in was not the same boy who had left me many months before. His shoulders were broader, his chest more filled out. His face had lost the last lingering curves of childhood and was now all decisive planes and angles; his hair had darkened to a mahogany color. His eyes were not as candid; they hinted at secrets that would not be revealed. More than ever, he reminded me of Louise.

Seeing him, I knew finally that I loved him. As much as I had ever loved Charles, perhaps even more. I was desperate to hold him, to claim him as my own.

Henri bowed, formal as a stranger, and we eyed each other across the distance of many long, lonely months. When I finally put my arms around his waist it wasn't just the man I embraced, but the memories and friends of another life that had been left behind.

"I used to lay awake at night and dream of what I would say to you," he said into my hair. "Now I am bereft of speech."

"Mayhap bereft of paper and ink, too, for all the messages I received from you," I said into his waistcoat, pressing myself hard against him. He felt strong as a beam around which a house could be built.

"Just returned, and I'm already being scolded," he said, grinning. "It's as if I never left. But did you not get any messages I sent?"

"One." I stepped back and glared, but felt like the richest woman on earth for having this man who blushed and stammered before me. I ignored the wetness in my eyes, but Henri wiped wonderingly at a single tear that escaped down my cheek.

"Well, Ohio is a rough place and the post is not to be counted on," he said. "I humbly ask your forgiveness for the missing letters I wrote but other people did not deliver."

"Accepted." We kissed then, and the embrace lasted long enough for a score of moths, attracted by the candlelight, to flit in through the still open door. All during our late supper they circled the candles on white gauze wings, glad harbingers of reunion.

Delilah and Joshua joined the homecoming feast. Little Aurore refused to sleep and would not stop wailing until Henri carried her downstairs on his shoulders—they had both grown! Aurore had to duck her head to avoid hitting the doorway—and she was set in her own chair at table. I sat at the head, Henri at the foot, and he questioned Joshua about plowing oxen and seed costs as the man of the house would. We were, I saw, already a family. I felt both joy and fear; here was a course I could not alter, I must see it through to the end.

Henri talked little of the rigors of the Ohio winter. Perhaps he already suspected what we would eventually realize. The opening of the Ohio frontier would be one of the many blows that would eventually reduce Azilum to dust and memory. Our colony would become merely an overnight stop for those eager to keep moving further west. We would no longer be a goal but only a temporary resting place.

Henri's winter had been a hard one of menacing snowstorms and much dangerous ill-will between the whites and the Indians.

"There was no more for me to do there," he said. He had left before treaties had been signed. "I received information that Senator Morris may have to delay his land purchases in that area."

"He is not well?"

"No. He's broken with his old partner, Willing, and begun new ventures with a man called Greenleaf. Greenleaf is a speculator and manipulator of the worst sort and Morris is verging on bankruptcy." Another blow to Azilum. One of our staunchest supporters was faltering under the weight of his own many problems, and could give no more assistance to us. "Greenleaf is greedy and dishonest and even if Senator Morris suffers no further financial losses through this partnership, his name will suffer."

342

"But your contract with him is expired," I said, uncomprehending. "There is nothing to cause you worry."

"It is expired. But he is as a father to me, and I worry for him."

"What will you do now, Henri?"

"It seems that decision is not entirely up to me." His eyes grew smoky as he looked at me, and I began to wish the meal would end and the candles be pinched out so we could be left to privacy and darkness.

But Aurore must stay up yet later to unwrap the presents Henri had brought her—miniature leather boots made of softest rabbit fur, a set of carved animals to complete the ark he had begun for her last year. Only when that was done, and both Joshua and Delilah presented with beaver vests, did we take each other's hand and go up the stairs, to the waiting bedroom.

"Now, madame, we have business that will not wait another day," Henri said, smiling. "And after, you can tell me why you have cut off your hair. Was it grief for me that drove you to it?" He stopped and put his arms around my shoulders, pressing against me until I was limp with the sweetness of his weight.

"No, only the summer heat," I said.

"Well, then. It suits you, those short curls. And it's going to get much warmer, I promise." His hands were already busy, undoing the laces of my gown.

The lark sang long into the night, and the mourning doves began their softer cooing well before dawn, and we were awake to hear both, more needful of that physical comfort that is love than sleep. The long months of waiting became a mere shadow in the corner, which we chased away with our lovemaking. The next day, for the first time in months, I sang as I worked and was content to do all the chores the day required to make the night come that much sooner.

But the next evening when my lover returned to me, he was petulant.

"You have been drinking," I said, going to greet him. He smelled strongly of rum.

"I have. In Beaulieu's public room. Drinking. And listening to gossip." His gait was unsteady; he had to reach twice before his hand found the doorknob and swung the door shut with a sharp crack.

"The talk was informative. I hear you have another suitor." He slumped in the chair he claimed as his own and scowled at me.

"Darnton is the man the gossips would have named," I supplied. "But . . ." Henri would not let me finish.

"That's the name. That's the man. I met him yesterday. He is a liar and a bore. I didn't know your tastes were so low." He struggled to remove his boots but they were wedged on tightly and his trembling hands could not dislodge them.

I went to him and pulled off the boots, then went and sat in my chair before the fire, opposite him.

"There is nothing between us. He is no suitor of mine," I said. "There could have been. I won't deny it. But there wasn't. He was not of my choice."

Henri glared at me. He was jealous as only a young man can be when he returns home to find that an older, more worldly and gallant man has been sitting in his chair before the hearth, wooing his woman. I should have pitied the boy in him who had never known family or love and had little reason to trust either.

Instead, I displayed the cold righteousness of a woman accused. Even just a year before I would have run to him and knelt at his feet. But I was no longer a young and tremulous creature who would weep into her lover's lap at the first sign of a storm. I stayed in my chair.

Henri unsteadily pulled his boots back on and tried to stand.

"Dirty Frenchman," he mumbled. "All slick and dandy and false."

"You are a Frenchman, too," I reminded him.

"No. I am an American. I want nothing more to do with France, it's a foul place filled with foul people."

"But I am a Frenchwoman," I said. "And I have seen enough of your country to think that it can be as foul as elsewhere. What is Azilum? Just a mud patch filled with log hovels." I was angry because he was angry and we used words like swords, to wound.

"Then go back to your damned France," he said, standing and moving toward the door.

"I will," I screamed.

The door slammed shut, and I was alone.

We parted a second time, and that parting was a more difficult one, for it was not mere distance but our own ill-will between us.

The weather grew unpredictable. When it should have been warm and sunny, it became cloudy and cold. Winds whipped the dust in the lanes into miniature whirlwinds that threw grit in our mouths and eyes. And then the rains started to fall . . . and fall . . . and fall. I thought we would all be swept away, before those torrential downpours ceased. The river swelled, and as the river swelled so did our anticipation, for with each day came new speculation about the whereabouts of the Dauphin.

344

Delilah continued to dream of disaster and grew tense and tight-lipped.

"The winter was a misery, but sometimes I think this is even worse," said Madame Farquet, staring gloomily out of the cookhouse window.

Delilah was working in the fields with Joshua, digging trenches for the overflow to drain into. I was rolling out biscuits for our dinner.

"I think if the rain doesn't stop soon, I'll go mad." she said gloomily.

"Try to see the bright side," I replied with false and bitter cheer. Since the quarrel with Henri, there had been no bright side to life. "Three of your chickens drowned in the trough this week. Less work for you."

"One of them was Prudence, my best layer," said Madame Farquet. "I was to have a new hat this summer because of her. And now she's gone." Madame, for the first time in her life, was learning to enjoy some of the reward of honest labor. I realized I could no longer tease her about the chickens.

"I shall roll out an extra batch for you and monsieur," I said apologetically, scattering a film of flour over the cutting board.

"Then knead them a little longer, dear. That last batch looked lumpy, not at all as good as Delilah's," she said, brightening a little.

The Great Wind Storm of 1795 began one late night with a gentle wailing that surrounded our cabins and flowed in and out of windows like a ghostly presence. Drowsy but sleepless because of the quarrel with Henri, I heard the tall oaks and pines of the forest sway and groan like lovers in heated embrace.

The next day I caught Delilah staring up at the sky. "Flying Head cloud," she said ominously, pointing to the western horizon. I've never before or since seen such a cloud. Its towering, billowed head all but filled the pale blue sky, blazing in muted colors of pink and violet and grey mixed into that huge whiteness. Behind it, long streamers trailed menacingly in a wind so high that only the boldest geese felt its cold strength.

"The trouble comes today," Delilah said, touching her medicine bag hanging on its leather neck cord.

"But the rain has stopped," I argued.

"Listen to the river," she said, frowning deeply. The rushing waters of the Susquehanna roared with a voice I had never heard before; the earth trembled beneath our feet with the force of the river's passage. "It's angry. And the wind will get stronger. Keep Aurore in the house today."

"All right," I said. "I'll tell Aurore now, and keep her with me during the day."

The wind came late in the afternoon, just as twilight was knitting the first grey shadows inside the cookhouse where I worked. The open door behind me was slammed shut by an invisible, icy hand; a sudden draft forced the smoke back down the chimney, and then cups and saucers and pots flew off their shelves.

I reached down, blinded by smoke and soot, to where Aurore had been playing under the table. She wasn't there.

Another gust of wind blew in one of the windows; the glass shattered at my feet. I screamed and Henri ran in, fighting his way through the smoke and debris.

"Root cellar!" he yelled over the voice of the wind, pushing me in the direction of the trap door that led to the root cellar from the cookhouse.

"No. Aurore. Gone," I yelled back. We could barely hear each other over the shrieking wind. Henri was out of the door again before I finished. I ran after him, clutching at the flying sails of my skirts, trying to keep my footing in a wind so strong that some of the smaller cabins were beginning to tilt easterly from the force of it.

We struggled first to the herb garden, bending forward to keep from being blown backwards. Aurore was not there, but my little wood pavilion had already been carried off by the wind.

My hair whipped across my eyes and I tore at it, wild with fear for Aurore. Henri pointed, no longer able to be heard above the wind, and we forced our way to the orchard, where the young trees were so bent they trailed their tops in the frenzied grasses of the orchard floor. She was not there either.

Henri was pale and I gasped from the effort of breathing; the wind tried to force the very air from our lungs. It howled about us, evil and menacingly strong. The air was thick with flying debris from cabins and gardens.

Aurore sometimes played at the river's edge, among the marshy cattails at the wharf, although this was forbidden when she was alone. We forced our way to the river, the wind pushing us back a step for every two we achieved. I was exhausted from the effort but I put foot in front of foot, bending deeply into the wind, numb to everything but the fact that Aurore was in danger. I did not wonder at Henri appearing so timely in my need; it seemed right and natural.

He saw her first, on the wharf, her small arms wrapped tightly around a post, her black hair streaming behind her. Her mouth was opened in a scream we couldn't hear.

"Hold tight!" Henri yelled. "Hold, Aurore!" With a last burst of strength he ran through the pushing, bullying wind and got her in the safety of his arms, just as her little hands were losing their grip on the post. Underneath them, revealed through open spaces of missing boards in the wind-torn wharf, the river roared and frothed, angry and dangerous.

"Sachema, Sachema!" Aurore screamed. "In the water!"

Henri, on his knees and holding Aurore to his chest, peered into the white spray but the dog had already disappeared from sight.

There was much damage caused by that storm. The forests around Azilum were filled with the long, dark forms of prematurely felled trees and our orchard looked as if some giant, vexatious deity had been playing at pick-up-sticks.

The smaller, less solid cabins of the colony stood open to the day, their roofs and windows and doors carried away. The wharf caved in and tumbled down-river just moments after Henri and Aurore left it, and with the wharf went the row of shanties that had been perched precariously on the banks of the Susquehanna.

There were no dead, but many were homeless. And even more had lost heart. How fragile we were, how easily destroyed.

Delilah and I put Aurore to bed and forced cup after cup of sassafras tea down her, to keep her from chilling and catching fever. She wept for Sachema. When we were certain, days later, that she would suffer no illness from her drenching and fright, Delilah brought home a new puppy for her.

"What will you name your dog?" I asked, lifting a black curl from her cool forehead.

"Sachema," she said with a grin that made her cheeks round and rosy as apples.

"No. New dog, new name," said Delilah.

Aurore frowned. I saw again how Charles's eyes had darkened when he was perplexed. "Smithy," said Aurore, and Delilah laughed.

"Good. Smithy-the-first-one will be proud and bring squirrel meat for his namesake. This dog will live a long life," she promised. She was right, as Delilah often was.

The storm also did some good. It washed away the anger between Henri and me. When danger threatened, I thought instantly of him. When danger threatened, he sought me. The bonds were deeper than we had known, too deep to cut of our own will. I relived a dozen times a day that moment when Henri rescued Aurore from the angry river and knew that both of them were precious to me beyond words. I could not lose either of them.

We wed just two weeks after that storm, when the repairs to the chapel roof still hadn't been completed and the birds in the trees could watch us make our vows.

Monsieur Talon led me to the altar; Victoire scattered handfuls of wild fern and ox-eyed daisies in my path. Delilah stood to the right of the altar, holding Aurore tightly by the hand. Bored with the pomp, and pouting because she had bot been allowed to bring her new puppy, Aurore squatted on the damp wooden floor and pulled the wild daisies apart. Henri smiled at her, and she smiled back at him.

Abbé Carles's low voice finished the reading from scripture and in the silence I could hear the birds singing in the overhead trees. How different it was from that other wedding. There had been a bird then, too, but it had been trapped in the overhead vaulting. It had beat its wings furiously against the stained glass windows, seeking escape. Charles had been somber and silent; Henri was cheerful and grinning. And there was Aurore, littering the floor with petals. I was very happy.

The abbé nodded at Henri, who sought my hand while Smithy stepped forward with a small silk pillow on which rested my new wedding band. Smithy smelled of bear grease and his fur cap gave off a pungent odor of ill-tanned raccoon. But he had donned clean trousers and trimmed his ginger whiskers.

I hadn't remembered to remove Charles's ring. Henri hesitated just one brief moment before he twisted the ring off my finger and replaced it with his own. I felt a brief pang, and then greater happiness. Outside, afterward, he returned Charles's ring.

"You'll want to keep this," he said, his voice gentle.

"For Aurore," I agreed.

The summer storms were over. The skies over Azilum grew pale and clear, the days halcyon, as the work lessened and the heat grew greater. I slept each night tangled in Henri's arms and legs and awoke early for the joy of watching him for a few moments as he slept.

All worries, all cares seemed suspended. Sometimes I would think of France and know that this marriage made my return difficult, almost impossible. Henri had no wish to return to a homeland that had given him so little. I missed France as much as ever, but you can't hold a country in your arms, a nation can't rub your aching back, pleasure you and give you babes. Charles had wanted to take me to America; Henri wished to keep me there. So be it. Beyond that, beyond the aching for home and my joy with Henri, I would not think.

The Queen's diamond still lay sleeping under the Old Man of the Forest. I had not told Henri of that matter. I told myself it was because the right moment hadn't appeared. It would certainly dismay a new groom to learn that his bride was in possession of a diamond that would help restore a King, ruin a Queen's reputation for all of history, and perhaps put the possessor under suspicion of theft.

But there was also a part of me that did not want to put Henri's loyalty to the test. He was not a royalist, he was not an admirer of Marie-Antionette. What would he make of all this? I'll tell him later, I decided, each time I thought of the matter. No need to worry him now.

By September I was already pregnant, and so lazy and indolent with heat and pleasure that Henri teased I was fit only for a seraglio. I spent my afternoons with my feet up on a hassock and my skirts and petticoats gathered above my knees to cool my legs. The heat lasted long that summer, as if to make up for the cruel weather of the late spring and early summer. The ladies of Azilum moved out of their stifling cookhouses and low-roofed cabins to spend the afternoons in the cool, airy parlors of the Queen's House, to rest and gossip.

I was already suffering greensickness and complaining goodnaturedly about women's lot, although I wouldn't have traded mine with a king.

"You'll feel more energetic in a few months," promised Madame Homet. "The first and last months are always the worse. Don't you remember?" She herself was as rounded as an apple ready to fall from the tree.

"I don't remember. When I carried Aurore I was in hiding. There were not good or bad months, only terrible days."

"Ah, yes," the ladies whispered. Fans slowed and petticoats rustled nervously as we each delved into our remembrances of last days and weeks in Paris, and the sorrow such memories bring.

"Is your new chicken coop finished?" Madame Homet asked Madame Farquet most pleasantly, after the moment had flickered past like a shadow in a doorway.

"Almost. It is far superior to the one blown away by the storm. But I wish the curtains for my sitting room were finished. I would so like to have them up before the little King arrives." She cleared her throat and looked pointedly at me.

"Next week," I promised. I had agreed to stitch them, but found the task discouragingly boring. The plain homespun panels were not even to be trimmed with lace; she couldn't afford it.

A knock sounded at the door and we sat up quickly, adjusting skirts and bodices for modesty. A black servant entered, carrying a large tray laden with glasses and a pitcher of lemonade.

"Monsieur Talon is so thoughtful!" sighed Madame Homet, after the servant left. "Yes," we all echoed, rousing ourselves just enough to empty the tray of its refreshment. The conflicting tastes of lemon and sugar overpowered the metallic greensickness taste in my mouth.

"No need to hurry with the curtains," Madame Homet told me.

"No?" asked Madame Farquet, bristling.

"Not if they are to please Louis-Charles. He will not come to Azilum until next spring or summer. He is very ill, and must rest in Albany until he is strong enough to travel."

"The Dauphin is in Albany?" we asked in one voice, setting down our glasses and looking at Madame Homet. I sat up, all attention. Madame Homet smiled and nodded. We did not ask whence came such information. It originated in Talon's office, and from there made its way to us through various spouses who muttered as they worked or talked in their sleep. We all of us, I suppose, came from France to Pennsylvania with a small gift for intrigue.

"How ill?" I asked.

"It is not known. That is why Talon is sending an envoy to Albany to present Louis-Charles with a petition of our continuing loyalty, and to see how matters are with him. Henri will no doubt be able to reassure us when he returns." Madame Homet smiled. "Surely you knew Monsieur Arraché was being sent to Albany?" she asked.

"Of course. The heat is affecting my memory. I forgot for the moment," I lied. He had not mentioned it.

I let the door slam heavily behind me. "Henri!" I shouted, running from room to room. He was not in the cabin. The back door slammed behind me as I ran into the herb garden. "Henri! Henri!" He was there, at the very back, pruning dead limbs from the honey locust.

"I was going to tell you this evening," he said, wiping his brow with the ragged sleeve of his work shirt. He was brown from the sun and glistening from labor and the softness in his eyes when he looked at me made me weak in the knees.

"Take me with you. To Albany," I said, throwing my arms about him.

"Sweet wife," he whispered kissing my forehead. "I won't be gone long. Don't be afraid."

"Take me with you," I repeated, not correcting his assumption that it was fear for him, rather than eagerness for my own purposes, that made me desire to go on this journey.

It was my chance to end this finally, to return the Golden Ransom to Marie-Antoinette's son and his guardians. I would not wait even one more

350

year while the Dauphin rested in Albany, to be free of this burden, to complete the pledge.

"I cannot take you," Henri said, stroking my hair. "Think of the baby you carry. You shouldn't make such a trip now."

"I will go," I said.

"No," insisted Henri. He lifted me in his arms and carried me to the wooden bench under the honey locust, where we sat and watched the sunset in the evenings. I sat on his knees, put my head against his chest and took a deep breath.

The time for secrets was passed. It was time to tell him of the diamond, and my pledge. Henri and I were joined for life. I had made a mistake before, of not confiding in the one closest to me, and it had brought Charles and me to ruin. I would not make the same mistake with Henri. I must believe in his faith in me. And I must now trust him. Completely.

"I will go, Henri. And if you will listen for a moment, you'll understand why."

21

. . . the diamond returned . . .

All is change; all yields its place and goes.

—*Euripides*

It is a vexatious task to convey a tender woman (as Henri thought I was) from the wilds of Pennsylvania to the more civilized roads of Albany, New York. We faced the dangers of unfriendly Iroquois, highwaymen, storm and wild animals. And of Henri's usually gentle temper, which was grown irritable with Indian summer heat, worry over my own person and health and the slowness of our pace.

Many times he came close to being irritable with me, for I was the reason our pace was slow. But he held his tongue and was careful to show only concern. Each time he looked at me I could see wonder and puzzlement clouding his expression.

The tale I had told him as we sat under the honey locust had made him frown and fall into a long silence. I omitted no detail. I told him of the Queen's trust in me, and of Charles's lack of trust; of d'Orléans's threats and Talon's warnings, and of the various hiding places of the Golden Ransom, which then was still buried under the Old Man of the Forest. I told him of the purpose of the gem, which was to help identify Marie-Antoinette's son, and restore him to his throne.

"Louis-Charles died in prison," Henri said, shaking his head.

"No one believes that. Certainly not Talon, else why would he be sending you to Albany?"

"Curiosity. Rumors. To ascertain this child is not the Dauphin."

"To ascertain he is the Dauphin," I insisted. "Talon is sending you to Albany to greet the Dauphin and assure him of our loyalty. And to discover when he may remove himself to Azilum. It may not be for a long time, if he is unwell. And I wish to be finished with this. I have my own son to care for." Delilah, after holding a stone tied in string over my wrist for several moments, had already announced that my second child was to be a boy.

Eventually, Henri gave in. I would accompany him to Albany, and discharge my pledge to the Queen. He also agreed that no one else should be privy to this strange history, for my safety and Louis-Charles's. My desire to visit Albany was passed off as the whim of a woman in a certain condition, who must be humored. Talon hired Smithy to be our guide, and so we went, the three of us.

"Damn female foolishness," Smithy muttered at least a dozen times a day during that journey.

Henri had rented a small wagon, light enough to travel quickly and narrow enough to maneuver paths that were often no more than deer trails cutting through forest and meadow. I equipped it with a huge sunshade, striped in red and white like a child's candy stick and trimmed with a long fringing of white silk tassels. I said it was to protect my complexion. But I hoped that the Dauphin would feel well enough to go riding, and that the gay sunshade would help lift his spirits.

Henri sat next to me on an amply cushioned board, holding the reins in his large hands.

"Never seen such a sight," Smithy had muttered, the day we started out. "I've heard of them traveling brothels that followed the army during the war, but never thought to ride shotgun along one of them."

"Enough, Smithy," said Henri peevishly. "You can't expect her to ride sidesaddle all the way to Albany."

"Didn't expect her to ride to Albany at all," said Smithy, spitting into the lower stems of a wild honeysuckle.

Henri, for the most part, held his tongue. But whenever we passed a settlement and the farmers and their children lined up to stare and giggle as we passed, my suffering husband would lower his head and stare straight ahead, urging us to a faster pace.

North of Azilum, following the river, we passed through dense, black forests where daylight never touched golden fingers to forest floor—the Shades of Death, they were called—and alongside high mountains where

353

clouds rested on the purple pinnacles. The size and beauty of the land astounded me. During my journey to Azilum grief still forced me to look inward; with Henri by my side and a new life beginning within, I looked outward, my curiosity restored. I was pleased, if sometimes frightened, by the green magnificence surrounding us. It was the world the day after creation, still new and untouched, filled with promise. Surely Louis-Charles would be pleased with his place of refuge.

In the cool evenings when tall pines cast shadows long as a city street we would stop to rest the horses and ourselves. I would stew whatever forest animal Smithy had shot that day, while the two men rubbed down the horses and made our wagon secure for the night. Often, we stayed at a hospitable farmhouse along the way, but my favorite nights were those spent sleeping under the black velvet sky where stars winked at us from a heaven that seemed close enough to touch.

Smithy slept on one side of the wagon, Henri and I on the other. The darkness and evening song of rustling winds afforded us a privacy which we amply enjoyed, for the life within my womb had awakened my senses to a pitch that rivaled even my young husband's. At night, at least, Henri had no reason to complain of my companionship on the journey.

One night Henri shot a catamount that had been threatening the horses; another time we hid in a cave as a band of Seneca Indians relieved the wagon of my case of ribbons and Smithy's stock of rum. But no harm came to us. We reached the city of New York in good health and with high spirits.

We stopped and rested a day at the home of Mrs. Ruth Moody, who had crossed the sea with me, for I was curious to see how she and her seaman husband fared. They had residence in a luxurious brick mansion in that green, pastoral section known as the Bowery, for it led to Stuyvesant's bouwery, or farm.

Ruth had grown even more dull-eyed and long of face than before, and the luxurious splendor of her ornate home made a poor comparison to her sallow complexion and dowdy manner of dress. But she, big already with her second child, was well contented. We spent happy hours discussing names for our children, and if Mr. Moody was absent at dinner and didn't come home until quite late, and then smelling strongly of rum, nobody was impolite enough to mention it. When he did come in he put his arms around Ruth and gave her a wet smacking kiss and called her his pretty lass, which put some color in her cheeks and a smile on her mouth.

Sleeping next to Henri in a feather bed so deep it all but enveloped us in warm softness, I reflected on Charles and Mr. Moody and all men who made wedding vows with hidden reservations. Having been married to Henri even for just three months, I could already judge that Charles had not been half as enthusiastic, nor half as willing, to play the role of husband. But there was no more room in me for anger. Charles had loved me, in his way, and he had died. The finality of death was a much larger truth than the smaller trespasses of the living. I hugged Henri who, even in his sleep, turned to hold me more closely, and like Ruth I was well contented.

From New York we elected to finish the journey to Albany by water, to break the monotony of overland travel. The sloop on which we booked passage was the *Magdalene;* while there were only twelve narrow sleeping berths we shared the journey with some twenty passengers.

Henri, to make me comfortable, let me have a berth to myself and spent the night on deck, exchanging long tales and longer glasses of grog with Smithy and a Mr. Campfield, a Scottish minister who seemed not to have known a sober moment in many years. They argued long and hotly over politics and in the morning I found them, mouths open as if ready to argue more, slumped over a table littered with bottles. Henri woke and shook off the cape with which I had covered him, and gave me a rousing kiss, for he had adopted the American custom of showing affection in public.

During the two days of our voyage—a very good time, I was told by Captain Donely—we spent our afternoons on deck, watching the verdant highlands of the Hudson roll by with easy grace.

"Happy?" Henri asked often, and I always nodded yes, even though I sorely missed Aurore. She had been left with Delilah, and it was the first time we two had been parted. "Aurore is safe," he would say then, reading my worry.

We landed at Albany on the third afternoon of our journey up the Hudson, after a large meal at a farmhouse called Bethlehem, which catered to the ferry travelers.

Albany. City streets, noises, scents. Crowds. The feel of cobbles underfoot, ringing as my heels tapped over them. My spirits rose to new heights. I was still young, I was loved, in half-a-year there would be a milky new babe to hold, and much sooner than that I would be free of the pledge, of the past. And crowning all that was the much-missed city smell that enveloped me anew. To be in the midst of seething commotion once again was like waking from a dream.

At that time, Albany was a city of some seven hundred wood and brick houses . . . not even a quarter as big as Philadelphia, but it seemed immense after a year in Azilum, with its twenty log cabins. The city was inhabited largely by descendants of strong-looking, tow-headed Dutch fur traders. Court Street was busy with merchants and housewives, most of whom displayed the blonde hair, wide cheekbones and round blue eyes of their ancestry. The houses, too, were in Dutch style, with their gabled ends facing the street, rigorous and straight as soldiers at attention, and each door was agreeably adjoined with two benches for sitting and visiting, for the Dutch were both orderly and friendly.

Whereas Azilum was suffused with sounds of French, German and English, Albany was loud with Dutch, Scottish and various Indian tongues. Because it was a port city busy with the turmoil and attractions of commerce, many houses were fronted with a shop. Everything in which the eye or palate or imagination could delight—Albany tobacco, London powder, German china, French silk, cloth of gold from India, Medford rum, sugar from the islands— was in such abundance my hands trembled with the desire to touch such luxuries. Afternoon tearooms for ladies quarreled for space against men's public rooms, and the perfumes of Dutch cakes melded into the stronger aroma of sausages and ale.

The women's salons both cheered and disheartened me. I was hopelessly out of style after just one year in Azilum. I might as well have been on the moon. From the salon windows cunning hats trimmed with flowers and miniature schooners and gowns trimmed to match beckoned. The women in Albany had not yet cut their hair and they eyed me with curiosity. But in New York some had, and New York, according to Mrs. Moody, knew more of fashion than Albany. Let the Dutch housewives stare, I thought. I will have one of those new gowns with the straight-hanging skirts and the kind of boy's cap that goes with it, and show them how a Frenchwoman pays tribute to fashion.

"After we've hired our rooms," Henri said, reading my thoughts. "We'll have time this afternoon to get some new things for you. You'll make the Albany wives look like scullery maids." I patted his arm, grateful yet still aware that a year in the wilderness does much to turn a woman into a drab.

"Bejesus," said Smithy. "These folk look like a sneeze would blow 'em over." But when a bold shop girl leaned over her Dutch-door and smiled at him his sneer disappeared, to be replaced by a look of such appraising lust that Henri laughed.

Her full bosom rested on the sill like an over-filled pillow. "Well," she said. "Where are you coming from, my fine woodsman?" She twirled a blonde curl around her forefinger. "*Houd uw bakuis!*" her master called from the back of the bakery. She winked at Smithy before disappearing inside. "Come back later," she invited.

Smithy tipped his raccoon hat and gawked at her.

We made slow progress down Court Street to State, where laborers were

356

busily tapping into place the cobblestones that were being installed over the remaining dirt streets of the city. There was much clamoring activity there, for the burghers were determinedly rebuilding the many houses and shops that had been destroyed by fire the year before. We stepped around piles of brick and lumber, able to still catch the smell of burnt timber and the despair that goes with it, until we reached the Sweetwater Inn on State Street. This was in sight of the Episcopal Church and its famed well. Residents of the city reasonably disdained to drink the river water. This part of the Hudson was as fouled as the Seine had ever been.

"I'll be leaving now," Smithy said as we left our wagon and horses in charge of the Sweetwater groom. He disappeared into the next-door bath house to scrub off a few months' layer of dirt and dust for his meeting with the baker's assistant. BATHS. FIRST WATER A NICKEL, SECOND WATER THREE CENTS, the sign read. I hoped he would be extravagant and pay for a first water bath. Perhaps he did; we did not see him again until the day of our return to Azilum.

Henri and I hired rooms at the Sweetwater. I tried not to stare like a country woman but the dining room, which was rustic by Parisian standards and extravagant by Azilum standards, had a large, sparkling chandelier and a mirror the size of a wall. A boy of about eight—two years younger than the Dauphin—guided us up the wide stairs to our rooms, struggling under the weight of our traveling cases. "My name is Jake." He grinned, settling the bags in a heap at our feet and holding out his small, grimy hand. "I'll fetch anything you'll be needing."

"Then fetch us a good bottle of port, and the largest batch of hothouse roses you can find," Henri said, spilling a fair number of coins out of his purse. Jake saluted smartly, closed the door, and Henri and I were alone.

He grinned. "A nap is in order," he said, lifting me in his arms and carrying me to the big feather bed. "I've had only Mr. Campfield for company the past nights . . ."

I rolled away from his embrace, hungry for a dozen things at once. "You've a lifetime to catch up on that," I said. "I've only a few days in Albany. We're going to the shops. And then we're going to find an eating room that will serve me all the oysters I have dreamed of and not had this past year in Azilum."

The next morning Henri straddled a chair in our rented room, pretending to frown.

"This was a large chamber yesterday, Julienne," he said. "Now I can't move without tripping over a box or hatcase." He was pleased, though he wouldn't show it.

"Pass me the scent bottle," I said. A serving girl from the Sweetwater poured another bucket of hot, sudsy water over my back and I closed my eyes, delighting in the feel of warm water scented with rose rushing all the way up to my shoulders. The tin tub was lined with the softest of linens and I had spent all morning deciding which of my three new gowns I would wear for my interview with Louis-Charles. Surrounded by such luxury, after a year in Azilum, I should have been lightheaded with pleasure. But I was nervous. I had waited years for this day; I wished all to go well.

Anna swathed me in fresh linens as I stepped out of the tub. A knock sounded on the door so I dried hastily and stepped into a violet dressing gown so new it crackled.

"That will be the hairdresser," I said. "Open the door, Henri."

"Hairdresser?" His reddish-blonde eyebrows rose in consternation. "Can't you do your hair yourself?"

"Louis-Charles will be expecting the manners and appearance to which he is accustomed," I said, "and I am not adroit with the curling irons." Henri opened the door and Monsieur de Laurence, another émigré from Paris, who had been recommended for his skill, entered. He exclaimed delightedly over my shorn locks and then spent a good hour bemoaning his fate, to be exiled in Albany where all the woman had white-blonde, pin-straight hair that would not yield, just would not yield, to the curling iron.

His chatter stretched our already taut nerves but I submitted willingly to his skilled, long-fingered ministrations, glad not to have to speak during this last hour of waiting to fulfill my pledge to Marie-Antoinette.

Henri and I did not mention the Dauphin's name aloud although we both thought of him. The Golden Ransom was with me, for delivery to Louis-Charles, and his guardians. I would ask for a moment alone with him; I would take the diamond from its hiding place and hold it out to that sad child, that exiled king, and he would know it instantly, and know me for the friend, the loyal supporter I was. There would be a shared moment between me, a seamstress, and my Dauphin, and we would remember that one other meeting, when he had been younger and happy, and his mother had put her arms about him and boasted of his cleverness.

For that prince, for that moment, I would dress as carefully as though I were being presented to him at Versailles. To remind him that Versailles, and the throne, were his future, once the madness in France was over.

"The Queen's own dressing room couldn't have been busier . . . or more ruinous," Henri said, smiling ruefully, as the maid cleaned boxes and ribbons off the floor and Monsieur de Laurence fussed over my hair.

"Ah, but it was," I sighed.

"You miss Paris."

"I do."

But that saddened my young husband, so I gave him a quick kiss and told him that should we ever be parted my longing for Paris would be nothing compared to my longing for him. The words were spoken lightly, as words often are when we are preoccupied with other matters, but they became more truthful with each year of our marriage.

After I had completed my lengthy toilette, we went to the dining room of the Sweetwater for our midday meal. Many eyes followed me as I walked, for the merchants of the city were unused to as formal a dress as I had managed that morning in honor of the Dauphin. My new shoes had three-inch heels, my skirt, with its train, trailed two feet behind me, my swanskin gloves were embroidered with silver, and my new walking cane had an ivory handle. I would not have been out of place in the Petit Trianon ballroom.

"I'm uncertain that Talon would approve of this," Henri protested over his plate of head cheese and *kool-slaa*. "We were not to draw attention to ourselves."

"Soon, it won't matter," I pointed out. When I gave Louis-Charles the Golden Ransom his future would be safe, and my debt to his mother finished. I thought it would be that simple. I wished it to be that simple.

My confidence dwindled after the meal, however, when we went on foot to our appointment with the Dauphin.

Following Talon's instructions, we left behind prosperous Court and State streets for the dark, foul-smelling alleys of the dockside of Albany. The streets were poor there, no cobbles came between our feet and the rutted dirt. The wooden houses leaned together for support like a band of cold beggars.

"It can't be here," I murmured, trying to hold my new skirt out of the mud and staring up at a decrepit wooden structure that hadn't been covered with fresh paint for many a year. Most of the window panes were broken and jagged pieces of raw lumber had been nailed over them. Beggars tugged at our clothes and hungry children with thin legs and matted hair followed us like a lost, clamoring flock of sheep.

What would the Dauphin be doing in such a place? He should be sheltered in the finest rooms that Albany could boast of, sitting in splendor and state. Not in this place, where I smelled poverty in the acrid, pungent odors, saw it in the heaps of refuse, heard it in the thin wails of the children who held their soiled palms before us, and felt it in the presence of the narrow-eyed men who slumped against the walls and eyed us speculatively.

Delilah told me once that life is a circle. We go back to from whence we came. My search for the Dauphin led me back to the hunger and poverty and misery of the Cité. This was a part of Albany that reminded me not of the gay, sunny afternoons in the Palais Royal with Manon, but of the darker, dire days of my own childhood.

I was all too aware of the weight of the Golden Ransom, stitched into the hem of my new skirt.

"This is the house," Henri said, pausing before a shabby, narrow house wedged between two larger ones. His voice was grim. He knocked on the low, wooden door and it was several minutes before the sound of footsteps approached that door from the other side. A man, old and decrepit as the house itself, opened the door partially and peered out at us.

"I am here to see Madame Jardin," Henri said, giving the name Talon had supplied. The door opened wider. The porter stepped aside and pointed his ancient knotty hand toward a dark stairwell.

"Upstairs, second door on the right, and be quiet as you go. Me missus is sick," he whined, holding up his palm as the begging children did. His breath told us his porter's tip would not be spent on a surgeon's fee for his wife.

The stairs were dark and narrow and covered with filth. We climbed cautiously to avoid stumbling. I reached out my hand to the bannister to steady myself but it was so greasy with slime I pulled my hand back, not wanting to soil my new gloves. Something furry brushed past my feet and made me shudder.

As a child I had not been afraid of mice and rats. When had I acquired these overly refined sensibilities? There was a wind in that stairwell that whistled past my ears and spoke of time past, time lost. Where was Julie of the Cité? Inside, deep inside. I called for her, for her fearlessness and stubbornness, and forced myself to continue up those stairs. The day had lost its bright promise.

Upstairs was no better. We could barely see; it was full daylight outside but inside was midnight darkness with an atmosphere of the despair that goes with that false night. We must get the Dauphin out of here, I thought. This is as unwholesome as his prison must have been. I only hope he has not been here overly long. What are his guardians thinking of?

Henri knocked on a second door and it opened to us. A draught carried to us the smell of illness and decay.

"Madame Jardin?" he asked. "I am sent by Monsieur Talon."

A woman, swathed completely in black, stood on the other side of the

360

threshold. Even her hat, which she had not removed, was veiled in black, so we could only guess at her features. But she had a haughty posture unhumbled by poverty or disgrace. She seemed very out of place in this sad location. Perhaps they chose those strange rooms simply because no one would think of searching there for the Dauphin. I was reminded that the child, Louis-Charles, had as many enemies as friends.

"Enter," the woman said. Her voice was cold and dark.

"This is my husband, Monsieur Jardin," she said in that quiet, wintry voice. But while she, in her black dress and concealing veil, stood upright and regal, her so-called husband bowed obsequiously to us. Afterward, back at home in the familiar comfort of our own bed, Henri and I whispered long into the night, speculating on who the woman and man really were. "It is always a mistake to have a footman pose as a husband," Henri concluded.

"Will you take refreshment?" she asked. We glanced at the pitcher of stale water, the tray of biscuits swarming with black flies. Her manner was one of a woman wearied of those amenities of life that add small comfort but no true substance. "There were fresh cakes yesterday, but the porter stole them in the night. They were almond cakes. The Queen's favorite. I was lady-in-waiting to the Queen," she volunteered. "Though you would not think so, to see me now."

I tried to discern her features through the veil, to see if she had a face familiar to me because of my own many hours spent at Versailles. I would have liked to talk of the Queen with her. But I could not make out her face, nor did she seem familiar. She seemed unwilling to be drawn into conversation.

"Thank you, but we will take no refreshment. May we see the child?" Henri asked gently. He was eager to finish our task. This hovel reeked of pestilence. I, who had waited so long, now wanted to delay the moment, fearful of what the next minute would reveal.

"As you will." The woman gestured to a closed door and then went and stood by the window, gazing out with a preoccupied, even indifferent, attitude. Henri opened the door for me. I went in, followed by Henri, and then by Monsieur Jardin, who closed the door behind us. I straightened my back and forced a smile with which to greet the Dauphin.

The room was dark and close as a coffin, and smelled as evil.

"He is still unused to fresh air," said Monsieur Jardin, who spoke in a whisper as good and unobtrusive servants are sometimes trained to do. "And light hurts his eyes."

The smell of sickness grew stronger as we approached the bed.

"My God," Henri said.

"He barely survived the ocean voyage," Monsieur Jardin whispered.

I gathered my courage and looked down at the child in the dirty mussed bed.

His eyes were open but unseeing, his mouth was twisted into a frozen grimace. His height, revealed by sharp bumps of knees and toes under the soiled sheet, suggested a youth of about the age Marie-Antoinette's son would be. He had the same arching eyebrows, the same full mouth.

But all semblance of a royal youth ended with those similarities. His flesh clung to his bones like rags on a scarecrow; he seemed to have lost all wit, all awareness. His eyes were vague and unfocused. The odor of his illness suggested a charnel house.

"He recognizes no one," Madame Jardin said. She had entered the room silently and stood at my side. Her voice was heavy with regret. "He has not spoken since . . . since events I cannot speak of."

"Tell me the name of this child," I demanded, turning to her. This could not be Marie-Antoinette's lively, intelligent, beautiful son. It could not. Don't let it be Louis-Charles, I prayed.

"You know his name, or you would not be here," she said cooly, meeting my gaze. "He is much changed, I agree. Are not we all?" She lifted her veil then to reveal her face. And I knew her. She had been younger then, much younger, that day long ago. Her voice had not been cold and filled with desolation, but merry and confident. She had sung, while another lady-in-waiting played the pianoforte in one of the Queen's reception rooms. And while she sang an aria, Marie-Antoinette instructed Louis-Charles to show me the flaw in the Golden Ransom and then give it to me for safekeeping.

"Yes. We meet again," Madame Jardin said.

"I never knew your name," I answered.

"It did not matter then. It does not matter now. Madame Jardin will suffice."

"Then tell me, Madame Jardin. How did this child come to be here, and where does he go from here?"

"Those are dangerous questions and the answers are not necessary for you to know."

"May I see him alone?" I asked.

Madame Jardin's eyes were inscrutable, but she seemed to hold her breath a moment before answering.

"As you will. But I will leave the door ajar. His safety is my responsibility."

"I assure you, I wish him no harm. Far from it."

Henri stayed in the room with me and watched as I ripped open the hem of my skirt and took the diamond out. My hands trembled. I waited for the child in the bed to display some interest, some curiosity, but he lay, inert and unseeing. The gem shone in the darkness, cold and yellow as the winter sun and Henri's breath grew sharp when he saw, for the first time, the size of it.

His eyes met mine. "That is a dangerous stone to have in your possession," he whispered.

"Then pray that this child recognizes it, and we may leave it in his keeping." I turned from him, to the sickbed.

"Louis-Charles," I whispered, kneeling by his pillow, my back to the outer room. "Look. I have saved it all this time for you. Do you remember, Louis-Charles? Do you remember the day the Queen, your mother, gave it to me?"

The Golden Ransom was cold and heavy in my palm. I closed my eyes for a moment, trying to shut out the dire poverty of the room, the smell of deadly illness, to remember a bright afternoon many years ago. The floor under my knees then had been cunningly patterned and polished parquet, not rough planks. The child's protector had been a Queen dressed in silver silk, not a silent, unknown woman in black mourning.

"Keep it for my son," her Austrian-tainted voice had whispered under the obedient singing of her ladies-in-waiting. The diamond, exchanging hands, had caught the afternoon sun and reflected it off a gilded ceiling where pink cupids chased each other across an immortal blue sky.

In that dark Albany room there was no light for the diamond to catch. Its fire seemed to have been quenched by time and distance.

The boy's eyes turned to me, but no recognition showed in them. His face, set in its grimace of terror and illness, did not change. His mouth worked, but no sounds came out.

Then, one hand slowly rose from the sheet and reached toward my hand, where the diamond rested. I held my breath, hopeful again.

He did not look at or touch the diamond. His bone-thin fingers captured the lace at my wrist. Then his hand fell limply back onto the sheet. He turned his face away. I, and the diamond, were nothing to him.

"For nought," I whispered over and over. "All this for nought." I looked at Henri. "He doesn't recognize the gem, as Marie-Antoinette said he must."

Madame Jardin stirred in the other room.

"I dare not leave the stone with her," I whispered, stricken.

"No." Henri agreed. "She is too much of a mystery. We do not know that her interests are the same as the Dauphin's. Or who this child is."

I wept as I returned the diamond to its hiding place and quickly restitched the hem with a threaded needle I had hidden inside my new hat.

We left shortly after. Henri gave Madame Jardin some money and she did not refuse it, indeed, seemed dismayed that the amount was not greater.

Outside in the now-dark street, I retched. I had to lean, panting, against the rotted wood wall before Henri could lead me back to the wholesomeness of Court Street. It seemed a familiar thing, to lean panting and unhappy against an unfriendly wall while the furies of death whipped by in the evening breeze, and I remembered the night of the old king's burial when Louise, pregnant, had leaned, panting, against a wall. Was the child upstairs Louis XV's grandchild? I did not know. I would never know.

"What will happen to them?" I asked Henri, when my stomach quieted and I could speak again.

"They leave Albany tomorrow. She would not tell me where they go. Several attempts have already been made on the boy's life. Apparently there are some who believe he is the Dauphin." Henri was holding my quaking shoulders.

"Jacobins," I said bitterly.

"Jacobins. And others. You saw the child, Julienne. Even those once closest to him would not let such a youth claim the throne of France. He is witless, I don't know if by birth or through illness and sorrow. Whoever the child is, and I'm not convinced he is the Dauphin, we can only hope his life will be spared. There are many who would want to kill him, Jacobins because they hate the monarchy and its heirs, and royalists who love the monarchy and would not want such a boy to claim the throne."

At the Sweetwater Inn, I changed from my extravagant costume into a modest one and admitted I had been foolish. Albany was not Versailles. And the child, even if he was the Dauphin, was no longer suited for royalty. He had not died. But the splendor of the old world and the old ways had been beaten and starved out of him. Now, he was a youth, ill and demented, no more, no less.

I had no appetite for dinner that evening, but Henri insisted I take some nourishment. He patted my still-flat belly as he reminded me of the importance of caring for myself and not giving in to an unhappy state of mind.

"Don't dwell on what is past, nor on what you can't rectify," he said.

I picked at a large platter of sausages baked in pastry, thinking all the while of that bone-thin, demented child in his reeking bed. The food had no taste.

"What do I do now?" I asked. "What would the Queen have expected me to do?"

"The Queen is dead, Julienne. And her son, whether that child or another is Louis-Charles, will never regain the throne."

It was dark and Henri's face was candlelit. I was thinking of the first time we had shared a meal together, in Senator Morris's rich and crowded dining room. He had fidgeted all night with his fish fork and overturned a glass of claret onto Mary Morris's pristine damask cloth. Now, he was calm and confident and more than a little protective as he reached for my hand. His fingers were warm and strong and helped to dispel the gloom caused by the remembrance of that other hand with the cold, skeletal fingers.

"That poor child is lost. But why do you say the throne is also lost?" I asked.

"Because it is the past, and men must look to the future. The time of monarchies is over."

"Charles said that, too," I said.

Henri's grasp of my hand loosened, his fingers slipped away from mine like a ship sailing from a wharf.

"Do you still think of him?"

"No," I said. "I think of you." I reached out, called his hand back to mine and our fingers twined around each other's and held tight.

The bustling streets and shops of Albany held no more attraction for me after our unsuccessful visit to that child. Henri, worried about my low spirits, decided we would leave Albany at once and return to Azilum.

We again boarded the *Magdalene* and of the three of us only Smithy was pleased with his journey to Albany, for he had purchased a new musket.

It was on board the *Magdalene* that Armand Darnton finally revealed himself. He had left Azilum the week after my wedding and I had hoped never to renew his acquaintance, for his wooing had caused me much trouble.

Henri and I were standing by the railing watching the rolling greens as we passed them at good speed, for we were in a deep part of the river and making time. Darnton appeared and stepped between us. I was surprised; Henri was not.

"You have followed us since we left Azilum," my husband said. "Did you think us fools that we would not see your campfire?" I, who had seen and noticed nothing, did feel a fool. I had thought heat and irritation had clouded my young husband's disposition. It had been worry and anticipation of something to come, something which he did not speak of to me.

"I have stayed close," Darnton admitted, smiling. There was cruelty in his face, despite that smile. And greed.

How did I ever consider him pleasing? I wondered, studying his face and seeing that it had none of the clean lines and openness of Henri's. Darnton looked sly.

"Madame Arraché knows my mission," he said. And at that moment I did know; I finally understood. Christ, how blind I had been. It was not curiosity that brought him to Azilum, but news of the Dauphin. It was not my company he had sought, but the diamond.

"The Golden Ransom. You want the diamond. You were to receive the message that Talon intercepted. You searched my room in Philadelphia." I paused, thinking. "But why didn't you search for it in Azilum? Why not there?" If he had been desperate enough to ransack the Pension Rose Noir, why not my cabin?

"Your manner told me the diamond was not in your home. And for the time being, I deemed it safer to let you safeguard the stone for me. I was, shall we say, between masters at the time. As you are well aware, a gem of that size is worthless without a buyer waiting to receive it. With d'Orléans dead, and then Robespierre, I had to bide my time till a new buyer announced himself." He spoke calmly, as if we discussed a mundane business transaction, not a Queen's reputation and an heir's future.

"Who is the buyer now?" I asked. "The Comte de Provence who wants the throne for himself?"

"Actually, you see before you a very fortunate man. There are three, not one, who are willing to bid on the gem. One who knows the harm this stone will do to Marie-Antoinette who, even dead, is not free of the scandals history will attach to her name. Another who, out of pleasure, collects stones, and another who wishes to remain assured that the Golden Ransom will never benefit Louis-Charles. Three buyers, three motives. I can name a price and a purpose. So you see, it is time to relinquish the stone to my keeping."

"I will not give it to you," I said. "It belongs to the son of Marie-Antoinette, to Louis XVII."

Darnton laughed and dabbed at his mouth with a lace handkerchief. "There will never be a Louis XVII," Darnton said. "So what good is the diamond to you? If you had left the stone with the child, I would not have stopped at murder to get it. Any child who inherits that gem will die for it. And the longer you keep it, the longer you place your own life in jeopardy. Be assured, I will possess the stone at any cost. Think of me as a friend, if you will. In the years to come many will claim that throne, that inheritance. Will you spend your life running back and forth from country to country, town to town, speculating on who is the true Dauphin?"

"If I must," I insisted, although the prospect was a bleak one.

"I have been warned of your stupidity," he said, and Henri, who had been silent, grew red with anger.

Darnton leaned against the ship railing to steady himself against the roll of a deep wave, for the current had grown stronger. His black coat melted into the blackness of the night but a full moon illuminated his confident smile.

"I will have the diamond, and now," he said. "Why waste it? Marie-Antoinette's son will never be king."

I was weary—of plots and missions and of carrying a burden that had brought great sorrow and no joy. If that child in Albany was the Dauphin, then the diamond was as useless to him as a lump of coal. I wished only to return home with Henri, to live a life that would be busy with work and child raising. The diamond was a talisman that brought suffering to all who held it and it seemed even the Queen herself would have wished no more suffering for her son.

"Give it to me," Darnton said again, "or I will take it from you," and his voice grew sharp with a greed that sees its goal in sight.

I bent and ripped open the hem of my skirt. The Golden Ransom fell onto the wooden planks with a heavy lifeless sound. I caught it up in my hand before Darnton could retrieve it, knowing what I must do.

It took but a moment but seemed an infinity. I stood, raised my arm and held it over the side of the *Magdalene*, over the rushing black waters. I opened my fingers and with all my strength cast the diamond into the night. It had come from the blackness of the earth, let it return there.

It arched high, catching the moonlight, and then, like a shooting star, it fell into the inky waters and disappeared.

A great weight lifted from me. Reckless with new freedom, I laughed at the expression on Darnton's face.

"If you want it, swim for it," I told him.

Darnton struck at me, catching his blow in the side of my face. My mouth filled with the salty taste of blood but it was a small price for my freedom and the Dauphin's safety. Henri, who had been motionless till then, lunged at Darnton. I had no more than a bloody lip. Darnton, when Henri stopped, had to be carried away and required a surgeon.

Later, when we were alone again, Henri put his arms about me and kissed me, gently, on the side of the mouth where a bruise was forming. I was peaceful and content. It was truly over.

"I have ended it, Henri. If Louis-Charles lives, let him live in safe obscurity. Let him have a future as a common man, so he may prosper and call his life his own. Let him live as a common man, rather than die as a prince. The Queen herself would have wished it, I think."

The diamond, and the past, were buried in the deep river.

22

. . . my story concludes . . .

The lines have fallen to me in pleasant places; indeed, a good
inheritance is mine. Thou dost make me know the path of life;
in Thy presence is fullness of joy; in Thy right hand are
pleasures for ever more.

—Psalm 16

We returned to Azilum, Henri and I. And all during that journey I had
the sensation that the entire world lay before me, and nothing was at
my back. There was only new future.

Talon, and many others, were disappointed to see us return without the
Dauphin. Henri explained that the child was too ill to travel, and that it was
not even certain he was the Dauphin. There was no irrefutable evidence of
his identity, except what his guardians claimed. I winced, then, realizing
anew that by turning the Golden Ransom into a shooting star that had
disappeared forever, I had obliterated history's chance to know Marie-
Antoinette's son. Then I remembered Darnton, and the many others like
him, and was glad anew that the child was safe in his anonymity.

"Perhaps it is just as well," Talon sighed. "We could not guarantee his
safety here. Just as well," and he went upstairs, to the Dauphin's bedroom,
and began packing away the books and toys. His limp seemed more
pronounced, his back not quite as straight.

368

Henri and I never spoke of the diamond, nor regretted its loss. My impulsive solution to the problem of what to do with the Golden Ransom freed us both from a past that could no longer claim us, and probably saved the life of that poor child in Albany, whereas the receiving of it would have been his death.

The child, and his guardians, disappeared.

Many royalists, frustrated by the disappearance of the Dauphin, became convinced that their futures rested in the elegant, beringed hands of the Comte de Provence. He, secure and well-dined in the various courts of Europe, had, since the beheading of his brother, planned to gain the throne. He did, in 1814. And lost it in 1815.

Hounded by Napoleon, who would not stay put on Elba, Provence, now Louis XVIII, vowed to defend the throne with his life, and then fled back to Belgium. Among the many items left behind in his hurried departure was a small box containing commemorative medals of the Dauphin. One coin bore the legend "When will the veil be lifted?" and a second: "Louis, second son of Louis XVI. Born the 27th of March, 1785. Set free the 8th of June, 1795."

I returned to Azilum glad for the solace of its night-singing crickets and rosy dawns, and its great distance from thrones and princes.

I was a wife again, barren widow no longer. And now that my pledge to Marie-Antoinette's son was completed as well as it ever could be, I was well content to pass time speculating on the increasing swell of my stomach. My belly rounded with the harvest time, and I grew clumsy and large through the winter snows. Henri's first son was born in March. We named him Louis, pronounced in the American way, and delighted in all he did, even when the event was no more momentous than a smile or step.

Henri, who hadn't known such devotion himself, wondered long hours over that sweet, infant replica of his own face. Many times I had to tell him to cease distracting the child from his sleep and feeding and attend to chores. Then I, equally adoring, would creep back to the nursery and watch my sleeping son, rejoicing in him and remembering that other son in Albany and wondering.

The next year our daughter Antoinette was born, and after her came little Marie, who was as gentle as the others were rowdy. Aurore was at first perplexed by the abundance of siblings but soon realized the power that comes from being the first. She earned a household reputation for tyranny that made us smile, for even when she made the little ones play at dogs and pull her sled they laughed gleefully, adoring the eldest and strongest as children sometimes do.

Halcyon years, sweet years, filled with talk of crops and teething . . . how quickly such times pass. What I would give to have those years back, to have my little ones rosy and plump and clinging at my skirts!

Yet even as my family thrived, Azilum began to close in upon itself like a delicate rose wilting in the heat of noon.

The plans to dredge the river and make it navigable for vessels other than the limited flatboats never came to fruition. Hence, our colony never realized its potential as a river port and commerce center; we remained isolated and rural, populated with a people who, for the most part, did not enjoy being isolated and rural.

Talon, discouraged by the colony's many failures . . . by the broken promise of the Queen's House that had never sheltered Marie-Antoinette, and the boxes of toys for a Dauphin, collecting dust and rusting in a closet, unused . . . returned to Europe in 1797 to explore other land development schemes. His return to France was premature, however; he was imprisoned as a royalist. Under confinement, his stalwart, quick mind lapsed into insanity. He died in France, broken and demented.

The same year that Talon left us, the tide of popular feelings turned again against the French. Washington retired to Mount Vernon, old and tired, and was replaced by an administration that felt no sympathy for the French, and the demands the French government, still at war with the rest of Europe, made against the Americans.

"It's a long time since the French sent arms and money for our struggle," Colonel Jamison pointed out. "The debt is paid in full."

The other farmers echoed similar sentiments and did not bother to differentiate between the demands of the French in France, and the French who were their neighbors. We French émigrés, who had once been warmly welcomed, were now accused of charging too much for our crops and paying our laborers too little. We were accused of holding apart from the Americans, of snubbing them with our aristocratic names and fancy manners.

I cannot say all of the accusations were false. We grew isolated by more than the difficult river and deep forest; we were surrounded by a fence of customs and ways that cut us off from our American neighbors. We remained foreigners.

Through all that, I busied myself in the summer by tending to babies and the herb garden. In the fall I preserved gooseberries and peaches; in the winter I helped the children with their lessons in Webster's Spelling Book. In the spring Henri and I, tired from busy, happy days, would hold each other in the big feather bed from Hollenback's trading post and listen to the wild song of the returning geese.

A day came, however, when I could no longer stay safe and secure within the circle of the family, the circle that shuts out all intruders and stray thoughts.

It was in August of 1802 that we learned that the Corsican, Napoleon Bonaparte, had become First Consul of France for Life. The revolution was over. After years of bloodshed and murder and war in the name of liberty, fraternity and equality, France again bowed to one all-powerful ruler.

I was in the orchard, picking the first red apples to make a sauce for dinner, when that distant First Consul set in motion events that would finally rend the delicate fabric that was Azilum. Aurore, already eight years old and strong and wild as an Indian, had climbed into the shaded lap of the tree and was tossing fruit down into my waiting basket.

"Julienne! Julienne!" Victoire came running toward us. She had grown from plump to heavy in her middle years, and it was alarming to see her move so quickly.

"What is it, Victoire?" I hadn't seen her so agitated since that day, years before, when she had come to tell me of the death of the Dauphin. Aurore, unheeding, dropped an apple on my head.

"Sorry," she said grinning. "It was gravity, not I." Henri had been lecturing the children about the laws of physics.

"Julienne, I have received a pardon. An official pardon, from the First Consul. My name has been removed from the list of émigrés." Victoire was breathless with excitement and exertion.

I stared at her, uncomprehending.

"It means I can return to France. And my estates will be returned to me, in trust for my sons' usage when they are of age."

"You are leaving, Victoire?"

"Oui." From that moment, she made no more attempt to speak the language of the land that had given her asylum. She left Azilum long before her actual departure.

A month later we met, for the last time, at the Azilum wharf. Her trunks were loaded on a flatboat, her two youngest sons, excited at the prospect of the journey back to France, danced around her.

We embraced for a long, painful moment.

"Remember the day we arrived?" I asked, fighting tears.

"Maman fainted!" Antoine slapped his thigh in glee.

But Victoire's face was set and determined; she would neither laugh, nor cry, nor be moved by maudlin memories. For her, the revolution was over and she could go home. "Au revoir," she said, stepping onto the barge.

Jacques-Pierre, her eldest, stood next to me as we waved and waved, until the barge slipped around the bend in the Susquehanna and we could see it, and its passengers, no longer. He, already seventeen, had decided to stay in Azilum and work the farm his mother was leaving behind. His voice had cracked when he announced his decision and Aurore, eating a hard, red apple, tossed it carelessly at him in play. Eight years later, when he first came to woo Aurore, he brought a basket of apples as a love token.

Generosity from First Consul Napoleon proved expensive for Victoire. The Revolution was over, but not the wars. She regained her château on the Loire, but lost Antoine in the frozen, corpse-strewn drifts outside Moscow. Louis returned to his ancestral home from Waterloo with an empty sleeve pinned to the right side of his uniform.

All that year neighbors—those I cared for and those I disdained—came with the same announcement. They had been forgiven for their crimes against the revolution. They could return to France.

Our colony withered until only a handful of us remained. Even those who did not wish to return to France found themselves wishing to be elsewhere. Some pushed deeper into the sunset, into Ohio; others journeyed south, to the warmer climate of Louisiana.

The streets, which had never been properly paved, grew narrower for lack of traffic, and cabin after cabin was boarded up and abandoned. The pastures were sold off to neighboring farmers; clearings not yet tamed by plough were invaded by the forest that had been felled ten years before. Gardens turned to marsh and wild meadow.

Azilum, abandoned by people, began to be reclaimed by nature.

Henri, the children and I gathered close about the evening hearth and became friendlier with the American neighbors about us. No letter of amnesty came for me, no pardon that would allow me to return to France. And would I have? Henri wished to stay in Pennsylvania. And the children were happy there, too. I swallowed my homesickness for Paris like bitter medicine and did not speak of it.

"Are you happy, Julienne?" Henri asked in the lonely winter of 1805, when the abandonment of Azilum was all but complete. It was evening, but no candlelight showed in the darkness, except for that within our own cabin. I wondered if Adam and Eve had felt this lonely in Eden, in their solitude. The children were asleep upstairs and Henri was pondering his ledgers on the dining table. I went to him and put my head in his lap.

"Ask me again," I said. "In French. I miss the sound of it."

"I think we could visit Paris for a short time. If you wish," he said. But he was frowning. He was planning to open a cabinetry workshop, for the income from farming no longer met our expenses. We measured things carefully that year, and wasted nothing, trying to save the money we would need for capital. Henri had no queen to get him started, as I had had.

I thought for a long moment. I ached with desire for Paris, for a city, as much as ever I had ached for any man. But you can't walk two paths at once, as Delilah put it. "No," I said. "We have no money for voyaging. And, the children are too young for the journey back and forth, and I could not leave them behind. Perhaps later, when they are grown."

But it was Aurore who went to France in 1814, not I. Aurore who received the letter of amnesty. It was from Charles's mother, though, not Napoleon. That cunning strategist had fallen and been temporarily replaced in the people's hearts and on their coins by Louis XVIII, the former Comte de Provence, who would himself soon fall.

I still have that letter of invitation. It is one of the most important mementos I have.

My dearest child,
I would be most pleased to have you come for an extended visit to your father's birthplace. Forgive an old woman for not writing sooner. The years have been sad ones for me, filled with many losses, beginning with the death of your beloved father, my son, so many years ago. Please come to me.

There was more, of course, explanations of how she had found us, details on the death of other children, other grandchildren. But the message was clear and it opened old wounds. The mother who had refused to receive her daughter-in-law wished to claim her grandchild.

I raged for days. "She shall not go!" I vowed. Aurore, nineteen then, looked at me with Charles's deep green eyes and kept silent until my anger turned to fear.

"I'll come back," she promised. "But think how exciting it would be for me to see the coronation. Grandmama said we would be invited to Paris and received at court!" I remembered Jeannette Mouret and how, years and years ago, she had been taken to Versailles to see the Queen and I had not. The old jealousy came back, along with new fears. I would lose my daughter to a future in which I played no part, had no role.

"The Comte de Provence is not the rightful King," I argued, thinking of that other one, Louis-Charles, and I wondered how the years sat on his shoulders, whether they were strong or bowed.

"That again," Aurore sighed, bored.

I could not keep her from going, nor could Victoire's son, Jacques-Pierre, with his baskets of apples. He had been courting her for three years. But the golden apple of Paris beckoned.

Six months later another letter came, that time from Aurore, who had voyaged safely to France. It was filled with the sentimental ramblings of a young woman in love for the first time, and details of her planned wedding to a Monsieur Jean Contat.

"What a trousseau the Queen's diamond would have provided," I sighed, grieved to be able to send so little to my daughter. But I knew that nothing purchased by the wealth of that stone could have brought pleasure.

Aurore wed, and stayed in France. I grieved at this loss until gentle Marie, my youngest, grew too quiet and no longer played. Concerned, I pushed aside my longings for France and the daughter that had been born to me there. I spent my afternoons teaching Marie needlepoint and soon she became lively again from the attention, and then climbed the apple trees as brazenly as her elder sister had done just a few short years before.

But in the Auvergne, in that ancient château where I was never welcomed, I have a granddaughter and great-grandchildren, Aurore's progeny, whom I have never met. I dream of them the way I once dreamed about that other woman, Angelina, my never-met mother.

When Aurore left us, there were only six farms left on the green Azilum crescent. Laporte bought up many of the abandoned farms and eventually moved his family into the Queen's House. Finally, that house realized the goal for which it had been created—it sheltered a family. Children's laughter echoed in its long elegant halls and the bedtime prayers of a farm boy whispered into the corners of a room once decorated for a prince.

Our own son, Louis, decided to read law rather than farm. Henri and I discussed it long into the night.

"We have to send him away, or go with him," my husband said.

"And Antoinette will need a husband soon. She needs more society, more choice. And Marie should be better schooled, she is too clever for our tutoring."

It was decided. We would all of us move, leave Azilum behind and go to Wilkes-Barre, where Louis could begin a solicitor's apprenticeship and Antoinette find ample dancing partners.

We waited until after the last harvest. It was my wish. In those hectic evenings of packing cutlery and deciding what to leave, what to take, I stole many moments to recall other harvests, especially that first, in the fall of 1794.

Despite the meagre results of our labors, we had celebrated with a dance on the meadow. Irish fiddlers from Wyoming, French aristocrats with mud caked on their fine clothes, and shy German farmwives met in a time and place that was called French Azilum. The young women captured fireflies and wore them in their hair like sparkling jewels, so that the night was alive with stars, both overhead and in the women's curls. We danced round dances and square dances; and when the fiddlers struck a more stately tune we, the French, the émigrés, lined up solemnly for a minuet as stately and regal as any danced in the ballrooms of Versailles. There was green Pennsylvania grass beneath our feet, but it was of Paris we thought.

And through that long, bittersweet evening of celebration and mourning, the log cabin home built for Marie-Antoinette presided over us like a queen on her throne, reminding us of all that would not be, and all that might yet come to pass.

&PILOGUE

*A*nd now, the Queen's House is being razed. It has outlived its purpose and its own time. I will mourn it.

The sun is up. Robins sing in the oak tree outside my window and the house stirs and creaks as though it, too, needs to stretch its weary bones. Matty, the new kitchen girl, pads back and forth, her footsteps sounding dim and hesitant from the back lower floor. I will have to remind her to skim the cream from the milk and save it for tonight's custard. She is not as clever as Delilah.

Though I pleaded, my Delaware friend would not follow us into this larger, cramped village where the sky is not as close as it was in Azilum. Instead she turned and walked back into the forest with Joshua at her side. I never heard from her again. How do you address a letter to a woman whose home is wherever the Great Father shines? Of all those I have known it cheers me that strong, determined Delilah may still walk those wildflower paths of the Azilum forest, her medicine bag swaying vigorously against her chest with the force of her steps.

And perhaps somewhere, in this country or France or perhaps England, lives a middle-aged man who has a dim memory of an auburn-haired mother who wore diamonds in her hair and at her throat. Perhaps it is only the dimmest of memories, like something barely remembered from a long-ago dream.

Two score of men have stepped foreward to claim the heritage of Marie-Antoinette's lost son. Henri and I follow each claim closely in the newspapers. The claimants are adopted sons of tailors, Italian inventors, titled barons and unknown watchmakers, all with the same claim of having been that lost child smuggled out of the Temple so many years ago.

None of the claims can be proved, or disproved. Not even that of a man known as Eleazer Williams who, after a brief stay in Albany many years ago, cared for by a family who called themselves Jardin, was raised by the Oneida tribe in upstate New York. His memories are vague, yet he has been often visited by highly-placed Frenchmen curious to know more about him. There are many who believe he is the missing Dauphin. He is a missionary and

377

has done much to improve the lot of the Indians; he is healthy and strong and his life has counted for much. Any mother would be proud of him. Even a queen.

But is he a Queen's son? It doesn't seem to matter as much as it once did. History has swallowed Louis-Charles, turned him into legend, but I hope that in the safe anonymity of his privacy he has walked in the sun and with a sweet breeze at his back.

Time to rise, now. Matty will be here soon with the weak tea I dislike, and then my granddaughter, Marie-Aurore, will creep in with a small cup of forbidden coffee poured from her own morning tray.

We will discuss what to serve at dinner and ways to keep her youngest, John, from sucking his thumb. Later, four generations will crowd at my table and I will tell them tales of the long ago. I will lapse into French, the language we stopped sharing when the grandchildren were born, and they will accuse me of forgetfulness. I do not forget. But I am old enough that I can live in the past as easily as the present, and sometimes it pleases me to hear the gentler sounds of French in my dining room.

Marie-Aurore will quarrel with her sister-in-law, Rose, and I will close my eyes, hearing in the angry timbre of their voices the close strife that bound Louise and Mathilde, those other high-tempered women. John will play his first tentative piano pieces in the parlor, trying to show off, and in his hesitant notes I will hear Victoire's determined but faulty music, as it once echoed in the drawing room of the Queen's House.

Henri will return to me in the evening, portly and dignified with success. We will complain about the apprentices in his cabinet shop, and the cost of rosewood and good beeswax. We will sit in the moss-green chairs, hands twined together on the little table between us, and watch the Susquehanna, the same river that flowed in its many moods past the Queen's House. We will slip together into the comfortable, silent evening that follows the long day.